Jewel

Heiress of the Lost Diamond

Readers agree
It's a MUST READ!

"Very engaging!"
Connie Abbott – St. Paul, MN

"A harrowing adventure... You feel and experience what happens."
Crystal Graves – St. Paul, MN

"The story is well-written and the characters are very compelling"
Christine Harder Mehl – Rosemount, MN

"A well-researched historical tribute with strong flesh and blood characters. I enjoyed the book."
Jimmye O'Connor – Boulder, CO

"The story grabbed me and wouldn't let go!"
Jean Thompson – St. Paul, MN

Jewel

Heiress of the Lost Diamond

K. J. Culpepper

Library of Congress Control Number: 2010905823
ISBN 13: 978-1-452-83416-0
ISBN 10: 1-452-83416-4

Cover Design Write Right Ink
Interior Set in Garamond, Benjamin
and Calisto MT fonts
by Write Right Ink

Printed in the United States of America

Jewel

Heiress of the Lost Diamond

K. J. Culpepper

This is a work of fiction. Although historical events and people in this book are referenced, all other characters and events are completely fictional.

Dedication

Dedicated to the Culpepper clan, I am very proud of the heritage I have as a member of the Culpepper family, and I hope that those who share this name will enjoy the story and the dream.

All my love to my daughters who have supported my dreams over the years.

Acknowledgements

Many thanks are due to a number of people: Paul, who lovingly continues to support me as I write; my daughter, Jessi, who helps me with her medical knowledge and personal encouragement; my daughter Jenni, who is a constant source of joy and encouragement; Joan and Barb H., without whose prayers I could not do what I do; and finally, my brother Steve, who helps me get the words right.

The information regarding the Cullinan Diamond was found on the following Web site:

http://famousdiamonds.tripod.com/cullinandiamonds.html.

Other diamond history was found on the Web site:

http://www.amnh.org/exhibitions/diamonds/africa.html

INTRODUCTION

In Transvaal, South Africa, a young shepherd boy traded the large, shiny stone he found for 500 sheep, 10 oxen, and a horse. The stone, actually an 84-carat diamond, was later cut down to 48 carats, and named the Dudley Diamond. Its discovery in 1867 was the first of its kind in the area, and it set off the great diamond rush to South Africa.

In 1905, the largest diamond ever found was discovered in Transvaal's Premier Mines by mine superintendent, Frederick Wells. Weighing just over one pound, the diamond earned its founder an award of $10,000 from the mine's owner, Thomas Cullinan. Named after its new owner, the Cullinan diamond was taken out of the country and purchased for $800,000 for the King of England in celebration of his 66th birthday.

Aptly named "The Star of Africa", the diamond was sent to one of the top diamond cutters in Amsterdam, Joseph Asscher and Company. The first fall of the hammer caused the chisel to break, but upon receiving the second blow, the diamond split perfectly. The diamond cutter fainted. The gem later produced nine major gems with 96 smaller cut stones.

Since that time, believing that the diamond had been stolen from its homeland and her people, the South African government has asked for its return. In spite of their request, the Star of Africa, a pear-shaped gem of 530.2 carats, remains in England upon the Royal Scepter, as do the remaining Crown Jewels.

No one has ever known about its rival, the Jewel of Africa, until now.

PART I
The First Generation

Chapter I

African Venture

March 15, 1858 – Oxford, England

Taller than most and in good shape for his 60 years, Sir Lawrence Pendleton easily stood above the large gathering of expectant young Oxford University students near the school's front entrance. They were listening to one J. Reginald Culpepper, the young man who had fascinated the assembled students at that morning's required chapel conference at Christ Church with exploits about his search for gold in Africa. He had concluded with a stirring exhortation urging the students to raise their sights to higher goals. Although Sir Lawrence had been as enthralled as his students, he missed the opportunity to speak to the young man after the conference. Now, already half past three, the day was slipping away, as was the professor's chance to speak with him. The senior-most professor of Oxford University's Humanities Department had not imagined anything as trivial as gold mining would have ever interested him, but alas, it had.

Although the younger man had originally gone to Cape Colony in the southernmost part of Africa to explore for ivory and other tradable commodities, he had come home to England with more lucrative entrepreneurial ideas. The topic had been well researched and well spoken, and the old professor was intrigued by the idea of adventure during these latter years of his career. Sir Lawrence wondered if he dared consider something adventurous – possibly even dangerous – but dismissed his doubts. He pursued the younger man across the commons where he joined the crowd with more interest than he cared to show.

Culpepper, a young man in his twenties, seemed to be an alien against the backdrop of gothic architecture at the university. He had a confident air about him as he leaned against the stone wall, wavy dark brown hair blowing in the breeze, surrounded by students who had also heard him speak earlier. Culpepper was a welcomed intruder during a time when adventure was still an uncommon commodity at Oxford. After his speech, he was interviewed by many of the students who were interested in a fortune hunt in the south of Africa. He stood looking amused with his thumbs hooked firmly into each side of his well-tailored suit vest as he fielded one question after another.

"Yes, Robert, I am sure there's gold there. I have visited the villages of the tribes north of the settlements, and have found they use gold in their tribal dress. Of course, they are not about to let us know exactly where it was found, but I have a resource there who can attest to the fact the tribes have been mining gold in Africa for centuries."

A young impish boy spoke up. "When do you plan to go again, Mr. Culpepper?"

"Why, I have just the other day made plans to enter into a contract with a Cambrian businessman," Culpepper replied. The boy's eyebrows lifted, surprised Culpepper would work with someone from a rival community. He was thoroughly enamored by thoughts of adventure on the "Dark Continent," and thought he would be someone Mister Culpepper might consider. His family had enough money to pay for his passage. Culpepper had truly given these 19-year-old boys something to dream about. Sir Lawrence stood behind them and paused to listen before interrupting the conversation. The professor cleared his throat with a gruff, "eh-hem," and a few backed away to clear a path for him.

"I dare say, young Smythe, you would do better to concentrate on your studies than on an adventure to unexplored lands," he said. "I am very sure your parents would appreciate that for all the money they have spent to send you to Oxford." Sir Lawrence looked down at the eager teenager who had jumped at the sound of his name and quickly stood at attention.

"Yes, Sir, Professor Pendleton. I will, Sir." Robert Smythe took a step back, and grabbing the hem of his friend's jacket, he quickly retreated. Culpepper turned toward the man who fairly towered over his own five-foot, six-inch frame.

"I apologize, Sir, if I seemed to be taking liberties, but I was only answering their questions." A little miffed by the interruption, Culpepper looked past him at the retreating students while he stuffed into his jacket pocket the piece of paper on which Robert Smythe had written his address.

"May I speak with you privately, Mr. Culpepper?" Sir Lawrence inquired. He motioned to the younger man to follow him.

"Yes, of course, Sir." Culpepper reluctantly bade farewell to the other students who still stood crowding around him, and followed Sir Lawrence. "How can I be of service?" he asked.

"Mr. Culpepper, I do appreciate your enthusiasm about your adventures to the south of Africa, but the boys –."

"I understand. You do not appreciate my filling their minds with nonsense – dreams of fame and riches." Culpepper frowned at the older gentleman. He thought the old codger seemed to think he had parental power over his protégés, which he was sure the professor did not.

"Yes, that's close to what I was about to say, but not entirely. The boys here at Oxford are greatly gifted. I would be highly displeased if any of them were swayed into giving up their opportunity here for a passing adventure."

Culpepper squinted. He wasn't at all sure he liked the old codger. Sir Lawrence had not learned what it meant to be tactful; but still he continued.

"What I mean to say is I would not want the *boys* to be swayed," he said with notable emphasis. "I, on the other hand, am older and more adept in handling a difficult situation away from home." He paused before continuing, leaving Culpepper tense with anticipation. "I find, Mr. Culpepper, that I am interested in your venture to Cape Colony."

Surprised by the professor's confession, Culpepper laughed. He had not alienated Sir Lawrence after all, he had simply recruited him! Perhaps the

3

old codger wouldn't be difficult after all. He pulled the paper out of his pocket again and took out a pencil.

"How interested?"

"Very, I should say. I would even be willing to help finance such a venture, were I be allowed to travel with you." Setting down his attaché case, Sir Lawrence lifted a meerschaum pipe from his vest pocket with a pouch of tobacco and stood there confidently, stuffing tobacco into the bowl. He wanted his counterpart to know he had money. Culpepper hesitated momentarily before responding, not desiring to appear too eager.

"I see. Well then, perhaps we should talk about this over dinner?" A grin crossed Sir Lawrence's face as he led the way to his favorite eating establishment.

Walking together, Culpepper and Sir Lawrence traded simple niceties during which time the professor asked his new friend about his family and education. Raised in India as a boy, Culpepper was alone in the world having lost his parents to war near his childhood home in Bombay. He was schooled in England, but had not attended a university.

Sir Lawrence, also alone after the passing of his wife 15 years before, explained he had been considering retirement for some time, but did not know until today what he wanted to do with himself. He was pleased to report he had decided he wanted to join the ranks of pioneers going to Cape Colony. Culpepper simply listened while making a silent survey of his host. Sir Lawrence seemed to be in good physical shape and could possibly handle the rigors of pioneering, he thought, but he wondered how long the old man would last in the deep, unforgiving jungles of Africa.

They soon arrived at Sir Lawrence's favorite establishment. The Gentleman's Lodge was paneled in dark mahogany, and smelled of aged tobacco and mildew, but it promised some of the best fish and chips anywhere in England. Sir Lawrence sat at his regular table, and while offering a chair to Culpepper, they were greeted by a friendly wench.

"'Ello, Sah Lar-rance." Sir Lawrence cringed every time he heard Rosie's high pitched Cockney dialect.

"Hello, dear. The usual, please," he said politely.

"Roit awaye, sah. 'Twill be moi pleashah. An' wha' wiw you 'ave, mate?" Culpepper noticed her wink at him, and could not help but smile. "I'll have whatever Sir Lawrence is having, thank you." With a small curtsy, she turned and worked her way through the crowd. He looked down at the chair Sir Lawrence offered, but the grin on his face was not lost on his new friend.

"A little while longer and I'll have her speaking like the Queen," whispered Sir Lawrence as he leaned in closer to him. Culpepper nodded and chuckled.

"So, Sir Lawrence –."

"Call me Larry, dear boy. If we are to enter into a venture together, we may as well be on a first name basis." Culpepper agreed and mentioned people referred to him as 'Reggie.' He voiced his thoughts about Sir Lawrence's physical health, but was quickly assured that the older gentleman was in excellent health and had actually been an athlete in his earlier years. Culpepper nodded doubtfully, but agreed to discuss his trip to Africa.

"I plan to leave the end of May or the first of June. If we want to avoid the winter snows below the equator, we must get there relatively quickly."

"I see. There's a ship traveling then, is there?"

"Yes. I believe 'twill be the Unity. She's a fast ship," Culpepper's voice cracked with excitement. He pulled a pencil and a sheet of paper from his vest pocket, turned it over and drew a map of Africa. Then, tracing the path he planned to take he said, "We should arrive in Port Elizabeth in about 18 days. Afterwards, we will take another trawler up the coast to Lourenco Marques in Delagoa Bay, and then travel up the coast by land to the Limpopo River. Traveling up the Limpopo should take about two weeks, barring any unforeseen circumstances." Culpepper wanted Sir Lawrence to understand their travel would be fraught with danger and hardship. They would have to be sure they were well armed, and their clothing would have to be of sturdy quality to provide adequate protection against the elements. Culpepper continued as Sir Lawrence took a piece of paper out of his attaché case and began to jot down some notes.

"I'll give you a list of items to take along, but we should travel light. I have a man who will meet us, but we will have to travel by small boat up the river and any large luggage will be an enormous hindrance. No large trunk, no suits." Sir Lawrence raised his eyebrow and made note – no suits.

"You said in your address today you had already found a mine?"

"Yes, but I am not willing to give away its location at this time." Sir Lawrence looked at him surprised. Culpepper continued. "You can understand I'm sure. These old mines were used by natives years ago and then abandoned. If anyone found out we were actually mining there, we could be overrun either by the natives or by pirates fully intent upon killing us or robbing us of any treasures we may have found."

"Of course, I understand," Sir Lawrence said, although he truly did not understand. He actually found himself a bit disappointed at Culpepper's refusal to divulge the mine's whereabouts, and he did not want to appear as if he had doubts already. "But you have already started digging, haven't you?"

"Yes! As you may already know, gold ore is an extremely difficult mineral with which to work," Culpepper explained. Sir Lawrence's obvious interest urged him on. "It is a soft metal, and easily marred. However, we have hired tribal men to help us since they are most knowledgeable. Nevertheless, we will still have to work very hard." Culpepper reached into his trouser pocket and withdrew a nugget of unprocessed gold weighing about six ounces. "Here is an example of what we can expect to find." Sir Lawrence's eyes sparkled at the sight.

"How much would you say that's worth, Reggie?"

"After processing, perhaps about £65."

"That much?"

"Why, yes, or more. You see, the gold standard is approximately ten and a half pounds to the ounce." Culpepper looked around to see if anyone was listening. "It will take a great deal of effort on our part, but I believe we are extremely close," he held up his hand pinching his index finger and thumb together, "to the greatest gold find ever made in Cape Colony. This mine could produce tons of gold and a wealth of other minerals, as well."

Several seconds ticked by as Sir Lawrence realized this was something he had to do. "You've convinced me, Reggie. You have my full support." Culpepper sat back in his chair almost shocked at Sir Lawrence's enthusiasm. The two men reached across the table to shake hands, ratifying their agreement.

The next day, Sir Lawrence met Culpepper at the Bank of England to withdraw £7,000. One thousand pounds would help to pay for his room and board while they stayed in Cape Colony, and the rest would be used to pay for passage on the ship, to purchase supplies, tools and equipment, and to finalize the legalities for a proper partnership. Culpepper had drawn up a contract for the two to sign, and the deal was made. The new company was named the "Culpepper/Pendleton Mining Cooperation." Culpepper had finally found his benefactor and he looked forward to the trip as much as the professor.

The next three months went by in frenzy as plans solidified for their trip to Africa. Meanwhile, Culpepper kept in close contact with his old friend, the Dutchman, to be sure everything was made ready for their arrival. Culpepper and Sir Lawrence became friends during their visits together, but despite their already close friendship, Culpepper could hardly wait to see the Dutchman, who had stayed behind in Cape Colony. When the day arrived for them to leave, Culpepper and Sir Lawrence stood on the deck of their passenger ship waving at the crowds of well-wishers, each believing they would soon return – richer and more gratified with life than ever before.

* * *

June 17, 1858. The ship, HMS Unity, departed London for Port Elizabeth, Cape Colony in the south of Africa. Sir Lawrence Pendleton, J. Reginald Culpepper, and 15 other passengers left London harbor in the early morning fog, looking forward to an adventure on the tip of the "dark continent."

Although sea travel on the Atlantic was often turbulent during the early months of summer, the voyage had been unremarkable. They traveled 18 days before arriving at Port Elizabeth where they were able to purchase many of the supplies needed for the rest of their adventure. In Port Elizabeth, they transferred to a trawler traveling north to a bustling Port Natal where they met Culpepper's friend and foreman. They would then travel by wagon to the Limpopo River, and it would take another two weeks floating north on the river before they reached their final destination. It had promised to be a strenuous trip for them all, but Sir Lawrence's determination was admirable. He promised he could handle it.

The foreman, Rikart Van Heusden, a Dutch immigrant to Transvaal, met the trawler at the docks in Port Natal. A stocky, red-haired man, at least ten years older than Culpepper, he stood an inch taller than his younger partner, and his rather square body was as strong as any athlete's Sir Lawrence had ever seen. His red hair was covered by a badly clashing red bandana, and his face sported a wide handle-bar mustache and a full chest-length beard. His demeanor was jolly and he reminded Sir Lawrence of St. Nicholas when he laughed. He had come with his parents to Transvaal as a young boy and had grown up in the Dutch colonies near Pretoria, north of the Orange River. A farmer by trade, he and his father had spent many a day looking for the legendary lost mine north of Transvaal.

"Hello, Culpepper!" The Dutchman said with his rich accent. "I haf looked forvard to your arrival."

"It is good to see you, Rikart. Thank you for meeting us." Culpepper reached out to Van Heusden. They embraced and shook hands.

"Yah. It is good." He looked at Sir Lawrence. "And velcome to you, Sir. I am happy to meet mit your acqvaintance." He bowed at the waist and waited for Sir Lawrence to respond before straightening up. Sir Lawrence was surprised by his formality.

"Why, thank you, Mr. Van Heusden. I assure you, the feeling is mutual." Sir Lawrence held out his hand as a gesture of camaraderie. Without realizing his own strength, Van Heusden made Sir Lawrence wince when he shook the professor's hand. The Dutchman then picked up all four of their suitcases and hauled them to the waiting wagon. Stacking them neatly on the back of the wagon with all the rest of the supplies from Cape Town, he jumped up to the seat and offered Sir Lawrence a hand. Sir Lawrence looked at the brawny Dutchman and laughed.

"Thank you, Sir. You are very helpful indeed!" Van Heusden literally jolted the older man into the wagon and slapped Sir Lawrence's back.

"Yah, Yah. It is a good ting I haf muscles, eh?"

Supplies were loaded, and Culpepper and Sir Lawrence were finally aboard. Van Heusden took the reins and slapped the solid backs of the two large work horses already hitched to the wagon. With a snap of the reigns and a rough jolt forward, the three unlikely friends began their new adventure to the River Limpopo.

Natives and horsemen had worn a trail over hundreds of years and even the jungle had not overrun the dusty path. Though winter rains were due, rain had not fallen much since May, and as they traveled north this time in early July, the hot temperatures blistered their skin. The arid weather was difficult for the old Englishman, but Sir Lawrence took it like the Oxford scholar he was. He simply raised an umbrella to protect his fair skin from the sun and waved his hand to signal them onward.

Traveling roads often overrun by vegetation was slow, but steady. After another 15 days' travel, they arrived at their destination, the gaping mouth of the Limpopo River. This fast-moving river promised yet another two weeks of laborious travel before they would arrive at their camp in the northern boundary area of Transvaal.

Van Heusden slapped at attacking mosquitoes as he urged the team backward and pushed the wagon onto a large river raft. The horses balked when the raft moved behind them, but he expertly managed to calm them while the raft captain firmly placed blocks under the wheels. Unhitching the horses, Van Heusden left them at the captain's home site and quickly joined the rest of the men on the raft as it began its way up river. Nightly, the captain pulled over to the bank so his passengers could rest. A campfire kept the coffee and food warm, but it was not long after dusk when the camp quieted down and they slept until the early morning when they would start their trek again.

Their base camp had been set up between the river bank and the jungle to provide protection from both the elements and any strays – animal or human – that might try to harm them. To the Dutchman, this was an ideal location; high enough to avoid confrontations from unfriendly natives, and low enough to gather water and supplies from the river. Sir Lawrence's generous contribution to the venture allowed him to complete the hiring of a few of the friendly Tsonga natives who would be helping in the mine. Tsongas gathered along the river bank as the captain deftly maneuvered the raft inland. Wading out to help, Tsongas jumped on board the raft to help him push the wagon to shore. Van Heusden called to one of the young men.

"M'mbulo! Over here! Help dem mit der bags."

A wiry young native jumped up from a rock overlooking the river and ran over to the wagon. "Yes, boss. I help you quick!" A member of the Tsonga tribe, M'mbulo was a good man, willing to do anything for the Dutchman who had befriended his father. He bowed repeatedly as he stood before Culpepper. "Sir" he said with a thick native accent, "You tell me do what you need, and I do. I work for you here wit my fader." Culpepper nodded his head.

"Good man. I expect you will help Sir Lawrence with whatever he needs, all right? Treat him well, M'mbulo."

"Yes, Sir, I treat him very well." M'mbulo picked up Sir Lawrence's baggage and walked behind the men as the Dutchman led them to their respective quarters.

Dust covered the tents, cots and anything that did not move, despite the dry wind, which was a constant factor. Sir Lawrence covered his mouth with a handkerchief so he could breathe when he dusted off his bed. He had M'mbulo set his suitcases by the tent wall and dismissed him with a thank you. M'mbulo bowed at the waist and thanking Sir Lawrence, he backed out through the canvas door. Lying on his cot, Sir Lawrence was rather dismayed when he found his legs dangling over the end, but his exhausted body needed rest, and he quickly fell into a deep sleep. Meanwhile, Culpepper and Van Heusden made their way through the dense jungle to the mine.

Culpepper had found the mine himself the year before while venturing through the area with Van Heusden. When they had first met, Van Heusden struck up a conversation about the lost mine legend which, over the years had circulated through the tribes and leaked down to Port Elizabeth. Van Heusden's father had frequently taken trips trying to find the mine himself, but had never been successful. When his father died, the Dutchman had inherited all his father's notes on the subject, and after he and Culpepper had become friends, the Dutchman shared what he knew about the mine with Culpepper who was the only one with enough adventure in his soul to pursue the findings.

The mining operation was small. They had less than half of the materials needed to do anything major, but the men were confident they had found the right place to start. Inconveniences were overcome by determination. The entrance to the mine was hidden by bushes so it would be difficult for intruders to find, but it was now secured with lumber supports. The mine opening was small – just large enough for Van Heusden to get through with a cart on wheels. However, the shaft opened to a larger area about 100 feet into the main artery. Men were hard at work, digging further into the hill than even Culpepper had expected. Since they were so close to the Limpopo River, there had been some water seepage, but the Dutchman assured the men they would be safe. Nonetheless, Culpepper told Van Heusden to be sure they put in some extra support beams and walls before they went much further to insure against cave-ins.

Only the most trusted of the natives were allowed to work in the mine at this point, and they had been sworn to secrecy by the cutting of a blood covenant, a tradition in the tribes which could never be broken, except by consequence of death. Not everyone agreed with the arrangement. A young man who had not yet been invited to help in the mine soon had an altercation with Van Heusden. Cocky and sure of himself, he went to his chief to accuse the white men of taking sacred treasures from the tribe. The chief rebuked him, reminding him of the covenant with their white brothers, and the young man was rejected by other tribal members. One day he simply walked out of the village. No one knew where he was, nor had they heard any news of him in any of the other villages. Van Heusden dispatched four men to go from village to village to search him out. He would have to be found lest he advertise the location of their camp, and possibly the mine.

Culpepper asked what the results were the previous six months while he was away. Van Heusden stated things were good. They had found a number of good-sized deposits, but it would be some time yet before they could process anything. Even so, Van Heusden said his practiced eye could determine these findings were of great value, and he was anxious for Culpepper to see them.

"I know Sir Lawrence will be excited about dese findings. Ve vill soon know fame and fortune, my friend, I am sure of it." The Dutchman also reported finding some kind of unusual element he had not recognized. He hoped Culpepper could determine what it was. Culpepper followed Van Heusden to the center of the mine. Looking up, he noticed clay-like green and red deposits.

"I must say, old man, I have never seen anything like this." He reached up to touch the clay. "I will have to check my mineral books to see if I can find something about it."

The Dutchman shook his head in agreement. "Neither haf I, my friend. Dat is vy I vant to take samples and send dem to Pretoria. I tink ve can get answers dere." They agreed, and wrapping a small sample in the Dutchman's bandana, they headed back to camp.

The next morning, Sir Lawrence carefully opened the flap to his tent, to look around to see if there was anyone about. The sun had risen an hour before, but he could still hear Culpepper's deep breathing as he slept in the tent next to his. Van Heusden was sitting in front of a campfire sipping coffee.

"Hello, Sir Lawrence. Sleep good?"

"Yes, thank you, Mr. Van Heusden. Considering the heat and the flies, I did sleep well." Van Heusden offered him a tin cup full of a black African brew, reminding the older gentleman to call him Rickart. Sir Lawrence nodded and sipped the steamy beverage cautiously. Bitterly strong, it did not taste like the watered-down coffee he was used to in England. Any weariness that might have lingered was immediately eradicated and Sir Lawrence's eyes bugged open. He sat on a stool next to the Dutchman.

My, that coffee would wake up the dead!" The Dutchman smiled at him.

"Yah, I make myself. Breakfast vill be ready soon."

"I would be eternally grateful, Rikart. I am famished."

12

The Dutchman chuckled. "You vill be more hungry dan dat, I am afraid. Hard vork, digging gold."

The two men's voices soon awakened their younger partner. Opening his dry eyes was difficult, but it did not take long for Culpepper to dress and make his appearance outside. He stood in the doorway of his tent stretching and voicing a yawn.

"Good morning!" The three spoke simultaneously. They laughed as Culpepper joined the others around the campfire. While the three enjoyed breakfast together, the Dutchman and Culpepper spoke confidently about their find.

"I am sure, Larry, you will be very impressed with what we find today. We have already collected some samples to send to Pretoria for analysis," said Culpepper. They showed him the green clay they had gathered, which very much interested Sir Lawrence who was glad to hear the report. This adventure was already becoming what he'd hoped it would be.

After a quick meal, the three men headed out to the mine. Sir Lawrence looked around him as they walked. The jungle was dense. Even though the path had already been cut, they had to use machetes to cut through some of the over growth. Eyes seemed to be peering at him through the vegetation, and it rather unnerved him. He listened carefully, keeping a watch on his surroundings.

"What about wild game, my boy? Will we be doing any hunting whilst we're here?" he asked, hoping not to sound alarmed.

"Of course, man. You've not eaten until you've tasted a fine cut of hyena meat! They say it tastes like chicken!" Culpepper and Van Heusden laughed at the joke, but Sir Lawrence was not amused. Unsure as to whether or not Culpepper was joking, he wondered if he could actually stomach the wild meat of a hyena.

It took almost twenty minutes before they arrived at their destination. Stifling heat and jungle humidity caused sweat to pour from their skin, soaking their clothes. Their breathing was labored, and their strength nearly waned. Sir Lawrence leaned against a tree to rest while both Culpepper and Van Heusden checked around carefully to guard against possible intruders.

Removing branches of leaves, they came to a small door, and opening it, they stepped in.

Sir Lawrence, standing tallest of the men, had to bend nearly in half to enter the mine, but his height was countered by his agility and he was able to maneuver into the cavern without a problem. When they reached the main artery, he was relieved to be able to straighten up to his full six-foot-three-inches, and relieved from the heat, he recuperated quickly. He looked around without saying a word, and not overly impressed. Dirt walls had been haphazardly supported by miscellaneous boards and studs, and some men were standing around doing nothing but talking. The walls had no gold vein in evidence, and he did not see a sign of any other elements. He stood quiet for a moment before saying anything, trying not to make any rash judgments.

"I do hope, Reggie, this is not the entirety of the mine. I see nothing here hinting at anything extraordinary."

Culpepper had been anxiously watching the professor, awaiting his reaction. He was sure Sir Lawrence would see the mine's potential, and he was disappointed by his partner's lack of enthusiasm.

"Oh, but you're mistaken, Larry. Watch this." Culpepper walked over to one of the carts and took up the shovel sitting against the wall next to it. He took a shovel full of dirt, sifted through it and then tried another. "Ah, here we are!" he exclaimed. Sir Lawrence came over to see what he'd found. Culpepper held out his hand. "There you are, Sir Lawrence, your first glimpse at gold dust."

Amazed, Sir Lawrence said, "Why, you don't say!" He gazed at shimmering flecks of gold mixed with the dirt in the palm of Culpepper's hand. It didn't seem to be much, he thought, but it was a start. Smiling, he looked up at Culpepper and said, "Let's get to work, old boy!" He took the shovel from Culpepper's hands, placed it over his shoulder, and started walking further back into the mine. Culpepper gave the Dutchman a congratulatory slap on the back, and the two of them followed their friend.

The work was as hard as Culpepper had warned; tedious and never ending. They carried one shovel load after another, sifting through each as they went, without much success. Many of the men were tired in just a few hours. By the end of the day, they had filled five carts with dirt, but had not found a decent sign of a gold vein the entire time. Sir Lawrence kept digging, though, tirelessly.

"We won't get rich sitting around the campfire, young man," he reminded Culpepper.

"This is true, Larry, but we have the entire summer to work, so don't tire yourself out in the beginning. This will take some time, and I don't want to lose my one and only recruit!"

Sir Lawrence lowered the shovel to rest against its handle. He took out an already filthy handkerchief and wiped grime off his forehead. "Right you are, my boy. Shall we retire then?" Sir Lawrence leaned the shovel up against the wall and started towards the front of the cavern. Culpepper looked at the Dutchman and shook his head amazed at Sir Lawrence's stamina. Of course, Sir Lawrence would never admit that he could barely move.

They called the natives up with them, shut the mine door and covered it up carefully. The sun was already setting, and the day was nearly gone. Food and a good cup of coffee was all they really wanted at that moment – sustenance and sleep.

The next day held much the same success. Little was found in the dirt hauled out of the mine. However, towards the end of the third day, Sulo, one of the miners called out to the Dutchman.

"Sah. I tink we have found someting!" The Dutchman put down his pickax and ran over to the young man.

"Vhat is it?" Van Heusden stood next to him to examine the finding.

The young man pointed to the ceiling of the cave where there was a small vein of gold-colored rock. The Dutchman looked up, and holding up a lantern, followed the vein over the top of his head, to the left and down the opposite wall. Biting the inside of his cheek, he patted the man on his back. "Good job, Sulo." He walked back to Culpepper.

"Reggie. Look at dis vhat Sulo found."

Culpepper followed him to the back of the tunnel with a lamp in hand. Looking at the vein, he smiled. "That's it, Rikart. We have found the vein! Get some men over here and start at this end. Sir Lawrence and I will work on the other."

Van Heusden quickly appointed three men to the task of cutting through the hard rock.

The crew worked feverishly for the next two days to break through the vein to see what was behind it. Sir Lawrence, nearly exhausted again by the end of the second day, decided to lift up his pickax one more time before he would quit. The ax went deep into a green clay deposit, which rather surprised him. He wondered about it without saying a word. Pulling the pick axe from the soft deposit, a large specimen fell from the upper wall, nearly knocking him over. Looking down at it, he saw it wasn't gold at all. He stooped over the piece of colored clay and called Culpepper over to look at it.

"Reggie. Over here."

"What is it, old boy?" Culpepper put his tools down and joined Sir Lawrence by the other side of the cave.

"What do you suppose this is?" Sir Lawrence picked up a small piece of the clay-like substance. "It's colorful enough, but it certainly is not gold." Disappointment registered in his voice. Culpepper took the piece from his hand and crumbled it in his own. There in the middle of that small piece of clay lay a small, yellow gem. Looking closer, Culpepper's eyes grew wide.

"By all that is Holy, would you look at that!" Sir Lawrence came closer as did the rest of the men.

"What? What have I found, Reggie?"

"If I didn't know better, Larry, I would say you have just found a diamond." Sir Lawrence stepped forward to look again. Culpepper spit on the specimen and rubbed it on his trousers. "It definitely looks like a diamond, wouldn't you say so Rikart?"

The Dutchman took it from Culpepper and held it up to a lamp. "Yes, my friend! I belief you haf found someting ve vere not expecting!" They looked back at the rest of the clay deposit still lying on the floor. All three of them dove for it and started rummaging through the clay.

"Here's one!" exclaimed the Dutchman.

"Here's another!" said Sir Lawrence. They pulled down what they could from the wall and spent the rest of the afternoon and evening searching through the colorful clay. They had truly found a treasure – 14 good-sized diamonds.

The mine took on a new life. Africans and white men alike worked feverishly starting at the front of the mine, now looking for veins of clay instead of gold. Every night, before turning in, Culpepper would record their findings, and their treasure quickly grew. Time seemed to stand still while they worked, but before they realized two weeks had passed. Sir Lawrence found the work exhilarating, and found himself looking forward to the day he could stand before his students and give a report about his adventure.

One night, after their supper, the Dutchman heard the faint sound of drums. Thinking it odd, but not wanting to alarm the others, he went to bed, keeping his pistol close at hand. The next day, Tsongas who had been staying with the Europeans for convenience, mysteriously left the camp, one by one. Van Heusden, Sir Lawrence and Culpepper were too busy working on sifting through the findings to notice the men had abandoned them. Culpepper, already having collected over 250 nice specimens, was preparing for the next day's work. He knew there was something more, but he was not sure just what it was or where they would find it. He only had a feeling they were close to something extraordinary, and he was excited about it.

After another day of hard work and recording, the three men quietly ate their supper. The camp was growing dark, and the fire had burned down to coals. Extremely tired, the men said good night to each other and headed to bed.

Sleep was only moments away when suddenly a wild scream shook them to their bones. Naked natives from the bush came running into the camp. Spears and shields in their hands, they surrounded the three Europeans. One man poked his spear at Culpepper and then gestured for them to leave the camp. Only then did Van Heusden notice their Tsonga friends had deserted them, and he remembered hearing the war drums the

17

night before. He knew then the natives were being warned of imminent attack. He had thought to mention the drums to M'mbulo that afternoon, but the young native had not come back to the mine that day. Now the Dutchman was angry at himself for not being more attentive to what he knew was possible danger. Surrounded by their attackers, the three Europeans were taken from their camp to the village of one of the Venda tribes.

Faces decorated with white dye, natives wearing nothing but colorful head dresses and loin cloths, danced around the three white men who were being guarded by very tall warriors. Helpless to do anything, the white men stood together silently while the natives performed traditional tribal dances. Swaying hypnotically back and forth, shoulders jutted forward and then back. Men jumped over a fire pit to prove their manhood and worship of an unknown god. The drums grew louder and were played faster until they finally culminated in a fever pitch. The Vendas had been held in great fear by the Tsongas, and Culpepper now knew why; they were not a tribe to be reckoned with. Though the Tsonga workers had never complained about their tasks, they never said much about anything; they had kept their distance from the white men not wanting to be associated with them in case of attack. He blamed himself for being so engrossed in the work he had not noticed what was going on.

When the dances stopped, the three of them were taken to stand before the tribal king. Standing next to the chief, Van Heusden recognized the man who had deserted the Tsonga tribe before Culpepper and Sir Lawrence arrived. The man was a traitor to his tribe – he had betrayed their whereabouts to the Venda chief and made covenant with them for protection. He tried to lunge at the man, but was held back by his captors. Even though the Dutchman could not reach him, the coward stepped back behind the chief and jutted out his chin like a defiant child. The chief, already tired of the man, gave him a signal to step back. He had cut covenant with the traitor and would stand by that covenant, but he did not have to put up with him. The chief stood with arms akimbo, preparing to speak. Van Heusden translated for the others.

"You come to our land, white man, to destroy it! You come to take our people as slaves and kill them when you have found your riches. You will not do so any longer. The gods will not allow it. I will not allow it!" Natives roared their agreement and the sound sent chills up Sir Lawrence's back.

Culpepper listened carefully to Van Heusden's interpretation, and then, despite shaking knees, he responded with as much diplomacy as he could muster.

"Sir, if I may speak." He waited for the chief's signal. "I have not come to take your people as slaves. I have come to help them. I come to give them food, clothing. I come to be friends with them."

"No!" The chief shouted. "The god of creation, Umveliqangi, says you lie! The penalty is death!" The villagers reacted again with shouting, raising their spears and cutting their arms.

"Wait!" Culpepper put up his hands. With Van Heusden's translation he said, "I, too, have a god! He is greater than the god Umveliqangi! I will show you what he can do!" He took out a match from his vest pocket and flicking the tip, it lit into a small flame. The natives stopped what they were doing and stared at the match. He dropped it onto the dry grass, which ignited with a burst of energy while they all watched. The natives jumped back, fear registering on their faces. Next, he reached inside his coat pocket and drew out a pistol.

"This is only an example of his tremendous power!"

Pointing it at the headdress of what appeared to be the medicine man, he shot a hole into it, knocking the headdress off the man's head. The man dived to the ground. The chief's eyes opened wide with fear, and the rest of the natives ran away from them.

"Do you see? My god could kill you all in a very short time," he said turning toward them and pointing the gun at the chief and the man hiding behind him. Spears were dropped in surrender and they fell to the ground in fear. "If you kill us, he will strike back at you!" The chief stood to approach carefully, but Culpepper threatened him with the point of the gun. The chief raised his arms to protect himself.

"May I speak?" the chief begged. Culpepper signaled his permission. He knew he'd won this battle. "If we do not kill you, you will make sacrifice to your god and we will not be harmed?" Culpepper nodded affirmatively. The chief motioned for the men guarding them to let them loose and give them safe passage back to their camp. They would never hear what happened to the traitor, but the Dutchman figured he would be the next sacrifice to Umvelinqangi. Van Heusden thought their safety factor back to camp had greatly improved. Nevertheless, Culpepper left the gun out in plain sight to be sure nothing would happen to them.

"Good save, old chap," was Sir Lawrence's only comment before they entered their respective tents. His eyes reflected his relief, and his shoulders slightly slumped with exhaustion. This had been a little too close for comfort. Culpepper responded with a simple thank you, and then upon entering his own tent, he fainted.

The Tsongas did not return easily. The Venda tribe's sudden interest in the white men was a sign the spirits might be turning against them. Nevertheless, Van Heusden rounded them up, convincing their chief it was safe to return. Three days after the attack, one by one, the natives finally returned, if for nothing else but a free meal. M'mbulo approached the Dutchman last.

"My fader says I must return," he said half-heartedly. "I am not liking it. My wife is with child and stays in our village alone, and the Vendas want pay back what was done to dem." M'mbulo's head bowed apologetically but he needed to let his friend, the Dutchman, know his fears. Van Heusden nodded his understanding.

"Ve are grateful for your return, M'mbulo. If you tink dat dere is danger, you will be permitted to go home. I promise." Relieved to hear this, M'mbulo returned to work in the mine with the rest of the men.

Guns were now kept in close proximity and the workers kept very quiet during their tenure in the mines. The work continued to grow more difficult with every bucket of dirt being taken out, and there seemed to be some unrest within the camp. Nevertheless, the men continued working as ordered. Culpepper and Van Heusden came up with a plan to have some of the men work in a place on considerably further away from them as a decoy in case the other tribe should be watching.

Thick vegetation growing around them was perfect camouflage for the natives. Culpepper knew they could be under surveillance the entire time without their ever being aware anyone was watching. He had the Dutchman take frequent trips to the decoy mine, making plenty of noise so the other tribe would watch him instead of Culpepper and Sir Lawrence as they made their way to the mine hidden in the bush – the decoy seemed to be working.

One day as the Dutchman walked, looking from side to side without turning his head, he could see African eyes watching him from the bush as he made his way to the decoy. Pulling his pistol from his side holster, he raised it and shot above his head. There was a frightened shout and the Dutchman watched a half dozen naked backsides disappear into the black jungle. He put his gun back in his holster and smiled. Once again, the great pistol god had protected him.

Chapter II

The Discovery

Tension filled the air. It had been over three weeks since the first attack, but Van Heusden had a gnawing feeling things were beginning to get tense again. The Tsongas had begun whispering during their meals, some left work early, some came late. Each day they seemed more nervous. One night after another day of hard work and little success, the Europeans sat around the campfire discussing their next move. Drums sounded in the distance, and all conversation stopped. By now they could tell the difference between the beats for communication and those calling for war. They all turned in, but none slept.

The next day, ominous clouds, heavy with rain, flew overhead hinting at danger in the air. The three white men had barely eaten when the vegetation was disturbed. They all jumped to their feet and grabbed their guns. M'mbulo came into the camp, limping. "Sah! Sah!" he cried. Van Heusden ran out to the young man, catching him as he fell.

"Vhat happened, M'mbulo? Your leg is bleeding!" The Dutchman laid him on the ground cradling his head in the crook of his arm.

"Vendas attack our village, sah. My wife dey take away, and my fader. Many run away." Pain crossed his face as he held onto a tourniquet he had wrapped around the gash in his upper leg. Blood oozed from the wound despite his efforts. His femoral artery had been nicked, but he did not bleed out immediately. Van Heusden ran back to his tent for his medical kit while Culpepper knelt over M'mbulo. He knew the young man had been spared by the Vendas to send them a message; they would soon be dead if they did not get out of there very quickly.

"Will he be all right?" Sir Lawrence inquired as he stood behind them. His eyes darted to the right and left searching the bush.

"I think so. But I don't think we will be if we don't leave very quickly," Culpepper replied. As he stood there, Sir Lawrence suddenly grabbed his neck and panic filled his eyes. He felt a small pin sticking into his skin. He had been shot with a poisonous dart. The poison, traveling quickly through his system, paralyzed him immediately. Sir Lawrence collapsed and fell over Culpepper, tumbling to the ground.

"Larry! Oh my God! Larry, what's happening?" Culpepper quickly examined Sir Lawrence's blue face and felt for a pulse on his neck. He found the dart. "Rikart! Watch out!" he called as he turned to warn his old friend. It was too late. Van Heusden had heard the commotion and had already started out of his tent. A dart flew out from the bush and hit him. He grabbed his neck and smiled at Culpepper.

"Good bye, my friend," Van Heusden muttered his last words as he fell face forward.

Culpepper hit the ground and crawled into his tent, darts whizzing past his head. He grabbed his pistol and a box of bullets, and then finding a hole in the back of the tent, stumbled through the canvas flap before the rest of the tribe attacked the camp to search him out. He stood up and started running, not looking back to see what they were doing, heading toward the mine. The Vendas did not know where the mine was, he was positive, so he ran as fast as he could, hoping they would be too preoccupied with the camp to worry about him. He was wrong. A dart caught in his holster as he ran.

He had to outrun these men, and he had to hide as quickly as possible or he, too, would be killed. He dodged tree after tree, being slapped by branches and tangled in vines then turned to travel opposite the mine to divert them away from it. He stopped long enough to catch a breath and aim at the men following him. A spear caught in a tree above his head. Trying to keep calm, Culpepper held his breath, but his hand shook as he held up the pistol. A shot rang out, and a bullet hit a man square in the chest. The other native stopped running. He momentarily looked at the dead man, picked up his spear and threw it at Culpepper. The sharp spear landed on the side of his foot. Culpepper fell back in pain, and dropped his weapon. The native scurried to finish the job, and just as he lifted his knife to kill his prey, Culpepper found the gun, turned over and shot him dead. He pulled the spear out of his foot, tied his bandana around it to try to stop the blood that might give him away, and crawled into the bush.

Back on his feet but limping, Culpepper started running again. There was no path to follow, and jungle vegetation impeded his way. Stumbling through the bush, he fell over a large, dead tree. His balance was already being affected by the pain and swelling in his foot and he had trouble standing up again. Using the end of the tree to steady himself, the rotten bark crumbled under his weight. The large tree was hollow! Investigating further, he realized he could use it to his benefit. A man of small stature, Culpepper found he could crawl inside feet first. Other branches had fallen over the old tree, which helped him to camouflage his whereabouts. He pulled leaves, dirt and debris over the open ends and scooted as far back under the branches as possible. Inside the tree, he lay silent and barely breathing not far from where he'd been wounded hoping a blood trail had not been left behind. Culpepper's foot had not bled much, but it may have been enough for them to believe he was still alive. He had a feeling they would not quit searching for him until they found him. Armed with just his pistol, he waited until he heard angry voices not far away. The men of the Venda tribe had found their companions and they were now looking for him. He did not move and he could barely breathe.

Leaves rustled under bare feet. Culpepper had stuffed as much refuse into the open end of the tree as he could to hide himself, but he wondered if it was enough. Insects crawled over his face, up his nose and into his ears, but he dared not move lest he be found. As he said a prayer asking God to help him, a familiar voice broke into his thoughts. It was the chief himself. He had seen the men Culpepper had killed and wondered about the holes in their bodies. He had never seen a weapon wound a man this way. He stood over the tree where Culpepper hid. Culpepper knew if he was found, he'd be burned together with the men he'd killed. In desperation, he sent a short, silent prayer to Heaven. *God, get me out of this and I will do anything for you*, he thought.

The chief took a spear from one of his men and shoved it through one of the holes in the tree. If it had been any closer, Culpepper would be missing his nose. He took in a quick breath and closed his eyes. *God, help me!* The chief pulled out the spear and again thrust it into the tree towards the other end. Culpepper's small stature helped him this time. The spear wasn't even close. Still he did not move. The chief looked into the end of the tree and saw nothing but leaves and dead branches. Turning to his men, he beckoned them to follow him. They left, Culpepper could tell by the sound of feet crushing the leaves and branches underneath, but still he did not move. Fear held him captive, and still barely breathing, he listened for nearly an hour until he fell asleep.

Culpepper awakened with a start. Darkness engulfed him and he had to determine where he was before he moved. Then he remembered. Listening for any sound, he lay another half hour before pulling wiggling out of the tree trunk. Night had fallen, and all was silent. He had been inside the tree trunk for nearly six hours. The moon was a sliver in the sky, offering little light, but it was enough for Culpepper to make his way to the mine. His foot throbbing, Culpepper cautiously approached the opening. Limbs and vegetation had not been disturbed. His native friends had not given away their secrets.

He wondered about young M'mbulo and how he fared after the attack on the camp. He had tried to save his friends, the good man he was, but Culpepper knew there was little hope he was still alive.

Culpepper did not try to return to the camp to see if anyone had actually survived. He knew better. He figured the tribe would have ransacked their supplies, taken any food the team had left behind, and then left the bodies for the wild animals. Instead, he decided to make his camp inside the mine. He knew he needed to act quickly, doing his best not to freeze in the damp cold. It was all that mattered. Blood had soaked his bandana. The wound would have to be cauterized. Looking for anything with which to start a small fire, he found one of the shovels. He stood on the bowl and pulled on the handle until it broke, and used part of its wood to fuel the fire. Cleaning the shovel's bowl as well as he could, he heated it over the hot coals. Finally, taking the blood-soaked handkerchief off his foot, he slid out of his boot and examined the wound. One of the main veins in the side of his foot had been severed. He could barely stand the thought of cauterizing, but focusing on the red-hot shovel, he knew if he did not burn his wound an infection could take his life. He had worked too hard and too long to allow a cut to take him down, he decided. He stood up and took off his belt then shoved it between his teeth. Turning his foot sideways and closing his eyes, he stepped on the hot metal. Screaming in pain, he passed out.

The sun's rays streamed through the cracks in the mine's cover before Culpepper opened his eyes. His foot still hurt, but it had stopped bleeding. Sitting up, he struggled to his feet to see if he could walk. When he fell again, he knew he could do nothing for at least another day. He crawled around the mine to collect what little equipment he could find, and he made camp.

An analytical man, Culpepper reasoned he needed to make plans and take stock of his supplies. He had his pistol, so he could hunt if he needed to. Otherwise, he would eat what he could find crawling in the mine. Water was not a problem, either, since there were plenty of leaks in the walls. He would be able to survive without a problem. When he was able, he would leave for America, taking what little gold or diamonds he could find and never looking back. Before the middle of the second day, he picked up Van Heusden's pick ax and, while standing on one foot, began chopping at the wall deep inside the mine.

For Culpepper, endless days turned into interminable weeks, and interminable weeks became ceaseless months; he was unaware when November arrived. Previously a man of means, a man of high esteem and integrity, Culpepper had evolved into something other than he knew himself to be – a wreck of a man, surviving on nothing but plump, unpalatable grubs; crunchy, tasteless insects; slimy, oozing worms. The first meal took all his strength to bear; now it didn't matter what he ate, as long as he ate. He passed each meal by imagining the delicacies he'd enjoyed in England, and he wondered when he would die. Nevertheless, he knew he must keep going, he must keep surviving.

After the month passed, Culpepper decided to return to the base camp to see what was left, if anything. The camp was waiting for his return, but he found no more than a skeleton when he arrived. He had practically crawled as he carefully made his way through the jungle. When he arrived, he found the tents still standing – a ghostly reminder to anyone who might try to trespass that others had been there before, and they had not lived for long. The Vendas had stolen the cots they had slept in, the trunks with their clothing and their tool chests. On hands and knees, Culpepper crawled through the back wall of his own tent to find nothing but a few scraps of material from tattered clothing; nothing worth keeping. His weapons were gone, his keepsakes and all the diamonds found previously. He cursed under his breath.

Slipping out of his tent and into Van Heusden's, Culpepper found a few small diamond specimens under the canvas flap. Otherwise, Van Heusden's tent was also stripped bare. Next, he quickly examined Sir Lawrence's quarters. Only three letters, already in their envelopes and addressed, remained where the cot had once been. Culpepper picked them up, deciding to mail them for his friend when he returned to Port Elizabeth. Turning to leave, his foot skimmed a small object under the back canvas flap. Bending down to see what it was, he found Sir Lawrence's Bible, worn but still intact. Culpepper thumbed through the small volume and stuffed it into his shirt with the letters. Taking another look around, he stopped to think about his lost friends. There was no evidence of their having been there – no bodies remained.

Culpepper prepared to leave. Somehow, he thought, he must notify Sir Lawrence's friends of his death. He decided to send a telegram to Oxford University when he posted the letters. They would be able to notify any surviving relatives, but he was sure Sir Lawrence had no one. Afterward, he could leave this God-forsaken country. Taking another quick look around, Culpepper scurried out, again careful not to be seen by any spies from the Venda tribe.

Back at the mine, Culpepper did not find any new diamond veins. Discouraged and hopeless, Culpepper finally broke.

"God! Where are you? God, please don't let me die here." He leaned on his shovel, crying like a child, when out from inside his shirt fell Sir Lawrence's Bible. He had kept it there for safekeeping, and as if Sir Lawrence was speaking to him directly, he knew he needed to read it for himself. Huddled in front of the little fire kept alive day and night, he read the page to which it had opened.

"Lo, I am with you always, even to the end of the earth." Culpepper held the Book to his breast, and bowed his head. "Thank you, God. Thank you."

Sleep did not come easy to Culpepper that night, but after it finally had come, he was awakened by a damp, cold discomfort. He had been sleeping on the cave's dirt floor, and turning over, his hand slipped across mud. Waking up suddenly, he realized the mine was flooding. The fire had gone out, and he was in pitch black darkness. Feeling his way to the door of the mine, Culpepper quickly went outside. The rains had come, and the river was rising. Culpepper had to find higher ground. With no available light, he moved slowly through the bush back to the camp, hoping he would be able to take refuge in the tent. When he finally got there, there was still one tent standing. Sitting inside, he shivered his way through the rest of the night.

Early the next day, Culpepper slid out the back of the tent the same way he had during his previous visit. He knew the Vendas could be watching, and he wanted no one to find him now. He hiked back to the mine, but when he arrived, Culpepper was shaken by what he found. The mine had indeed been flooded, with at least four feet of water standing towards the rear. He groped around in the six inches of water on the floor towards the front of the mine to find the small stash of treasure he had left behind. Then he grabbed everything he could salvage to take it back to the tent, realizing he would have to give up his dream and leave this place before he made his great find. Hopelessness was all he owned now, and it threatened to take his life. He made his way back to the tent and spent another lonely night at the abandoned camp.

Culpepper was prepared to leave the next day. He had buried all the tools and made a satchel out of his jacket to carry what few possessions remained. As an afterthought, he decided to stop again at the mine before heading out. Stepping down into the cavern, his boot sunk deep into slimy mud. Fashioning a small torch out of a branch and some grass he had picked and dried out the day before, he headed cautiously back into the cave.

It was still flooded, but the rains had calmed a little, and the flooding had at least not increased. He made his way back into the main artery, muddy water up to his chest. Looking up at the walls, he examined them carefully. He had not seen those colors in the walls before. Evidently, water seeping into the mine had washed away part of the wall. Holding the torch up, he examined the wall and then he saw it – the largest vein of greenish clay they had found yet. A feeling of excitement bubbled up inside, and he quickly waded back to the front of the mine and out to the camp to unbury his tools. Only two lanterns remained, but they would be enough for him for now. He checked the kerosene supply. One was half full, the other was nearly full: they would have to suffice.

Culpepper knew the mine walls, extremely weak by now, could collapse any time. He would have to hurry if he was to work through the clay fast enough. Chopping at the vein, he pulled down bucket after bucket of clay, examining it as he went. Soon he had 20 good-sized diamonds in his hand. He knew he was almost there. He worked feverishly into the night and well into the next day before he stopped to rest. Sleeping for only an hour, he continued.

The vein was immense. It covered the entire back quarter of the cave. Culpepper knew he would have to get what he could out of the largest part, and then perhaps in the future, he would return. Perhaps then the Vendas would be gone and he could renew his mining efforts. He had always known there was something great in store for him, and he was sure this was it. Finally, he had success. Finally, he had something with which to make a new life. Working feverishly to bring the wall of clay down, his pick ax suddenly hit something extremely hard. Pulling back, Culpepper was unable to move it. Persevering with the axe, he worked around to the left and right of where he had hit the hard deposit. Hitting the wall with as much strength as he had, the pick axe passed through leaving a gaping hole where water poured in around him. He had broken through to the river.

The wall began to crumble. Panicked, Culpepper tried to swim out, but the current headed him the wrong way. He grabbed a lantern floating in front of his face. Knowing he was in another fight for his life, he began to tread water, holding up the lantern to get his bearings. Light bounced off the water and reflected the greenish clay in the way. That was when he saw it: a diamond bigger than his hand. The water had removed all the dirt and clay surrounding it and the diamond just stared back at him, inviting him to get it. Now floating near to the top of the cavern, Culpepper reached up and took hold of the rock, pulling with all his might. When the stone let loose, he fell back into the water, the diamond in his hand. He could not believe his eyes! Here was the vein he had been looking for all this time. It had to be the greatest find known to man!

With water threatening to bury him, he realized he would drown if he did not make a move. Looking around, the light all but gone, he dove under to see if there might be a way to swim out. After three diving attempts, feeling the wall in the darkness, he found the large hole where the water was coming in. He slipped through it into the raging waters of the Limpopo. Swimming towards the light underwater, he soon was able to reach the surface. With the heavy seasonal rains, the river had swollen over its banks. It took all his strength, but he finally reached the southern banks of the river. Exhausted, he pulled himself from the rushing water and collapsed onto a huge boulder. Looking up at the gray sky, he closed his eyes and passed out, the huge diamond still in his hand.

Chapter III

A New Land

March 9, 1859

Salt air slapped Reggie's face and wind mussed his short-cropped hair as he leaned over the rail of the Cape Colony sailing ship, Alacrity. Weary of the trip already, Reggie imagined himself on the shores of Massachusetts, hoping he would be able to avoid any of the formalities of customs in America. With people gathered to his left and right watching the festivities of departure from Port Elizabeth, he grinned to himself as he thought about the treasure he had hidden in the large carpet bag at his side. The Cape Colony venture had indeed been profitable. He raised the bag close to his chest and fell back through the crowd.

Nearly a year had passed since Reggie had first met Sir Lawrence Pendleton. The Culpepper/Pendleton Mining Corporation had been short lived, but it had been beneficial for him, anyway. Culpepper had spent five long months alone in the jungle looking for the diamond treasure which was now held in his hand. Walking back to Port Natal after his near-death experience in the Limpopo River, he realized his African adventure had been more a disaster than a success because of the loss of his two good friends and the natives who had worked the mine with him. He'd had to live in rags, eating grubs and rodents to survive, and he had a horrible scar on his right foot to prove his story.

After he'd awakened from passing out on the river bank, he had returned to the campsite to check for any remaining usable items. There was hardly a sign of his having been at the camp. The mine had been completely destroyed, except for the highest area where he had been camping. He found his jacket and a bucket in which he'd kept the smaller diamonds discovered during his months alone in the mine. He'd had to dig through the mud to find tools and anything that may have dropped during the flood, but other than those two major things, there was nothing much else to claim. He left them behind and started his trek back to civilization.

The jungle was unforgiving, and travel back to Natal was hard. Rather than try to fight the jungle, he followed the river south until he saw the river raft coming toward him. The captain recognized the Englishman, and pulled him aboard. Culpepper slept for three days as they traveled back to civilization.

He would never forget the first meal he ate when he reached Natal. The first morsel of bread had tasted heavenly as it melted in his mouth and he'd savored each bite before he swallowed and then ravaged the rest of his meal. Topping it off with a glass of wine, he toasted his lost friends.

Returning to Port Elizabeth had been both a sad and a happy occasion: happy he finally returned to civilization, but sad for the loss of his companions. He missed his old friend, the Dutchman. He found Van Heusden's few friends just outside of Port Elizabeth and notified them of his death. The letters he'd placed inside the cover of Sir Lawrence's Bible were ruined completely during his swim in the Limpopo River, but the Bible had survived. He had carefully cleaned and dried the pages, and wrapping the book in brown paper, he sent it to Oxford University with a letter explaining what had happened. During their trip to Africa, he had learned Sir Lawrence had no kin; having been widowed early in life, he never remarried. The University would be his only beneficiary. With great remorse, but also with some gratification, he had given the package to the postman and turned toward his new life in America.

The little money left from the venture was his own since Sir Lawrence belonged to both he and his partner. He went to the bank and retrieved it. He considered stopping into the assay office where he could claim cash for the over fifty small diamonds he had sown into his jacket lining, but standing in front of the assayer's office, he decided not to enter. He knew if anyone heard of the mine, the place would be overrun by miners, and he wanted to leave it there untouched as a memorial to the two brave men and Tsongas who had lost their lives searching for a treasure only he knew existed.

He did have the jewel, though. Yellow in color, and as clear as crystal, Culpepper named it the Jewel of Africa. He figured it was the greatest find in Cape Colony – in all of Africa for that matter. It appeared to weigh at least five pounds, but he had no idea of its real worth. When buying the ticket for the trip to America, he decided he would trade in the smaller diamonds for cash there and keep the huge diamond as collateral for his future home. He boarded the Alacrity, made himself comfortable in his cabin, and slept for 14 hours in the comfortable softness of a good mattress and expensive bedding.

The first month of the cruise was enjoyable and restful. Reggie took full advantage of this time of rest to write in his diary about his experiences in the jungles of Transvaal. It was therapeutic, and he felt better after confessing his regret at having involved his newfound friend, Sir Lawrence Pendleton of Oxford, in such a dangerous venture. He grieved for his friends and longed to be able to see them again. Nevertheless, he knew he must overcome the depression assailing him. America promised a new beginning, and the Jewel of Africa provided a way back to prosperity.

By the end of the first month, however, sickness was found among the passengers. For years, consumption had been rampant among travelers between England and South Africa, and had caused not a little difficulty in the cities of Cape Town, Johannesburg and Port Elizabeth. A man named Joseph Humphrey, who was in charge of the company on the ship, kept people in their cabins so as to avoid infecting anyone. Another Humphrey – William – died from an unknown illness, despite Joseph Humphrey's efforts, and was buried at sea. Fearing the worst, the ship's doctor checked the Humphrey family, but he found no one else with any evidence of consumption. It had taken over two weeks, but the scare ended as quickly as it had started. People began to feel at ease again, and relaxed more often on the main deck.

A young lady, Victoria O'Neil, sat comfortably on a deck chair the day everyone was finally allowed out of their cabins. She loved breathing the salt air, lying in the sun, watching sea gulls fly over head. They had just passed through the Azores, so the birds were plentiful, even this far out at sea. She set aside the book she had been reading to enjoy the birds. Closing her eyes against the bright reflection of the sun off the waves, she soon dozed off. She was awakened when she felt someone's eyes watching her and realized a shadow blocked the heat of the late afternoon sun. Her eyes flickered open and she raised her hand over her face to look up at the man standing over her, silhouetted by the glare of the sun.

"Miss, if you don't mind my saying so, I believe I am looking at the loveliest sight I have ever seen."

"Sir? What are you looking at?" Victoria sat up straight to see over the ship's rail. Her reddish blonde hair gleamed in the sunshine, and her fair skin was only slightly freckled.

"You, Miss."

"I?" Surprised, Victoria blushed and looked away from the man. "Well, I cannot say I mind your observation, sir, but I dare say it is rather forward." Trying to hide her pleasure, she mentally rebuked herself for being flattered by his comment.

"Perhaps," said Reggie Culpepper, sitting in the lounge chair next to her. He was clean shaven except for the small mustache above his upper lip. He wore a fine woolen four-button suit and sported a top hat in his hand. "But I could not help myself since it is the truth. You are indeed the loveliest thing I have ever laid my eyes on." Putting her hand up to cover her smile, she looked away again. She was shy, he thought. "Have I offended you?"

"No!" she responded, a little too exuberantly. "I mean, no sir, I am neither offended nor hurt by your comment. I am simply taken by surprise." She sat up straight and turning to the other side of her chaise lounge, she readied to leave. The light in her blue eyes reflected her pleasure and her rosebud-shaped lips twitched as she tried to hide yet another smile.

"I had not expected such a fine compliment, Sir, but in truth, I cannot deny it pleased me," she said honestly. She stood up and reached for her book, but before she could retrieve it, he picked it up for her. Reggie introduced himself and invited her to lunch.

"You would not leave me now, would you, lest I be left thinking I had indeed insulted you. I would be miserable, to say the least, believing I may have wounded such a delightful creature such as yourself." Mischief, which she found quite charming, registered in his eyes.

"Sir, I would not want to leave you in such a state as that. I shall accept your kind invitation." Reggie bowed and offered her his hand to escort her to the dining room.

Victoria O'Neil had traveled with her parents to Cape Colony from Dublin when she was only 10. Her father, Patrick O'Neil, was a businessman who had found an open market in the banking business in Port Elizabeth where they had lived quite comfortably until her father was taken ill just two years before. She was only 17 when he died. When she and her mother buried him, just six months before the voyage, they decided to travel to America where they could start a new life together there. Patrick O'Neil had provided a substantial inheritance to her mother, but not enough on which to live the rest of their lives. She and her mother would have to find work before long.

"And what will you do there, Miss O'Neil?" Reggie asked. His eyes never left hers. He was sincere in wanting to know more about her; another captivating characteristic Victoria liked about the man.

"I am afraid I truly have no idea. Mother is a seamstress and a housekeeper, so she should be able to find something in Boston, but I, I am just the daughter of a well-to-do businessman. I have no real education, except for what I learned from Mother and Father, so I expect I will help Mother in her duties. Whatever we do, I know God will provide for us." Reggie nodded. He knew the same. God would provide, if they could but trust Him, for God had provided for him.

"And you, Mr. Culpepper? What will you do?"

"I hope to farm. I have some small monies to buy land, and I plan to build it up from there."

"Oh? You are a farmer then?"

"Heavens, no. I have never farmed in my entire life!" he laughed. "But after my experiences in Africa, I expect I can do just about anything I set my mind to. I love animals, and I am very interested in learning about the native plants."

"So you'll buy some acreage," she replied. Reggie nodded. Victoria had a mind for business like her father, and she unwittingly found herself calculating expenses and income. "How much land do you plan to purchase?"

"Perhaps 300 acres or so. It depends on the going price in Georgia. Once we arrive in Boston, I have some business to take care of. Afterwards I will head south."

"Oh, I see." For some reason, Victoria found herself disappointed. She thought he could be her first friend in America – her only friend, at this point. "Perhaps we could see each other before you leave, then?"

"Definitely," he said, taking hold of her hand and kissing it.

Victoria, Reggie and his precious carpet bag spent most of their extra time on the ship together. Victoria wondered about the carpet bag Reggie always kept at his side. She asked him once what was so important, and he responded with, "A surprise for the future, my dear." She asked if it was very valuable, and he just smiled. She realized he was not going to reveal his secret, but she didn't really care. She found herself falling in love with him, and his secrets did not matter to her. She decided not to pursue the subject any further, at least for the time being.

Reggie's journal was nearly complete by the time they docked on May 17, 1859. His prose was poetic, describing the loving relationship and he and Victoria had developed during the time they had spent together on the voyage. It was obvious to all who were acquainted with them they were meant to be with one another. Reggie's journal had taken a turn from the adventure and excitement of diamond mining to the love he found in Victoria.

Margaret O'Neil, Victoria's mother who was better known as Maggie, a robust Irish woman in her early 50's, was more than relieved to see the two of them together. The loss of her husband, Victoria's father, had been very difficult for her only child, and she knew she wouldn't live forever. Victoria needed a right-standing young man like Reggie. Her daughter had blossomed into a beautiful woman, but she was giddy as a school girl whenever she spoke of her new beau. When they landed in Boston, the first place Maggie O'Neil planned to go was the millinery shop to purchase material for a wedding dress. Of course, she had not mentioned this to Victoria, but she knew all the signs, and there was not a doubt in her mind that Victoria and Reggie belonged together.

The voyage came to an end soon enough. Maggie stood between the two love birds as they docked. She would keep a close eye on them from here on out, she decided.

Like the Port of London, Boston was all business. Cargo lay on the docks ready to be loaded onto ships readying to head to other ports both across the Atlantic and south around the South American Horn leading to the Pacific. Victoria and her mother were amazed at the hustle and bustle of the town, and it rather unnerved them.

Cape Colony had been a busy place, but not like this. Reggie took charge, making sure Victoria and her mother and every piece of their luggage was safely on a coach headed to the Tremont Hotel before he left to take care of his own business. He had little luggage himself – a parcel with three shirts, two suit coats, two pairs of trousers, stockings and underclothes – besides the carpet bag that never left his side.

With Victoria and Mrs. O'Neil tucked safely into a carriage, Reggie started walking toward the downtown area. It was a beautiful spring day in Boston Towne and he was enjoying the sights. He looked up at tall buildings, visited the newspaper stands and other street vendors, and took note of the fashions of the day. The walk was a pleasant adventure with new discoveries on every street corner. He finally came to the Benjamin Franklin Savings Bank on a corner opposite him. He crossed the busy street, dodged a rushing carriage in the process, entered the bank and walked up to a teller.

"I'd like to speak to the president of the bank, please," he said. Looking over his spectacles, the teller eyed Reggie carefully. He noticed Reggie's sweaty brow, his frayed jacket sleeves and overall unkempt appearance.

"I'm sorry, sir, there is no peddling here."

Reggie's right eye squinted and he chewed the inside of his cheek. "Is that so? Well, I'll make a note of that the next time I meet a peddler on the street, sir." Reggie placed the carpet bag on the window counter. "Would you care to lift this?" This time the teller squinted. Slowly, he reached over to pick up the bag, noting its weight. "There is a goodly amount of cash in that bag, sir, as well as a very large item of considerable value. Now, if you care to keep your job, you'll get me the president."

"W-why, of course, sir. Just a moment," the teller stuttered. He looked up and raised his arm signaling for the bank overseer. When he came over, the teller whispered in his ear, and the overseer quickly went to retrieve the bank president. When he arrived, the teller introduced him. "Sir, Mr. Engle. Mr. Engle, this is –."

"Culpepper, Mr. Engle, J. Reginald Culpepper. I've just arrived from the south of Africa. I'm in need of an account and a safety deposit."

"I'm happy to meet your acquaintance, sir. Shall we go into my office?" He turned to lead the way.

"Mr. Engle, about your teller." The teller stiffened as Mr. Engle looked back at him. Culpepper looked at him and smiled. "Good man. You might offer him a raise." Wide eyed, the teller watched the two men retire to the president's office.

"Now, Mr. Culpepper, what is it you'd like to deposit?" Mr. Engle asked as he pulled a chair out for Reggie. After his guest took his seat, Mr. Engle seated himself behind his desk, and placing folded hands on his desktop, he patiently waited for the younger man to show him what he had to offer.

"This, sir." He reached into the carpet bag and pulled out the money left from his venture with Sir Lawrence. There were £3,000 from Sir Lawrence and a little over £4,500 of his own money, all in small bills and change. From the bottom of the bag, he pulled out the undersized strong box holding the small diamonds from his mine. Handing the box to Engle, he added, "And this."

Culpepper ripped open the lining of the carpet bag and retrieved the jewel from its hiding place. "And finally, this." He'd tried polishing the gem himself, but it was still uncut and lacking the luster of a finely crafted stone. No one in South Africa could have known how to cut it. He had reasoned a diamond cutter in America could do the job correctly, if indeed there was one.

Engle had opened the strongbox, his eyes already agape as they took in the brilliance of the many stones inside. And then looking up, he gasped when he saw the singular diamond in Culpepper's hand. He'd never seen anything like it: yellow in color, a perfectly clear and incredibly large gem, it was notably the most remarkable specimen he'd ever seen.

"What is it, Mr. Culpepper?" He pushed back his chair, almost fearing to touch it.

"This, sir, is a diamond, greater than any ever found, I believe. No one except you and I are aware it even exists. That is why I need a safety deposit. It's what we shall call my collateral on some land I want to purchase in Georgia."

Engle's mouth went dry, and he could barely speak. "H-how much do you suppose it is worth, Mr. Culpepper?"

"I estimate around £750,000, if not more. I'd like it insured, of course, and I want to get it appraised when possible."

"Of course." Engle reached for a file. He happened to have a list of some of the most reputable jewelers in Boston, Philadelphia and New York. Looking up and down his list, his eyes fell upon a foreign name. "Ah, here is someone; a Jacob Rosenbrand. He originally haled from Amsterdam, but now a jeweler in New York, and considered as one of the best diamond cutters in the country."

Reggie nodded. "Jacob Rosenbrand," he said, rolling the name around in his mind. "Perhaps we should contact him. Meanwhile, this carpet bag is getting very heavy after carrying it with me for nearly three months, and I would appreciate leaving it behind."

Engle chuckled. "I understand. Let's see what we can do for you, sir." He reached for the forms for Reggie was required to fill out. Engle then figured the exchange rate on the cash Reggie had, and made out a deposit slip for him. With all the paperwork out of the way, Engle showed Reggie to the safety deposit area in the banks lower level. They deposited both the jewel and smaller diamonds in the special box and locked it into a wall. Reggie hesitated, almost deciding not to leave his treasure behind.

"I assure you, Mr. Culpepper, Benjamin Franklin Bank has an excellent security record. Your items are as safe as they can be, and much safer than your carpet bag," Engle said. Reggie chuckled, and as Engle escorted him back to his office, Engle offered to contact Jacob Rosenbrand personally saying, "We can meet as soon as tomorrow if I send a telegram right away and he takes the first train from New York." Reggie agreed. He was anxious to meet the diamond cutter. Engle gave Reggie some instruction about the Boston area – where to stay, where to eat – before they parted.

"Mr. Culpepper, it has been a pleasure doing business with you. I look forward to seeing you in a couple days, if not sooner." Mr. Engle shook Reggie's hand and opened the bank door for him. Culpepper glanced back at the teller who still stood behind his cage, looking amazed at this foreigner who was so favored by the bank president. Reggie tipped his hat towards the teller, and he quickly turned to shuffle some papers. Reggie gave Mr. Engle a cordial farewell and left the bank.

Noting he'd been given the name of the hotel where Victoria and her mother were staying, Reggie decided it would be a good idea to join them for dinner. After only two hours, he already missed Victoria and wondered how her day had progressed. He caught a carriage and after a bumpy ride over Boston's cobblestone streets, he soon arrived at the entrance to the Tremont, an elegant hotel in the main business section of the city. Although the warm, red brick walls were inviting, the doorman's greeting was cold and stiff as he opened the door.

"After you, sir."

"Thank you, my good man," Culpepper responded giving him a tip. For the first time in nearly a year, Culpepper felt good – he felt very, very good.

Chapter IV

A New Life

Victoria awakened with a smile on her face. She stretched and threw the goose down coverlet off to the side, then scooted off the tall hotel bed like an enthusiastic school girl. The Tremont Hotel was indeed grand, and she loved the soft mattress and the crisp bed sheets she had never had the pleasure of getting accustomed to in Cape Colony. Although they were well-to-do, her father was close to his wallet, and never sent home to obtain the niceties of Ireland. South African linens were rough and plain, but it was good enough for them then. Now it was a new day, and time to start a new life in America.

The wash stand held a pitcher filled with cold water. She poured water into the bowl, and the icy liquid splashed her awake. After washing and putting on her best everyday dress and shoes, she knocked on the door to her mother's room, which adjoined her own.

"Mother, are you awake?" She listened for a moment and knocked again. The door swung open, and there stood Maggie O'Neil wrapped in a shawl, wearing a hat on her head.

"Of course I am, child," she said in her thick Irish brogue. "It's nigh eight o'clock in the mornin'! Do ye think I'd be in bed at this hour when there is so much to do and see? Are ye ready to go?"

"Yes, mum, if you could help me with my hair." Victoria flashed a frustrated look at her mother and held up her long, strawberry tresses. "I think you should have named me Rapunsel, Mother."

"Get on with ye now, girl. Let's see what we can do with it," Maggie said, pushing her daughter back to the vanity to sit down. Victoria watched her mother's reflection in the large oval mirror as she thoughtfully combed through her long tresses. Wondering what her mother was thinking, she quickly heard the answer.

"Victoria, I've changed me mind about going sight seein' right away this mornin'. I have a few things I want to accomplish downtown today. I expect you have some things you want to do also, so I'll just go me way today and meet ye later. Is that all right?"

"Yes, of course, Mother, if you insist." A sparkle gleamed in her eye as she considered the possibility of running into Reggie Culpepper. "Perhaps we could have tea this afternoon in the hotel then?"

"Of course, me dear. Tea at four o'clock sounds very nice." Her mother slipped the last pin into her daughter's unruly hair and kissed her on the cheek. "Love ye," Maggie said, and she was out the door. Victoria wondered what she was up to. It wasn't like her mother to change plans suddenly, and she hadn't been this excitable since before Victoria's father died. A little disgruntled at the quick retreat, Victoria picked up her parasol, gloves and handbag, and then slowly made her way down the corridor to the lobby. As she walked by, every male head turned to look at her, including those escorting a woman already on their arm. Victoria was easily the most refreshingly beautiful sight they had looked upon this morning. Innocently unaware anyone was in the least bit interested in her, she passed the front desk and entered the hotel restaurant for breakfast. She squinted in the darkly lit room trying to see where she was going, and was greeted by the maitre'd who escorted her to a table. She was unaware that seated in the lounge having his morning tea, Reggie had been waiting to see her. Noticing the stares of men twice her age, even if she had not, he was not pleased. He folded his newspaper and followed her into the restaurant.

"May I join you, Miss?" he asked. Victoria responded happily to the familiar voice.

"Oh, Reggie, I'm so glad you're here." He smiled down at her and lifted her soft hand to his lips.

44

"It is my pleasure, my love, as well as every other man's in the hotel," he added, not without an edge in his voice. Victoria's eyes opened wide in surprise.

"Why, Reggie, whatever do you mean?" Fumbling with her napkin, she laid it across her lap. She did not want to spoil the day with an unpleasant discussion. He sat down at the table across from her.

"I only mean, my dear, that every man who has eyes is watching your every move. I must say, it rather disturbs me. I don't relish sharing you with any of them." Victoria looked down, folded her hands and smiled.

"Well, dear Reggie, you will not have to. I am only yours," she looked up at him sideways, batting long red-brown lashes, "if you want me to be." She blushed as a half smile formed on her lips. Reggie thought nothing else would matter, if she were only his.

"You honor me," he said, his voice husky with emotion. They sat looking at one another, not saying a word. Their eyes held each other in a warm embrace, and no conversation was needed. Reggie knew then Victoria O'Neil was his last chance for love in this lifetime; there would be no other who could fill that void for him. Their visual embrace was broken by the voice of the waiter who stood over their table. They both cleared their throats and looked up.

"Excuse me. Are you ready to order?"

Shaken by the sudden realization that he could no longer live without her, Reggie was unable to respond. Victoria looked up at the waiter and requested tea for them both and asked for some time before ordering breakfast. The waiter bowed and left.

Reggie took her hand again, and held it to his lips. "Victoria, since the crossing from Africa, I have come to learn I am desperately in love with you." She blushed again as tears filled her eyes. "I realize I am just an adventurer, and I have nothing in this world really to give to you, but I have to ask you, would you consider – I mean could you ever – He hesitated, feeling stupid. Pardon my clumsiness, but I've never done this before." Her smile encouraged him to continue. "May I ask you to be my wife?"

"Oh, Reggie, I –." Tears formed pools in her crystal blue eyes, and then spilled over to her cheeks. "I'm so surprised! I love you, too; but are we ready for marriage? I mean, we've only just known one another a short time and with everything that has happened this year, I simply do not know if I am ready." Holding a kerchief to her eyes, she sat back in her chair wondering if she should cry, shout, or do a jig on the table. "I do so love you, but you must give me some time to think!" she said with finality. Reggie looked back at the waiter and waved him over.

"Sir, your best champagne!" Reggie requested with an air of confidence. "We are celebrating today."

"Yes, sir," the waiter responded. He signaled for the steward to come over and instructed him to set up their table before heading to the wine cellar to collect the champagne.

"What are we celebrating, Reggie? I did not say I would marry you," Victoria laughed.

"True, but you did not say you wouldn't. Besides, now I know there's a chance, if only a small one, that we will be together. To me, that is worth celebrating, is it not?" She only smiled.

* * *

Maggie O'Neil had asked the clerk at the front desk where the finest millinery shop in the area might be. The clerk called the hotel tailor who escorted her to a shop only four blocks away from the hotel on Harrison Avenue. The tailor bowed at the waist, leaving her staring through the window. Maggie could see bolts of cloth on shelves touching the ceiling. Samples of bridal gowns dressed mannequins along the side, and notions of all kinds decorated a store case next to the window. She could not wait to go in. Opening up the shop's door, a little bell announced her arrival. Maggie entered the shop to find a plump, middle-aged woman sitting on the floor straight pins held in her mouth, and a concentrated frown on her face. Jasmine Sunday looked up from her work. Spitting the pins out, she forced a smile.

"Hello, ma'am. What can I do for you?" Jasmine said as she poked a pin into a cushion and stood up. She had been working on her newest creation for Mrs. Prendergast, of the Boston Prendergasts. It took her a bit before she could stand straight from her awkward sitting position, but when she did, she stood to her full four feet, eleven inches and Maggie had to look down at her. Jasmine's salt and pepper hair was tied up in a tight knot on top of her head, and her round shape was evidence she was well-to-do, with plenty for her table. Maggie liked her right off.

"Yes, I'm lookin' for some cloth for a weddin' dress," she said matter-of-factly. "Fer me daughter."

"You sew?" Jasmine asked, "Or are you looking for someone to make the dress for you? If you are, I'm afraid I can't. I'm over worked as it is."

"Are ye now? Well, do ye need any help? I'm lookin' fer work."

"As a matter of fact, I am considering hiring, but I can't pay much," Jasmine said as she set the pin cushion on a nearby table and straightened her dress.

"Would it be enough to support me-self and me daughter? We're just arrivin' from Africa and we're stayin' at the Tremont Hotel. It won't be long before all our money's used up there."

Jasmine smiled and her round face flushed as she walked over to the counter to pick up some keys. "Come with me." They walked to the back of the store, through a set of curtains, then up the dimly lit back stairs where the only light came from the window above them. Two flights up, Jasmine introduced Maggie to a complete apartment which was vacant and ready to rent. There were two small bedrooms attached to a sitting room, and a small kitchen with a common bath to be shared down the hall. "The only thing I ask is you keep it clean, and no men allowed." Maggie's eyes lit up with delight.

"Oh, Mrs. Sunday, this is perfect. How much would you be askin'?"

"You work for me and I'll pay you a commission on anything you sell, and then you pay me $15.00 a month for your daughter's board. Fair enough?"

"Oh, by all means, Mrs. Sunday. I'm so excited. I can't wait to tell Victoria!"

"Call me Jasmine. When can you start?"

"Right away, if you wish. Then this afternoon, I'll meet me daughter for tea and we'll get ready to move in tomorrow, if it meets your approval." They agreed and Jasmine and Maggie became fast friends.

Jasmine showed Maggie around the place, explained the duties of the shop and then showed her the wedding material Maggie was looking for when she first came in. They decided upon her finest white satin, found just the right lace to apply to the bodice, and chose perfect cultured pearls to decorate the skirt. They'd work on it together, Jasmine said. It would be a pleasure to see Maggie's dream for her daughter come true.

The day passed by quickly, and before Maggie realized it, three thirty had come and gone. She told Jasmine she would be there bright and early in the morning.

"Seven o'clock to be sure, Jasmine. Oh, I am so excited," she repeated for the umpteenth time. The entire day had been spent working on outfits for Mrs. Prendergast. Maggie was an avid seamstress, and Jasmine was pleased with her new discovery. They would have a good working relationship, she was sure of it.

The carriage dropped Maggie off at the hotel just at the stroke of four. She quickly hurried into the restaurant where she found her daughter awaiting her arrival. Reggie Culpepper was sitting with her.

"Hello, you two. Did ye spend the day together?"

"Why, yes, Mother. And it truly was a glorious day!" Victoria exclaimed. Her eyes sparkled and her cheeks were aflame with excitement.

"I've had quite a day me-self, child. I can't wait to tell ye about it." Maggie pulled a comb out of her hair and whisked a few unruly hairs from her forehead. Reggie stood and held a chair for her. Sitting down, she took in a deep breath and smiled at the two of them. "So, how are you two love birds doin'?"

Victoria looked down at her hands, surprised at her mother's remark. "Oh, Mother, really."

"Don't really me, young lady. If I don't recognize two people in love, me name ain't Maggie O'Neil," she laughed.

"Mrs. O'Neil," Reggie began, "you're a very astute woman." She nodded her thanks. "And I realize, because you have a great many things to handle at this time, my timing may be off, but I should tell you your assumption is correct; I have become enamored by your daughter. I had hoped to ask you for her hand, if she cared to have me; however, she has already told me she is not ready for marriage, and I am extremely heartbroken." He pouted and placed his hand over his heart. Maggie's eyes lit up with humor as she listened to his sad tale. "I fear I may lose the one person who could tame my wild ways."

Victoria's fair skin blushed easily as Reggie spoke. She looked at her mother and then at Reggie. She may as well have been in another country, for the way they spoke about her. She was still at the table, in case they had not noticed.

"Me boy," Maggie countered. "Victoria is far too young to know what she wants let alone what she needs. I have every confidence in the world that the two of you belong together, and I have already taken steps to prepare for such an event." Victoria looked at her mother, waiting to hear what she was talking about. "Victoria, you'll never guess where I have been all the day long."

"No, Mother, I suppose I would not." She picked up her tea cup and peered at her mother over the rim, her Irish temper beginning to rise. Maggie could tell she was miffed, but it didn't matter. She was used to Victoria's sudden flares of temper.

"I have been down at Jasmine Sunday's Millinery."

"Who is Jasmine Sunday?" Reggie and Victoria asked in unison.

"Only the best seamstress in all of Boston, so I hear. She has a lovely shop! And she has offered me a job working with her for room and board. You may also come, if you wish, for only $15.00 a month. Can you imagine that?" Then, looking back at Reggie, she added, "Unfortunately, you cannot. No men allowed, me boy. That's not to say you can't see each other, meetin' at a restaurant or somethin'."

"Mother, I'm sure Reggie has plans of his own. Don't you, Reggie? You're going to Georgia soon, aren't you?" Victoria hinted. She had thought about his lovely proposal all day, but when they returned to the restaurant earlier in the afternoon, she realized she was indeed not ready for marriage, and she was not ready to take an adventure with a man she barely knew to a place about which she knew even less.

"Quite right, Victoria. I do have plans, some of which include you; and whether you like it or not, I won't give up, you do know that don't you?" Their conversation amused Maggie. He reminded her of her own dearly departed Paddy, may the Lord bless his soul. "For now, though, I must say good bye. I have a very important appointment at the bank. I bid you farewell," he said standing to his feet. He held Victoria's hand to his lips. "My love, I *will* be back." He kissed her fingertips and said good bye to Maggie, leaving enough money to pay for their bill. He passed by the window on the sidewalk. Tipping his tall hat, he pointed at Victoria and he mouthed the words, "talk to her." He then turned to board a carriage and was gone.

"What's with him?" Maggie asked. Victoria simply shrugged, not wanting to mention he had actually proposed. She knew her mother would pounce on the information like a female lioness after her prey. Victoria, still a bit miffed at Maggie for keeping her out of the earlier conversation and accusing her of being too young to know what she wanted, did not say a word for quite some time before her mother finally broke the silence.

"So, what do ye think?"

"What do I think about what, Mother?"

"About Jasmine. Do ye want to come see it?"

"Are you pleased, Mother? Is it what you want?"

"Yes, me luv, it 'tis. I would be doin' what I love best, sewin' for people. And Jasmine will teach me what I don't already know. It's a new start, darlin'."

"Well, then, perhaps we should go pack our bags and prepare for the move. If you're happy with it, I'm sure it would be just fine for me, as well."

Victoria's ire never lasted long. She wiped her mouth with her napkin and stood up. "Shall we?" Maggie stood to her feet and the two of them went upstairs to pack.

Reggie stepped down from the carriage in front of the Benjamin Franklin Bank at the same time a genteel-looking older man stepped down from another. The man had long, wavy gray hair under a plain black top hat. He wore a stiff four-button black suit, and heavily starched white shirt decorated by a poorly tied bowtie. Carrying a cane, he stood a bit stooped over. He politely allowed Reggie to go before him and they both entered the bank. When the man stopped to speak to a guard, Reggie could not help but notice a heavy Scandinavian accent as he heard him ask for Mr. Engle. The guard started to escort the man to Engle's office when Reggie stopped them.

"Pardon me, sir, are you Jacob Rosenbrand?"

"Vy, yes, I am he. Are you da von I am supposed to meet today? Mr. Culpepper?"

"Yes, sir! J. Reginald Culpepper, at your service," said Reggie as he offered a slight bow from the waist. I've just recently arrived from the South of Africa, and Mr. Engle advised me he would contact you. I'm very happy to meet your acquaintance." The two of them shook hands and started walking towards Engle's office together, leaving the guard behind. The men had not gone unnoticed by Steven Engle who quickly met them in the lobby. Mr. Engle explained they would have to go to the safety deposit area to retrieve the merchandise Mr. Rosenbrand would be examining. Reggie could hardly contain his excitement.

When Mr. Engle pulled the safety deposit box from the wall and carefully placed it on a nearby table, he motioned to Reggie to use his key to open the box. It felt heavier than he remembered. Reggie lifted the diamond from its resting place and held it up to the light.

"Mr. Rosenbrand, I present to you the Jewel of Africa."

Rosenbrand gasped when he saw the gem. He had never seen a diamond of this magnitude.

"Vere did dis come from, Mr. Culpepper?"

"Alas, sir, I hesitate to say. It did come from Africa, but I care not to divulge its actual location. The mine has since been destroyed, and I lost two dear friends and many other helpers in its finding."

"I am sorry to hear zat, but I do understand, Mr. Culpepper." He hesitated thoughtfully. "However, I knew nussing of diamonds in Africa before."

"Neither did I until a year ago," Reggie responded. Rosenbrand asked permission to examine the gem, picked it up from its container and mentally calculated its weight. Taking out a magnifying glass, he examined the diamond as carefully as possible in the poor lighting.

"My, my. Zis is unbeliefable. I haf never seen anysing like zis in all my life. Ze clarity is egzelent, ze color is magnifizent. Zer are no flaws, zer is only perfection. I am amazed!" Rosenbrand carefully placed the diamond back into the box, then examined the other smaller diamonds holding a loop to his eye with care to look deep into the facets of the gems. "Yah. Ve can do somesing wis zese vones."

"Could you venture a worth, Mr. Rosenbrand?" Engle asked anxiously.

"Off hand, I could not say for sure. But I vould venture to say you haf nearly $1 million vorse of gems here. Ze large gem, I could not tell it's vorse right now. I vill only say dat it is vell vorse $750,000 uncut. I vould be honored to be ze von to vork on zis prize." He looked up at Reggie with hopeful eyes.

"Mr. Engle has highly recommended you, Mr. Rosenbrand. I will be happy to have you do the work."

The two men made arrangements to have all the diamonds packed and sealed . Mr. Engle offered an armed guard to travel with them as they traveled back to New York, suggesting they could never be too careful.

"One, thing, Mr. Rosenbrand: No one must know about the Jewel of Africa. It is to remain a secret for now, anyway." Reggie looked steadfastly at Jacob Rosenbrand. "No one. Is that understood?"

"Yah. It is as you say, Mr. Culpepper. It could be very dangerous for anyvone to know. Zese times are very unstable." Rosenbrand and Reggie shook hands, agreeing they would travel by the evening train. The older man headed back to his hotel to gather his things while Reggie made final arrangements with Engle. Rosenbrand could not wait to get back to New York to start working on the jewel.

Steven Engle had made another contact in the Georgia banking system with a listing of land availability in the area. He handed Reggie the name of his contact explaining he had properties available whenever he was able to go south. "Of course, I'll help you with anything you might need, Mr. Culpepper," he added amiably. "Perhaps a letter of recommendation would help?" Reggie loved it. Things were falling into place very nicely. He was now known as the rich man he always knew he would be with contacts in both New England and the South.

Victoria sat pouting on the edge of her bed, rehearsing the news of Reggie's departure for New York. He had sent a note by messenger the previous evening. Reading the note over again and again, she realized he had not even bothered to stop in to say good bye. His note only said he loved her and would contact her when he was able to return. She and her mother had already made arrangements for a porter to load their luggage in a carriage early in the morning, but she would not be able to notify Reggie where they had gone. Sadly she put the note in her handbag and checked to be sure everything was out of the room before she left. Leaving a letter at the desk in case of Reggie's return, Victoria and her mother left the grand Tremont Hotel for the little apartment only four blocks away.

Rosenbrand unlocked the door to his little shop on the east side of New York. Dismissing the armed guard and lighting a couple of lamps, he lifted the shade at the window to let in the morning light. He was now able to see well enough to take a good look at the jewel. Reggie drew it out of the box and laid it on the table. Rosenbrand was even more amazed. He could not believe the clarity and the perfection of this gem. He studied the lines time and again and then set the rock aside.

"I vill vait on zis until after I finish ze oser specimens, Mr. Culpepper. If I hurt ze osers, it will not be so bad. Zey can still be sold. Zis vone I must take special care of. Is zis all right wis you?" Reggie agreed hesitantly. At least he tried to convince himself it was all right. He had carried that diamond 14,000 miles, and leaving it in a stranger's hands was difficult. He had to entrust it to Rosenbrand now, and he found it more difficult than expected.

"Are you sure you can cut it, Mr. Rosenbrand?"

"Yah, I am sure I can cut it. I just vant to be sure I cut it right!" he chuckled. Reggie's confidence was slightly shaken, but he said nothing. Rosenbrand picked up the first of the 50 other stones. Measuring carefully, he said, "5.4 carats. A nice vone."

None of the stones were less than two carats in weight, and having never seen African diamonds before, Rosenbrand was thrilled to work with them.

Reggie would not leave Rosenbrand's side, actually standing in his way at one point. Rosenbrand could not work with Reggie leaning over his shoulder, and asking him to kindly leave, he ushered Reggie to the waiting sitting room.

"I am sorry, Culpepper, but you are in my vay. Please to sit in the front of my shop, yah?"

Disappointed, Reggie agreed. He had wanted to watch, to learn everything he could about the process, but instead he reluctantly returned to the sitting area and fell asleep in a chair while the master worked well into the night.

"Yah, here you are." Reggie started at the sound of Rosenbrand's voice. The old man stood over him with a couple differently cut stones held out before him. "Perhaps you vould like to see zese under ze glass?" Reggie rubbed his eyes and set aside the newspaper resting across his chest. He stood up and stretched before following Rosenbrand back into his work area.

"Yes, of course. Have you started on the jewel yet?"

"No, zat vill be again anoser day. I still vant to study it to be sure vere to apply my chisel before I start." Reggie was relieved to hear the man was thorough. Rosenbrand man showed Reggie the stones under a magnifying glass, then took a loop and showed him how to inspect the diamonds for flaws. There was a small inclusion under only two of the surfaces. Every other one was perfect in clarity, color and cut. Reggie was pleased. He had indeed found a treasure in Africa.

"How much are they worth, Jacob?" Rosenbrand smiled at the question and signaled him to follow him into the back end of his shop. Opening up a safe, he brought out a diamond necklace which had 28 one- quarter to one-full carat diamonds inlaid in gold. "Oh, my, but it's beautiful, Jacob. Did you make this?"

"Yah. I made for my vife before she died. She only vore it vone time, to ze opera. I haf since kept it under lock and key. Zese diamonds without the settings are vorse $230,000. I brought ze diamonds from Amsterdam ven I come to America. Your diamonds are better. I vould say zis many vould sell for $300,000. When put in settings, maybe you get over $380,000." Culpepper whistled. He really had no idea since he had never been an expert in the area of diamonds. He was simply a gold miner who had had a great deal of luck.

"How do we sell them?"

"I do it for you. I make ze jewelry zen ve have a show. I vill take my pay from ze sale and give you vhat ze diamonds are vorse. It vill take a great deal of time, but it vill be vorse it."

"How long will it take?"

"Ve look at hafing ze show in about six months. I vill vork very hard for you."

Reggie looked at the diamonds one more time before giving them back to Rosenbrand. Searching through the uncut gems, he found one that especially refracted the light perfectly. "This one, Jacob. I want this one made into a ring. Can you do that for me?" He picked up a medium sized sample still lying on the table. "I want something special like this for a very special lady."

Rosenbrand set the diamond aside and marked it for a ring setting. Placing his wife's necklace back into the safe, he locked it in with the jewel and Reggie's other diamonds.

"She is a good friend, yah?"

"Yah," Culpepper laughed, mimicking Rosenbrand's accent. "How long will it take to cut the jewel, Jacob?"

"The first cut vill tell us zat. Come. Ve go to supper." Walking up to the front of the shop, Rosenbrand lifted his hat from the hat rack on the wall and put it on his head. Opening up the door to the little shop, he ushered Culpepper outside and then locked the door behind him. Outside the shop, not another word was mentioned about the jewel or any of the other diamonds during their evening together. Rosenbrand was as tight-lipped as he needed to be.

Jacob Rosenbrand did not sleep well for weeks. All his life he had dreamed of cutting a diamond as magnificent as the jewel, but never did he imagine he would actually have the opportunity of doing so. One morning, after nearly a month, he awakened at four o'clock after another fitful night of sleep. He rolled out of bed and went downstairs to his shop to look again at the jewel. He had been studying it, dreaming about it, forgetting to eat, forgetting to go to bed, and then once he got to bed, unable to fall asleep for hours. This diamond was unlike anything he had ever seen. Its size was immense, weighing just under seven pounds, and its clarity, perfect. Even the diamonds from Israel had not been as perfect as this. He continued to study the gem until he was sure he knew every facet of it.

Early morning passed into afternoon before he attempted his first cut on the magnificent stone. The sun was high, and light streamed into the windows just at the right slant to illuminate all the facets Rosenbrand needed to see before the cut. With the stone in a vice, he placed the chisel on the line just left of center. He raised his hammer and just as he was about to hit it, the door opened.

"I say, old man, how are you? I overslept at the hotel, and it has taken me over an hour to get here." Reggie walked in and saw Rosenbrand holding his breath, with the hammer still in the air. He stopped talking.

"Culpepper. Don't ever do zat again. I am vorking on ze jewel," Rosenbrand rebuked him.

"Oh, sorry, chap. I didn't mean to disturb. I'll just sit in the front room until I hear you call." Reggie ducked through the door again and went into the sitting room where he had spent entire days and weeks. He had undertaken a writing project to keep himself from being anxious about the jewel. Having written about his exploits in Africa, he had been able to conduct some business with a New York publisher; but his main interest was the jewel. Daily he would check with Rosenband, and daily he had been disappointed to learn Rosenbrand had not yet begun working on the gem. Rosenbrand had to explain time and again he was not ready to attempt cutting the jewel because of its complexity. Instead, Rosebrand concentrated on cutting the smaller gems, putting off cutting the jewel until he was sure how to cut it. The time had finally come to cut the great stone, and Reggie felt he could move forward. He would soon see Victoria again.

Rosenbrand watched Reggie go through the door. "Silly Englishman," he muttered. Turning back to his task, he again placed the chisel and lifted the hammer. Holding held his breath, sweat poured from his brow. Anticipating the results, down he swung, the hammer hitting the chisel with perfect accuracy.

The normal ring of the chisel sounded like a thud. The chisel broke, and Rosenbrand was amazed as he watched it fly across the workbench. He had never lost a chisel to a diamond before! Wiping the sweat from his brow, he examined the tool. A frown registered across his face as he studied the stone again.

Yes, he had hit the diamond correctly, but there was not a scratch on its surface. Loosening the stone from the vice, he turned it over in his hand. Perhaps there was another place he should try. He stood to his feet, placed the diamond back into his safe, walked to the waiting room and silently signaled for Culpepper to follow him. Locking the door behind them, he led the way to a nearby restaurant. He would not attempt to work on the jewel again until he was sure of the cut.

The gem was examined many times over the next few days until Rosenbrand felt he had nearly memorized every facet. Holding a loop in his eye and turning the gem over in his hand, he searched again until he found the right spot – a fault where the diamond was sure to break. He placed it back into the vice, and finding another chisel, he sat back down to see if he could crack through the surface this time.

Rosenbrand felt his heart beating heavily in his chest and his eye glasses fogged slightly from the perspiration on his brow. Ever so precisely he placed the chisel on the fault. Slowly, he raised the hammer.

The hammer swung down, the chisel rang and the diamond fell into 11 different pieces.

The old man sat back in his chair, amazed at what he saw. A tear fell down his cheek as he realized his dream had actually come true. He had just cut into the largest diamond ever discovered.

The largest of the eleven pieces weighed 652.4 carats and had 89 facets. Reggie looked at the stone with awe written across his face. What indeed had he found? The other stones weighed as much as 417 carats and as little as 23. It would take Rosenbrand a very long time to cut all the stones into workable pieces, a total of 84 gems, but carve them he would. He began to immediately work on the piece that would retain the name Jewel of Africa, but he could not promise when it would be finished. Showing Reggie the largest piece, he could only say he was amazed.

In the end, the jewel remained with him for nine months before he finished the cut. It was his last great work.

Chapter V

Fairland

"**J**. Reginald Culpepper, Sir, at your service. I'm happy to meet with your acquaintance." Reggie held out his hand to a tall, blonde gentleman who stood behind a desk at the Atlanta Property Investment Company office in Macon, Georgia, a subsidiary of the Franklin Bank in Boston. Behind his salesman's smile, Charles Lind was summing up Reggie with one look. What he saw was a proper English gentleman with not much business sense. Although Lind was considered a fair judge of character, in this instance he was 100 percent wrong. Although he was rather scruffy in appearance and was well-mannered, he had come from the North, and Lind did not care to do business with him. Lind, however, had received a directive from the bank's headquarters, and knew he had to at least hear the Englander out. He sat down in his executive's chair and leaned forward with folded hands.

"Culpepper was it? Would you happen to be related to the Samuel Culpepers of Virginia?" He gave Reggie a smug smile. Reggie shook his head smiling back at him.

"No, actually. The William Colepepers from London."

"Well, Mr. Culpepper, what can I do for you?" He looked at his pocket watch and snapped it shut, calculating the 15 minutes he would allow for the meeting. A feeling of tension passed between them as he waited for Reggie's answer, preparing to turn him away. An astute judge of character himself, Reggie knew Lind had already made an error in judgment. Chewing his lower lip, deciding what to say, he said nothing for a moment. This rather unnerved Lind, but he sat silent with a half smile on his face. Without realizing it, Reggie had already out-maneuvered the snob. Slightly shaken by Reggie's silence, Lind retrieved the letter he had received from Steven Engle. Engle had written an excellent recommendation, suggesting it would be a great help to them both if he would, "Assist Mr. Culpepper in any way necessary." Lind read the short letter, twice, and then looked back up at Reggie, who finally broke his silence, crossing one leg over the other, appearing relaxed and unhurried.

"Before I tell you what I'm doing in Georgia, Mr. Lind, I want to assure you I am very interested in some of the commodities I've heard so much about here in the colonies."

"That's states, Mr. Culpepper."

"Of course, forgive me – the states. I'm sure Mr. Engle has made my reputation clear enough, but I will need your assistance to accomplish my goals here.

"How did you come to meet Mr. Engle?" Lind asked, only half listening as he gazed at Engle's signature.

"Mr. Engle was the first person I contacted the moment I landed in Boston. He was kind enough to recommend you as well as another man who is working on a special project for me. I believe if you contact him, he will assure you I have substantial funds to finance what I have in mind."

Lind looked over the letter a third time then set it aside on his desk. Sitting up a bit straighter, he smiled amiably. "Well, Mr. Culpepper, what do you have in mind?"

Reggie produced a pouch filled with American money. "I have here what Mr. Engle seemed to think would be a good down payment for what I need. I understand land is available outside of Macon, and I would very much like to purchase at least 300 acres. I have an idea to grow cotton and other crops as well as opening a large stable for anyone who may need to board their horses."

"So you want to be a farmer?" Lind asked doubtfully. Do you have any experience along these lines?"

"Actually, no," he replied. "As I mentioned earlier, I grew up in London, and am unaccustomed to farm life. However, I have traveled extensively, and I believe I am finally ready to settle down. I plan to marry soon and have hopes to grow a family here in the colo—er—states. Mr. Engle mentioned you might be the person who could help me find the right property and to build the estate."

"Of course, Mr. Culpepper." He turned to reach for a small box sitting on a credenza behind him. "This is the file where I keep all my recent listings. I'm sure there will be something here worth looking at." He pulled up a card. "Ah, here is one. This piece has just come in. It's just under 200 acres, part of which is a little wet; but a good piece nevertheless. Since you have no real experience, it might be just the place to start."

Reggie's right eyebrow lifted, and a smirk registered across his face. Lind could tell he was not pleased. "Mr. Lind, you may not be aware of my considerable research regarding this effort, but I am not an idiot. I know what I need. I requested 300 acres of good farm land, not swamp. If you have nothing else to offer, perhaps I shall go to someone who has."

Lind was caught off guard. Culpepper would not be an easy sale after all. Lind wondered how badly he had actually misjudged the man. He knew what he wanted, he knew where he was going, and he wasn't going to go for any folderol.

"I apologize, Mr. Culpepper. Didn't mean to offend," he said insincerely." Looking the through the cards again, he pulled up another. "Here is another parcel not particularly far from town. It is good farm land, previously owned by a man who recently passed away. He and his wife have lived here for many years, but she is unable to continue handling the property. It has 320 acres, is partially treed and there's a small home on the property where the woman still lives."

"I see. Perhaps we should go out to look at this property, Mr. Lind." Reggie put the pouch back into his bag. He had already grown tired of Lind's foolishness and was anxious to be done with this transaction. If the property was not acceptable, he would end his relationship with Lind immediately.

Shutting the card file as he walked around his desk, Lind led Reggie through the door where his private carriage stood waiting. The most expedient route out of town and to the property would cover over five miles, or about an hour for the two men to get to know each other a little better. The men climbed aboard and with Lind at the reins, the carriage soon reached a steady pace.

He loosened the tension on the leather strap he held wrapped around his right hand. "So, Mr. Culpepper, tell me a bit about your travels."

Lind's query brought a sudden rush of pleasure which surprised Reggie, and just as quickly, he responded with a summation of the more than six months he had spent in the African bush country – the adventure, the dangers, the victories, and the losses.

"Through it all, I learned some important lessons, especially that a man alone can become a lunatic if he's not quickly rescued. I survived only by the grace of the Almighty, I can assure you."

He didn't tell Lind about the treasure, for Lind seemed to be at best untrustworthy. But when he said he had just sold his memoirs to a publisher in New York City, Reggie offered to forward a copy should Lind wish to have it.

"I'd be very interested in reading about your adventures," Lind assured him, knowing he would quickly dispose of the book once it arrived.

Lind seemed less and less interested as they traveled, so Reggie made quick work of the conversation by saying he would not be returning to Africa. They spent the rest of the ride talking about Lind and his business.

Mary Watson Lee, a slim brunette woman in her late forties, stood at the door of her home on the farm named Fairland, watching the two men step down from Lind's carriage. She and her husband, Edward, had migrated to this land from their home in northern England when she was only 17. She had raised her eight children here and had helped her husband build the farm from forest to one of the best producing farms in the county.

Together they had raised 140 head of cattle, cotton and tobacco; vegetables and a small peach orchard were harvested annually. She was proud of the work they had accomplished, for she had helped to carve out a living during both drought and flood. After more than 20 years of hard work, they planned to set back and let their sons run the farm, but Eddie had taken sick and soon died.

After her dear Eddie died, she wanted a rest. Her children had helped on the farm when they were young, but the five oldest of the eight children were girls. Most of the children had married over the past 15 years. The two boys had moved onto their own farms, but the third had died at an early age. Mary had finally determined to sell the farm and live with her youngest son, Matthew.

Mary stood quietly on the porch as the men approached her. The smaller of the two was dressed in a fine waist coat and trousers. As soon as she saw Reggie, she knew he was the one who would buy the farm. She could tell he was English by the way he was dressed. He appeared to be proper and someone who, unlike others before him, would care for the land. He stood with one foot resting on the lower step to let Lind introduce him and she stepped out onto the porch to greet them.

"Hello there! How can I help you fellas?" she asked with a heavy southern drawl. She had lost her English accent after more than 30 years in the back country.

"Hello, Mrs. Lee. I have a man here who might be interested in buying your farm," Lind said happily. "Would you mind if we looked around a bit?"

"Not at all, Mr. Lind. You men go ahead and do what you need to, and when you come back, I'll have some peach pie set out for you."

Culpepper and Lind walked the land together. The west 40 acreage was high and well-treed with a creek running below it, a small tributary of the Ocmulgee River. There were 110 acres of cotton; 100 acres of corn, tobacco and potatoes; the back 40 was an orchard. The rest of the land was used as pasture for the cattle. He looked at a couple of the cows, examining their teeth and checking for any disease. They seemed to be well-nourished and in good health. Lind picked up a handful of soil to show Reggie it was good, rich soil for crops.

Reggie was especially impressed by the peach orchard. He imagined his children running toward the trees to steal a peach. The dream continued to form.

"How much is she asking for this land again?" Reggie finally asked. Lind smiled. He knew he'd made a sale.

The lady owner sat knitting in her rocking chair on the porch of the little farmhouse. Reggie watched her for a moment before approaching. She looked right on that porch, he thought. She was at peace there. Mrs. Lee welcomed them with a smile and invited them in. She gave Reggie a tour of the old home, showing him the kitchen with a working pump, a bedroom downstairs and two on the second story where the children had slept. The outhouse was in the back yard. He was very satisfied with what he saw, but although he judged the house to be in good condition, he knew it was not his home, and it never would be.

Mrs. Lee indeed did have peach pie ready for them. They had taken enough time during their inspection of the land for her to make a pie and a small lunch, and she set the whole meal out for their return: corn bread, fried chicken, potatoes and peas – all from her farm. She was pleased to be able to offer it, for she believed it would be the last time she could. When she stepped out of the kitchen, the men ate heartily, enjoying her food and talking about Fairland – its past and its future. Reggie sat back in his chair very satisfied with his meal.

"Mrs. Lee, I do not believe I have ever eaten so well. You are an excellent cook, Madam."

"Why, thank you, Sir," she said with a curtsy. "I was pleased to do it. Did you find the farm to your liking?" she asked. He heard the slight nervous quiver in her voice.

"Yes, Madam, I certainly did. I would like to buy it. I understand you want $10,000 only for the land, crops and animals."

She nodded in confirmation.

"I shall meet your offer but only under one condition."

Surprised, Mrs. Lee cocked her head anxious to hear the condition, yet unsure whether she could satisfy it.

"What would your condition be, Sir?"

"That you remain here in this house and work as my housekeeper. I will pay you for your services, of course, and you'll be able to run your home as you always have. I plan to build a larger home on the other side of the property, and when the home is completed, you can continue to live here while I move my family into the new building. Are we agreed?"

Mrs. Lee was beside herself. She had not dreamed she could remain in her own home, let alone make money doing it. Tears came to her eyes as she stepped back to lean against the wall.

"My heavens, Mr. Culpepper, could this really happen?"

Folding his napkin, he stood to his feet. "I would not have offered it if I could not make it happen, Mrs. Lee. Am I to assume by your reaction that you approve?"

"Why, yes, of course! I would be happy to help you here at Fairland!"

"It's settled then," Reggie said as he smiled down at her. "I have to say, I am very pleased with the way this whole transaction has transpired," he said looking back at Mr. Lind. Lind was already busy writing down figures to calculate his commission.

"I, too, Mr. Culpepper," Lind said eagerly. Shall we go back into town and draw up the papers?" He was already on his feet and heading to the door. When they left Fairland Farm, Mary Lee still in shock over the news. She had so much to do, but first, she must contact her son. She would not be moving in with him after all.

Time flew by, and before Reggie knew what was happening, it was September. He had finally started working on the plans for the house. An assayer was hired to calculate whether the land by the creek would meet all the necessary requirements for a large home. Once the assayer determined the property was suitable, Reggie began making arrange-ments for the build. Hiring one of the best architects in Macon, they decided the front of the home would face Fairland's green pastures. The back would lead down to the creek so water could be easily accessed until they could sink a well.

While the carpenters began the daunting task of building Reggie's new home, he continued to be in contact with Victoria O'Neil. Time had passed quickly while he became involved with the legalities and various duties included with the purchase of Fairland. The crops were harvested in time to go to market, and he received a very good return for the cotton and tobacco, as well as most of the peaches. They had food to get through the winter, and everything was in order for the next planting, thanks to Mary Lee and the help of her two sons.

Mary loved her home. She took good care of it and her new employer. Unfortunately, although she was pleased with the arrangement, her eldest son, Noah, was not. He did not like the fact his mother was working for a stranger – let alone a foreigner – a man who was connected in the North. She, however, was looking forward to Mr. Culpepper bringing home his bride when the time came. It would be good to have another woman around to talk to. Nevertheless, even in early 1860, politics were very unstable. Noah Lee kept watch on the situation and voiced his concern frequently.

"He's an Englishman, Ma. He's in tight with the Unionists. I just don't like him," Noah said. As a rebel activist, he was in favor of Georgia's secession from the Union. He wanted no one who even hinted at supporting the Yankees to be on his father's farm.

"Shush, boy. Now you listen to me, Noah Lee," Mary retorted. "He's a good man. He's taking care of Fairland just the way your pa would've wanted. He's building his own home so I can keep mine, and I thank him for it. Now if you don't have something nice to say about the man, then jes' leave."

"All right, Ma, if that's what you want, I'll take my leave. I am not goin' to abide his bein' here takin' advantage of you or me." Noah mounted his horse and left Fairland. She would not see her son again.

Fairland Farm continued to prosper. Although Reggie knew very little about farming, he educated himself with books and listened carefully to Mary and her younger son's advice. Fairland House was nearly completed and he had already begun to purchase furnishings. In another month, Reggie could finally go to collect his bride from Boston. First however, he had to stop in New York to see Jacob Rosenbrand.

Rosenbrand had finished his work on all the smaller diamonds, and he was nearly finished with the jewelry he planned to show in the spring. The Jewel of Africa, a round brilliant cut, would not be finished for yet some time. Since he knew it would not be a part of the collection at the sale, Rosenbrand held it until last; but now it had all but consumed him who, as a perfectionist, could not help but work on it continually. He had hired another diamond cutter to finish the smaller diamonds and he completed the second of the eleven pieces from the original cut, a 323 carat brilliant, which would be placed on the head of a gentleman's walking stick and shown at the exhibition.

Rosenbrand had designed some exquisite pieces for the sale, including a gold tiara, which held both diamonds from Reggie's collection and rubies from Rosenbrand's own collection. He had also made a necklace with a fine gold chain, a pendant with a pear-shaped 10 carat diamond surrounded in gold lace and a locket with a small diamond inlaid in the center. Another piece was a man's ring which included five diamonds taken from the jewel and sapphires sent in from a mine in North Carolina. In all, there were 35 pieces of fine jewelry to be sold beside the walking stick with the 323 carat brilliant. Reggie was amazed at its beauty, but equally amazed at the fine work Rosenbrand was doing on the jewel.

"Tell me, Culpepper, what do you plan to do vis zis diamond. You vill keep it for your children, yah?"

"I am not certain, Jacob. I would like to sell it in the future, I think, because something this rare, this perfect should be shared, would you agree?" Rosenbrand nodded. "However, I am not at all certain about what I should do. The memories connected with it are too painful for me even now, and I cannot consider parting with it at this point. As you can imagine, I am anxious to see the final cut, but I am not concerned about the time you need to take to make it."

He held the magnificent piece up to the light. When the sun hit it, it sent gold-colored prisms of light onto every wall. Reggie was enthralled and he knew even though he had said the length of time did not concern him, he could not leave it with Rosenbrand much longer. Since the political situation grew increasingly precarious, he also knew he would need to keep it for a time in a secret place yet to be determined. "So, my friend, do you have some idea when?"

"Vhen vill I finish? Soon, my boy, soon," was all he would ever say. He had no plans other than to make this the most perfect creation of his lifetime, even though no one except Reggie may ever see it. Reggie squeezed the old man's shoulder knowing patience was called for, even in these precarious times.

Being anxious to see the woman he had grown to love more each passing day, Reggie took the afternoon train to Boston. He often checked his vest pocket to be sure he hadn't lost the pouch Rosenbrand had given him for her, and each time let out a breath of relief when he saw it.

While he was gone, Victoria had become the head housekeeper and nanny for the Harrison family in one of Boston's wealthier homes. Her good business sense, which she inherited from her father, was recognized immediately by Mr. Harrison, and he also permitted her to manage the Harrison's household finances, while working with the children in their studies. Victoria was not completely happy with the way things were going, though. She longed for Reggie to return.

Victoria and Reggie had been writing frequently and had continued to remain very close over the past many months since he left for Georgia. His coming to Boston was especially exciting for her. She had become bored with her job, and yearned for children of her own and a life with the one she loved. She had told her mother he had proposed the previous summer and that she wasn't ready at the time to marry; but she was now, and hoped he would soon come for her.

"I love him with my very being, Mother, and I will simply die if I don't see him soon," she had told Maggie. Her mother had heard those words before, and she rolled her eyes when they were repeated. Maggie remembered saying the same thing to her own mother so many years before, and could not help but smile. She had continued working with Jasmine in the millinery shop while she secretly worked on the wedding dress she had planned from the beginning of Victoria's and Reggie's relationship. When she heard about Reggie's soon return, she stepped things up a bit. By the time he arrived, the dress, the veil and all the accessories would be completed.

A knock came at the door early in the evening of December 23rd. Reggie had bought a new suit, shined his shoes, greased and combed his hair and waxed his mustache. He was ready for the big night when he would once again ask Victoria O'Neil to marry him. Having received directions to Jasmine's shop, he climbed the back stairs and entered the hallway by Maggie's suite. When Victoria opened the door, he just stood there not able to say a word, taken aback by her beauty. Although he thought he had remembered her every feature, he had not been prepared for what he saw this evening. There was a depth of maturity and loveliness he had not seen before. She looked at him curiously.

"Hello, Reggie. I'm so glad you've come," she said. He could not respond. Finally, nervously, he held out the flowers he had brought for her. When she reached out to take them, he grasped her hand in his and pulled her toward him.

"Oh!" she exclaimed, very surprised. He held her for a moment, then as tenderly as he could, he touched his lips to hers. He could barely hold back his desire for her. Dropping the flowers, he smothered her with a passionate kiss.

"Are these yours?" Maggie O'Neil asked standing behind him. Startled he turned around to face his future mother-in-law who held the bouquet in her hands. "You'd be better to hold these, young man, than my daughter." He took the flowers from her and stepped back from Victoria.

"Yes, Madam. Of course. I was so overcome by her beauty, I –."

"It's good to see you, Reggie. I'm glad you've come," Maggie interrupted. She gave him a hug and pushed him through the door into the apartment. "As you know, men are not allowed up here, but tonight I'm willin' to make an exception." She gave her daughter a stern look. "I'll just leave the two of you alone – that is if you can keep your hands off one another." She shot a glance at Reggie who blushed and looked down at the floor. When she went into her room, she shut the door, then opened it a crack to be sure she could hear everything.

"Reggie, it's lovely to see you. I've missed you so." Victoria took the flowers from him and put them into a vase on a wall shelf. She turned, took him by the hand and led him to a couch. They could only sit for a moment before they were again in each other's arms.

"I don't hear any talkin' out there!" called Maggie O'Neil. Exasperated, Victoria sat up and straightened her dress. Her mother would keep close tabs on their conversation, she knew. Reggie sat closer to her again and held her hand.

"Victoria, I know we have been apart for a very long time, and so I was hoping you would be glad for my return. Can you forgive me for having been away for so long?"

"Yes, Reggie, of course. I know you have a dream to accomplish in Georgia, and I am very glad you have been able to do what you needed to. I do wish we could have seen more of each other."

"I, too, my love. That is why I've come. When we last met, you told me you were not ready for marriage, but it has been such a long time." Reggie looked at her longingly. He felt the resentment she held toward him.

"Yes, Reggie, nearly six months" she reminded him with a noticeable bite in her voice. She had tried not to be angry with him, but she had to admit, she was. She glanced down at her hands which were demurely folded together in her lap. Reggie tried to avoid the confrontation.

"You know, I have established myself very well in Georgia. I've bought a running farm, and I'm building the grandest mansion on the land. I cannot wait for you to see it."

"Oh, Reggie, it sounds wonderful," she began. Then she hesitated. "But when could I? I'm a working girl, you know. I have responsibilities, and a family to care for here in Boston." She sat there, hands still folded on her lap, looking at him with large fawnlike eyes that nearly melted his heart. He reached into his pocket and found the pouch he had carried from New York. Opening it, he retrieved the ring he had asked Rosenbrand to make for him. He held it out to Victoria.

"Victoria, my love. May I ask you again to come with me to Georgia? I love you ever so much, Darling. Will you marry me?" Victoria's eyes grew wide as she looked down at the perfect two-carat marquis surrounded by six smaller brilliant shaped diamonds on either side. She couldn't believe what she was seeing. "I brought this for you. These are the diamonds I carried from Africa."

"In the satchel?"

"Yes. I couldn't tell anyone, but I will tell you. I am a very rich man, Victoria. I can provide very well for you, if you'll have me." Holding her hand, he slid the ring on her finger. She held it up in the light, enthralled by the way colors bounced off the facets. She nearly melted into Reggie's arms, but then reason took over.

"I don't know, Reggie. This is all so sudden. What about Mother and the Harrisons?"

"Your mother can either come with us or stay here as she wishes. She is always welcome. I hear the Harrisons are very rich. They will not want for another housekeeper."

Victoria smiled. She realized it really was as simple as he said, and even though hearing she was expendable humbled her a bit, she realized she could use some humbling. She had become far too proud of her own independence these past few months. She sat there staring at the ring while Reggie became more anxious to hear her answer.

"Please, Victoria, please do not tell me you have to have time to think about this. You've had over six months. I don't think I can bear being without you any longer. Will you marry me?"

"Answer the poor boy, girl!" Maggie yelled from the back room. Victoria and Reggie looked at one another and laughed.

"Yes, Reggie, I will marry you. I'd be honored." Reggie pulled her into his arms and kissed her hard on the lips.

"Well it's about time," Maggie said as she entered the sitting area. The couple pulled away from each other again. Bringing with her the dress she had so lovingly created, Maggie stood in front of them. Candlelight white satin gown had been decorated with fine lace around the bodice and down each of its long hand-length sleeves, and each little leaf in the design of the lace had been filled with pearls on sequins. The veil, made from the finest mesh, had the same lace decorated with pearls and sequins flowing down the back of the dress. Victoria stood up from the sofa and touched the fine fabric.

"Oh, Mother, it's absolutely beautiful!"

"'Tis me gift to you, dear. 'Twas your father's wish that we get ye the finest bridal gown ever, and who best to make it for you than me-self, with Jasmine's help, of course." Victoria embraced her mother, and before the night was over, Jasmine, too, came up to congratulate the two of them.

The wedding was planned for March 9, 1860, the same day a year after they had sailed on the Alacrity from Cape Colony to the United States. The next three months were a whirl of activity with planning for both the wedding and the late spring gem event.

The day finally came, and as people arrived, wedding bells sounded from the church bell tower. The celebration included friends from Boston, New York, and Georgia. Jacob Rosenbrand came to the reception with a gift for both the bride and the groom. Before the service, Rosenbrand found the groom and pulled him aside so they could speak privately.

"Here is ze special item you ordered so long ago, my good friend." Rosenbrand's face was drawn, and he had dark circles under his eyes. His suit coat noticeably hung loosely on him, and it was obvious he frequently missed his meals. He handed a box to Reggie who was surprised by its weight. He looked at Rosenbrand, who simply nodded, sure he knew what Reggie was about to say.

"Thank you, my dear friend. You have been so kind to do this for me."

"It is my pleasure. In zese last days of my life to have had the srill of vorking on such a vonderful treasure, I am very happy." Rosenbrand embraced Reggie. He also had a package for Victoria. "I hope your new vife will like her gift. It is somesing very close to my heart." He gave Reggie the package, and shaking his hand, Rosenbrand said good bye and took his seat. Finally at peace within himself about the loss of his wife, Jacob Rosenbrand had given Victoria the necklace he had made for his wife so many years before. Reggie knocked on the bride's door and was pushed back by a commanding Maggie O'Neil.

"Don'tcha know 'tis bad luck to see the bride before the weddin'?" Reggie lifted an eyebrow before making a protest, but then handed her the package from Jacob.

"Give this to Victoria, Maggie. Ask her to wear it for me." She assured him she would and pushing him away, quickly closed the door.

The young bride opened her gift and swooned when she saw it. Maggie helped her to put it on. It perfectly fit above the neckline of her gown. Rosenbrand's eyes filled with joyful tears when he saw his necklace on the young Mrs. Culpepper as she walked down the aisle. She looked as lovely as his own dear wife. He wiped a tear from his eye, and did not stay for the reception.

The wedding ended too quickly, and Victoria too soon found herself waving goodbye to her mother at the train station. Reggie stood next to her holding her hand as tears were allowed to fall freely.

"Don't worry, child, I'll be visitin' ye soon. Ye just be happy now," Maggie O'Neil shouted over the noise of the train engine. She hugged her daughter and ushered her to the train steps just as the wheels started to move. Reggie helped her to board.

"I'll miss you, Mother. Take care!" Victoria shouted back as the train pulled out of the station. "Good bye, Mother!" Maggie stood waving her handkerchief back at her daughter until the train was nearly out of sight. This was the first time Victoria would be separated from her mother. Maggie held a handkerchief to her eye and gave her nose a blow. She stood on the platform watching and waving her handkerchief even though the train was already out of sight.

In their private car, Victoria cried openly. Reggie held her close, trying to soothe her pain. "Oh, Reggie, I don't know if I can do this. I don't know if I can do anything without Mother. We've never been apart! What if I'm not a good farmer's wife? What if I don't make you happy?"

"My darling, there is no possibility of that. Nothing you could ever do would make me unhappy." Placing his finger under her chin, he tilted her face up to look at him. Drying the tears with a handkerchief, he kissed each cheek. "I love you so much, Victoria. Please don't be unhappy." She apologized for being so silly, put on a brave smile and snuggled under his arm. She felt safe there. She was at peace there.

"Thank you, Reggie. I know we'll be just fine. I know we will," she said doubtfully.

Chapter VI

The Secret Revealed

Victoria stood in the entryway of her new home turning circles as she looked up at the spiral staircase leading to the upper floor. She had never been in such a grand place, except for the Tremont Hotel in Boston. The thirty-foot ceiling enhanced by an enormous crystal chandelier welcomed the weary travelers with the warm light of a hundred candles. Even the Harrison's home could not compare to this, she thought. South American mahogany rails highlighted by bright-white painted spindles led the way up the stairs which were covered by a fine, woolen carpet. Reggie indeed had not spared any expense in building this for her.

"What do you think? Do you like it?" Reggie asked hopefully. Victoria turned around looking at him in amazement.

"Why, Reggie, it's absolutely beautiful! I have never seen anything like it in all my days!" She threw her arms around his neck and kissed him once each time she spoke. "Thank you, thank you, thank you!"

Reggie turned her in a circle. "This is not all of it, darling. Just wait until you see the land! It's positively wonderful. I truly believe you will be happy here."

"Oh, Reggie, I know I will. I just know I will!"

What little luggage Victoria brought with her was taken upstairs by one of the servants. Her belongings were few since she and her mother left Africa, and she had needed little while working for the Harrisons. A trunk and two small suitcases was all she carried to Georgia. Maggie would give the few things left behind to a charity in Boston. Victoria followed Reggie up to their bedroom where Mary Lee was setting out her clothing.

"Mrs. Lee, this is Mrs. Culpepper – here at last!" Reggie said proudly.

"How do you do, Ma'am. I'm proud to meet you." Mary Lee curtsied as best as she could remember her mother teaching her when she was in England. She was the servant now, and she had to mind her manners.

"Mary Lee? May I call you Mary?" Mary nodded. "I am very sorry to hear about your dear husband, Mary, but I am very glad you can stay here at Fairland." Victoria held out her hand to her. "Fairland: I love the name. Did you pick it out?" Mary nodded again, not quite sure what she should say to this young lady. She could tell by both her accent and her red hair that Victoria was Irish, and she remembered her parents didn't like the Irish. She wondered if the stories she'd heard about the Irish were true – scallywags, always looking for a way to get your money – but she seemed sweet; rather charming, actually. Mary decided to give the new Mrs. Culpepper a chance. Victoria continued.

"I know we will be wonderful friends, you so remind me of my own mother. I will be relying on you to help me make the transition here at Fairland."

"I'm happy too, Mrs. Culpepper. I look forward to working here with you." Mary finished hanging up Victoria's dresses and proceeded to unpack her undergarments.

"I'll take care of it, Mary. Perhaps we could have supper soon? The trip was very long, and I'm quite hungry."

"Of course, Ma'am. I'll start it right away." Mary tucked some stockings into a drawer and nearly skipped out of the room, happy to have someone there to keep her company at last.

Reggie held up a pair of bloomers and looked at them curiously. "It's been a long time since I saw anything like this," he chuckled. "My mother's were a bit larger, as I remember them."

Victoria grabbed the bloomers and stuffed them back into the suitcase.

"Mr. Culpepper, I will not have you rummaging around in my undergarments, if you don't mind. Now, I would like to freshen up a bit before supper, so if you could just show me where the facilities are –." Reggie scooped her up in his arms and placed her on the bed.

"Not yet." He leaned over her and kissed her neck. "I think we need to get better acquainted first, don't you?" Shutting the door with his foot, he unbuttoned his shirt.

* * *

Life at Fairland was comforting to Victoria in her third month of pregnancy. In less than six months already, a child would be born into their home, and Reggie was amazed how their lives had changed. Over the first few weeks, Victoria found her fears regarding her inability to be a good farm wife were unfounded. Her keen business sense helped Reggie immensely as they worked the farm together. She was able to figure out the income and loss statements, the necessary amounts to pay house staff and hired hands, and all the other household management duties. She was happy both with herself and with her new-found talents.

Mary Lee and Victoria did become good friends, and because Victoria relied on her heavily, Mary was less a servant than she thought she should be. Still, she had a problem convincing her sons they should be neighborly and join them sometime at the farm.

After his argument with his mother about the Englishman, Noah never showed up on her doorstep again. Young Matthew Lee, however, helped his mother when he could, but he had a family of his own to look after, and was not available as much as she hoped he would be. Feeling his mother's disappointment caused Matthew to withdraw from her more and more until finally one day in July, he advised Reggie to get himself some "boys" who could do the cotton picking and harvesting of the tobacco and fruit that year. Shocked at the suggestion, Reggie told him he wouldn't hear of keeping slaves. Slavery had been outlawed in England years before, and should have been in America by now, in his estimation. The Constitution, as he understood it, was for all men, not just white men he told Matthew confidently. Matthew looked at Reggie realizing he was unsure of what to think about this Englishman. Was he the good man his mother had said he was, or was he the Unionist his brother had accused him of being? In the end, he decided Noah's judgment had been correct; Culpepper was a Unionist, and could not be trusted. He had to talk to his mother.

"Mama," he said hesitantly. Mary could see the consternation in his eyes. "Mama, I guess I gotta say I agree with Noah. I don't trust this Culpepper, even if'n he is from your country."

"What're you tryin' to say, Matt?"

"I guess what I'm tryin' to say is I cain't stay here and work with him no more. I'm takin' my leave; I'm sorry as I can be, Mama." Disappointed by her son's shortsightedness, Mary gave him a kiss on his cheek and bid him goodbye. It was not many days later before Matthew sent her a message through his oldest sister that he had joined the Confederate army. He suggested she go stay with his wife and help take care of the children. Angrily, Mary tore up the letter. She faced her daughter squarely.

"Thank you very kindly for bringing me the news. I hope you do not take your brothers' views, but if'n you do, you can leave, too." Her daughter said not a word. She simply gathered her shawl about her shoulders and took her leave. Mary was extremely saddened by this turn of events. Her children had deserted her for a cause she knew was futile, but she would not turn back from her original decision. She happily stayed in the home she had built with her dear Eddie many years before.

Times become more unstable by the summer of 1860. States, including Tennessee, Alabama and Georgia were threatening secession from the Union, and the economy was suffering badly. In spite of the economy in the South, however, the North was still thriving. Reggie and Victoria decided to attend the exhibition in New York where they were going to sell his diamonds.

Jacob Rosenbrand met Reggie and Victoria at the train station. He escorted them downtown to the New York Commodities Building where they would be holding the sale of their diamonds. Jacob and his staff had done a beautiful job of mounting the gems, and he was very pleased with the end results despite the delay they'd had in holding the event. Even though

Rosenbrand seemed even weaker since their last meeting, Reggie noticed the excitement in his step as he hurried them along.

"I cannot vait for you to see vhat has been done!" he said happily. "I know you vill be as pleased as I, my friend. Come through here." He literally pushed Reggie and Victoria through a large double door where the diamonds were on display.

"Oh, Mr. Rosenbrand, these are beautiful!" Victoria stood in awe. She looked over each piece wondering about their worth and whether all their treasure would sell.

"Yah, and it vill bring a pretty penny, I know," Rosenbrand assured her. He had already been in contact with some of the brokers in the city, and there was great excitement about the debut of the Culpepper/Rosenbrand collection. Invitations had been sent to wealthy businessmen, the mayor of the city and even New York's governor. Reggie had also been in contact with some of the businessmen he'd met in Boston, including Steven Engle, who was happy to join them for the debut. Reggie shook Jacob's hand again once he finished examining each piece. Indeed he was pleased with his friend's expertise and congratulated himself for taking Stephen Engle's advice in the beginning.

The sale began at precisely two o'clock the same afternoon. After the long train ride, Victoria had to take a rest at the hotel, but was able to join Reggie again before the sale started. To Rosenbrand's surprise and great pleasure, she was wearing his wife's necklace beautifully displayed on her long neck. She stood next to Reggie quietly as he and Jacob made plans for the pieces left from the sale.

"It's settled then, Jacob. The pieces will go to Washington for the Union cause."

"Yah, if you insist, Culpepper. I vill do as you say. It is a good cause, is it not? The government vill be able to sell the stones in Europe, yes?"

Reggie nodded. "Yes, I believe so, Jacob. This is a good cause. Since living in Georgia, I have come to believe that war is imminent. It is my opinion the state will be one of many to secede by next spring, if not before. We must keep as much money in the North as we can." Rosenbrand agreed and made arrangements with the auctioneer to send the leftovers to Washington.

The sale went beautifully with excellent results. Reggie and Jacob split the money amicably, and Reggie sent his portion of the $930,000 to his bank in Boston. The few pieces left behind only valued $11,000, but they were shipped by messenger to Rosenbrand's contact in Washington D.C. They agreed their contact was to hold them until it was determined whether or not the money would be needed by the Union government. If war did not occur, the money would be split between the two men.

Reggie felt he had done what was necessary to help the war effort, if there was to be one, and he was satisfied with that. Writing a personal letter to President Buchanan, Reggie explained his reasons for donating the funds and encouraged him to press on for the cause of freedom. He signed it J. Reginald Culpepper, Esq., Fairland Farm, Macon, Georgia. The contact was asked to give the letter to the President only in the case of actual war, for if news of his donation ever reached Macon, Reggie's reputation would be completely destroyed in the South. They were living in very precarious times. Reggie and Victoria returned to Fairland satisfied he had not only provided well for their family, but had also done a service for his newly-adopted country.

Victoria's pregnancy went well over the summer months and into the fall until, just before the dawn of December 15, 1860, a light-haired, seven-pound, five-ounce girl came out screaming her dissatisfaction at the injustice of the world. After being shown her mother, who was now resting, she was handed to her proud father. Reggie held her up to the morning light coming through the bedroom window.

"My darling daughter, why are you so upset? Your mother sleeps quietly, why don't you?" Reggie held her close and whispered soft words of encouragement into her ear. "What shall we call you? I think I shall call you Jewel, Jewel Victoria – after your mother and the Jewel of Africa, my darling. I'll show it to you someday. It's beautiful, but not as beautiful as you." Jewel fell asleep in her father's arms as he spoke to her. Her father's deep, resonant voice would always soothe her from then on, he decided, and they would be as close as a father and daughter could be.

Fairland's fall harvest profits had been affected by the unstable economy. The cotton crop did not bring in what they had hoped, and the tobacco brought in less. Reggie was not poor, by any sense of the imagination, but he was aware that the next year's crops could be adversely affected by this turn of events.

Against his better judgment, Reggie had had to hire Africans to work the fields. He fed and clothed them, never considering them slaves. He felt obligated to pay them as employees, and they were treated as equals, free to come and go as they wished. His days in the African jungle and the hard working Tsonga men who had helped in the mine and lost their lives because of him, were fondly remembered. He would tell Jewel those stories when she could understand, he thought. She would grow up to be like her father, believing God had made all men equal, in spite of race, religion or education. He would teach her to know right from wrong, and the Confederate beliefs now tearing America in half were wrong.

Instability in the markets and in politics bred talk of secession from the Union even more fiercely. Riots in Macon and Atlanta caused loss of life and property to many, while Rebels held their meetings in the streets. The Georgia flag with the words, "Don't Tread on Me" flew over cities and small towns replacing the American Union Jacks torn from their masts.

Reggie stood on his porch watching the glow of flames hovering over the city. Rebels were having another bonfire, most likely, with furniture belonging to someone who did not agree with their cause. He wondered how this would all end, and he was concerned for Fairland and for his family. Nevertheless, determined he would not abandon this place if he could help it, he stayed. Reggie had spoken to Victoria frequently about returning to Boston, but she would not hear of it. Her place was by her husband. They would stand for the Union together, she had said, even if they stood alone.

One cold night in early January 1861, Victoria was awakened by the voice of Mary Lee calling from the porch below their window. She slipped out of bed and padded over to the window looking out over the porch.

"Mary Lee? What's wrong?"

"Oh, Victoria, please come! They've set fire to the orchard and my house has caught!"

"Oh, my God! We'll be right there, Mary! Call Samuel from the bunkhouse and get the other men!" She turned and looked at Reggie who was already sitting on the edge of the bed putting on his shoes.

"I heard, Victoria. I'll be back soon."

"I should go, too, Reggie. It's Mary's house!"

"No, stay here with her and the baby. I don't want you out in case they should come back here." With that word of warning, he rushed through the door and down the stairs. Finding Mary outside, he gave her orders to stay behind. He and the other men would take care of things the best they could. Running to the barn, he mounted a horse and rode bareback to the servants' quarters to awaken the men.

By the time Reggie and the men arrived at Mary's home, it was fully engulfed in flames. There was no need trying to save it; they just stood by and watched, keeping water nearby in case the fire should try to spread. Most of the peach orchard was gone. Thankfully, there still were no crops planted, so nothing else would be harmed. Reggie clenched his teeth as he thought about what he would tell Mary when he returned. He stood there helpless, unable to stop the raging fire, unable to stop the rage of hatred spreading throughout the South.

The next day, Reggie and Victoria found Mary rustling through the charred remains of her home. Literally everything had been destroyed, though she did find one of her children's shoes under what was left of her cedar chest. No tears fell. She could only sigh at the loss. She could not believe her fellow Georgians would have done such a thing to her home. Her Eddie would never have done anything like this, if he had lived. Victoria put her arm around her friend and led her over to the wagon.

"Samuel and the men will clean this up, Mary. If they find anything, they'll bring it to you," Victoria said, trying to console her.

Mary looked at Victoria, hopelessness showing in her eyes. "Where do I go now?" she asked. She thought she might live with one of her daughters or even with Matthew's family; but in truth, she knew she would never be at home there.

"Why, Mary, your home is with us. I would never want you to go anywhere else, unless you want to. I need you here." Mary looked at Victoria whose arms held her steady as they walked away from the last bit of security she had – her home. With her lips pursed, she nodded and climbed into the wagon. Words were very inadequate just then.

Fairland suffered great losses during the winter of 1861. More fires and more loss of life in and around Macon caused the economy to plummet, and Reggie knew he would have to sell off some of the livestock. They had enough grain for a few, but did not have enough for future crops. He sat in his library quietly looking over the books with Jewel Victoria in his lap.

"Little Jewel, we might have to leave Fairland. I hate to do it, but we might have to. Perhaps we'll move back to England for a while. I want you to be safe, little one. Look, here is the diamond for which you were named."

He had opened the hiding place in the bookshelf where he kept the gem. Hidden in the back of the bookcase behind a well-camouflaged door, Reggie lifted the Jewel of Africa from its encasement.

Walking back to his chair, he sat down to examine the great stone under the lamp. He turned to see his daughter's eyes follow excitedly the refracted light streaming onto the walls.

"See here, sweetheart?" He said. "It's as fair as you."

Reggie placed the jewel on the desk and extracted his diary from the desk drawer. He needed to record some kind of clue as to the whereabouts of the jewel in case anything should happen to him. He looked across the room at the picture he'd had painted of Fairland Farm, then back at the bookcase where the family Bible stood on the shelf in front of a hidden door. Carefully, he inscribed the following into his journal:

> *Fairland overlooks the picture of God where the door opens by pressing toward the mark.*

"There, little one. Some day you'll read your father's diary and you will know his treasure is hidden from everyone but you." He folded over the corner of the page to mark it as another clue.

Reggie still had not told Victoria about the jewel, but he knew he had to; there was urgency in his gut he knew he could not ignore any longer. Lifting his daughter to his shoulder and putting the Jewel of Africa into his pants pocket, he stood up and started for the kitchen. Victoria and Mary stood together cutting up apples for pies for the next days' meals. Reggie watched the two of them for a moment before entering.

"This little one says she needs to go to bed, Mary. Would you please take her upstairs? I'd like to talk to Victoria for a moment."

"Of course, Mr. Culpepper. I'm sure she'll settle right in." Mary wiped her hands with a towel and took the infant from her father. She left the kitchen, closing the door behind her. Over the previous weeks, she had made it a habit of hiding behind closed doors to listen to conversations. The times had required it. It wasn't because she enjoyed spying on them, but if something was going to happen to Fairland, she wanted to know about it.

"Victoria, I have something to show you," Reggie began. Victoria looked at him with tired blue eyes and gave him a half smile.

"Is it bad, Reggie? Things have been so bad lately."

"No, My love, it's our security. Look." He took the heavy diamond from his pocket and placed it on the table next to an apple. The gem was larger than the apple, and perfectly shaped. Victoria's eyes grew large as she looked down.

"Oh my, Reggie. Is that a diamond?"

"Yes, Darling. I call it the Jewel of Africa. I brought it with me when we left Cape Colony. I didn't want anyone to know about it for fear it would be lost; but now I believe it is time for you to hear the story." Reggie had already told her about his experience in the jungle with the natives there, and how he'd barely escaped with his life, but he had neglected to mention the gem in all this time. Victoria was angry.

"And you didn't trust I could handle this information?" she asked, her voice on edge. Her look was threatening as her Irish temper flared.

"It's not because I didn't trust you, Darling. It's because I couldn't bring myself to tell anyone of the horrible things that happened to Larry and Rikart. The jewel is my memory of those days. I wouldn't have brought it up now if I didn't trust you, and I didn't think it was absolutely imperative you were aware of it."

Victoria's eyes softened and she reached out to touch Reggie's arm. "I do understand, Reggie, truly I do. But what do we do with it now? With things the way they are, shouldn't we have sold it with the other treasures?"

"Perhaps, but I could not bring myself to sell it. I've thought I'd rather it be a family heirloom. However, if there ever is a necessity we cannot meet for our children, we will sell it then. Jacob has told me it will only become more valuable with time."

"What is it worth now, Reggie?"

"Over $850,000. It's the collateral I used to buy this farm. I was able to pay off the loan with the sale of the other diamonds, but this one I wanted to keep for the future. No one should know about it, Victoria. No one," he admonished her sternly. "Not even Mary," he added to be sure she understood.

"All right, Reggie, if you insist. Where do you keep it?"

"I have it hidden in my library. I will show you where later, but I wanted you to see it now before things become worse politically. I wanted you to be assured that you and the baby will be well taken care of."

Mary Lee, listening quietly at the kitchen door, backed away with little Jewel still in her arms. She knew she could never tell anyone what she had overheard, but it was information she would remember in case she needed it. Fairland must remain, she thought, and if it meant having to cash that diamond in some day, she would do it.

The political strain of early 1861 continued to cause Fairland Farm to suffer financially. Hearing Reggie had a heart for slaves, however, and hoping for amnesty, Africans began coming to them by droves. He knew he could not help them if he hoped to survive this horrible time. His neighbors shunned him when they met. Even the pastor of the local church turned his back on the Englishman. Reggie decided he would feed the renegades; but if their masters came by to get them, they were made to understand, he would not protect them. Neither did he feel he could engage their help on the farm since they did not belong to him. He would feed them, but that was all. Soon, a few of his own men abandoned Fairland and went north, taking some of the renegades with them. This left Reggie to do much of the spring planting alone.

Victoria watched helplessly as he worked the fields. Mary Lee stood beside her holding little Jewel.

"My Eddie killed himself tryin' to keep this farm goin', Miss Victoria. Maybe y'all should think about movin' north."

"It'll be all right, Mary. We have enough to keep us going."

Mary Lee looked at her knowingly. "Yes, Ma'am, I know you do. Just keep in mind that things here are not going to be easy, him bein' a Unionist. He might get things planted, but I don't know anyone who will buy from him."

Victoria looked at her with concern in her eyes. "Are we in danger here, Mary? Is there something we should know?"

"Maybe you are, but don't worry, Miss Victoria. I'll be here if you need me." The older woman gave the younger a pat on the arm as she turned to go into the house. She could not help but stand in the library door looking in, wondering where the diamond could be.

On January 29, 1861, Georgia declared its secession from the Union. A long dissertation was given and approved by the people of Georgia which dissolved their association with the Government of the United States of America. Due to their stand on possession of the human property known as slaves, and claims against the Union of fraud against the Constitution of the United States, the Union accepted this decision. The document expressed many Georgians' beliefs that the northern government acted without consulting the southern states regarding the slavery issue, and though it was not the only issue causing the secession, it certainly remained the most turbulent.

The document also mentioned complaints about the territory acquired from Mexico in the recent war. Congress now governed the Southwest Territory and outlawed slavery in Mexico. Angry slave owners demanded the return of their property, slaves who had escaped to the North, but the North would not give them up. Other complaints included the monopoly of fishing businesses in the North, as well as the associated costs of building lighthouses and buoys, and the maintenance of their seamen, which were all being supported by the treasury. Senseless accusations were tossed into the mix to further enrage southerners, keeping them in strong opposition to the Union.

The belief that the African slave was not equal to the white man either physically or mentally, gave Confederate supporters reason to believe their very lives were at stake, should slaves be allowed to govern themselves. Reggie knew better. He had seen their hard work, their creativity and their originality. He had seen the love they had for their families and for God. He knew they would die for their new country, should they have to. Reggie could not and would not give into the pressures of his neighbors and business associates.

Fort Sumter, South Carolina, an artificial island made with granite from quarries in the North, was one of the last Union-held forts in the southern states. In the same month Georgia seceded, President James Buchanan sent the U.S.S. Star of the West to Fort Sumter to bring in supplies. Shore batteries at Charleston Harbor fired upon the ship, and she retreated without leaving the badly needed supplies. The fort's commanding officer, Major Robert Anderson, was ordered to protect Union-held forts such as Fort Sumter, but he had little with which to defend them since the supplies did not get through.

After winning the presidential election, Abraham Lincoln was inaugurated in March 1861. Hearing Major Anderson had less than a month's supply left with which to keep Fort Sumter open, the president struggled over the decision whether or not to keep the fort open. In the end, it was decided Fort Sumter must not be lost. He sent another ship to bring supplies to the fort.

General P.G.T. Beauregard from New Orleans, Louisiana, took the opportunity to seize the fort on April 11, 1861, demanding Major Anderson hand over the keys. Major Anderson, unable to make a decision that would satisfy the general, delayed his answer. The next day, angry with Anderson's inability to act, General Beauregard fired upon Fort Sumter.

President Lincoln's relief supplies never reached the fort, and the War Between the States had begun.

Chapter VII

Casualties of War

Reggie never again took the diamond from its hiding place. He didn't have time. Before the end of April, confederate soldiers were standing on the steps of Fairland House pounding on their door. He stood in his doorway, an ancient musket in his hand, hoping to protect his home, but knowing he was out numbered. Except for his run-in with the natives in Africa, he hadn't had to use a fire arm since his days in the English army. Nevertheless, he stood his ground hoping he could convince these men to leave peaceably. Victoria stood on the staircase behind him with little Jewel in her arms, fearing the worst.

"Sir, I expect you will leave my land immediately. You are trespassing," Reggie said as boldly as he could. His knees were knocking, but he'd never show it.

"On the contrary, Sah, it is you who are trespassin'," responded the captain who stood in front of a small troop of soldiers. They held their rifles up, pointing them directly at Reggie. "This land is bein' confiscated by the Confederate States of America. We believe, Sah, that you are a traitah to our Confederate States and demand your immediate surrendah. As a Unionist, you are not allowed to retain property in Georgia. As such, we are immediately takin' over your home to use as our headquartahs."

Reggie could not believe his ears. He had come to America in good faith, believing that living here would bring him freedoms he had not experienced in his homeland, his family would be safe here and he would be able to prosper as did other people who came from other lands to seek refuge in this country.

"You can't do that!"

"Yes, Sah, we can. Georgia is no longer a member of the Union, and we have full jurisdiction in this instance. I hereby remind you of your trespass, and command you to stand down."

The captain signaled the guards behind him to arm their guns. In unison, the rifles were cocked and ready to fire. Reggie took a step back and set his musket aside. He knew he would be dead in a moment if he did not obey the order. Raising his arms in surrender, he stepped outside onto the porch.

"Will my family be safe, Sir?"

"Yes, they will. You, howevah, must come with us." A soldier stepped up behind Reggie and pulled his arms behind his back. Handing the baby over to Mary, Victoria ran down the stairs to see what was happening.

"Reggie! Where are they taking you?" she cried. When a soldier grabbed her to keep her from going to him, Reggie escaped the hands of the man holding him and rammed his shoulder against the soldier who restrained her.

"Leave your hands off her!" he shouted. The soldier felt the full blow of Reggie's body against his and fell across the porch rocking chair. Turning on him, the rebel pulled a dagger from its sheath and plunged it into Reggie's ribs. Reggie staggered back, and with his hands still tied behind him, lost his balance when he hit the top stair. Falling into the captain, the two of them toppled over the side rail and onto the ground.

The soldier landed on top of Reggie, but when he moved to get up, he noticed Reggie had stopped breathing. He checked Reggie's pulse, looked up at his commanding officer and gave him a negative shake of his head.

Victoria escaped her captor and ran down the steps to find Reggie sprawled on the ground, his neck broken. She fainted.

Months later, Mary Lee held the spoon up to Victoria's lips. She had not been able to eat since the dreadful day her Reggie died. "Come on, Miss

Victoria, take one sip. You need your strength to hold onto this new little one. If you don't eat, you'll lose more of Mr. Culpepper than you already have."

Victoria's eyes closed. She did not want to face another day. She did not want to believe she would have to raise one child alone, not to mention two. How could this have happened? She turned over on her side and feigned sleep. Mary Lee stood up straight and sighed.

"All right, Missy. I'll give you one more day, and then I'm gonna pull you right out of that bed," she said sternly. It had been a month since Reggie's death, but Victoria's depression grew deeper daily. She couldn't face anything or anyone, and except for going to the bathroom, she never got out of bed again. After Mary lifted the tray from the bedside table and left Victoria's room, tears silently flowed down Victoria's cheeks. She tried to block out the memories of seeing her husband lying on the ground dead, blood oozing from his belly, but she could not.

The Culpepper family and Mary Lee were held captive at Fairland House. Soldiers walked in and out of the house as if they owned it, but Mary patiently worked around them. She would cooperate with them as long as they left her and her family alone. This was still Fairland House. It was her home as much as it was Victoria's, as far as she was concerned, and she was not about to let it deteriorate just because it was occupied by a bunch of strange men. She refused to allow any of the rebel soldiers up the stairs, for the second floor was Mrs. Culpepper's personal quarters. The military could have their run of the downstairs and use the property as needed, but nothing else, and she frequently reminded them of their boundaries.

The captain who had come to arrest Reggie had been sorely admonished for allowing the capture to get out of hand. He was demoted to lieutenant by his commanding officer, Major Wilson, who also made sure his men understood Mrs. Culpepper was not to be molested in any manner. Her property was to be kept intact, and she was to have full privacy.

Letters to Victoria's mother were confiscated for security purposes. Mary Lee knew Maggie O'Neil would wonder why she suddenly had no contact from her daughter. Talking to the Major, Mary finally convinced him she needed to tell Mrs. O'Neil that Victoria was all right and not to worry. The war made it impossible for them to have any further communication, but

Mary felt Victoria's mother should know she would soon have another grandchild. She also requested that Mrs. O'Neil be allowed to come to care for her daughter during this difficult time. The major agreed, but after it was written, the letter was thoroughly examined for any other kind of hidden information.

Maggie O'Neil received news of Victoria's second child with mixed emotions. As soon as she saw the handwriting on the envelope, she knew something was not right; it was not Victoria who had written the letter. Maggie hesitated before opening the envelope. She had been worried for her daughter in that strange place with only Reggie to lean on. Now he was gone and her daughter was alone. Victoria had written before about Mary Lee being her good friend, but she was a southerner, Maggie reminded herself. She decided to leave immediately to gather her family home. The next day, when she checked if she could purchase a ticket to Georgia, she was denied.

"Sorry, Ma'am," the ticket master said, "No trains in or out of Georgia these days 'cause of the war. It'll probably change in a little while, but for now, there's nothing we can do."

Maggie sent a letter to Victoria to tell her she would come as soon as the borders were opened. She did not realize they would remain closed for most of the rest of the war. The letter never arrived.

Mary managed the household and the farm to the best of her ability. Victoria was in no shape to do anything either physically or emotionally, so Mary had to take over. Her daughters would come to visit at times, but she never again saw her son, Noah. At times she would ask her daughters to bring her sons' children over to see their grandmother, but Noah's oldest boy, Nathaniel, was difficult. He was bitter over his father's abandonment and bitter about the war. Already in his mid-teens, he made it his mission to remind his mother and grandmother of the reasons for his misery. Although it was difficult, Mary tried to love the boy despite his rebellion, but after a while he stopped coming.

Time passed ever so slowly during those first months of the war. The summer was hot and dry and the winter promised to be cold and wet. Victoria successfully carried her child through the heat of summer. The pregnancy was shortened when, early in the evening of November 25th, birthing pains began. Mary knew it was too soon, but Victoria's health had deteriorated to the point where Mary was unable to manage her without help. She needed constant care, so Mary had one of the servants who had stayed voluntarily to help the family come in to watch over her when she was unable to. Victoria was both weak in body and weak willed. The pains came faster and harder. Victoria had not kept up her strength as the pregnancy progressed, and she was in no condition to go through the birth. She wanted to die and she told Mary as much.

"Mary, I can't do this! Help me, please!"

"Now, Miss Victoria, I told you we'll be jes' fine. You need to hang on. You've had a child before, you know how it goes. You've got to help me to help you, all right? Now push!"

Sally, the servant girl, stood behind Victoria's head and helped her sit up to push. Victoria screamed as a sudden pain shot up her spine and the baby's head crowned. But with the crowning, came blood – too much blood.

"Oh, my God, Sally, get over here, quick!" Mary shouted. Sally eased Victoria back down on the bed, but Victoria felt and then saw the blood now oozing out from under her.

"Mary, I'm bleeding! I don't remember this from before!"

Sally tried to calm Victoria down, but Victoria knew there was something very wrong.

Mary encouraged her to push again, and Victoria bore down. Then, it was done. Over a month premature, a tiny boy child was born.

Sally brought hot water and cotton cloths to clean up the child while Mary tried to stop the bleeding. The bleeding couldn't be stopped. She had already sent for the doctor, but the call for help had been ignored. No one wanted anything to do with the Unionist's household, not even the doctor. There was nothing she could do to help Victoria.

"I'm sorry, Miss Victoria. I can't stop it. I don't know what else to do!"

Sally stood back wiping her face with her apron, trying not to let Victoria see her tears. Saying nothing to alarm the young mother, she only watched the tiny body of the little boy who had survived his early birth.

"I'm dying, then." Victoria quietly resigned. With an odd peacefulness in her failing voice, she comforted Mary. "It's all right, Mary. I can go and see my Reggie now. Is it another girl?"

"No, Darlin'. It's a little boy. What would you name him?"

"I think David," Victoria responded in weakened bare whisper. "Yes, that's a good name, isn't it? David was the man after God's own heart. I think David Reginald, after his father."

"It's a nice name, Miss Vic –." Mary's face fell as she abruptly stopped speaking. Victoria's eyes looked back at her blank and empty of life.

Mary scooped the whimpering child up in her arms to allow Sally to cut the cord. Sally, a new mother herself, would have to nurse him until he could be weaned.

Mary then washed and quickly wrapped the newborn in one of Jewel's baby blankets. Then, with David in her arms, she quietly walked out of the room and down the stairs to the library.

Standing in the doorway, she scanned the library hoping for a clue as to where the Jewel of Africa was hidden, but it was no use. There were too many soldiers there and no way to find it now. The major looked up at the haggard Mrs. Lee with a knowing question in his eyes.

"Yes, Major, Mrs. Culpepper is dead."

PART II
The Next Generation

Chapter VIII

The Tradition

Mary Lee sat on the porch in her rocking chair watching gray-clad boys walking past their property. She kept searching their faces, hoping to see one of her sons. It had been almost exactly four years since the first horrible shots rang out at Fort Sumter, South Carolina, beginning the War Between the States. Finally, on April 9, 1865, General Ulysses S. Grant, under President Lincoln's command, offered General Lee, general of the Confederate army, an opportunity for the first quiet surrender. They met in the home of Wilber and Virginia McLean at Appomattox Virginia Court House where General Lee gave his word that the army of Northern Virginia would no longer take up arms against the Union. Mary Lee thought it ironic that she would have to share the same name as this man whom she had learned to respect and despise at the same time. He was a great leader in his time, but he had taken her sons from her whom she had little hope of ever seeing again; he had led a war that had all but destroyed her home, and killed two of the finest people she knew – J. Reginald Culpepper and his lovely young wife, Victoria.

The Civil War was a victory for Lincoln, but it remained a source of tragedy for the United States. Lincoln had suffered a great deal of persecution at the beginning of the election year, but by the end of 1864, the war had started to turn. Fanatics, still enraged over the seeming atrocities of the North, were pleased when, on the 14th day of April, 1865, one fanatic in particular – John Wilkes Booth – ended President Lincoln's life. Tragically, Lincoln died the day after he was shot. On April 17th, General Sherman accepted the surrender of the Confederates in Durham Station, North Carolina. Lincoln never saw the official end of the war that had divided his country.

Day after day, men and boys still dressed in rebel gray would pass by Fairland Farm. Mary recognized a few faces, but none of them were her sons'. Her other children had rejected her over the years because all their men were either at war or helping with the war effort in some way, but in faith, she continued to wait for her sons' return. Finally, one rainy afternoon, a wagon pulled up in front of the gate. Her son, Matthew was driving.

Mary practically jumped off the porch and ran to the wagon, tears streaming down her face. "Oh, Matthew," she called to him, "Matthew, I'm so happy you're here! Thank God, you're alive!" He stood with his rebel hat in hand, looking down at the ground. Mary could tell he was defeated mentally as well as physically, but he was here, and she was glad. She stood back.

"Yes, Ma, I'm alive. But Noah ain't," he said woefully.

Mary's countenance fell when she heard the words. All her prayers for Noah seemed to have been for nothing.

"He died near Richmond, Ma. I saw it. He got hit bad, and the doctors couldn't save him." Matthew broke into tears. "I tried to get to him, Ma, but it was too late. I tried hard as I could." He fell into her arms looking for the solace he had never been able to find.

"It's all right, Matthew. I know you tried. It's all right." Mary held him close and helped him to cry. "Just get it all out, Son. I'm here now." She walked with him over to the porch and had him sit on the step. Four-year-old Jewel, who had been watching from the door, came out of the house and sat next to him.

"Mama? Is this man cryin'?" she asked. She hadn't seen many men in her few short years, and of those she'd known, she had never seen them cry.

"Yes, Hon, he's cryin'. Go on back into the house, now."

"What's he cryin' 'bout? Should I git him a cookie?"

"That would be a good idea, Jewel. Ask Sally for a cookie."

Jewel ran up the steps, and meeting her little brother who stood in the doorway, she took his hand and went into the kitchen to get Matthew a cookie. Matthew couldn't help but smile at the little girl. She was all business, he could tell, much like his eldest.

"Who's that?" Matthew asked finally.

"She's the daughter of the lady who used to live in this house. She died, and I became her mama." Matthew nodded.

"I s'pose you had to then. Don't forgit you got grandkids, too." His voice sadly held the resentment he had felt against his mother, who had become a traitor in her son's eyes.

"I won't forget if you don't." There was meaning in her voice, as well. Matthew nodded again. He knew the rift between them had to be mended. He thought perhaps this had already been started by a treaty between the North and the South. Jewel soon returned with a large sugar cookie in her hand.

"Here, man. You eat this and you're gonna feel better."

"Thank ye, Missy. What's your name?"

"Jewel. My daddy named me after a diamond," she said proudly. Mary stiffened. She hadn't told anyone about the gem except Jewel herself.

"He did? Well, Jewel's a nice name."

"Go on in the house now, Jewel. I'll be in after a while," Mary said quietly, hoping the secret hadn't been spoiled. She had been searching the library since the major pulled away from Fairland House, but she had not found the Jewel. She knew if she could find it, she would give it to the children, but if anyone else found it, the Jewel would be lost. Matthew stood up.

"Thanks for the cookie, little miss."

"You're welcome, I'm sure," came the refined response. She curtsied and ran back up the steps, golden curls flopping about her pretty head. She took little David's hand again and went back into the house. Matthew looked at his mother and nodded his good bye. Getting back into the wagon, he turned it around and gave a half-hearted wave of his hand.

"See ye, Ma. I'll be around if'n ye need anythin'."

Mary waved back as she watched the wagon lumber down the road. Her fair-haired boy had grown into manhood the worst way. She knew the war had dramatically changed him, as it had everyone, and he would never be the same. Putting her thoughts behind her, she quickly turned around to go back into the house. She knew she must find that diamond.

Over an hour later, with books strewn everywhere, Mary stood up from her knees to gaze at the mess she had made. She had already searched every shelf, every book had been opened, every desk drawer pulled out of the desk and turned over, and every carpet corner pulled back. She had checked for false bottoms in drawers, loose floorboards, and false pages in books, but she could not find the illusive diamond. How she wished she had followed Mr. Culpepper to the library the night she overheard his conversation with Victoria. She might have seen where he'd hidden it. Perhaps she had heard wrong, she thought. Perhaps he was joking! She dismissed the idea. Victoria had been too astonished and downright angry when she saw it. Remembering their muffled conversation, Mary decided it must have been a huge thing for her not to even recognize what it was. Mary shook her head.

"Ma'am?" Sally stood at the library door, eyes wide, wondering what Mary was doing. Mary started.

"Oh! Sally! Don't ever sneak up on a body like that! You liked to scare me to death."

"I's sorry, Ma'am, but I needs to know what you want me to do with the chillun today. They's askin' 'bout goin' fer a ride."

"That's fine, Sally, if you want to take them. I have to clean up this mess," Mary said absent-mindedly. Sally looked the room over again.

"Does you needs help, Ma'am?"

"No, no, Sally. Thank you. I'll take care of it." She dismissed the maid with a wave of her hand. Sally nodded and left the room without saying another word, but she sure wondered what the Missus was doing. Maybe, she thought, the war finally got to her. Mary proceeded to put the books back onto the bookshelf in the order she had memorized over the years.

Later in the day, Mary sat on the porch with a small notebook. Some of her deepest thoughts had been journaled over many years so she could remember them later in life. She had hoped to give something to her grandchildren by which to remember her, and since everything had been destroyed in the fire of her small farm house, she had been forced to start over again. She had already recalled a bit of her childhood, her travels from England to America and the early years of her marriage. Later she had written about Eddie and the children. She wrote fondly of her years on Fairland Farm, and silently wished it could be hers again, but Reggie Culpepper had made it prosperous, had built this beautiful home, and had left it for his family. Now the farm belonged to Jewel and David, as it should.

Davey and Jewel played in the yard as Mary sat wistfully thinking about times gone by, jotting a note down every couple minutes. It was a joy for her to watch the children since she rarely saw any of her own family. Jewel was very much Davey's second mother, and Mary smiled as the little girl bossed her brother around.

"Davey, now you bring me the tea cups and we will have tea," said Jewel.

"Aw wight, Jewew," the three-year old answered. He clumsily brought two tea cups over to his sister who plopped down on a blanket in the yard, petticoats flared around her. She filled them up with water from her little tea pot, and offered it to him.

"Don't spill, young man," she warned. Of course David did spill, and watching, Mary could not help but laugh. "I told you not to spill, Davey. Now we have to start all over again."

When Jewel brought the cups to the steps, she stood there with hands on her hips, a curl at the corners of her mouth, and her little foot jutting out to punctuate her frustration. "Mama, Davey spilled! I just don't know what to do with that boy!"

"Don't worry, honey, it will dry," Mary soothed. "Why don't you go give him a hug so he doesn't feel so bad?"

Jewel looked up at her with a smirk on her face. She rolled her eyes, went back to her tearful little brother, helped him up, and gave him a hug.

"It's all right, Davey. I know you didn't mean to. Let's go see if Sally has any of those cookies left."

She was very much a mother, Mary thought.

Mary looked back at her notes. She had finished her thoughts about Victoria and Reggie and started writing about the lost diamond.

I know I heard Mr. Culpepper talk about a diamond that night. It seems like it was so long ago. He called it the Jewel of Africa. From what I could tell, this is where all his money came from, diamonds from Africa. I have wondered ever since the night I heard it where he could have it hidden. I have searched and searched, but from what I can tell, it is nowhere in the library where I heard him say he kept it. When the soldiers came, I was never able to get in there to look. Perhaps they found it and took it for themselves. Maybe the diamond is gone forever, just like the Confederacy.

She closed her journal with a sad sigh. Indeed the Confederacy had come to naught, and she was held in captivity in a home not her own by the fallen dream of an unknown relative named Lee.

Over a month had passed since Maggie O'Neil received permission to go to Georgia to collect her grandchildren. Mary Lee had written her a number of times saying she would be willing to keep the children, but since Maggie was the rightful grandparent, she had to have Maggie's permission before she tried to adopt them. Maggie wasn't sure what to do. She worked for a thriving business in Boston, and was happy living in her little apartment. If she went to collect the children, they would be ripped from the only home and the only mother they ever really knew. It could be very unsettling for them all.

Still, she couldn't bear knowing her only surviving relatives were so far away. She finally decided she must make the move to Fairland Farm to take care of her grandchildren. Since she had learned so much about business from Jasmine, she was convinced she could make a living anywhere, even in the South. Finally deciding to pull up her roots in Boston, she followed her decision and left for Georgia.

The ride seemed interminable, but finally the train pulled away from the station in Macon, leaving Maggie O'Neil alone with all seven pieces of her luggage. Beyond weary, she looked around to find a train station worker who could direct her to a hotel. She had planned to spend the night there and then hire a wagon to go out to the farm the next day. However, she had not planned for the poor reception of the clerk at the hotel.

"Hmmm," the clerk said with one eyebrow raised and a disapproving look pasted on his face. "O'Neil. Irish?"

"Why, yes, young man. Thank ye fer askin'. But it has been fairly a lifetime since I seen me own country," she answered wistfully. Coming back to herself, she looked up with a smile. "I'm told ye might have a warm room for a weary traveler," she said jovially.

"Yes, I s'pose we do. Two flights up and on the right," he said handing her a key, knowing there was a more favorable accommodation on the first floor. She stood there looking back at him.

"And my luggage?" she asked. He didn't respond immediately, but then rang for a bellman.

"Henry, take this woman to 216." He barely looked at the boy who was so small, he could barely pick up one of the bags let alone all of them.

"I dare say, Sir, you could help!" Maggie exclaimed with a sniff. She picked up the two largest of the bags in both hands and marched up the stairs leaving the rest for the young man to carry. If this was the way they were to be treated in Macon, she would not be here for long, she murmured to herself.

Maggie was tired after the long night at the hotel. "I barely slept a wink last night with all the hootin' and hollerin' they were doin' out on the streets. A bunch of rabble rousers, they were," she complained to the hotel clerk. He simply nodded his head, rolled his eyes, and dismissed the complaint. There wasn't a thing he could do about it, he said.

Typically Irish, Maggie was broad shouldered and thick waisted. She was no longer the small woman who married Mr. O'Neil over 25 years before, and it was not easy for her to get into the wagon hired to take her to Fairland Farm. The little bellboy who had helped Maggie with her luggage the night before gave her a hefty push so she could board, and wiping the sweat from his brow, he waved her off.

Mary Lee sat quietly on the porch watching the rising sun and writing in her journal. She had been extremely tired of late, and she had a terrible time moving quickly these days. Sally came out with a cup of tea and handed it to her.

"Sally, I 'spect to be hearin' from Mrs. O'Neil any time now. She should be arrivin' in Georgia today or tomorrow. Make sure the children are ready for her, won't you?"

"Yes'm. Deys up an' runnin' already. Dos two kids 'r jes as happy as dey kin be a'waitin' fer dere grammama. Hee, Hee," she laughed, "Can'ts wait fer ta see her m'self." Sally laughed again as she went back into the house. Her laugh, rich and full, made Mary Lee smile every time she heard it.

Sally had been a great help and companion to her over these difficult war years after Victoria's death. She had stayed despite her family's decision to travel north. Her husband left her with the children, so what little she had was shared with them. Having been in a similar situation, Mary offered her a place to live and raise her children. She's said, "I's got no place else to go, Miss Mary. I 'spect I'd be more useful here than anywhere." Mary smiled at the memory and then returned to her journal.

> *I sit here waiting for the children's grandmother, Maggie O'Neil. My hope is for the children, that she will treat them well and love them. I understand her wanting to be here for them, for they are all she has left of her own daughter. I wish I could adopt them, but I know it would be difficult for them to carry the Lee, especially now. Times are so –."*

She stopped writing. Looking up, she saw a dust cloud rise on the horizon, and realizing there was a wagon coming, she knew she would meet Maggie O'Neil at long last. Mary Lee went into the house to get the children ready to meet their grandmother.

The wagon pulled up in front of Fairland House, and Maggie O'Neil was dropped off without so much as a, "Thank you, Madam." She barely got her last bag off the wagon before the driver pulled away. He did not care to have a Yankee in his wagon, let alone an Irish one. She had tried to strike up a conversation with the old man, but it was of no use. He snuffed her, and the long ride from town was made even longer by his silence. Finally she stood in front of the mansion in a place she'd never been, waiting to care for children she had never known, and start a business in a town in which she'd never lived. She was suddenly very weary, and felt like running back to Boston. Then she heard the noise of little feet and tiny voices, and she was greeted as she started up the steps.

"My, my! What lovely children ye are!" Maggie exclaimed. "I have waited so long to see you both!" She looked down at Jewel and recognized her daughter's eyes. Jewel also had her mother's golden hair, fair skin and freckles. She took in a quick breath to quell her tears as she remembered her lovely daughter who had died so young.

Mary Lee stood by, not knowing what to say or do. Here she was with a strange woman, who was about to come into her home to rule the roost, but worse; she was Irish! Her mother had warned her about the Irish. She remembered being as leery of Victoria, at first, but they'd become friends quickly, and she hoped her relationship with Maggie would work as well.

Questions bombarded her mind. She wondered how the children would take her. She wondered if she would be welcomed to stay in their home. Perhaps she'd have to find a place in town, or maybe tuck her tail between her legs, and beg for a place with Matthew.

The two women had been writing back and forth for over four months now, so she knew she shouldn't feel estranged, but those feelings could not be quelled. She stood to the side trying not to interfere, but wanting to very badly, and butterflies in her stomach would not stop their fluttering, especially when Maggie acknowledged her.

"And ye must be Mary Lee. I'm so happy to finally meet ye in person! My daughter spoke so fondly of ye, my dear. Thank ye for carin' for the little ones all this time."

"It was my pleasure, Ma'am. I believe I've taken to them as much as they have to me."

The two women stood looking at each other for an uncomfortable moment before Mary finally asked her to come into the house. Davey and Jewel struggled trying to carry in her luggage, but only Sally could move it.

"My gooness, Granma, what you got in here?" Jewel asked.

"These, me lovely, are me treasures, the things I've been holdin' onto to give to you!" Maggie touched Jewel's nose and was rewarded with a giggle.

"Pirate treasures, Granma?" Jewel asked eagerly. Mary Lee had read the children all the best pirate stories.

"Oh, no, darlin'. Just treasures from me past. They need to be passed on to the younger now. We'll talk about it later, I promise." Maggie caressed Jewel's cheek with her hand, and Mary could not help but feel a twinge of jealousy. These children were as much hers as they were Victoria's, maybe more so since they never really knew their real mother.

Mary dismissed the youngsters and taking one of the bags, helped Maggie upstairs to her quarters. Mary had been staying in the front bedroom next to Victoria's room. No one had gone into Victoria's room since she died except to keep it clean, but she gave Maggie the option of staying there. When Maggie saw the room, however, she couldn't bring herself to staying there either.

"Is there another I might have? I don't want to disturb Victoria's things."

"Of course," Mary replied. There were actually seven bedrooms in the house, so Mary gave Maggie the nicest one next to the back stairs so the children would not awaken her in the mornings.

"Yes," Maggie said relieved, "this will be perfect, Mary." She looked at her counterpart. "I do appreciate it so very much." Mary gave her an uncertain smile and left her to unpack her things. In the uncomfortable tension of the moment, Maggie hesitated, wanting to say something to Mary to make it easier for her, but nothing came to mind. After the door closed she started to unpack.

The day passed quickly as Maggie learned about her grandchildren. She opened her suitcases and brought out the ribbons, pearls, threads and materials with which she would begin her business. Then she gave the children the toys she had collected for them over the years. Gleefully, the children played with their new toys all day until bedtime when they were ready for their nightly story. Jewel asked Mary to again tell the story of the lost diamond. Mary hesitated for a just a moment wondering if she should repeat the story in front of Maggie. Knowing the truth would come out sooner or later, she sat on Jewel's bed and recited what she knew.

"And so, Jewel, you were named after the diamond your father brought with him from Africa," Maggie finished. She said nothing more about the story until the children were safely tucked in bed.

"Mary, is it true, that story?" Maggie asked as they sat together in the sitting room.

"Yes Ma'am, every word of it. I heard them talking in the kitchen one night before the Mister was killed by the rebels. I've been searchin' for the jewel ever since. I jes can't find it. I'm thinkin' the Mister hid it in the back yard when we were all asleep or somethin'. I have searched the library over and over. It's jes' not there." Mary sat in the chair across from Maggie and pulled a quilt over her lap to stay warm. She was tired and longed for a good night's sleep. Maggie sat there thinking about the jewel. She had known Reggie was rich after his exploration in the jungle, but she had thought all his money had dwindled during the war. Then she remembered the diamond sale Victoria and Reggie had attended in New York City.

"What happened to the rest of it then?"

"I'm not sure. Miss Victoria said she knew Mr. Culpepper had given some money to the Union for the cause. He left enough for her and the children to live nicely, though. We have never been without food or clothing the whole time the war was on. Not until now." She paused and sighed. "I have never had the heart to go through her things, but I suppose we should now that you're here. I did go through the Mister's desk and found some bank statements from Boston. Maybe we should start there."

Mr. Engle from the Franklin Bank told Maggie the amount remaining in Reggie's account. Since Reggie had no living relatives except the children, the money could be split between them. Maggie opened two accounts in the children's names and Mr. Engle transferred $14,850 into each. The money would be a good start towards both their futures, Maggie thought.

Weeks passed before the two women decided to go through Victoria's belongings. They had revisited the library a few times since Maggie arrived, but time and again found nothing. Mary and Maggie both decided Victoria's chest was the most likely place she would have hidden anything. A tear fell down Maggie's cheek when she opened the chest where Victoria kept her wedding dress. Memories of the wedding flooded her mind as she remembered her beautiful daughter standing with her new husband on her wedding day in the gown she had so carefully sewn. Under the gown, Victoria kept her jewelry box. Maggie hesitated before picking up the velveteen container, and her hand shook as she opened the lid to find the Rosenbrand necklace. The gems refracted the sunlight and rainbow colors bounced along the wall. Mary stopped short and stared at the amazing piece.

"I've never seen anything so beautiful," she gasped.

"She wore it at her wedding," was all Maggie could say. She replaced the necklace and repacked the box. She had no idea of its real worth, but she did not want to know. "It should be Jewel's." Mary silently agreed, and the two women left Victoria's room.

Mary had not realized what a heavy load she had been carrying all these years, but with Maggie in the house, the load lightened for her. She was able to spend more time with her own children and grandchildren, and she was happy again for the first time in many years. She helped Maggie start her business at the plantation by advertising to her family and friends. Soon the business took off, and the two women were kept very busy.

News of Noah's death had been hard on Mary's daughter-in-law. She contracted pneumonia and died a few weeks later. Maggie had Mary bring the children into the big house where Noah's offspring could be comfortable. But the strain was as hard, if not more so, on Mary. Her fatigue held her back from helping much with the children and soon her son Matthew had to take them in.

Two years passed before Mary finally went to the doctor. The fatigue she felt only became worse, and she had dropped about 40 pounds. The local doctor listened to her chest, then pounded on it and listened again. An ignorant man, he told her there was nothing wrong and sent her home. She was bedridden just days later. Insisting Mary see her own physician in Boston, Maggie notified Matthew of his mother's illness. Within a week, Maggie, Mary, Matthew and the children all boarded the train to Boston.

Matthew hadn't wanted anything to do with Yankees, but he knew they had the best of everything there, and his mother did deserve the best. Maggie's physician examined her and believing the worst, had Mary hospitalized immediately. She had contracted cancer, and was only given a few weeks to live. Instead, it was only a few days before they gathered around her to say good bye.

Mary was barely able to keep her eyes open when they came into her room, but she had Jewel and Davey sit on the bed next to her. Davey played with a wooden top Matthew had made for him, while Jewel laid down next to her. Jewel knew her mama was sick, and she said not a word. She only put her hand up to touch Mary's arm and patted it to comfort her. They laid there quietly for only an hour before Mary took her last breath, and Jewel and Davey lost the only mother they had ever known.

* * *

Jewel grew to be as lovely as her mother. Her blonde curls were replaced with auburn locks, but her blue eyes, round and bright, reminded Maggie more of her Victoria than anything. Jewel had been aptly named.

Fairland's property was restored to its heirs by federal decree, but since Mary had nothing left to give to her real children, Maggie gave Matthew and Mary's daughters some acreage with which to work their crops. She felt they deserved to have something of their parents, especially after the hard years of the Civil War. Each of the remaining four children received 15 acres.

Jewel was to receive Fairland when she was old enough to manage it, Maggie decided, and Davey, his father's tools and livestock. Fairland Farm now only consisted of the house, the orchard and about 200 acres of land.

Maggie also kept Victoria's jewelry, but after a while, she put the diamond ring and the Rosenbrand necklace into a safety deposit box at the bank. Jewel would inherit the necklace and Davey would receive his mother's wedding ring, while the small amount of estate money set aside for the children would remain in their accounts to gain interest.

The Jewel of Africa was never found.

Maggie taught her granddaughter the fine art of sewing, and the young woman was soon working alongside her grandmother. By the time she was 17, with her mother's sense of business, she also handled her grandmother's bookkeeping. She would someday go to a fine college, meet a fine man and marry, Maggie dreamed. But time passed all too quickly, and now at the age of 20, Jewel still remained at Fairland sewing in her grandmother's shop.

As handsome as his father, David had girls swooning over him early in life. Jewel had to constantly remind him he was still young and had plenty of time for girls, but he still had to take care of the farm. Nevertheless, at 18, David soon found himself engaged to be married. Miss Lorraine Skuggins was from a farm down the road, and he had fallen head over heels in love with her. When he told Jewel about it, she scoffed.

"Why, Davey," she said, sitting down on the lawn under the big oak, "You're way too young to be thinkin' about marriage. Why here I am, over a year your elder, and I haven't even got a beau."

"Oh, Sissy, that's 'cause you got your nose in those books all the time. Maybe if you'd come out with us to one of the parties, you could get a beau." Jewel looked at him sideways.

"If I had time for beaus, Mr. Culpepper, I would have one. I don't. Tell you what. When you marry Miss Lorraine, you can name your first daughter after me and carry on the family name."

It was a happy conversation, Jewel remembered, but two years had already passed since then. In October 1881, Ms. Lorraine Skuggins married young David Reginald Culpepper. Within a year, a little girl was born and Davey named her Jewel Victoria because of that very conversation. They all laughed at the fact she was Jewel's absolute opposite – blonde hair and brown eyes – but just as beautiful as the one for whom she was named. Maggie had given Davey his mother's ring to give to his bride, keeping the necklace in the bank for Jewel. She decided she would show it to her granddaughter when she had time, but Davey's wedding took her attention, and she quickly forgot.

The fervent July sun beat down unmercifully as Jewel pulled up the last bucket of water she would need for her weekly laundry chores. Times had become hard at Fairland Farm over the past year, but undaunted by trial, Jewel was determined she would not give up. Today was like any other day, and she must be about her business. She took these times of aloneness to think about the events of recent days.

Maggie O'Neil's Bridal business had kept them in food and clothing for many years, with most of their business coming from the North, but the land had remained dormant. Neighbors who could have leased it, still chafing from old war wounds, refused the opportunity. Jewel and her grandmother were still considered Yankees in their eyes, and Maggie was Irish to the bone. Jewel had no understanding or training in running a farm, so it had become overgrown. Nevertheless, as wild as it was, the land was still beautiful, and by 1883 it had become valuable. They had retained only 280 of the original 320 acres up until now, but it would be only a matter of time before Jewel would have to sell it off, if something wasn't done with it soon.

Maggie had grown old over the past eighteen years. Born in 1799, she was now in her eighties. She was a spry old gal up until a year ago, and she continued to work. Jewel thought it was time for Maggie to retire, and she could take the business to a new location in town. Maggie, stubborn as she was, would not hear of it. The shop stayed out at Fairland Farm, until one day while Maggie was working, she took ill.

Maggie had been her jovial self when the day started as she flittered from one customer's order to the next. She had mentioned to her granddaughter earlier she was feeling a bit tired, but any fatigue she had been feeling was not evident to anyone else. Right about noon, Mrs. McGillicutty from Butler stopped by the farm to check on her daughter's dress. Maggie had been working hard on the gown; the wedding was only a week away, and final alterations were finally complete.

"Here we are, dear, just the way Miss Evelyn requested. Maggie flared the dress across the sofa as Mrs. McGillicutty looked on. Made from satin imported from Paris, the material caught the light from the fireplace. Swiss lace adorned the bodice and wrapped around the back to incorporate the bustle. Mrs. McGillicutty said nothing for a moment. Maggie held her breath. Finally Mrs. McGillicutty spoke.

"I don't believe it looks right, Mrs. O'Neil. I was sure Evelyn had said she did not want hooks in the back, but buttons." Maggie stared at her. The woman had been a thorn in her flesh from the beginning when she had burst in the shop and announced the dress would be needed in less than a month. First the material wasn't right, and then the hem was crooked.

"And now buttons?" Maggie spoke her thoughts. She looked at the order slip. There was nothing mentioned about buttons – only hooks. "I think, Mrs. McGillicutty, we better have yer daughter come and confirm the order."

"That will not be necessary. I always put buttons on my daughter's dresses."

Maggie tried to hold her Irish temper. "Perhaps that's why she asked for hooks and eyes." Mrs. McGillicutty caught the meaning of Maggie's words.

"Look here, you Irish Yankee –." Maggie's face reddened as she faced the woman.

"Irish Yankee? I might remind ye, my dear woman, your name is McGillicutty, a fine Irish name if I ever heard one." Maggie's temper flared. She felt blood flush her face and her head felt like it was going to explode. Pain shot through the left side of her skull and suddenly her right side became numb. She collapsed to the floor, leaving Mrs. McGillicutty standing there with her mouth open. Jewel dropped the material she was working on and rushed to her grandmother's side. Maggie was unconscious, but still breathing.

Medical help was slow in coming, but Maggie had a fighting spirit. She survived the stroke. Nevertheless, the attack had left her partially paralyzed and unable to talk. After finishing up Evelyn McGillicutty's buttons and their current customer orders, Jewel retired the shop for a time to take care of her grandmother, planning to reopen it after Maggie's recovery. She believed her grandmother would never return to the shop, so she began preliminary plans for finding a new location for the business and transforming the house to accommodate Maggie's disability. But the more Jewel planned to move the shop, the more she realized a shop in town would not work. She knew Maggie would be very upset about taking the wedding shop into Macon, so until a proper building could be found, she decided to arrange the house to make enough room for people to come in and out.

Maggie may have been partially paralyzed by the stroke, but she refused to be considered helpless. She wrote a nearly imperceptible note with her left hand and handed Jewel the key she kept in the drawer next to her bed. Understanding that Maggie wanted her to go into the bank to check her accounts, Jewel left for Macon to meet with the banker. Although she had been handling the bookkeeping for the business, she was unaware that her grandmother not only had one bank account, but several. She had opened an account in Jewel's name, one in Davey's name and another in her own; but thrifty Maggie, who had saved nearly every spare penny for over 20 years, kept the secret that she was not a poor woman. She also had the business account, which Jewel had known about.

Jewel also learned that she wasn't poor, either, much to her surprise and relief. Thanks to her grandmother's efforts, Jewel was pleased to learn that she and her grandmother could survive on the interest from these accounts alone. Maggie had been wise enough to put Jewel's name on all the accounts so she could manage them, so Jewel made arrangements with the banker to come back another day. She no longer had to worry that the shop would be closed and she could make plans for renovations.

While she was at the bank, Jewel also found a safety deposit box in her name. The diamond necklace passed down to her from her mother had been saved as well, but Jewel had no idea its worth. Even though she knew the history of her father's treasure, Jewel did not connect the Rosenbrand necklace with that treasure; she simply knew the necklace was her mother's and it was very likely expensive. She put the necklace back into the box, slid it into place, and left the bank confident that they would be all right.

Word that Jewel had visited the banker to take care of her grandmother's affairs traveled fast in town, and like the vultures they were, people started to hover. Bit by bit, neighbors who had yet to introduce themselves stopped by to see how "dear Mrs. O'Neil" was faring. Even the parson, who had turned them away from his church when her foster mother died, stopped by for a visit. Women Jewel had only known by their account status came with food and good wishes hoping to speak to Maggie before she "passed on." Jewel turned them away apologetically thanking them first for the food and promising to return the dishes when they were done with them. They hadn't eaten so well in many a day! One day, after visiting with a few people who had stopped by, Jewel took her complaint to her grandmother.

"I'm appalled, Grandma. These people are like bees to honey!" Jewel said. Maggie's eyes twinkled in her silence. She raised her left hand and waved at Jewel as she busied herself in Maggie's bedroom. She couldn't speak and aphasia kept her from understanding everything Jewel talked about, but she knew her granddaughter's face and was always happy when she walked into the room. "Never you mind, though, Grandma. I'll keep those hornets away from you," Jewel had assured her. She leaned over Maggie to adjust her pillows. Her grandmother patted her cheek and gave her a happy half grin.

Time passed too quickly, and because the bridal shop was faring so poorly, money was melting away faster than Jewel realized. She still had plenty in the bank, but inexperience forced her to let the servants go. She soon found herself alone in the big mansion with only her grandmother for company.

Jewel found it increasingly difficult to take care of Maggie, and though money was getting shorter, she never touched the diamond necklace still hiding in the safety deposit box. They were sacred; a memory of the mother she could not remember. For all she knew, they were really only glass, and worth nothing but truthfully, she was afraid to check. What if a jeweler did appraise them and found them worthless? She would be heartbroken. She couldn't face it, and refused to let anyone know of their financial straits.

The laundry basket was heavy as she hauled wet sheets out to the lines. Jewel was amazed at the amount of laundry a little old lady could cause. Maggie was incontinent, she drooled and spilled frequently, and her care was beginning to become burdensome for young Jewel. She would not give up on her dear grandmother, though – she loved her with every fiber of her being – but she realized it would be only a matter of time before she would have to let someone else do the care.

It was already late in the morning, and Jewel knew the heavy humidity would prevent the wash from drying today. She chided herself for complaining. It was Monday, and the laundry must be completed as it was every Monday for as long as she could remember. The sheets were hung to dry despite the heavy heat which caused her to be so weary.

Maggie lay in her bed facing the sunny window in her bedroom. A tear fell from her eye as she watched her lovely granddaughter bend over the load of laundry, pulling at the heavy, wet material of one of her own dresses. She knew Jewel would stay with her until she died, and it was at the same time a comfort and a sorrow to her. She reached for her note pad and scribbled out three words: "Davey New York."

Jewel prepared lunch a little later than usual, but when she delivered her grandmother's meal, she tried to appear as cheerful as possible. She greeted her patient with a smile on her face and a lilt to her voice.

"Why hello, Sunshine. I hope you're doin' as well as you look!" Jewel greeted her patient.

Maggie's eyes softened as Jewel entered the room. It had taken her nearly five minutes to write out those three words, and she was determined to give the note to her granddaughter. The note pad fell from her lap as Jewel placed the tray on the table, and she heard the pad hit the floor.

"What's this? You writin' me notes again, Grandma?" She reached down to pick up the pad. "Davey. New York. Hmm." She looked at her grandmother curiously. "Davey's not in New York, Silly. He's right here in Georgia farmin' right outside of Augusta. You know that." Maggie shook her head and sealed her lips. She would not let Jewel feed her until she understood what she meant by her note.

"C'mon, Grandma, eat," she said impatiently, "I don't have time to fool around today. You know Monday's always busy for me around here."

Tears came to Maggie's eyes and she clamped her mouth shut as Jewel held the spoon up to her mouth.

"What is it? What's wrong?" Maggie held up her hand and pointed at the note. "Grandma, this doesn't make sense. Do you want Davey to come? Is that what you want?"

Maggie nodded. Looking at down at her grandmother, Jewel sighed. She promised she would send for Davey right after Maggie ate something. Maggie gave a half smile and opened her mouth to accept a spoonful of soup.

Davey Culpepper rode into Fairland on his horse less than a week later. Jewel had sent him an urgent note saying Maggie was not eating and he needed to come quickly. He left his wife and two children at their farm and came as quickly as he could. He looked fine atop his horse, a brimmed hat on his head and wearing a gentleman's coat. He had become a handsome man, with deep brown eyes and thick dark hair framing a square jaw and strong chin. Jewel was proud of her little brother as she peered up at him.

"Hey, big sister!" he said giving her a proper salute.

"Hey yourself. Come on down here and give me a hug!" Jewel held out her arms as Davey dismounted and ran up to her. Twirling her around, he gave her a loud smack on the cheek. As he set her down on her feet, she said, "It's about time you got here!"

"What, I just got that letter two days ago. I can't fly!" he teased. She looked at him sadly.

"Oh, if only we could fly, Davey. I'd fly from here." Davey looked at her concerned.

"What's the matter, Jewel? Is Grandma alright?"

"Oh, I'm just tired is all. I don't know if Grandma is alright or not. She's not eatin'. She's losin' weight. The doctor seems to think she's on a hunger strike, and we don't know why. She just keeps pointin' at this note." She held the note out to Davey. He looked at it and frowned.

"This don't make no sense 'tall. I ain't in New York."

Jewel shook her head. "I know it. She just won't take any kind of explanation from me and I don't know what she's talkin' about."

The two of them went into the house. Davey noticed the house had lost its luster. Though it was clean, some things were in ill repair, including the door knob where they entered. Jewel had to jiggle it a little before the door would open. He didn't say anything. He had known Jewel would be unable to keep the farm as hard as she had tried to do so, and it would not surprise him if she decided to sell it off. Tapping on the door, they entered Maggie's bedroom.

"Grandma, what're ya doin' in that bed?" Davey joked. He had not been home for nearly three months and he always told Maggie she would have to start getting out of bed if she ever hoped to come and visit him at his new farm. Maggie looked up and with a gleam in her eye, she waved at Davey. He took her in his arms and sat with her on her bed.

"Davey, you always had a way of charming Grandma. Don't you go givin' her any ideas," Jewel laughed.

"Why, Jewel, whatever do you mean? I have nothin' in mind other than good things for my grandmother!" He turned to whisper in Maggie's ear. "How about you and me bustin' outta this hole and take a trip around the world." Maggie laughed and patted his hand. Davey stood up again.

"Okay, Grandma. Why ain't you been eatin'? Jewel said you've been a naughty girl." Maggie nodded and patted her tummy. "You wanna eat now?" he asked her. She nodded again and pulled on his jacket. "You want me to eat, too?" Her eyes sparkled with affirmation, and the three of them sat together eating sandwiches and hot soup.

At the end of the meal, Maggie was tired. She held Davey's hand until she fell asleep. Jewel and Davey left her room, deposited the dishes in the kitchen and strolled out to the front lawn arm in arm.

"You look exhausted, Jewel," he said sitting down on the ground. She sat down next to him.

"I must admit to you, Davey, I am. I never thought taking care of Grandma would be difficult, but it is becoming very burdensome. I can't seem to keep up with her care and the care of the farm."

"I wouldn't expect you to, Jewel. You're not equipped. Why don't you sell off the place?"

"Davey, I just can't. I don't know why, but I can't. There's too much history here; Mama's history and the Culpepper history." She never considered Victoria or Reggie as her mother and father since she never really knew them. She only remembered her mama, Mary Lee, who had taken care of her from the time of her birth until Grandma Maggie came along.

The bridal shop would be revived, she was sure of it. It would just take a little longer than she had anticipated.

"Jewel, I couldn't help but notice some of the repairs needin' to be done around the house. How do you think they will ever be accomplished when you're here alone?"

"I don't know, Davey, but I'm still young. I might have a husband in my future, you know." Jewel picked a piece of crab grass, placed it between her thumbs and blew on it to make a buzzing sound. Davey smiled at her and did the same. They were still playmates after all these years. She looked at him sadly.

"Maybe I am just a dreamer, Davey. Maybe my life will never amount to anythin'. I just know I can't sell off Fairland. I may live here the rest of my life, an old maid." Davey stood to his feet and pulled his sister up to her feet.

"We'll figure it out, Jewel. Don't you worry about it," he said putting his arms around her. He held his sister close as they walked back into the house.

Maggie greeted Davey with a limp smile the next morning. They had spent the previous evening together and she knew Davey was preparing to leave that day. She had to get her message across to him. She held up the note she had scribbled the night before.

"Sew. New York." Davey looked at the note and then down at his grandmother.

"What are you tryin' to tell us, Grandma? Do you want to go to New York?" Maggie closed her eyes in exasperation. Pounding her leg with her hand, she signaled he was way off track. "You want me to go to New York?" Again she said no. "Do you want someone from New York?" Maggie started to cry. "Oh, don't cry, Grandma. I'm only tryin' to understand. You sent for me, didn't you?" She nodded. "Why?" Maggie patted his hand and pointed at him, and then patted her blanket. "You want me to stay here?" Maggie nodded. She took her pad in hand and started to scribble, "Sew New York," just as Jewel walked in. She laid the breakfast tray on the table and took the pad Maggie held out to her.

Jewel read and re-read the note. At first it made no sense to her. "Sew New York." She repeated it again. "Sew New York." She looked down at her grandmother. "Grandma, do you mean sew in New York?" Maggie nodded and pointed at her. "You want me to sew in New York?" Maggie nodded and patted her chest signifying it was her wish for Jewel to go New York to sew.

Jewel had shared her dream of attending a college in New York to study domestics and business administration. Even with all the training her grandmother had given her about sewing over the years, she could never have educated her in the areas of design and fashion that would give Jewel the well-rounded knowledge she would need to continue in the industry.

She smiled as she remembered having often been caught looking through literature from the fine schools in New York when she was supposed to be hemming a dress or sewing on a button for her grandmother. But Maggie hadn't forgotten Jewel's dream of becoming a famous designer. She wanted it for her as much as Jewel had wanted it for herself, and Maggie knew it was time for Jewel to leave her cocoon and make her way in the world.

"But, Grandma, who would take care of you?" Jewel asked, dismissing the idea. Maggie pointed at Davey who stood over her looking very concerned. Finally, they deciphered Maggie's intentions; Davey could stay at Fairland and take care of her and the farm while Jewel went to New York to get her education. Davey loved his grandmother, but knew he would never be able to take care of her – not here anyway. He had a wife, two children and a farm of his own to be concerned about. He sat next to her on the bed and pulled her into his arms.

"Grandma, I would love for Jewel to be able to go to New York. It would be a wonderful opportunity for her; but you know I couldn't take care of you, don't you?" Maggie looked up at him with tear-filled eyes and patted his hand. She knew it very well. She hadn't wanted to admit it, but she had known all along. More than anything, though, she had wanted Jewel to know she remembered the dreams of a young girl who was willing to give up her entire life to care for a crippled old woman. She waved at Davey, closed her eyes, and leaned back on her pillows. Davey was released to go, if he wished. He stood up, gave his grandmother a kiss on the forehead and they left her alone. It was not until her grandchildren left the room that she allowed herself to cry.

Jewel could not sleep. Davey had gone, and Maggie was asleep. The house was empty again. It was too hot this night to even cover up with a cotton sheet. She pushed the sheet away. Tossing and turning for more than an hour, she finally gave up trying to fall into a restful night's sleep. She stood up, threw her shawl around her shoulders and stepped into her slippers before heading toward the kitchen. Perhaps a glass of warm honey milk would help her to sleep, she thought.

Honey milk was the remedy Grandma always gave her for any ailment she'd ever had. If her stomach hurt, Maggie gave her honey milk. If she hurt her knee, honey milk would help it. If she couldn't sleep, honey milk was the answer; and it would be the remedy for her sleeplessness this night, as well.

Jewel peered into her grandmother's room to see if she was alright and saw that Maggie seemed to be sleeping peacefully. With the hot cup of honey milk in her hands, she made her way to her father's library.

"J. Reginald Culpepper" was the name embossed on the diary's cover, which had been kept in the left-hand drawer of the massive mahogany desk since after the war. Maggie had often pulled the diary out to read it to Jewel when she was young. She'd say, "Darlin', this was your father's last words. He was a man with adventure in his soul, but your mama tamed him. It's your diary now, darlin'. It holds many secrets and perhaps you're the only one who can solve the mystery of the lost diamond."

Jewel touched the gold embossing and wondered about her father. He was hated by their neighbors, she knew. He'd said so in the diary. But at the same time, he seemed to be a man of peace and integrity, and she had never been able to understand why he'd been so despised. She remembered hearing Mary say he was a Unionist which she supposed was the reason. It was because of his bond with the North that they were alone now.

Opening the dog-eared page, she read her father's words, *"Fair land overlooks the picture of God where the door opens by pressing toward the mark."* She had never understood those words. She wondered why the page corner was bent and questioned whether there was some sort of clue within the page. Maggie had never understood the words either, but she had told her the story of her name and the lost diamond. Jewel wondered if these words were referring to the mystery treasure, but she had never been sure. She sighed and put the diary away in its place in the drawer. Maybe some day she would be able to figure it out. She leaned back and thought about the possibility of finding the Jewel and taking a trip around the world, or just attending a college and getting the education she had always wanted. She soon fell asleep and found herself dreaming about diamonds and strangers in a place called New York.

Sunlight streamed through the eastern window of the library before Jewel awoke. She had slept in her father's chair most of the night. The milk had cooled in its cup on the desk and her neck was slightly stiff from her head leaning over to the side. She stood up to stretch, collected her cup and saucer, and then went to check on her grandmother.

Maggie lay quietly on her bed, the sun shining down on her face. Jewel smiled as she looked at her grandmother with loving concern. She was a little Irish angel, lying there so peacefully. Jewel watched her for a moment before going in. She wondered if she would be able to continue here at Fairland. She wondered if her grandmother would be better off with Davey at his farm. She walked over to her grandmother's bedside and brushed away a wisp of silver hair. Maggie did not stir.

"Grandma? It's time to wake up," Jewel said cautiously. She put the cup and saucer down on the table, and felt her grandmother's arm. She was cool to the touch. "Grandma? Wake up!"

Jewel took Maggie's hand into hers, but her limp hand slipped away. Her legs failing to hold her up, Jewel nearly collapsed at the realization of what she was seeing. Only partially recovered, with tears streaming down her cheeks, she carefully tucked her grandmother's arm under the blanket, lovingly combed her hair and washed her face. Fluffing up the pillow and kissing her forehead as if to bid her dear grandmother good night, Jewel closed the door behind her after saying good bye to the grand lady named Maggie O'Neil.

Chapter IX

An Unexpected Education

No one could have described New York to Jewel's satisfaction, for nothing in the entire world was like it. The city spread across miles with seeming oceans of streets in between mountainous buildings. Jewel had not imagined any place could be so exciting. After their grandmother's funeral, she and Davey had decided to travel together to the city to see what it was like and to find out if she truly belonged there. Jewel was enthralled by the excitement of the city, but after seeing the teeming streets, buildings over ten stories high, large families living one on top of another, garbage strewn everywhere, and the hideous combination of sewage and cooking smells, Davey whole-heartedly refused to let her stay.

"You belong at Fairland, Jewel. I will have no sister of mine in this hovel of sin," he admonished her.

"My dear brother, it is not for you to say whether I stay or do not stay. I have always wanted to study in New York, and it was Grandma's desire for me to do so. If you want, you can go back to your dear Georgia, and I will stay to study at the women's college." Jewel stood with her hands on her hips looking at her brother in her most determined way. He knew there would be no arguing with her. Instead, he followed her around like a puppy through the streets of New York City while she went from shop to shop trying to learn how to get the education she would need to enter into the fashion industry.

It took three long days of aching feet and useless information before Davey finally called it quits. He kissed her good bye at the train station telling her he would keep watch over Fairland so it would be ready for her when she decided this fool hardy endeavor was over and she was ready to return home. She assured him she would make a decision in a week. If she found nothing by the following Sunday, she would be home by Monday. Holding her to her promise, he boarded the train. He stood on the steps of the passenger car waving back at her.

"Don't forget, Jewel, one week. I expect you home in one week!" His voice was drowned out by the noise of the departing train.

"What, Davey? I can't hear you!" He tried to repeat what he'd said, but Jewel simply waved good bye and watched as the train left her alone on the platform.

The week went by quickly, with little to no success in finding out how she would go about entering a college in New York. On the final day before she would be forced to admit she was defeated, Jewel walked into "Madmoiselle," a French boutique located on Madison Avenue, which was owned and managed by a woman named Dominique. She had emigrated from France as a young woman and made her way in America. With olive-colored skin that was as smooth as silk and black hair piled into a neat chignon on her head, Dominique appeared to be in her 40's. She was actually over 60. Her heavy French accent was difficult to understand, but she had the look of a worldly woman, and she seemed to be very knowledgeable. Pretending to look at the dresses, Jewel struck up a conversation with the woman, matter-of-factly questioning her about obtaining an education towards a fashion career. Dominique laughed out loud.

"Surely you do not expect to enter ze fashion industry in New York. You would have to be crazy, mon ami." Dominique stood behind the register next to the store clerk.

"And why not?" Jewel asked defensively. "My grandmother encouraged me to do so, and I certainly have the determination."

"I understand you are determined, my dear girl, but Paris is really ze only place to study fashion. All of ze great ones are from zere. I know. I have worked wis zem for years."

Jewel looked at her directly. "Then you know how important it is to me." Raising her eyebrow, Dominique returned her determined look but said nothing. Instead she reached under her register and handed her a card.

"Go here. Tell zem Dominique sends you. Zey know me well enough."

Jewel hesitated for a second before retrieving the card. Looking at it, she saw the name Henrietta Williams, Art History Professor. "What's this?"

"Zis is your opening into Vassar. Take it. It will help you." Jewel stood there reading the business card, her head cocked to the right. Dominique could not help but see herself in this simple young woman. She offered Jewel some coffee and a snack before she sent her on her way.

Vassar, a women's liberal arts college established in 1861 by the English brewer and businessman, Matthew Vassar, was known for its high quality education. It was the first in the country to offer women a well-rounded education in art history, physical education, geology, astronomy, music, mathematics and chemistry. Only the highest educated women in the country were admitted, much to Dominique's chagrin. Her educational background had not met the requirements for an education at Vassar, so she learned the fashion industry on the job until she could open her own little shop on Madison Avenue. The woman whose name was on the card had been instrumental in helping Dominique to establish her business.

When she was an adventurous young woman, Henrietta Williams had volunteered to be one of the first exchange students from Vassar. She had crossed the Atlantic in the mid-1800's. Henrietta studied by day, painted by night and sold her wares on the weekends, making her living by selling art on the Champs-Elysées near the Arc de Triomphe.

She was very attractive to the opposite sex, not only because of her looks, but also because of her citizenship. Many of the French desired to go to America. Rich men would buy her artwork and then try to buy her. Putting their money in her pocket, she would hand them a painting and pinch their cheek before turning them down. Somehow they never minded losing the money.

During her time in France, she met a young girl named Dominique who had big dreams of working in the fashion industry in Paris. As her aide, Dominique had followed her around Paris helping her with her French and making contacts with many important artists like Gustave Le Gray, who was considered to be the most important French photographer of the 19th century. He developed some of the technical aspects of the medium producing such great works as the Zouave Storyteller in North Africa, and beautiful seascapes and architectural photography in Paris. Henrietta also studied some of the works of Theodore Chasseriau and Eugene Fromentin, as well as other lesser-known artists. Her well-rounded understanding of French art later enabled her to obtain her master's degree and finally a doctorate in art history, after which she returned to Vassar to complete the full circle by teaching other women what she had learned during her travels in Europe.

Dominique had not been as fortunate. She traveled back to the states with Henrietta and tried desperately to enter Vassar, but time and again she had been deterred by her seeming lack of education. But Dominique fooled them all just a few years later by opening her own shop in the fashion district of New York. "Mademoiselle" became one of the most popular boutiques in the city. She was now a very well-to-do, independent woman who provided some of the great designs of Europe to the rich of New York. Dominique had had the last laugh.

Not sure what she was getting into, Jewel took the morning train to Poughkeepsie and walked from the station to Vassar College. Looking at the massive gates, she wondered why she had decided to follow through with Dominique's suggestion. Who was this Henrietta Williams, anyway, and how would she be able to help her?

Entering through the administration office door, Jewel walked up to the woman who stood behind the counter. A short, chubby, older woman with fine graying hair wrapped into a tight bun at the nape of her neck, she stood straight-shouldered looking up at Jewel. Her round spectacles and graying hair gave away her age, but when she smiled, ten years disappeared from her face.

"Hello, young lady. What can I do for you?" Esther Beasley asked jovially.

"I – I am not sure, actually. I was given this card and told to look for Henrietta Williams." Esther took the card and noticed Dominique's name on the back. She smiled and gave it back to Jewel.

"The professor is in room 103 of the Women's Studies building." Esther gave her a map of the campus, marking where she had to go to find Professor Williams. Jewel said thank you and left Esther to her paperwork.

Henrietta Williams rolled her wheelchair into position at the front of her classroom. An intelligent, well-educated woman, she was highly respected by her peers as an excellent communicator and an even better historian. Having studied at Vassar and during her career as an intern and now professor, she helped to develop the Women's Studies program at the college. More than that, she was Dominique's oldest friend.

"Miss Williams?" Jewel asked.

"Doctor Williams," Henrietta chided.

"Yes, forgive me, Doctor Williams. I was told to find you." Jewel could feel the blood rush into her face as she stood tall before the woman in the wheelchair. She was not accustomed to looking at someone who was disabled, and her discomfort was evident. She avoided the professor's gaze by looking around at the walls of the class room, wondering if she would ever be able to sit under the tutelage of someone so respected.

"I'm down here, dear." Dr. Williams sat confidently in her chair looking up at the girl. Jewel shyly handed her the card Dominique had given her. "Oh, do you know Dominique? I'm surprised I have never seen you before."

"We've only just met," Jewel confessed. "I'm hoping to be educated in the art of fashion and design." Dr. Williams looked surprised.

"And what makes you think I can help you?"

"I don't." Williams was even more surprised by her response. "I mean, I have only just arrived in New York a week ago and I met Dominique by accident, and after we spoke, she gave me this card. So I came here as quickly as I could to find you. I only have today to get into Vassar."

Her naivety amused the professor, and it touched her. She could tell this was a very determined young lady. The professor wondered who she was.

"Have you qualified to enter Vassar?"

"Qualified? I'm not sure. I can sew. I can do bookkeeping – I handled all my grandmother's business affairs when she moved to Georgia." Jewel could feel the perspiration roll down the back of her leg and she wondered if she looked as nervous as she felt.

"Miss – I don't think I have caught your name."

"Culpepper. Jewel Victoria Culpepper, Doctor Williams. I've just traveled up from Macon, Georgia, where I lived with my grandmother. She died recently."

"I'm sorry for your loss. Do you have other family?"

"Just my brother and his family," she answered eagerly. "I live in my father's house on Fairland Farm. My parents came from Cape Colony and were very well to do before the war. After they died, my grandmother came to take care of my brother and me, and that's how I learned how to sew. I have always wanted to learn how to make designs, though. I would often show my drawings to Grandmother for her bridal shop." The last few words rather trailed away as Jewel realized she was babbling. It seemed a curtain had fallen over Doctor Williams' eyes, and Jewel knew she was losing her audience. She pushed her fingernails into the palm of her hand to calm herself down and unsteadily looked down at the humorless face of the professor.

"I see. And so you came to New York and met Dominique who just happened to give you my card." Doubt exuded from Doctor Williams as she rehearsed what she had just heard.

"Actually, yes. I told her I must learn the industry so I can continue my grandmother's business successfully. I believe she trusted I was serious."

"Serious." Doctor Williams' eyebrows lifted and a light shone in her eyes.

"Very." Jewel clasped her hands in front of her and with her back straight as an arrow, she stood nearly at attention. There was nothing else to say. She knew this was the only chance she could possibly have of entering

Vassar. It was the only chance she could possibly have of staying in New York. Her lips shut in a straight line as she waited for the gavel to fall. Henrietta sat in her chair evaluating the young woman and silent minutes passed before she responded.

"Come with me," Doctor Williams said finally. She rolled her wheelchair out the door, down the hall and through the side door of the building. Jewel walked as fast as she could, opening doors as they went, trying to keep up with the older woman. They passed through the doors of the Administration Building and soon found themselves back at Esther Beasley's desk.

"Miss Beasley, please administer the entrance tests to Miss Culpepper. I would like to know the results of the tests this afternoon." She looked back at Jewel. "The tests will take approximately three hours. I don't doubt you will do well, but it will take the majority of the day before we have the results. You will stay at my quarters tonight as a favor to Dominique. I will never hear the end of it if I do not treat one of her constituents well. Good luck to you, my dear. I will see you in three hours." With that, Doctor Williams left Jewel at the mercy of Esther Beasley.

Jewel had no idea she would have to take a college entrance exam that day and she was totally unprepared for it. Esther gave her the instructions, two sharpened pencils and a large rubber eraser and paper, patted her shoulder, and with a pitiful shake of her head, left Jewel to her misery. Jewel wasn't sure whether she should run and hide or simply put her head down on the table and cry. She opted for the latter. Ten minutes later, she sat up straight, found a tissue in her handbag, dried her eyes, blew her nose and gathered her wits about her to begin the tests. She slowly read the first question. Surprised she knew the answer, she quickly went to the next, and happily to the next gaining more confidence as she continued. The test was long, and though some parts were relatively easy for her, others were tortuous. Undaunted, Jewel completed the test without complaint.

After just under three hours of answering questions regarding everything from philosophy to political science, Jewel laid her pencils down. Her greatest abilities were in mathematics and English, but she especially loved history. She was miserable in geography, however. Her grandmother had taught her everything she knew about Ireland and the South of Africa, but the rest of the world had been ignored. Esther Beasley entered the room a few minutes later, gathered up the papers and supplies, then left Jewel to herself again. It was another hour before she returned. Jewel had fallen asleep in her chair.

"Miss Culpepper?" Jewel jumped at the sound of Miss Beasley's voice.

"Hmm?" Her eyes were still foggy with sleep. "Yes?" She tried to focus in on Miss Beasley.

"You passed, Miss Culpepper. You barely passed, but you did pass." Esther's face glowed when she gave the announcement. Jewel stood up in disbelief.

"Really, how?" Jewel grabbed Esther's shoulders and hugged her. "I can't believe it! I passed? I've never been in a school house my entire life, and here I am passing tests at Vassar! I can't believe it!"

"Not only that, Miss Culpepper," Henrietta Williams had entered the room unawares. "The deal I have with Dominique is she sends someone to me, and they work in her boutique as an intern when the time is appropriate. When Dominique determines someone has talent, it is rare they do not succeed. She is an excellent judge of character."

Classes began a month later. Jewel had returned to Georgia to visit her brother and finish the final plans for the caretaking of Fairland. She and her brother went to the bank in Macon and withdrew the money her grandmother had saved over the previous 20 years. She gave half to Davey, and kept half for herself for her education and room and board in New York. They made arrangements with the bank to pay Davey a portion of the profits for any crops harvested and the rental of land to anyone who might be interested. Afterwards, Davey found and hired a caretaker for the grounds who would maintain Fairland as long as Jewel was away. He would farm out the land for the planting of crops, as well as manage the peach orchard and any profits from it. Fairland was again in safe hands, and Jewel did not worry as she began her new career as a student at Vassar.

Life at Vassar was certainly more interesting than life on the farm. Jewel loved the camaraderie of the girls at the college who, unlike her, had mostly grown under the ease of rich living. Politicians' daughters, girls from industrial families, and many from the farthest parts of the country had come to receive the best education available to women in the United States. Though her maturity level was high above theirs, Jewel enjoyed them all. She was in a new world now, one her brother would never come to understand.

Henrietta Williams decided to take Jewel under her wing. Although Jewel had desired an education in the fashion industry and her "fashion sense" could be developed, her test scores revealed her high intelligence, and it was determined she would make an excellent history student. She definitely had the ability to teach, so Henrietta Williams decided Jewel would be her protégé, if she had the mind to. She even planned a possible trip to Europe together after Jewel's final year. Nevertheless, the political situation remained tense not only in the United States, but around the globe. Spain and America were now at odds with each other. Henrietta Williams' plans for her protégé would not come to pass, and Jewel's sheltered life would soon change completely.

* * *

José Martí looked over his audience as he prepared to make his opening remarks before the morning assembly. Here he was, a 29-year-old hero, addressing a crowd of women as if he had been a statesman his entire life. In truth, he was simply an exiled Cuban who had immigrated back to the United States from Spain just two short years before. His time in Spain had been spent writing about his life in Cuba where he had been imprisoned for denouncing a pro-Spanish classmate during Cuba's Ten Years' War, their struggle for independence. In 1869, when he was only 16 years old, he had started the newspaper, "La Patria Libre" or Free Fatherland. After a short time, he was freed from prison, but was exiled to Spain. While he lived there, his literary protestations continued when he developed "El Presidio Político", a paper attacking Cuban prisons. After completing his education in Madrid and Zaragoza, Spain, he became too visible. He was forced to return to America only two years before to fight for the freedom of Cuba from his offices in New York City.

Martí stood looking over the crowd of women at Vassar College wondering if his address regarding his cause for Cuba would make any difference here. Many stared back at him, starry-eyed and dreaming of a life with this handsome Latin man. He straightened his collar, pushed long, black hair back from his forehead and smiled uncomfortably before he began. He was well versed in the political climate of the world, but he did not believe these silly women would be able to understand a thing he was about to say. Nevertheless, he had been invited and he would make the address politely, using only words women would understand; words like, "starving children forced to work in the cane fields 18 hours a day." Those kinds of words always seemed to get a good response from women, especially here in the North.

Martí's heart truly ached for his people, and the slave issue was still very fresh in many peoples' minds, so any reference to that kind of abuse usually helped his cause. The plight of his people in Cuba gave Martí an agenda he wanted to press. Cubans were mercilessly oppressed by the Spanish governor, while he lined his own pockets with money made from their sweat and toil.

Jewel listened intently to his elementary speech noticing Martí was patronizing his audience. It was her senior year and it was obvious to her he had indeed underestimated the women of Vassar. Some of the country's greatest political and social minds of the time were sitting in the auditorium listening to this man. She thought he should realize many of these women would day affect national policies behind the scenes. She perked up when the speaker asked for questions from the audience. A young sophomore stood to her feet.

"Señor Martí," she began. He looked down at her with a smug smile awaiting her question. "I understand you were exiled from your country for many years. Since your communication lines are limited, to say the least, how can you be sure the political atmosphere in your country hasn't changed? Would it be safe to say the oppression your people are enduring may be over stated more because of your painful memories than certain facts as they are today?"

Martí straightened his back to try to stand taller than his five-foot-seven-inch frame would allow. He blinked a number of times before answering. *How brazen*, he thought.

"My dear woman," he responded, his Latin accent dripping with as much sweetness as he could muster. "Until you have actually seen the oppression of my people, you will never be able to know what they are experiencing. If you are aware of the political atmosphere in my country, then you must know things cannot continue the way they are. My people are starving, and they are living in squalor. If you had such an experience, my dear, you would know the memory is more than enough to spur anyone into action regarding these circumstances. However, I will also state that I have excellent communication with certain government officials who are not supportive of the current governor. Therefore, I would say I am aware things basically are the same as they were when I left Cuba more than 10 years ago. People are being imprisoned daily by a wicked man who must be deposed. I hope I have clearly answered your question." He looked up to answer another question as the young woman sheepishly sat down. Jewel smiled as she listened to the banter before she finally raised her hand.

"Señor Martí." He looked down at her small frame and waited for her question. He had noticed her when he first walked in and wondered if he might introduce himself later. "Perhaps you have an opening in your office for someone who might be interested in helping your cause?" This surprised the young statesman, as well as the other women in the audience. He hadn't really expected to recruit anyone, but he was always open to people joining his cause. He told her to meet him after the meeting and took another question.

Henrietta Williams was as surprised by Jewel's question as was Martí. She hoped she could get to Jewel before she talked to Martí, but because of the crowd, the professor's wheelchair could not get there in time.

"Thank you, Señor Martí. I so appreciate your time. I will see you on Saturday, then." Jewel smiled at their guest and turned to leave, running directly into Henrietta Williams' chair.

"Oh! Dr. Williams!" Jewel practically fell into the professor's lap. Martí reached for her and helped her to steady herself. Flustered, Jewel clumsily introduced the professor to Señor Martí. Dr. Williams held up her hand to the younger man.

"Professor," he said as he bowed and caught her hand, "I am delighted to meet you. I have heard of you in some of the art circles in France and España." He leaned over and kissed the top of her hand. Jewel's eyes opened wide having never been exposed to such gallantry in her lifetime.

"It is my pleasure, Señor. I was surprised to see my young protégé becoming involved in your cause, however. I wonder if she will be over worked by helping you while continuing her education here at the same time."

"Do not fear, Professor. I will watch her like an eagle so she does no such thing. I have some administrative things she can do in the office on the weekend only. I promise."

Jewel cut in. "I hope I wasn't stepping out of line, Doctor Williams. I have been looking for a worthy cause to which I can put some extra effort in my spare hours. It would do me good to be away from the school for a day and I am thrilled to be able to be of some small help to Cuba. Being from the South, I feel it is my duty to help the oppressed." Martí smiled at that. He'd hooked her after all. Henrietta Williams looked doubtfully at her student.

"I suppose one day a week would not hurt, but I will keep an eye on your grades, Miss Culpepper." She nodded and turned to José Martí. "I pray you will notify me if you need further assistance, Señor. Perhaps I might contact one of my friends at Harvard." Martí bowed and watched Professor Williams as she wheeled away.

"She's a bit protective," Jewel commented apologetically.

"I would say you are correct, but in meeting you, Miss Culpepper, I can understand why." Humor sparked in Martí's eyes as he prepared to leave. "I will see you this coming Saturday then." Jewel smiled and gave him a positive nod.

Saturday came quickly, and before Jewel realized it, she was taking a carriage from the train station to a small business building in South Manhattan. The red brick, three-story building did not look impressive as she stood looking at it. Her own Fairland House was larger, it seemed. Nevertheless, she opened the door to go in and started up the three flights of stairs to the offices of José Martí, Attorney at Law.

Knocking before she entered, Jewel stood by the door looking at the near-naked room wondering if Señor Martí had forgotten she was coming. Indeed, she wondered why she had come at all. He had seemed to be a man of means when he spoke at the college, but these meager surroundings proved otherwise. She heard voices in the next room and tiptoed to the door. Listening carefully, she could hear two men having a heated discussion in Spanish. Just as she was about to knock, the door opened and one of the men nearly ran her over. He held her close as he steadied himself, and Jewel looked up into the most handsome face she had ever seen. Coal black eyes met hers with a look of both surprise and irritation.

"Señorita, me perdona. I am sorry," he said in a thick accent. "I did not know you were here. May I be of some help to you?"

"Who is it, Alberto?" José Martí's voice came from behind. Jewel peeked behind her captor.

"'Tis I, Sir," Jewel responded. Martí stood up from his desk and welcomed Jewel into his office.

"Alberto, I want to introduce you to the young lady who will be helping here on the weekends. Señorita Jewel Culpepper, this is Alberto Recalde Nieves. Alberto, Miss Culpepper. She will be assisting us with basic office duties."

Martí eyed Recalde sternly and Recalde hesitated momentarily before he bowed at the waist. She wondered if she had been the subject of their discussion when she walked in. "Mucho gusto, Señorita. I am happy to meet you."

"Mucho gusto, Señor Recalde. I am afraid that is the extent of my Spanish. Perhaps I will learn more while I'm here." She looked up at the man with child-like innocence and Recalde's face softened as he smiled back at her. Jewel felt electrified by his smile. She had never met a man so charming in her life. As she thought about it, she had barely known any man, as protected as she had been both at the plantation and at Vassar.

This indeed would be an adventure. The sparkle in her eyes did not go unnoticed by the two men.

Recalde kept Jewel busy in the office until noon when the men left together for lunch. Martí had invited her to come along, but she refused saying she had brought a lunch and was looking forward to finishing her tasks so she could get back to the college before dark. The two men walked briskly down the stairs without saying a word. The tension between them was still high, but Martí did not want Jewel to hear their discussion.

When they reached the street, Martí looked directly at his companion and reiterated what he had said earlier in his office. Since he met her, he had been unable to stop thinking about Jewel. She had become both the subject of his desire, and a raw point of contention between himself and Alberto. He had not wanted to cause an argument with his friend, but Jewel was different than anyone he had met before, and he continued to press the matter.

"I tell you, Beto, I am taken with this woman. She is lovely, no?" Recalde returned Martí's glare and nodded. "Even though we have met only once, I believe there is a reason she has come into my life at this time. Once the freedom of Cuba has been determined, I will court her, and she will be my wife." Recalde turned and led the way down the street toward a café.

"José, I can see you are very determined," Recalde said. "We will discuss the matter at another time. I am sure your father would not approve, and that is why I am here, ¿no? I am to protect you from dangers, even the dangers of an innocent child such as her. Certainly there is a woman in Cuba, or even España, who would be more fitting than this girl." They reached the café and Recalde signaled to the waiter for a table. Martí followed the waiter without saying a word. When they were seated, he picked up the napkin and shaking it, set it in his lap.

"Perhaps a girl from España would be more fitting in the eyes of a Cuban nationalist, but my eyes have caught the elegance of this young lady. There is something special about her, and I intend to find out what it is." He picked up his water glass, held it up to Recalde in the form of a toast and took a drink. Recalde said nothing more about the subject. There were more important things to consider now, like how they were going to help finance a revolution in Cuba.

Chapter X

An Evil Plan for a Just Cause

Alberto Recalde was more than charming to Jewel the next time they met. He stood to his feet as she entered the office the following Saturday, walked over to her and kissed her hand. Jewel nearly swooned as she caught hold of the scent of his cologne.

"Why, Señor Recalde, what brought that on?" Jewel's blue eyes sparkled as he looked down at her. He was clearly another four inches taller than his counterpart, José Martí, though their coloring was nearly the same. They were surprisingly fair, despite their jet black hair and eyes a Spanish deep-coffee brown.

"I simply wanted to make up for my cool welcome last weekend. We are much more hospitable in Cuba, I am sorry to say. Will you forgive me?"

"Why, of course, sir. I must say, I am surprised by your kindness." Jewel fairly blushed as she spoke. She looked away to try to hide her embarrassment and then quickly walked over to the small table that had been made into a desk for her. "I really must start work."

Putting her gloves into her bonnet, she clumsily placed them on the corner of the table. Unbalanced, the bonnet fell to the floor. Rolling her eyes, she chastised herself before picking them up. Looking back at him, she gave him a demure smile, but her fluster did not escape Recalde's notice; he immediately knew it would take little to get her to fall for him. He would do anything to keep his future president from falling into the arms of this young woman, as lovely as she seemed to be. His initial plan to steal her away from Martí would work after all.

Martí arrived late after having spoken at a businessmen's breakfast. He walked over to Jewel. "How are you today, little one? Are you ready for another busy Saturday?" She looked up and greeted him with a smile. She was indeed a lovely woman, he thought. He decided would ask her out for dinner this afternoon.

The day had gone by quickly. There had been a number of new donations sent in toward the cause in Cuba, and Jewel was kept busy organizing the books for the ministry Martí and Recalde had started in the small office. Martí had written a number of articles for papers in Caracas and Buenos Aires which had to be transcribed and posted. He had also started a magazine for children called Edad de Oro (Golden Age). Jewel spent hours together with him in his office while Recalde worked separately. Realizing this could pose a problem to working his plan, Recalde approached his friend.

"José, perhaps Señorita Jewel would like to go with us to supper tonight." Martí looked up, surprised. He shot a look at Recalde which was ignored as he stepped up behind Jewel's chair.

"Actually, Beto, I was about to ask the señorita if she would like to –."

"My apologies, gentlemen, but I really must get back to Vassar," Jewel interrupted. "Dr. Williams is waiting for me. She is quite strict. She wants me home by eight o'clock, and waiting for transportation does take quite some time. Perhaps we could do it another time, a little earlier?" She stood up and turned toward Martí.

"Señor Martí, I cannot tell you how much I'm enjoying working with you. I am already learning so much, and I know my working here will somehow have an impact on things in Cuba. Thank you so much for allowing me the privilege."

Martí stood to his feet and bowed. "It is entirely my pleasure, Señorita. Thank you for your hard work and commitment to my people." He took her hand and kissed it tenderly. Blushing, Jewel carefully removed her hand from his and flashed the two men a quick smile before leaving the office. Somehow she felt uncomfortable between the two of them. She decided she would discuss this with Dr. Williams. Then she recanted. Perhaps she might not be the best one to talk to about the affairs of the heart. Dominque would be a better choice, she decided, and she could stop at her shop before returning next week.

The bell above the door rung as Jewel entered the boutique. Dominique looked up from her customer and a smile crossed her lips as she raised her hand in welcome. Excusing herself from the matron whom she had been helping, she signaled for another clerk to assist her, and then fairly floated across the floor to greet her young friend.

"Mon amí, what are you doing here? Should you not be with ze charming young Martí?" Jewel looked at her surprised, unaware of Dominique's knowledge about her new position. "Oui, mon amí, I am already aware of your employment. Henrietta told me almost immediately. I have been awaiting your visit."

"You have?"

"But of course! You would not go to stuffy Henrietta for advice about a man. How silly would zat be? Now, tell me about him, will you?" She drew Jewel into her parlor and ushered her to the sofa. Dominique's maid brought them tea and biscuits while the two women discussed the subject of José Martí.

"Dominique, it is not Señor Martí I'm concerned about. He has a friend. His name is Alberto Recalde Nieves." The name tasted as sweet on her tongue as the honey milk her grandmother had given her in times of need. She closed her eyes and sighed. She had truly become infatuated with this man. Dominique let her head fall back as she laughed. Her reaction stung Jewel's tender feelings, and she straightened her shoulders defensively.

"My little sweet pea, you are very young, no? You must understand there will be many opportunities for you to meet young men. You also must be discerning in your choices." She passed a cup of tea to her young friend, and eyes sparkling by her thoughts, she continued.

"Let me tell you about my Franc. He was, oh, so beautiful." Her eyes looked to the ceiling as she remembered. "He had ze most beautiful eyes and his voice was so elegant when he spoke. But Franc was only after one sing, as are all men, my dear." She shrugged her shoulders as if the matter was already understood. "When I told him I would be coming here to America, he vowed he would follow me. Unfortunately, he missed ze boat and I never heard from him again. I later learned he had been married ze whole time I had been wis him. Tsk, tsk. Such a waste," she said, and then sighed at her memories. "Never ze less, if I had waited for him, I would not have come here to America and made my fortune." She clasped Jewel's hands in hers. "Please, mon ami, do not waste your time so early in life on zis one man."

Jewel listened, but she did not hear what her friend was saying. She immediately surmised that Dominique had been hurt early in life by a relationship, but Franc was not Alberto. Surely this was a different set of circumstances. She decided she was a grown woman and already had had to make many difficult choices in her short lifetime. Dominique was from another era; only Jewel would be able to determine the best course for her relationship with Alberto Recalde.

Three weeks passed before Martí was able to talk to Jewel again. Recalde kept him busy and away from the office as much as possible. He had numerous speaking engagements and other meetings to attend to, and Recalde stayed by his side continuously. In the meantime, Martí continued working on his articles, which he asked Jewel to proofread before they were wired to their destinations in South America. He was a very effective communicator, and Jewel was pleased with the final outcome of the articles. But José was not Alberto.

The office seemed empty when Alberto wasn't there, and there were times when Jewel found herself daydreaming about him as she gazed out the window next to her small work table. Jewel continued with her varied duties and tried not to think about him, but she found it increasingly more difficult until one Saturday afternoon when Martí opened the door and poked his head into the office.

"Hello, my dear Jewel. I have returned at last." Daydreaming again, Jewel jumped at the sound of his voice and looked up surprised.

"Why, I should say it is about time, Señor. I had begun to wonder if you were indeed a figment of my imagination." She smiled at him as the door swung open, but when she saw that behind him stood Alberto Recalde, her eyes lit up. Recalde raised his eyebrow identifying the look of love in her eyes. He nodded and crossed over to his desk.

"Yes, I was beginning to think the same. At least I had been imagining being able to spend the evening with you and wondered if it would ever happen. Will it be possible for you to join me this evening for dinner?" He stood over her table as she finished gathering the envelopes she had just addressed. Feeling a bit uncomfortable by the invitation and intimidated by Martí's anxious look as he stood over her, she stood to her feet. Glancing at Alberto, she noticed he had busied himself by the bookshelf, but was looking directly at her. She hesitated before answering.

"I would be happy to join the two of you for dinner," she said, not blinking an eye. Martí stepped back.

"I am sorry, Señorita, but I thought it would just be the two of us." His face flushed and she could see the disappointment in his eyes.

"Forgive me, Señor Martí, but I have been warned by Professor Williams that it is improper to be seen with a man in public without a chaperone, and it is not allowed for a Vassar girl to do so. I am sure Señor Recalde would appreciate that on your behalf, as well. Perhaps he has a friend who would like to come along?" She looked at him confidently, guessing as much as she hoped he did not, he probably did have a woman, or maybe two, who would be happy to be escorted by the second officer of Martí's movement. Martí turned toward his friend to give him an urgent look. Recalde raised his eyebrow and returned her gaze with a confident one of his own.

"But of course, Señorita. That is very wise of you." Martí sneered at his old friend and then turned back to Jewel with a brilliant smile.

"It is settled, then. We will have dinner in a little restaurant of which I am very well acquainted where they serve the best Cuban cuisine. I am sure you will be pleased with the taste of our food, Señorita." His message did not escape Recalde's understanding. Martí was preparing her for her future in Cuba. He glanced down at the book he still held in his hand, replaced it on the shelf and excused himself to "prepare for the evening," leaving Martí and Jewel alone to finish out the day's work.

New York was growing a mile a decade, according to the experts, and the lower West Side Warehouse District was not normally a pleasant or even a safe path to travel. The unpleasantness of the Warehouse District was lost, however, when they entered the festive atmosphere of Café Cubana. Not many people came to the café in the evening, but Martí stopped in frequently to visit his old friends, Alfonso and his wife, Pilar. Refugees from Cuba, they were staunch supporters of Martí's ideas and desire for independence. When they saw him enter through the door with a beautiful young lady on his arm, Alfonso gave them the best table in the house. Pilar, meanwhile, closed the doors to the rest of the public.

Martí was pleased to have the first few minutes alone with his intended. He had been attracted to her at Vassar, but had fallen desperately in love with her. When they first met he recognized her special attributes, but he had no idea the spell she would cast over him as they worked together. He had memorized every freckle crossing over her upturned nose, the lilt of her voice as she spoke, her smile and the way she crossed her legs at the ankle as she leaned into her table to write. He believed he had found the next first lady of Cuba. He glanced at her and looked away, hesitating to say what was in his heart. Instead, he filled their wine goblets with the wine Alfonso brought to the table.

"Señor, did you have a question?" Jewel looked at him directly. It was the American way, looking directly into the eyes of a person. In other countries, it was considered prideful, and Martí had difficulty bringing his eyes up to meet hers. Finally, he took courage and began to tell her how much he cared for her.

"Señorita Culpepper – Jewel, if I may." She nodded and smiled. She had wondered if he had been taken with her, but having been blinded by her own feelings for Alberto Recalde, she did not have an inkling of the depth of his true feelings. "Señorita Jewel, you should know you have more than captivated me. You have captured my heart." Her eyes widened and she started to interrupt, but he continued. "I must tell you, I have never in my life, in Cuba or in España, ever met a woman as delightfully challenging as you. I find I can barely do my work for thinking about you. I have wanted to ask you if I may perhaps be able to court you, and soon after to ask you to be my wife."

Jewel gasped. Never had she even thought of José Martí as a gentleman friend let alone a husband. She thought he liked her, but had not thought he had fallen in love with her. In her naiveté, she had sincerely believed that even though he might have been taken with her, his cause was truly the only thing on which he was focused. She barely knew how to react or what to say. She picked up her wine goblet, gave him a quick smile, and gulped down its entire contents, choking on the final drops. Martí politely refilled her glass.

"Forgive me, Señor," she said trying to cover her total inexperience in these matters, "I don't know –."

"Please, call me José. If we are to become closer, it would please me if we could be a bit more informal."

"Of course, José." Her talk with Dominique had definitely not helped, and though Dominique was much wiser than Jewel in the ways of the world, not even Dominique would have expected this. Her friend had failed to prepare her for this particular situation. Dominique knew men and their habits, but Jewel was relatively clueless having been so protected throughout her lifetime. The only man she ever really knew was her brother, and he was nothing like this romantic Cuban. Totally taken by surprise by this turn of events, she took another gulp of wine.

The door opened and Alberto Recalde walked in with the most strikingly beautiful woman Jewel had ever seen. Coal-black hair flowed over her bare shoulders, and she glanced about the room with large, almond-shaped black eyes. She wore a satin teal dress with ruffles about the neckline that had been pulled around her shoulders, exposing the tops of her arms and a well-developed chest. A dark beauty mark on her upper left cheek highlighted her eyes, and high cheek bones gave her face a look of maturity and perfection. She was crowned with a Spanish comb which held a black lace mantilla veil in place. She was the picture of the pure Cuban woman.

Jewel's eyes widened and her face flushed at the sight of them together. Martí could not help but turn at her reaction, to see what she was looking at. Recalde waved at his friend, and placing his arm around the woman's waist, led her to the table. Martí stood to his feet to greet them as Jewel downed another half glass of wine.

"Margarita Ramirez Estrada, this is José Martí, the future presidente de Cuba." Nearly forgetting to introduce Marti's guest, he hurriedly added, "Oh, and Jewel Culpepper from Vassar College."

"Pleased to meet you, I'm sure," Margarita said. Her eyes sparkled as she looked at the man she most admired. Martí kissed her hand and bowed, and then bidding her to be seated, he held her chair before the men sat down. Jewel had been struck dumb by the woman's gentle demeanor and beauty, and she could do nothing but sip her wine. She was out of her element, and totally unprepared for her reaction to Recalde's choice of women. He continued to explain how he happened to invite her.

"After our conversation today, I decided to go to the market to see if my sister would be interested in joining us this evening. I met Margarita by the orange stand where she was buying fruit for her employer. She works for the Honorable Judge Horatio Leeland of the District Court."

With cat-like prowess, Jewel studied the young woman who, in her estimation, could not have been older than 18. "And what do you do for *him*, Margarita?" she hedged. Jewel smiled, and checked to see if her claws were sharp. She downed some more wine as Recalde shot her a serious look. Margarita returned the smile innocently.

"I am working for his daughter, actually. I am her nanny."

"Oh," Jewel said sheepishly. She drew back her claws, swallowed her pride, and took another sip of wine. The girl was too perfect, she thought. Somehow she felt amazingly relaxed, and perhaps a bit groggy.

"She is such a sweet child, Beto," Margarita continued in her honey-like Latin accent. *Beto,* Jewel thought to herself, *I don't even call him Beto, and I've known him for over a month!* "She is only eight years old, but she is very wise for one so young. I am often amazed by our conversations together."

"I'll just bet you are," Jewel slurred under her breath. She picked up the wine decanter and refilled her glass. Martí looked at her surprised and then at Alberto. He leaned over to Jewel and whispered in her ear.

"Are you feeling all right, my dear? Perhaps you have had enough wine." He took the decanter from her hand and placed it on the other side of the table. Jewel smiled at him as her entire body seemed to go numb.

"Sahtenly, sah," she replied in her finest southern, "I am feeling sahtenly fine. A little light headed, p'haps, and I find I am rather thusty." She picked up her goblet and once again gulped down its contents. Looking into the glass, she continued, "Grandma never told me 'bout this stuff. It is sahtenly delishus. MMM, mmm. We nevah had this on the plantation. Only good, solid whiskey that, mind you," she pointed her index finger to the ceiling, "was only for medicinal pahpesses. My, my, but it is warm in heah." She held her napkin up and fanned herself.

"José, perhaps Señorita Jewel should lie down," Recalde suggested.

"Me? Oh, no. I am sahtenly fine. Beto, did you know José wants me to marry him? What do y'all think o' that? Why, I nevah even thought about it and heah he jes' come right out an' said he wants to court me! Why, I nevah!" Embarrassed, Martí stood to his feet.

"Yes, perhaps Jewel should be excused." She had embarrassed him publicly. Martí waved at Alfonso who rushed over to the table. "I think the wine was a little more than the señorita is used to, my friend. Would you please call for a carriage?"

"But, Señor Martí," Alfonso protested, "your food is being prepared, and your friends have only just arrived."

"It is all right, my friend. Please, let my friends take the food while I escort the señorita to her hotel. Here is the money for the bill." He looked down at Recalde. "Enjoy, no? I will take Jewel home. I am sorry for this inconvenience." Alberto stood and drew Martí to the side.

"José, Margarita wanted to meet you. She only came on the pretext that you would be here. You are her hero, hermano, and I promised her dinner with you."

"But what about Jewel? She cannot remain here. She drank nearly the entire bottle of wine. Soon she will not be able to sit up." He looked back and watched Jewel stick her finger in her glass to get the final drop and then lick the wine off her fingertip. He shook his head and rolled his eyes. "This is certainly an unfortunate turn of events, Beto." Recalde chuckled.

"I will take her back to the office and she can sleep it off on your sofa. She will be safe there, I will watch over her and no one will know about it." Martí nodded then helped Recalde take Jewel to the carriage. She was barely able to walk, so Recalde picked her up in his arms and placed her inside. Martí leaned into the carriage, took Jewel's hand and kissed it lovingly while Recalde entered on the other side. "Don't worry, my friend. She will be better by the morning," Recalde assured him. The carriage left Martí at the curb waving after them.

Recalde sat straight shouldered against the backside of the carriage as Jewel slumped in her seat across from him. The carriage hit a bump, and Jewel started to slide. Recalde jumped to her aid and pulled her back up to sit beside him. In a euphoric fog, she opened her eyes and looked up at him.

"Hi there, Beto," she slurred.

"Hi there, Jewel." He could not help but smile down at her as her head snuggled into his shoulder.

"I am not sure, Beto, but I think I am quite drunk. I have never felt like this before."

"Yes, I am afraid you have had too much wine, my dear."

"My deah. That's nice. That is very nice of you, Beto. I love you so much." She closed her eyes and snuggled into his arms a little further.

"I care for you as well, Jewel, but José must never know. It is a secret, ¿no?" He had planned to plant seeds he hoped would germinate quickly from the first day Martí had spoken to him about her. His mission was to keep her from distracting Martí from gaining his future office as Presidente de Cuba, and he could tell his plan was definitely working. He thought if he could keep her off guard, he could seduce her away from his friend. It would hurt José for a time, but he would go on, with God's strength and leading.

"Yes. Sssshhh," she replied holding her finger to her lips. "Some day I'll tell you my secret, if you want. I have a secret hardly anybody knows."

"I think you have already let your secret be known." Recalde turned her toward him and laid her in his arms.

"Nope. I ain't tol' nobody heah in New York 'ceptin' Henrietta Williams. She's the only one who knows about it." Recalde did not take her seriously thinking it was the wine talking, but something deep inside told him he should pursue the subject.

"Then, if I knew the secret, I would not tell anyone either. I am sure it is a very important one," he hedged.

"Yes, sah, very important," she mused. She was half asleep until the clip clop of horse's hoofs barraged her mind. "Beto, what is that noise?"

"It is only the horses, my love. Now, what were you saying about a secret?" He kissed her forehead and held her closer.

"Yes, I have one, you know. I am a very rich woman," she said pointing upward with her index finger. Recalde took her hand, held her index finger and kissed it. She sat up momentarily, but the wine affected her equilibrium so she sank back into his arms. "Ohhh. I don't feel so good."

"Driver! Pull up!" Recalde shouted. He stood to his feet, jumped off the carriage and pulled Jewel down to the side of the street where she promptly lost everything she had consumed earlier in the evening. Afterward, he helped her back into the carriage and they went a little further down the street where they stopped in front of Martí's office building. Recalde gave the driver his money and then gathered Jewel up in his arms. The driver opened the door to the building and Recalde carried her up the three flights of stairs. Breathless, he deposited her on the sofa.

"I am so sorry, Señor Recalde. I have never in my life acted like this." Tears flowed down her face as she lay there mortified. "I don't know what came over me!" Recalde brushed the hair away from her face and sitting next to her on the sofa, he handed her a cup of water.

"You needn't worry about it, my love. Wine can be a very disturbing drink if you are not used to it. Have you never had it before?"

"My Grandma would whip my hide if I ever did anything like that. She always said strong drink had been the death of many a good Irishman, and she would have none in her house." She took a sip of the water and lay back down on the pillow. "I am dreadfully sorry."

"Sleep now, my dear. Sleep. We shall talk tomorrow." Recalde covered her with his coat and she fell into a deep sleep holding his hand. Letting loose of her hand a few minutes later, he picked up her handbag to search its contents. It only held a few dollars and lip rouge. Nothing in her handbag would have given him a clue about the riches to which she had referred. Tossing the bag on the sofa next to her, he left Martí's office to go into his own to do some paperwork. Martí came in about two hours later to find Recalde asleep in his chair. He jumped at the sound of the door closing.

"Oh, mi hermano, it is only you." Recalde yawned and rubbed the sleep out of his eyes.

"Yes, how is she?" Concern was written across Martí's face as he stepped over to his office door to peek in at his beloved.

"We almost made it here when she became sick, but she is fine now, José."

"Yes, wine on an empty stomach is no good." Martí could not help but chuckle. He was glad Alberto handled it instead of him, but his heart melted as he watched her sleep. "She is beautiful, is she not?" Recalde walked over to his friend and placed a hand on his shoulder.

"Yes, my friend, very beautiful," he agreed disdainfully. "And how is Margarita?"

"She is safely at home. We had a nice dinner and talked about her childhood home in Havana, and then I took her to her parent's home not far from the café. They are true believers in Cuba's independence. They will support our cause." Recalde nodded then picked up the papers on which he had been working.

"José," Recalde approached him carefully. "I must ask you, who is this Jewel Culpepper?"

"What do you mean? She is a girl from the college." Martí still watched her as they spoke.

"Yes, I am aware of that, but have you checked on her background? One does not go to Vassar or any university for that matter, without some money." Recalde tried not to sound too urgent in his curiosity. He flipped through the papers and placed them into a satchel.

"I do not know, my friend. She told me she lived on a plantation in Georgia, and because her parents had both been killed during the war, she had been raised by a grandmother. The only other thing I know about her is she has a brother who is married with two children. Why do you ask these questions, Beto?" Martí turned and walked toward his friend.

"Oh, it is probably nothing, but while she sat with me in the carriage, she happened to mention she had some secrets only her professor knew about. I hope her being here will not jeopardize our cause."

As Recalde moved toward the door, Martí took his arm and turned him around.

"Alberto, I think you are walking on thin ice, as these Americans say," Martí warned.

"José, you are my dearest and closest friend and brother. I am only watching out for you and your future back in our country. Will you promise me to be careful with this woman?" Martí let go of Recalde's arm and they stood a moment looking at one another before he answered.

"I will, my friend. I am sure you need not worry about her, but I will do as you say." Recalde gave him a stiff nod and left Martí alone with her.

Sunday morning dawned much too quickly. Sunlight broke through the window panes and fell upon Jewel's face, but as she opened her eyes, pain shot through her head.

"Oh, my heavens, what happened!" She moved slightly and felt Recalde's coat slip off her to the floor. Martí heard her stir and was quickly at her side with a cup of tea and a cool cloth for her head.

"My darling, here. Take this tea. It will help to clear the cob webs from your brain." She looked up at his silhouette and took the cup from his hand. "Do you remember where you are?"

Hesitating before answering, she replied, "Señor Martí, I vaguely remember a thing, except I do recall acting very badly last night." She blushed at the memory. "I am sorry I ruined our dinner."

"On the contrary, Señorita. It was I who acted badly. I had not realized you would be adversely affected by the wine, and I should have known better." Martí kissed her forehead and bade her to remain lying down. "I would like to ask you something, if you would not mind."

"Of course, Señor, what is it?"

"Do you remember what I asked you last night?" Martí looked down at the floor hoping she would answer positively. Jewel did not speak for a moment as she thought about the events of the previous evening.

"Oh!" she exclaimed sitting upright. The cloth fell into her lap, and she swooned momentarily. "I mean, oh, my, yes. Señor Martí, I hope I have not led you to think that I, well, I hope I have not been forward." Setting the teacup aside, she stood to her feet, weaved a bit more, and sat down again.

"My love, are you all right?" Martí sat next to her and held her hand. He was a good four years older than she, but very immature where women were concerned. He had left home as a very young man, but had been very protected by both friends and family. He had not had any close relationships with a woman for a number of years until he met Jewel, and knew nothing about how to handle an awkward situation like this.

"No, actually, I am not feeling well at all. I think I should go home." Martí helped her to his private area where she could freshen up while he hailed a carriage to take them back to her residence at the college.

The ride was long and quiet as Jewel considered her options, and Martí suffered the agony of not knowing what she was thinking. Even when he tried to start a conversation, she just looked at him, gave him a little smile and a nod, and went back to her thoughts. How could she tell this gentle man she was not in love with him? How would she ever explain her feelings for Alberto? Did Alberto actually feel the same about her? How would this affect his relationship with his friend? Questions continued to barrage her mind, but answers escaped her.

When Martí left her residence, he felt very much alone. Jewel had simply shaken his hand and wished him a good day saying she was not sure if she would be able to come to the office the following Saturday. He spent the rest of the day working, trying to deny the fact that Jewel as much as rejected him, and he now knew she did not love him.

While Martí took care of Jewel, Alberto Recalde made it his mission to visit the Brooklyn Daily Eagle, hoping to find out something about Jewel's background. Standing at the reception desk, he simply explained he had some research to do on the history of the United States and its relations with Spain, and "if you could help me with some information from, perhaps, a few issues dating back twenty or thirty years – during your Civil War. Perhaps I would be able to grasp the historical perspective I will need to write a paper I must present to the governor on behalf of our government in Cuba." He hoped he sounded like he knew what he was talking about. The clerk looked him up and down before responding.

"Oh yeah, sure. So you're from Cuba, eh? It sure looks like things are getting hot down there." He didn't trust the stranger, but it wasn't his place to judge a person just on his nationality. He'd learned that much from the previous war. He looked Recalde in the eye, and then said, "Well, follow me, and I'll take you to our archives. It pretty much covers everything from the Revolution to current world events." The young man was eager to show off the newspaper as they walked. He explained the different jobs people were doing around the office.

"That guy's the managing editor. He makes all the final decisions about what goes into the final copy of the Eagle."

Recalde nodded politely, but did not actually hear a thing. He was thinking about Jewel's supposed riches. *If she indeed did have money, I might be able to convince her that Cuba's desperation is so great her money would be better used there than here raising a few head of cattle in Georgia.*

He reasoned his intentions were honorable; it was all for Cuba.

The young man closed the door after him leaving Recalde alone in the library. He pulled out Sunday papers dating back to 1860. Searching each one carefully, he looked to see if he could find anything pertaining to Jewel or her family, or something he hoped would be fruitful to the cause. He searched the society pages, the business news and headlines, and noticed a small advertisement for a jewelry sale in New York City, but found nothing remarkable. He stopped when he read an obituary of a Sunday paper.

"Culpepper, J. Reginald – A staunch supporter of the Union, was killed by Confederate soldiers in his home outside of Macon, Georgia on April 27, 1861. Making his fortune in diamonds, Culpepper arrived in America in

1859. Culpepper donated a large sum of money to the Union cause at the start of the war, and though considered a traitor by the Confederate government, the Brooklyn Eagle salutes this American hero. He is survived by his wife, Victoria and daughter, Jewel."

Recalde looked back at the jewelry sale advertisement he had found in another paper, and read the small print. A man named Rosebrand, a jeweler in New York, was offering the Culpepper collection. He sat for a moment contemplating what he had just discovered. This had to be Jewel's father. Did Jewel have money left over from the diamonds her father and Rosenbrand sold so many years before? Perhaps she actually had diamonds left from her father. They would be worth more than a fortune in today's market, he thought. Quickly gathering his belongings, he left the building through a back door.

Henrietta Williams sat in her wheelchair overlooking her protégé as she slept. She had stayed up late the previous night awaiting Jewel's return, and arose early in the morning checking to see whether Jewel was home. She breathed a sigh of relief when she saw the carriage pull up in front of the residence, but she was not pleased to see Martí step down and help Jewel to the door. Dr. Williams was sure the girl had taken ill or she would not have been away over night. Certainly that was the only explanation. Jewel had never been foolhardy in the four years she'd known her, but still, she was with José Marí. Professor Williams sipped her tea as she waited for Jewel to awaken. Finally she stirred and opened her eyes to see the matron looking at her.

"Oh, Dr. Williams. What are you doing here?"

"I have been waiting for you to wake up. Are you feeling all right?" She set her tea cup down on the bed stand and folded her hands across her lap. "I saw you come in this morning."

Jewel looked up surprised and then her face flushed. "Oh, Dr. Williams, it is not what you might think. I had a little too much to drink last night and I. . ."

"Excuse me, did I hear you say you drank alcohol last evening?" Henrietta leaned forward in her chair.

"I mean to say, why, I suppose I did. I hadn't thought of wine as alcohol, but I suppose it is, in a manner of speaking." Jewel sat up and leaned against her headboard pulling the coverlet up to her chin. "Señor Martí asked me out to dinner, but I countered with inviting his friend, Alberto – er – Señor Recalde to go along with us so I would have a chaperone. And so Señor Recalde met us there with the most beautiful girl. Dr. Williams, she was the most beautiful woman I have ever seen, and he certainly looked taken by her. He just kept looking at her, and so I just sat there and sipped my wine. But do you know, as I recall, that wine glass never did empty out. The next thing I knew, I was in a carriage with Beto, uh, Señor Recalde. I don't recall ever having been so sick in my life. The carriage seemed to be spinning in circles and he had to hold me up on the street. I was so embarrassed. I don't remember anything else except for waking this morning with Beto's coat jacket over me."

"Señor Recalde's coat jacket?"

"Yes, ma'am. Señor Recalde covered me with his coat," she responded lamely. She sat Indian style on her bed with her still aching head leaning back on the wall behind her.

"Quite the gentleman," the professor said doubtfully. Dr. Williams pulled her wheelchair away from the side of Jewel's bed and returned with a cup of hot tea a few minutes later. "It sounds like you had quite an adventure."

"I am afraid I don't remember much of it, except..." She hesitated looking fearfully at her teacher. The professor waited for her to finish. "Except Señor Martí proposed to me last night. Well, he said he wanted to court me. I was simply shocked, Professor. I had no idea he had intentions toward me."

"And how do you feel about that?"

"I have no feelings about it. My feelings are for..." She stopped. She had not admitted her feelings about Alberto to anyone except Dominique who had promised it would be kept absolutely secret.

"Beto?" Dr. Williams smiled. Jewel blushed. "I thought so. You are a very transparent young lady. My dear, may I offer you some advice?"

"Of course, Professor Williams." How could she refuse? She had broken every rule set down by the college. She was caught, and she knew it.

"I have had, shall we say, encounters with young men in both Spain and France. Latinos are romantic, mysterious and sometimes even sincere, but they are also fickle. They fall in love with women many times over because they are not ruled by their hearts, but by their flesh. Women, on the other hand, usually are ruled by their hearts and not their heads.

"Because of the station in which you stand and the responsibility you have to your estate, you need to be very careful about the gentleman with whom you fall in love. I am sure this Recalde is an honorable man, if you believe he is, but I would suggest you tread very lightly in this matter. As for your young Martí, his country needs him, and you would be wise to quickly end that affair."

"Of course, Professor, I'm sure you're right."

"I know I am right. Now, in the matter of your indiscretion last night, if you were seen drunk in public, this could have a dire reflection on our institution. This will not please the dean. I am very thankful Mr. Recalde had the good sense to take you to their private office so you would not be seen. I will have to report your absence of last night."

Jewel looked at her fearing her career at Vassar would be cut short just before she graduated.

"However, I promise you the incident between you and these two men will be kept a secret between the two of us. I believe this was a circumstance brought on by your inexperience in the world and it was beyond your control," Professor Williams said matter-of-factly. "These two men have taken advantage of your naiveté and I shall certainly speak to Señor Martí about it."

Jewel held up her hand to protest, but the professor dismissed her protestations with a shake of her head.

"Now, you have missed the morning worship service. I would suggest you spend the day in prayer seeking the Lord's guidance about your relationship with both of these men." She nodded stiffly and turned to leave the room. Turning back she said, "Jewel, I am very relieved you are home safe." She gave Jewel a reassuring smile and left her to her thoughts.

Jewel did not leave her room the rest of the day. Her slight indiscretion had indeed caused her to feel extremely guilty. What had she done, she wondered, but more than that, what had she said? At the end of the day, after she had cried a bucket of tears and had used a dozen handkerchiefs, she decided to write Martí a letter. She would post it the next day before her first class. The letter would simply tell him she was very honored by his kind offer, but she was not disposed to being courted at this time. Perhaps he would find a more suitable relationship with someone like Margarita who hailed from his own country and understood his customs better than she ever would. She signed it, "Respectfully, J.V. Culpepper."

The dean called Jewel into his office early the next morning. She sat quietly as he listened to Professor Williams expound on Jewel's attributes, her excellent record and her bright future.

"Miss Culpepper is an honor student, Dean Fitzgerald, a woman of great talent with a desire to teach after she leaves Vassar. Her actions while on this campus have been nothing less than exemplary."

Jewel blushed at the accolade, for her recent activities had been much less than exemplary, she knew.

The dean looked at Jewel and back at Professor Williams before he gave his judgment in the matter. "Dr. Williams, I am sure you know the rules here at Vassar are extremely stringent due to our standing as one of the first women's learning institutions in America. These rules are not only present to protect the institution, but they are in place to protect the students. Miss Culpepper is well aware of the strict guidelines regarding night hours to which every student must adhere, no matter who they are."

Dean Fitzgerald turned to address her. "I understand, of course, you were under the weather and unable to travel after hours, so I will make an exception in your case. However, staying in a public office over night not only was highly irregular, it may have put your very life in jeopardy. For that reason, I demand you resign your position with Mr. Martí and commit yourself to your studies here only. If you cannot abide by my demand in this respect, I will have to dismiss you from the college altogether, which would be very unfortunate this close to your graduation." He leaned back behind his desk, looking sternly over his spectacles, hands folded, face paled by his demeanor. "Do I make myself clear?"

"Yes sir." Jewel could hardly speak. The words were barely audible, and she cleared her throat to try again a bit louder. "Yes sir," she said plainly.

"You're dismissed." He turned to speak again to Dr. Williams as Jewel stood up and turned to go. Hesitating, she looked back to say something to the dean who waved her out the door. She left quietly.

The next few weeks were miserable for Jewel. The semester was nearly over, and Jewel was to graduate that month after four long years of education. These weeks held the most difficult of all her classes, the last in a series of art history courses. Then she had to face final examinations. She tried to concentrate on her studies, but all she could think of was Alberto Recalde and José Martí. She wondered how José was managing, now that she had broken his heart. She more than wondered if Alberto was still seeing the beautiful Margarita, and instead of Jewel, she imagined him wooing her.

After nearly a month with no contact, Recalde received the invitation Jewel sent to the office to attend her graduation. Recalde quickly hid the invitation from his friend. He would attend the graduation himself giving Jewel José's apologies for his absence. He did not want Martí to see the woman again.

During her time away, Recalde had continued his research into her background and had learned much more about her inheritance. He had contacts in the South who were eager to check into the Culpepper estate in Macon. He had found out about her bank accounts, financial situation, and the safe deposit box still listed in her name. He was also told the unfounded legend about treasure buried on the estate, and he wanted to check into that himself. She indeed did have the potential for helping with their cause, he thought.

"Yes, my love. I will attend your graduation, and I will even travel home with you to your Fairland." He folded the invitation into the envelope and tucked it into his breast pocket. That evening, he sent a message to Jewel asking her to meet him.

Chapter XI

Home to Fairland

On graduation day, an arrangement of white and yellow roses arrived at the Vassar College Administration Office where Esther Beasley was sneaking a peek to see who they came from. Jewel had been notified of the delivery and was already on her way to Administration to pick them up. While reading the card, Miss Beasley heard footsteps in the hallway and quickly tucked it back into the envelope. She slipped the card into the bouquet and stepped back to her desk just as Jewel opened the door.

"Beautiful flowers. Who sent them?" Miss Beasley asked innocently, pretending to be hard at work.

"A friend," was the coy reply. "A dear friend." Jewel sniffed one of the roses. With a broad smile written across her face, she picked up the vase and looked back at Miss Beasley. "As if you didn't already know."

"Well!" Miss Beasley huffed, but she could not help but smile when she saw Jewel wink at her.

After responding to Jewel's invitation, Alberto Recalde started visiting her secretly on a regular basis. Every Friday and Saturday evening, they would slip away to spend time together going to dinner and talking. She had regretfully resigned her position with Martí not only because of the dean's demands, but because she did not want to hurt him any more than she already had. She had been concerned when Recalde corresponded with her, but despite her concerns, Recalde had picked up where he'd left off a few short weeks before, and continued courting her on the sly. During dinner the Saturday before graduation, Recalde proposed.

"My darling," he said. His liquid eyes bore into her soul. "I have cherished these stolen moments with you. You are in my every thought."

"Thank you, Beto," Jewel responded, hypnotized by his voice and thrilled by his touch. Her eyes glistened with expectant tears. She had come to love him desperately, and their relationship seemed to have bloomed exponentially. Her young heart was so tender in his hands, and he knew it.

"I know it is a very short time before we will be apart, and this saddens me greatly, my love." She nodded her agreement, unable to speak through her emotions. "But I never want our relationship to end."

"I too, Beto. But I have to return to Georgia."

"Yes," he said. His voice seemed almost dark. "I know." He picked up his wine goblet before he said another word, wrapping his arm around hers and taking a sip of wine.

"Jewel, my dearest, I want to stay with you. Will you do me the honor of being my wife?"

Jewel was just taking a sip her wine when he asked the question for which she had been waiting since they had met. She choked on her wine, coughing directly into his face. He backed away and flipped out his handkerchief to wipe off the red liquid as it made its way down his chin.

"Oh, I'm sorry, Beto. You caught me off guard!"

"I can tell," he snapped. Catching himself, he quickly recanted. "I mean, it is all right, my dear." He pulled her to him so close their noses nearly touched. She gasped.

"I love you, Jewel. Marry me."

Jewel looked up at him, and barely able to breathe, she relaxed into him, placing her head against his chest. Reaching up, she caressed his cheek with her hand, and he took her hand in his to kiss her palm. Feelings surfaced she had never felt before, and she fairly melted into his arms.

"Yes, Alberto, I would be honored to be your wife."

Recalde knew he had conquered his prey. He held her close to him, satisfied he would finally be able to complete his plan.

Davey had been unable to come to the graduation, but he wrote saying he had prepared Fairland for her return and looked forward to meeting her at the railroad station. She had no time to write a letter, so she sent a telegram saying she would be bringing her dear friend with her. She hoped Davey would approve of her choice for a husband despite his Cuban heritage. His customs were very different than theirs, but she was sure her brother would grow to like him.

At the graduation, names were recited one by one. Jewel was ninth out of just eighty in her class. Henrietta Williams stood up from her wheel chair to greet her protégé as she walked across the stage to receive her diploma. She had turned out many students over her many years at Vassar, but never had she been as proud as she was of Jewel. Dominique stood to her feet, as well. She applauded her two dear friends as they stood together upon the stage, knowing she had played an important part in the development of this fine young lady.

Recalde sat next to Dominique wondering what all the fuss was about, but when he did not stand to applaud Jewel's accomplishments, Dominique's look of disapproval spurred him to respond. He stood up with her and applauded showing as much enthusiasm as he could muster. He was glad they would soon be able to leave and get away from the crowds. The noise of this very boring celebration was more than he cared to deal with.

Speeches were given, awards provided, and finally the closing remarks ended the Baccalaureate. Suddenly Jewel's education was over. After a small reception in the Fine Arts Building, Recalde escorted Jewel back to her residence. Bidding her good night, he promised to be there early the next morning to travel with her to the train station.

Jewel had been longing to see her beloved Fairland, and the day after graduation, she was finally able to return. She had so many plans for the farm, and with her dear Alberto by her side, she would accomplish them all. Her lifelong dream of working in the fashion industry would never be fulfilled, but Jewel had a remarkable education in art history, and she looked forward to working with it in Macon. She had become an accomplished artist and had planned to open her own art gallery in the city.

Alberto had claimed similar interests stating he also looked forward to his life at Fairland. He told her he did not plan to return with Martí to Cuba, for he knew there would soon be a war. He also told her of his desire to stay with her in Georgia to raise their children. This, of course, made Jewel love him all the more and want to share the rest of her life with him, but she knew he would always be torn over his decision not to return to Cuba. She left the door open to the possibility of living in both places. Fairland would remain in the family, she was certain; but whatever happened, she was sure they would forever be together.

Recalde was amazed by the amount of luggage the girl had in comparison to his own simple suitcase. She reminded him she had lived at the college for four years, and most of her life's treasures were with her. He gritted his teeth as, one after another he loaded the many pieces of luggage onto the carriage.

Dominique stood next to Professor Williams' wheelchair as they said their goodbyes. Asking Recalde's permission, Jewel presented the flowers to her professor, giving one of the white roses as well to Dominique, and telling them they had truly been wonderful friends and mentors to her. She said she would never forget them as long as she lived.

"I hope you will come to visit me in Georgia, the two of you. I would love to show you Fairland," she said with tears in her voice.

"But of course, mon amí, I would never refuse such a lovely invitation," Dominique said wiping a tear from her own eye.

"Nor would I," the professor agreed. She looked at Recalde with a keen eye. "And you, sir, will take care of our Jewel, will you not?"

"Of course, Doctor Williams," he responded with a click of his heels and a slight bow. "She is my Jewel as well as yours, remember." Recalde kissed Jewel's hand to punctuate his response. Williams frowned. There was something about his smooth attitude she did not like. He seemed almost dangerous, though she could not determine why she had that feeling. She had, in essence, become Jewel's guardian – not just a mentor – and her parental instincts were extremely sensitive at this moment. She turned to Jewel and reached up to pull her down to kiss her cheek.

"Jewel," she whispered, "Be careful of that man." Jewel straightened up and looked surprised by her comment. "Won't you?" Dr. Williams said aloud.

"Of course. Of course I will write as soon as I can." She glanced up at Recalde wondering if he had heard the professor's warning. "As soon as I get settled I will send you a note." Dominique kissed both her cheeks and stepped back so Recalde could help Jewel into the carriage. Waving goodbye and throwing kisses, the young couple was soon off to the train station. He helped her onto the train and then walked ahead of her to their seats as if they were not together.

Traveling with Alberto seemed like a dream come true for Jewel as she snuggled next to her intended. Recalde's attention was on other things, though. He finished up some papers he would be sending back to Martí as soon as they arrived. Her clinginess was beginning to get on his nerves.

"Please!" He said, moving closer to the edge of the seat.

She sat up straight and looked at him. His eyes blinked rapidly a few times before continuing. He smiled. "Please go to sleep, my darling. I will awaken you when we arrive. It has been a very strenuous day for you." He reached for her hand and kissed her palm, then turned back to his paperwork.

José Martí had been traveling back and forth to Brazil and would soon be returning to New York. He had an appointment with President Arthur who had made it plain he was strictly against the independence of Cuba, and desired to keep a quiet relationship with Spain. Despite the president's feelings, Martí had hoped he would be able to convince him to at least consider his pleas on behalf of the Cuban people.

When Martí asked Recalde if he could join him at the meeting in New York, Recalde said he would be traveling to Georgia to meet with some of the politicians there regarding funding. Martí, blind to Recalde's plans for Jewel, but concerned the cause was always in need of more funding, did not question his leaving at such an important time. Martí's demeanor had changed – he had become very businesslike since he lost Jewel, which had not escaped Recalde's notice; another reason for resenting this woman. He would be sure her money was his, and then he would end the relationship as soon as it began.

Davey stood at the station with his land manager, Noah Lee II, waiting for his sister at the station. When Jewel stepped onto the platform, they greeted each other with the enthusiasm of two lost children having just been reunited.

"Oh, Davey! I am so happy to see you! I've missed you so!"

"As have I, Sissy. Hey, you're lookin' pretty good since the last time I saw you. New clothes, new hair; I should've sent you off to school earlier," he joked. Jewel laughed and playfully slapped his shoulder.

"Really! You were the one who was trying to keep me home. I seem to recall some words like, 'No sister of mine will be stayin' in this den of iniquity.'"

"Sin – a hovel of sin – is what I said," he countered. "But you seem to have fared well, Sis. Are you well?" David looked down upon his older sister who stood a half foot shorter than he.

"Yes, Davey, I am. I am very well," she said. She reached for Recalde's hand. "Davey, please allow me to introduce my friend, Alberto Macías Recalde."

Davey looked past her at Recalde who was standing politely to the side listening to their banter. David stretched out his hand.

"My pleasure, I'm sure."

"Mucho gusto, Señor. I am pleased to meet with your acquaintance." Davey was surprised by Recalde's Cuban accent, but said nothing. The train ride had been tiring for Jewel, so Davey decided not to mention anything about their relationship on the trip back to Fairland. With Lee driving the team and Recalde sitting next to him in front, Davey kept the conversation light hoping to corner her later.

Servant staff had been restored to Fairland under Noah Lee's and Davey's management, and they happily welcomed Jewel home preparing her bedroom with fresh flowers and new bedding. Davey had done a wonderful job of renovating Fairland House over the past four years. After they arrived, Jewel retired to rest in her own room while Davey gladly showed Recalde his quarters and gave him a tour of Fairland. He wanted to take this time to find out Recalde's intentions toward his sister. Recalde countered with questions of his own.

The two men strolled down the walking path towards the peach orchard. Davey wisely spoke little, but Recalde was a volume of information.

"Yes, I came to America shortly before I met your sister. She has been a delight to me ever since."

"You seem very close," Davey hedged.

"You might say that," Recalde responded, smoothing down his mustache. He did not want to give Jewel's brother any more information than necessary. "She is very dear to me," he lied. He looked down at the ground when he said it, which did not escape Davey's notice.

They walked through to the other side of the orchard. Davey plucked a peach from one of the few fruit-bearing trees still left on the property. He had plans to bring the orchard back to its former glory, but that would take more time and more money. He offered a peach to Recalde.

"Very nice," the Cuban said as he examined its red-gold skin. "Fairland is aptly named. I understand you own another farm some ways away.

"Yes, southeast of here. My wife and children will be joining us later."

"So, Jewel has the responsibility of running this property alone?"

"Yes, in a manner of speaking. But I've hired a property manager for her. He's done a great deal to improve the place. Lee's the name. He's a relative of my late foster mother – a grandson, I believe."

"I see," Recalde said. He will not be here for long, he thought to himself. "And you have no other relatives?"

"Not that I know of. Maybe some in Ireland or England, but we have no record of anyone."

"How sad for you," he said. *How glad for me,* he thought. "I look forward to meeting your children. I hope to have children some day, as well."

"Will they be Jewel's children?" Davey asked bluntly. Recalde's right eyebrow raised, and a half smile registered on his lips.

"Perhaps," was all he said. He and Davey walked back quietly to Fairland House. After her rest, Jewel met Davey in the back yard.

"Davey, you are so handsome! I can hardly believe over four years have passed since we last saw each other." Jewel shook her head as she leaned over to kiss his cheek. They were sitting together in the chairs under their favorite climbing tree. They were quiet for a moment, enjoying just being together again. Finally, Jewel took a chance to talk about Recalde.

"I'm sure you'll like Alberto, Davey. He's truly a wonderful man. He is a patriot to his country, you know, but even so, he wants to stay here with me at Fairland. He's asked me to marry him." Davey looked at her, unsure about what to say. "We thought we would marry in a couple weeks."

"I'm sure you're right, sister. He seems very nice." Davey said no more about him. He had felt an underlying tension between Jewel and Recalde, but could not discern the cause. "Lorraine and the children will be joining us for the week," he said not wishing to pursue the other subject any further.

"That's nice." Jewel looked at him, wondering what he really thought about Recalde's proposal. She knew her brother well enough to know he was not telling her everything. "Is she well?"

"Yes, very well. We will have another child near Thanksgiving." He smiled proudly when Jewel nudged him.

"Oh, Davey. What a blessing! And I will have another niece or nephew." The conversation fell into silence once again. Jewel had never felt uncomfortable talking with her brother before. What had changed? "Well, I'm sure supper must be about ready. Shall we go in?"

"Yes, of course. You go on ahead. I want to check on the livestock before we turn in. It looks like there may be a storm." He looked up at heavy clouds above them. Jewel stood up and leaned over to kiss his cheek.

"Davey, it is so good to be with you again. Truly it is!" She hoped she didn't sound as unsure as she felt.

"I feel the same way, Jewel. Go on in now before it starts to rain." He returned a kiss on her cheek and headed for the barn.

Recalde had been watching the two of them from the upstairs window in his room. Anxiously wondering when the brother would be leaving so he could search the house, Recalde watched Jewel as she entered the back door. He backed away from the window. He was here under the pretext that Cuba needed his help, and Jewel's money. Recalde knew he would have to handle this mission very carefully, and to him it was a mission.

Later that night, insomnia kept Davey from sleeping. The weather had turned violent – another tropical storm had come up from the Caribbean threatening the entire Southeastern Seaboard. Knowing the livestock would be unsettled in the barn, he had a couple of the men servants, Samuel and Jacob, run out with him to see if they could quiet the animals down.

Opening the massive barn door was nearly impossible, for the wind fought the three men as if they were its enemies. Then, as they entered the barn, a tree was struck by a bolt of lightening. A large branch, still burning from the blow, fell onto the roof of the old structure caving it in. Just to the right of where Davey was standing, a beam fell over him, knocking him off his feet. The beam landed on his leg, and Davey screamed as pain from the broken tibia seared up his leg. Cinders from the branch fell onto the straw next to him, and it was quickly ablaze.

"Samuel! Samuel, help me!"

"I's a comin', Misah David. Hol' on!"

The old African man ran over to help Davey, calling out to Jacob who was in the stall working with one of the geldings, trying to calm him. Fire licked at Davey's foot and crawled quickly up the old wooden wall by the stable. Sam pulled up on the beam as Samuel dragged Davey out from under it. He then released the horses from their stalls as the first and third stables caught fire, dry hay lighting up like match sticks. It seemed like only seconds before the entire building was ablaze. The men barely got Davey out in time. Helping Davey cross the yard, the three of them stood in the pouring rain to watch the structure burn. The old, dry wood burned quickly despite the rain, and there was nothing they could do to stop it.

Jewel still slept regardless of all the commotion. She had had a long week preparing for her graduation and then the trip south. Recalde, on the other hand, was very much awake. He stood at the window in the hallway watching the men pull Davey from the barn and then watched as cinders blew up through the hole in the roof. The barn would soon be nothing but a cinder itself, he thought, and he realized his plans for searching the house had been spoiled. He supposed he should awaken Jewel so as not to cast suspicion on himself, so he quickly walked over to her room and knocked on the door. Jewel did not stir. Opening it slightly he stepped in and watched her sleep for just a moment before he approached her bed. She was a beautiful woman, he had to admit, but he had a mission to accomplish, and her beauty could not deter him from it.

"Jewel. Wake up, my love." He touched her cheek with the back of his hand.

"What?" Jewel looked into Recalde's face. She sat up. "What is it, Alberto?"

"You must come. There is a fire in the barn," was all he said. Jewel was out of her bed in a second, grabbing her robe and running out the bedroom door leaving Recalde to follow. Before he did, he glanced around her room trying to figure out where she would have hidden her treasures. He spotted the cedar chest at the foot of the bed and decided that would be the best place to start. *But when*, he wondered.

Jewel ran down the staircase quickly, meeting the servants as they brought Davey into the house. She immediately took charge of the situation.

"Bring him into the library, Samuel," she said urgently. Davey yelled out in pain as they hefted his leg onto the sofa. Although the bone was obviously broken, it had not protruded through his skin. Nevertheless, Jewel knew it would have to be set immediately. Samuel stood back dripping water on the carpet, hat in hand, looking mournfully over his mistress' shoulder.

"I's sorry, Miss, I tries to he'p him, but that timber jes' come down right on top o' him. I's sorry to say, Miss, de barn's los'." The old man had been with Jewel's family since before her father's death, and was the only one who had stayed on throughout the war, despite the release of the other servants. He had raised his family on Fairland, and Jewel's loss was his own.

"Thank you, Samuel. You've done just what you needed to do."

Davey opened his eyes and looked at his sister, pain written across his face. "The barn burned down, Sis. Couldn't stop it. The horses are out, though. The boys'll have to round them up in the mornin'." Even in his agony, he was the epitome of reason.

"Oh, pooh, Davey, forget that ol' barn. It needed to be replaced anyway. It's you I'm worried about. We need to get the doctor," she said looking up at Samuel with pleading eyes. He simply smiled and put his hat back on his head.

"I be back in jes' a little bit, Miss. Ol' Doc Beal live jes' down de road." He and Jacob ran out into the rain and rode as fast as they could to retrieve the doctor.

Davey passed out shortly after Samuel and Jacob left the house. The storm seemed to be calming a bit, though lightening could still be seen in the distance. Jewel stood at the window of the library looking out at the burning barn. Though the barn had been completely gutted, thankfully, the rain had kept the fire from spreading to other buildings, including the mansion. *Thank God for small favors*, she thought to herself. Recalde came up behind her wrapped his arms around her waist.

"Do not worry, my love. We will replace it soon enough. We will build a temporary shelter for the animals and then we will restore the barn." He nuzzled her neck.

"Of course you're right, Beto. It's just such a sad beginning to our life here." She turned towards him.

"Oh, but you are wrong!" Recalde said confidently. "It is just a new beginning. You will see, my love. Everything will turn out for the best." He kissed her lips and then led her to the door. "I insist you go back to bed. Your brother will be fine here on the sofa. I will watch over him."

"Oh, but I couldn't, Beto. He's my brother. You go on upstairs and get some rest. I will be fine here in the chair. Go on up, now." Reluctantly, Recalde turned to go up the stairs.

"You are sure you do not need me?"

"I'm sure, thank you." She looked at him with longing in her eyes. "I love you, Beto."

"I, too, my love." Her hopeful smile could have warmed the coldest fish, but Alberto Recalde hadn't noticed. Hesitating before going up the stairs, he wondered if his response lacked sincerity. He hoped not. He needed her to believe him now during these final, important steps toward Cuba's independence. As he turned to go up the staircase, Jewel retreated to the library, closing the door behind her. Hearing the door close, Recalde hurried up the stairs.

At the top of the staircase, instead of turning left to go into his bedroom, he turned to the right into Jewel's. He followed the wall first to check for squeaky floorboards, and felt behind the pictures for a possible safe. Nothing was behind any of the four pictures in the bedroom. As quietly as he could, he slipped over to the cedar chest he had identified earlier as the easiest target. Trying the lid, he found it locked. Cursing under his breath, he looked up at her dresser and eyed a box where she kept small items. When he opened the lid, music tinkled from the box. Quickly closing it, he stood still for a moment to listen for footsteps. He disengaged the key and peered into the box. Nothing was in it except hairpins.

One drawer at a time, he ran his hands through Jewel's personal wear, stocking drawer and petticoats until he happened upon another small box. Lifting up the lid carefully, he deftly searched its contents to find two small keys. The first key did not fit the lock to the chest. Throwing it back into the small box, he picked up the other, and then dropped it on the rug where it bounced and slid under her dresser. Recalde dropped to his knees to look for the key when he heard voices coming up the staircase.

"I'll find the bandages as quickly as I can, doctor," Jewel called. "Lizzy," she said to her maid, "Go tell Samuel to find some strong splints while I go upstairs to find something to make bandages for the doctor."

"Yes'm. Right away!"

Recalde flattened out on his stomach and slid under Jewel's bed. Looking to his left, he saw by the foot of the dresser, the key that had dropped from his hand. He reached for it just as Jewel walked into the bedroom and stood by her dresser. Pulling his hand back slowly, he watched as her foot pushed the key under the heavy furniture. His frustration was nearly audible, and he caught a sigh before it escaped from his mouth. Jewel opened the drawer to her dresser and pulled out one of her old petty coats. Recalde heard a loud tearing noise as she ripped it apart one piece at a time. Agonizing minutes passed before she finished, and her foot just barely kicked him as she leaned over the bed to collect all the material she had torn. She finally turned and quickly left the room.

Relieved, Recalde let out a breath of air and slid out again from under the bed. Before he stood up, he reached under the dresser for the key, but it was beyond his reach. Standing at the end of the dresser, he tried to move it, but with the combination of the looking glass attached to the weight of the heavy oak wood furniture, he was unable to draw it away from the wall without making some noise. Looking around the room for something with which he could reach the key, he spotted a parasol in the corner. Tiptoeing over to it, he grabbed the parasol and headed back to the dresser just as Davey screamed in pain. Recalde's heart jumped and the parasol nearly hit the floor. He thought thievery was certainly a nerve-racking business and he was not well-practiced. Catching his breath, he knelt to the floor, made the sign of the cross over his chest, and believing God was certainly behind his mission, said a quick prayer asking for help. He then lay down and reached for the key with the parasol. Slowly he dragged the small piece of metal forward until he could grasp it in his hand. He turned and knelt before the cedar chest.

The tumbler clicked as the key turned in the lock. Finally Recalde was able to see into the chest. On top was a beautiful wedding dress, most likely the one Jewel had spoken of many times as having been handed down to her from her mother. She had mentioned there was also a necklace given to her of which Recalde had made a mental note. Lifting up the material of the dress, he saw another box. He reached for it, and carefully opening it, he found nothing but a pile of papers. He searched through them to see if there was anything that could give him a clue as to the whereabouts of the necklace. There were some bank papers and underneath those papers was yet another key. He carelessly replaced the top of the box leaving papers sticking out the bottom and threw it into the bottom of the chest. He knew he would not find the necklace this night. Shutting the cedar chest, he replaced the key in the small box and placed it back into the drawer under the petticoats.

Slipping out of Jewel's bedroom, he returned to his own. He took off his robe and threw it on a chair in the corner. Pacing, he chided himself for yet another failure. It had been a night of fumbling and stupidity. Recalde knew he would have to be cleverer if he was to ever find the diamonds that would pay for the war in Cuba.

The morning sun was just rising when Recalde finally slept. Jewel had been awake with Davey most of the night, as had the rest of the household, so the day began later than usual. Davey's wife, Lorraine, drove up in her carriage with the children shortly after brunch. At first excited to see Jewel and her new intended, she was quickly distressed when she heard about Davey's unfortunate accident.

"Who will manage our farm, now?" she asked selfishly. Davey had learned over their many years of marriage that Lorraine did not handle stressful situations well. He was the master of their property, and coddled greatly, she was the perfect Southern Belle in their home.

"Oh, come on, Lorrie, I ain't dead," Davey assured her. "If I can handle both my sister's property and our own at one time for over four years, I am sure I can handle ours alone from a sitting position." Somehow Lorraine, still the spoiled youngest daughter of the Scruggs family, was not comforted. Davey told her he would only have to be bed ridden for a week or two, and then he would be able to walk on crutches. In the meantime, they would be able to get to know Jewel's new husband, show him the ropes and help him get started on the plantation.

Recalde played his part well, he thought, and playing up to Lorraine made her believe him. His attentiveness to Jewel was very impressive, from her sister-in-law's point of view. Davey, on the other hand – a keen judge of character – was not fooled. He had a gnawing feeling Recalde was not everything he pretended to be, and before Jewel got married, he would have a serious talk with his sister.

The family had been together for three weeks preparing for the big celebration. Finally, the day before the wedding, Davey pulled Jewel aside and asked her to speak with him. They met in the back yard under the old oak tree.

"What is it, Davey?"

"Sissy, I have to ask you a favor."

"Why, anything, Davey. You know that." Jewel touched his cheek with her hand.

"Jewel, I know you are planning to marry this man, but I can only say I encourage you to hold off for a bit." Davey looked at her with steady eyes.

"David Reginald Culpepper. I am getting married in less than one day. We have all this food and we have people coming in from as far as New York. What are you talking about?" Jewel's face reddened as she confronted him. She turned her back on him for just a moment, and then facing her brother again, she said, "I think you're just jealous."

"Jealous? Of what?" he demanded, struggling to stand up on his crutches.

"Of Alberto, of course. He's taking your big sister away from you."

"My dear Jewel. You have been away for nearly five years. What in the wide world would make me jealous? I am simply saying I don't trust this man." Davey moved wrong and turned his bad leg. Wincing, he sat back in the wrought iron chair.

"Serves you right," she mocked him vehemently. "Now if you will allow me, I intend to return to my duties for this wedding. You may be a part of it if you wish, or you may leave. That is entirely up to you, my dear brother." Jewel sniffed, held her head high, and stiff backed, she retreated to the house. Davey had not seen his sister this angry since she was a little girl. He knew she was under too much pressure from the wedding and having to juggle her duties on the farm while caring for him. He sat there angry both at himself for not handling things better, and at Jewel for getting herself into something bigger than even he knew.

Jewel went back into the house, and inquiring of Lizzy where Recalde was, she headed up the stairs. Looking into his room, she noticed he was not there, so she continued on to her own. There, standing over her cedar chest, was Alberto Recalde with a box of receipts in his hand.

"Alberto, what are you doing?" Recalde nearly dropped the box when he heard her voice.

"Oh! Excuse me, my darling, but I was just looking at your beautiful dress." He tried to look confident with his answer.

"Alberto, that chest was locked. Where did you find the key?" Jewel looked at him with questions in her eyes. The guilt written across his face and the look in his eyes quickly enabled her to see what it was he had done and why. She looked at her open dresser drawer and then back at him.

"Oh, no. No, no, no, Alberto, please tell me it isn't true. How could you have known? I kept them a secret all these years." She asked. "But it only makes sense. All the tension, your coldness toward me on the way here. You only wanted my father's diamonds?" Recalde's face reddened as she spoke, but his eyes were as cold as iron. Somehow he had found out her secret; somehow he knew she had the Jewel. As the truth made it course from her brain to her heart, Jewel looked at him with tears in her eyes and pain stabbing her heart.

"The gems are truly all you ever wanted. It wasn't me after all, it was the diamonds." Her legs gave way and she sunk into a pile of hoop skirts and petticoats. "I can't believe I fell for such a lie," she said more to herself than to the one who had torn her heart in two. Alberto Recalde looked at her, refusing to give in to the pitiful sight. He threw the box into the cedar chest and slammed the top down.

"And why not? You would have your man and I would have your money. It is for a good cause, the cause of Cuba's independence from España, which you fully support, do you not?" He walked over to her and pulled her to her feet. Holding her arms in the vice of his strong hands, he kissed her lips with a fervency he hadn't used before. Jewel backed up and slapped him. The Irish fire in her soul had indeed been kindled as she stood away from the man with whom she had been so infatuated.

"José would never take your filthy money, Señor. He is an honorable man. You low-life dog, get out of my house!"

"I shall never leave, my love. I have you now no matter what you say." His accent oozed with disdain and Jewel knew he was right. He stood at her bedroom door looking back at her silhouette in the sunlight. Laughing he simply turned to go to his room. Suddenly Jewel could no longer hold back her fury. She ran at him and pushed his back with such force he stumbled towards the stairs. He caught himself, and grabbing her arm, pulled her around in front of him. Her foot slipped on the carpet. Screaming as she fell, Jewel was all cotton material and petticoats tumbling down the flight of stairs. She lay at the bottom, unconscious. Recalde stood motionless at the top of the stairs, looking down on Jewel's still body. If he'd killed her, he knew he was dead himself.

Meanwhile, Lorraine, having heard part of the argument from the library, had called Davey from the back yard. Just as Davey came through the hallway on his crutches, he saw his sister pushing Recalde from her room. It was as if the whole scene occurred in slow motion. He saw Recalde reach for his sister and turn her toward the stairs, and then watched helplessly as she fell. His crutches fell to the floor as he put up his arms to yell at Recalde.

"No! Jewel!"

Davey did not know if she had fallen to her death, but reacting to Recalde's abuse to his sister, he pulled his revolver from his vest holster, aimed and fired. Davey had never been a good shot, and his aim was proof of that. The backlash knocked him off his feet, and Recalde was only winged in the shoulder. After recovering from the initial shock, Recalde only looked at the blood on his hand before he turned back into Jewel's room and jumped out the upstairs window.

Downstairs, Lorraine was quickly by Jewel's side. She picked up Jewel's limp hand to check her pulse, and finding it still strong, she patted Jewel's cheek to awaken her. Davey crawled over to Lorraine who assured him she would be okay.

"Thank God! She's not dead," he said. He held his hand over his chest, and took in a breath, relieved.

"W-what happened?" Jewel said, trying to sit up. She saw her brother with the gun in his hand. "Alberto, he's –."

Davey held his sister in his arms. "I know, Jewel. I know." Jewel could only cry.

Recalde became a hunted man. Knowing he had dishonored his friend and brother, José Martí, he could not return to New York for his support. Instead, he made a run for Florida where he caught a ship to South America. Recalde planned to hole up with acquaintances he knew through Martí.

Hearing about Jewel's misfortune and Recalde's betrayal, José Martí sent her a large bouquet of flowers with a note expressing his regrets.

> *My dearest Jewel,*
>
> *My heart was greatly saddened to hear about your loss. I am grieved I brought this horrible betrayal into your life. You will always be close to my heart, and though I know we can never be together, I hope that some day you will find someone who will love you as much as I do still. I shall never stop hunting Alberto Recalde until he is found and punished.*
>
> *Ever your servant,*
>
> *José Martí*

Martí's words never comforted Jewel. She was heart broken by the only man she had ever loved, and she now also knew the pain she had caused her friend, José Martí.

Years passed before Jewel recovered from the harrowing experience of knowing and loving Alberto Recalde. Sleep often evaded her, and she would wander downstairs at night to the library to pull out the diary left to her by her father. She traced his handwriting with her finger and wondered if she would ever find a man who would be like the one who'd written these comforting words. But the Irish fire within her had been quenched, and she had no further interest in following her father's dream. She no longer wondered where the adventurer she had never known had hidden the diamond. She didn't want to know. It seemed that anyone with whom it was associated was either dead or harmed in some way. She figured it was better off lost forever.

Taking the Rosenbrand necklace from the safety deposit box, she gave it to Davey for safe keeping, giving him instructions that her oldest niece should have it on her wedding day. Even if it was glass, which Jewel still believed, the necklace might be of value some day; and since she knew she would never have a daughter of her own, it was only fitting the one who carried her name should have it.

Jewel Victoria Culpepper the second grew to be as beautiful as her namesake. Her aunt left her entire estate to her for her brothers would share their father's land. It would take forty more years before the land was legally her inheritance, but one day she walked onto the plantation and did not leave it until late in life.

Having undertaken the same course as her aunt – Art History at Vassar, and having spent so much time over the years with her Auntie Jewel, she had caught her vision. She became determined to make Fairland Farm into something worth remembering – a museum and art gallery in honor of her aunt and those who had gone on before.

The Jewel of Africa was never found, but the tradition and mystery of the diamond lived on through the generations. Every first Culpepper daughter was named after the gem for a hundred years.

Part III
The Final Generation

Chapter XII

A Jewel is Born

December 15, 1960, Minneapolis, Minnesota.

Early morning light streamed through metal blinds to brighten the dreariness of a sterile hospital room. Joseph Culpepper stood by his wife's beside at St. Barnabas Hospital holding his newest child in his arms. He and his wife, Gwen, had already birthed three boys and this one would be their last. The two of them had been at odds over a boy's name, believing their chances of having a girl had been lost, but he was satisfied now, for this baby was a girl. He could finally follow through with the family tradition.

Joseph's father had told him the legend, how Jewel Victoria I had been named after her mother and the lost gem, and though each generation had searched for the gem, the mystery diamond had never been found – even after 100 years – and so the name had continued down through the generations. Every first Culpepper girl born since 1860 had been named after the Jewel of Africa, and this child would be no different. Joseph found out later his daughter had been born on the exact day as her namesake, the first Jewel Victoria.

There had been four Jewel Victoria's all together. Joseph remembered his own Aunt Jewel fondly. An aristocratic woman, she remained in Texas where she and his father had been raised. She had married a fine officer of the Air Force and had had three children of her own. She was not an extremely attractive woman, but she was kind and loving. With a wonderful Texan drawl and a fine sense of humor, Aunt Jewel was always available to her brother, no matter what the circumstances.

Joseph's grandfather had moved the family from Georgia in the early 1930's, after deciding to make a living in the oil business near Houston. Unfortunately, his entrepreneurial efforts had never rewarded him successfully, so plumbing became the family trade. The only two children born to him were Joseph's father, Jason and his sister, Jewel. The rest of the family remained in Georgia, but little was known about them.

Joseph had heard stories about the plantation near Macon inherited by Aunt Jewel, but in his mind Fairland Farm was a thing of the past. As far as Joseph knew, there was little property left, if any at all. None of that history ever really touched him, at least until now when his own little Jewel was born. Even if the little one in his arms inherited the family farm because of her family name, it may not be worth the bother. He figured he would have to do some studying on the subject when he got some time.

Nevertheless, all the time in the world would not have been enough for Joseph Culpepper. He was a working man with a family to feed and a part time student. The university had begun offering night classes two years before, so he had started an education in engineering. He believed the low income he received as a plumber would grow considerably when he was finished. For the time being, however, he laid pipe for a major contractor in the Twin Cities. He looked forward to the day after he graduated when he would not have to do so much physical labor. Instead of the boss telling him what to do, he would tell the boss what needed to be done.

By the time Joseph finally graduated from the university, blonde and blue-eyed Jewel was an action-packed, blue-jean-clad, three-year-old tomboy. Joseph's education had taken longer than he expected because he had a family to support, but he finally accomplished his dream. Little Jewel waved at her daddy from the stands when he stood before a crowd of hundreds to receive his degree.

Life had been financially challenging up until then, but the Culpepper family was happy. Elvis Presley, the Platters and the Beatles all made it to the top of the charts during the time Joseph worked on his degree, but in the fall of 1963, Joseph's '56 Buick was replaced with a brand new '64 Cadillac Hardtop, and Jewel no longer had to wear her brothers' hand-me-down pants. The boss had been pleased to promote him to assistant engineer on one of the new high rises in North Minneapolis. Things were finally really looking up; at least, for a while. The world was again in turmoil, and it would not be long before Joseph's world would change.

Joseph and Gwen sat together on the couch watching in horror as the news story flashed across the television set. Governor and Mrs. Connelly, and Jackie and John Kennedy sat across from one another waving to the crowd in a motorcade ambling along the route from Love Field to Dealey Plaza in Dallas. Suddenly, three shots rang out from a building across the street. The President's car sprang forward in a desperate attempt to escape from an assassin's bullets; but President Kennedy had been mortally wounded, and it was already too late. Joseph sat there, tears streaming down his face, realizing life in the United States would never be the same.

John F. Kennedy's administration often paralleled the administration of Abraham Lincoln a hundred years before. The similarities between the two men were uncanny. A secretary had advised Kennedy not to go to Dallas; her name was Lincoln. Kennedy had been an American hero during World War II and was highly regarded by most Americans. Tragically, he fell to an assassin's bullet in November 1963, as had Lincoln nearly 100 years before. Vice President Samuel Johnson took Lincoln's place, as did Vice President Lyndon Baines Johnson after President Kennedy's death. The Civil War tore the Union apart during Lincoln's administration, and the Vietnam War would tear the Union apart in this generation. The war was in its beginning stages in 1963, and all-out conflict was imminent.

Joseph was confident war could not touch him. He had already served four years of active duty when he was younger. Now he had a family and too old to serve. Nevertheless, he was a reservist. Engineers were sorely needed outside of Saigon by 1965. The Seabees had already started working in Vietnam, but the brass wanted someone who knew the best way to design the required aircraft and military bases. Joseph was one of the first reservists to be recalled.

He and Gwen sat quietly together at the airport awaiting his flight to Fort Irwin in California. He held her left hand with his right, and held Jewel on his lap with his left. He wondered how long it would be before they'd see each other again, if they'd ever see each other again. Gwen didn't say much as she sat there, trying to hold back her tears. Joseph knew her. She'd wait for the children to go to sleep and she was alone to shed the tears she so bravely kept from falling.

Peter, Joseph's oldest son, now twelve, sat quietly next to him, ten-year-old Joe, Jr. and seven-year-old Thomas played at his feet.

"Dad?" Peter asked tentatively.

"Yes, Son?"

"I had a dream."

"What about?"

"I dreamed you were flying in the clouds without a plane," Peter, looking down at the floor, didn't want his dad see him cry. Four-year-old Jewel smacked his arm.

"Peter," she said matter-of-factly, one hand on her hip and her chin jutting out slightly, "Only Jesus can fly in the clouds without a plane." Mature for her age, Jewel sat on her daddy's lap with lips in a tight line, her bright blue eyes looking up at her dad, awaiting his affirmation.

"That's right, Jewel," said Joseph quietly. When he thought about Peter's dream, it bothered him. "Unless you go to meet Jesus," he added. Jewel thought for a moment.

"Oh, Daddy," she laughed. "You can't meet Jesus if you're not in heaven!" She giggled at the thought, but Peter looked at his father with an ominous feeling in his gut. He stood up, staring down at Jewel.

"Shut up!" Peter shouted. Gwen grabbed his arm.

"Peter, that's enough," she said. "This is hard enough on your father without you starting an argument." Peter frowned, pulled his arm away, and walked over to the large windows to watch the airplanes take off.

"It's okay, Gwen. Leave him alone," was all Joseph said.

"Daddy? Why's Peter so mad?" Jewel looked up innocently at her father.

"He's not mad, Jewel. He's just sad Daddy's going away." Jewel's lower lip protruded in a pout.

"Me, too, Daddy. I don't want you to go away."

"Me, too, Jewel." He hugged her and let her off his lap. The plane was about to board. Turning to Gwen, he simply told her he loved her and not to worry. They had already said their good byes, cried together and tried to work through their premature grief. It would be a hard six months. Nevertheless, Joseph had a duty to perform, and he was bound to it.

Walking out the terminal door, he waved back at his family from the field before he boarded the DC-8 that would take him to Fort Irwin for his briefing, and then on to Saigon.

Six months turned into nearly ten years before Major Joseph Culpepper permanently remained on U.S. soil. Over the years, he had returned home for visits, but after Vietnam, he was never quite the same. He had seen too much death, too much pain. In the end, after it was all finished, he had been wounded only emotionally.

Assigned to the military headquarters near Ho Chi Minh City, Joseph had been part of the final evacuation there before the Communist takeover. At the American Embassy, helicopters were overrun with people trying to escape occupation. As the aircraft rose into the air, he watched as women ran to the helicopters, trying to get their children onboard to safety. And then he saw their expressions of grief as they were pushed to the ground, their final hopes were dashed. Months later Joseph still heard their screams in his sleep.

Jewel was nearly grown by the time Joseph returned home permanently, but she never forgot sitting in her daddy's lap at the airport that dreadful day. She remembered her dad, quiet and loving, not wanting to leave his beloved family. Now, here she was nearly 14 years old at the end of the horrible war that was not a war. She didn't understand it all, but she was glad to have her dad home again.

She had often sat on her dad's lap asking him to recite the story behind her name, until one day her father said, "I don't remember a story like that. Leave me alone."

The adolescent stood to her feet and saw the faraway look in her father's eye. Somehow she knew she would never hear him tell the story again. Their relationship would never be the same again, either.

Away at college, Peter would often write to his sister to encourage her to keep up her studies so she could go to the university. He had taken Joseph's place as the father of the family during his long absences. Every time Joseph left after a short leave from the service, he would say, "Now, Peter, you're the man of the family. I want to hear good reports from your mother." And Peter had always taken his responsibilities very seriously. Now, tired of being "the man of the family," he was glad to be away at college.

Tommy and Joe, on the other hand, did not take their roles seriously. Joe was nearly 20, but never considered attending college. He wanted to skip out of anything requiring commitment. Tommy, however, had his mind on girls – lots and lots of girls. Every time he came home from school, he had another name on his tongue and another picture in his pocket.

Tommy and Joe were very close and shared many of the same interests – women, drugs, and alcohol. Tommy seemed to be a lost soul, and Peter knew Joe was into more than he was letting on. Peter had met him more than once at the door to help him into his bed. He couldn't help Joe, and Tommy wouldn't let Peter help him; Jewel, on the other hand, was different. Even if he couldn't help his younger brothers, he was determined his little sister would not fall into the traps of adolescence if he could help it.

One Saturday afternoon when Peter was home, Jewel sat on the couch staring at Monty Hall's, "Let's Make a Deal" one of the most popular game shows of the day.

"Pick door number three," she said urgently to the woman standing next to the host. The woman picked number two. She rolled her eyes. Number three was almost always the best door. She switched off the TV and slumped back in her chair as Peter walked through the door with a load of books in his hand.

"Hey, Sis, what's up?"

"Nothing," she responded. Peter looked down at her knowing better. He'd been her suedo father for too long not to know something was bothering her.

"Okay, what's the matter?" He knelt down in front of her and gave her a grin. She sighed.

"It's Dad. He's just not the same any more." Peter patted her knee and stood to his feet.

"You're right, Jewel. He isn't the same. I don't think he ever will be. War does that to people," he responded, wise for his years.

"He doesn't even remember the story about the diamond."

Peter looked down at her, rather surprised. Even he remembered the story though he couldn't have cared less about it. He knew it meant a lot to Jewel, though, because it was their dad who told her the story from the first. He thoughtfully bit the side of his cheek and stood up to his full six foot height.

"Tell you what," he offered. "We'll sit down with dad and write the story down for him. That way he can remember it better, and you'll have it to look at when you want to." The teenager did not accept his suggestion. She sat up straight in her chair, tears welling up in her eyes.

"You don't get it, do you?" she asked vehemently. Eyes wide, Peter was taken aback. "Dad isn't the same. It's not the story. It's Dad. I don't ever want to hear that stupid story again!" she shouted at him. Then crying, she ran out of the den to her room, slamming the door behind her.

Peter just stood there, stunned. His little sister was growing up.

Chapter XIII

An Archeological Discovery

Among Jewel's favorite activities during her first years at the University of Minnesota included autumn walks between University Hospital and the Northrup Auditorium. She enjoyed the scenery, the rustling of dry leaves under her feet, and the people she'd meet along the way. Individuals of all ages greeted her as they rushed by to get to their classes. One of her favorite people was Professor Cole. He easily stood a head taller than Jewel, and his wiry build made him look a little like a marionette. Jewel always smiled as he approached, for she could see him sauntering down the lane from a distance. She wondered if the beard he sported made up for the lack of hair on his head. Wearing an old tweed jacket and matching Homburg hat, a walking stick and briefcase in one hand, a pipe in the other, the elder history professor would walk with her to discuss the events of the day.

The weather this mid-October day in 1981 was pleasantly warm. The sun was shining through red and gold leaves on campus and Jewel was enjoying it immensely. Being born in Minnesota, however, did not mean she enjoyed Minnesota's cold weather. She shivered when she thought about it. Today though, it was a lovely 74 degrees – not too hot and not too cold. She sat on the bench across from the Administration Building just as Professor Cole greeted her from behind.

"Hello, young lady. How are you on this lovely day?" he asked, tipping his hand.

"Why, hello, Sir. I'm fine, thank you. It's good to see you," she answered, flashing him a winning smile. He sat on the bench next to her, propping up his briefcase as a proper barrier of separation between them. Jewel smiled. Professor Cole was a married man, and he had mentioned to many a student that improprieties could be detrimental to both a student's and a professor's career. He did not want any gossip about him to start this late in his life; he preferred a quiet retirement in his old age.

"I have something for you, Miss Culpepper." He pulled a piece of paper out of his case and handed it to her. "You were asking about some different pathways, were you not?"

The paper contained the name of the head of the Archeology Department and a description of courses required for a degree in the subject.

"I realize not everyone can be a History Major, though I believe you would do well in it." The professor said, eying her to give her a chance to recant; she did not. Sighing with a smile, he continued. "However, Archeology is more than history. It's art, communications, history and more. I believe you will enjoy it."

Her eyes opened wide with excitement. She had only mentioned it in passing, but when Professor Cole described it, it sounded exciting, and she became extremely interested.

"Thank you!" she responded, slipping the paper into her pocket. They sat together amiably for a moment before she continued. "You know, I have thought and thought about what you said, Professor. You're right. People don't know enough about world history and the ramifications of their actions. That's why Vietnam was such a disaster. The history of those Asian countries is full of war and destruction, and Americans just weren't ready for the war, let alone the culture shock. Maybe if we had sent some archeologists over there first to study the history and the people, we might have been better prepared."

The twinkle in his eye confirmed her theory. Professor Cole wasn't fooled. He asked, "How is your father?"

He had met young Jewel just a year before, but he already knew her well enough to understand that when she started to talk about Vietnam, she was referring to his experiences there.

"Oh, he's about the same – doesn't talk much. I visit the Veteran's Hospital where he's staying just about every weekend." She didn't look at him. Tears fell too easily when she talked about her father. Peter and her two other brothers had pretty well written their father off, but not Jewel. He was her hero as a child, and he remained her hero as a young woman. She had decided many years before that he would move into her home some day and she would take care of him, even if no one else cared to.

"That's very commendable of you," the professor responded. He puffed on his pipe thoughtfully. "Well, I must be off. I have a class in just a few minutes. We're studying the Egyptian pharaohs this quarter. I have some time lines to draw."

He smiled down at her as he stood to his feet. "Have a nice day, Miss Culpepper. I look forward to seeing you in one of my classes again soon."

He tipped his hat and she responded with a smile and a relaxed salute before he sauntered down the lane, briefcase and walking stick in one hand, pipe in the other.

Later in the evening, Jewel checked her pants pockets before throwing her blue jeans into the wash machine. She pulled out the paper Professor Cole had given her.

"Hmm. Professor Noah Lee V, Doctor of Archeology. Huh. I wonder if he's anything like Professor Cole?"

* * *

The Archeology 101 classroom smelled musty when Jewel walked in. Dust particles floated past her face in the sunbeams from the windows and old wooden desks and chairs carried many years of history, which was obvious by their appearance. Hundreds, maybe even thousands, of men and women have been in these chairs, she thought. Names were carved in the desks, gum was stuck to the bottom of the chairs, and cracks were in the legs.

Looking around at a few of the other students who were slumped in their chairs, she noted none of them seemed particularly thrilled by their attendance. Jewel, on the other hand, was ecstatic. She finally knew where she was headed after four excruciatingly long years of decision making. She had vacillated between her love of art history and music, and the idiotic concept she might be able to teach some young minds some day. She knew she had no real talent in the area of teaching, but she could dissect a passage of an encyclopedia in no time flat.

The professor looked up at her from his creaky chair hidden behind an old oak desk at the front of the room. Loudly clearing his throat, he stood to his feet to signal he was about to begin. When Jewel took a seat on the end of the last row, Professor Lee looked over his glasses rims at her. She self consciously moved up to a vacant seat in the second row.

Uncomfortable under his stare, she could not help but notice he was rather attractive. A man in his early-to-mid thirties, she guessed, his hair was a sandy brown. She couldn't see his eyes from where she was sitting, but she imagined them to be blue. Average in stature, about 5'9", he moved around the room easily; not like old Professor Wood, her old English professor, an elephant of a man who could barely get out of his chair to write on the blackboard. Jewel closed her eyes and shook her head. *Concentrate!* she reprimanded herself.

Professor Lee was a good teacher. Originally born and educated in Georgia, he was new at the university. He spoke with a soft, southern drawl while he explained the syllabus for the quarter, adding there would be two important projects due before the end of the quarter. One would be a paper on the findings of the archeological diggings in the Badlands, and the second would be a paper based on the family history of each student. They would have to provide a genealogy of their family, historical evidence of that genealogy, and physical proof of their family roots.

"Why would I ask you to provide to me your family history?" he asked, answering everyone's question before they asked it. "I'll tell you why. Each one of you has a past. You may not even know what that past entails, but it is a past, nevertheless. I suspect some of your ancestors came over from the Old Country, as I have heard a number of the Scandinavians here say it." The class laughed. "You may have treasures in your parents' attic which you have never explored. You may have ancestors dating back to the Vikings themselves – any of you with a Scandinavian background. Young people today have neither taken the time nor the energy to find out the least important facts of their families."

He looked at Jewel, who squirmed under his scrutiny.

The truth was Noah Lee knew exactly what was in Jewel's past. He had made a special point of investigating her when he saw her name on the list of incoming students. He had even suggested to Professor Cole that if he knew of any "bright, promising women" who would be interested in a career in archeology, he would take them under his wing to train them up in this most lucrative field. "As a matter fact," he said to the professor, "I was wondering about the Culpepper girl. Isn't she one of the honor students graduating in May?" Cole had said she was, and he would mention it to her the next time he saw her. And here she was, just as Lee had hoped.

He continued lecturing the students. "That is the foremost reason for archeology – to discover what happened to people in our pasts so we can improve our futures. Perhaps there's a treasure buried in your background and you don't even know it."

He looked directly at Jewel, but any innuendo he may have intended escaped her.

The class was an hour long, but for Jewel, it only seemed moments before Professor Lee dismissed his students. She sighed to herself when she stood up thinking she wished it could continue.

"So, Miss Culpepper," Professor Lee said standing next to her. "Did you enjoy the class?" Turning around, Jewel was surprised at how close to her he was standing. Backing up a step before she spoke, she smiled.

"Why, yes, Professor Lee. I thought it extremely interesting. I was telling my friend, Professor Cole, the other day how excited I was to be in the class. I was so pleased to find it would be open during this quarter."

"Yes, Professor Cole did mention you to me. He's a good man." Lee pushed the door open for her. "I'm sure you will enjoy the class, Miss Culpepper, as I will enjoy your being in it."

Jewel's eyes opened wide. Was that a pass? She dismissed the thought as quickly as it came to her.

* * *

Jewel was preparing to end her time at the university, and weeks passed quickly in this second quarter of her senior year. She had met many wonderful friends since starting there – her roommate, Jill, Charlie the mad biologist, and of course, Professor Cole; but no one could replace her childhood friend, Jonathan Tyler. They had met in fifth grade when they both sang for a community children's choir. They'd gone through the tempestuous adolescent years together, and now here they were, attending the university. Jonathan often accompanied her to classes, carrying her books for her or helping her with some difficult math problem. He was studying for a mechanical sciences degree, so they had few classes together, but he was always there when she needed him. He reminded her of a faithful puppy; he was always good company. They talked about everything, but for some reason, she dreaded telling him about Professor Lee. Though he was her dearest friend, she instead developed the fine art of avoidance.

"So, kiddo, what's going on?" Jonathan asked as they sat together in the U of M library. Their table stood between the stacks and the librarian, who looked at them sternly over her reading glasses. The matron held her index finger to her lips as a not-so-subtle reminder to stay quiet.

"Going on?" Jewel whispered. "Why do you think something is going on?"

"Because in the many years I've known you, you have always seemed to be in control. Except for the times you got involved with stupid guys, you knew what you were doing and pretty much where you were going – that is until now. What's going on with you?"

"Oh, nothing, really. I'm having trouble with one of my professors," she hedged. "I'm not doing very well in that class."

"Which one?"

"Archeology. I really can't say why." And she couldn't. She hadn't realized how infatuated she had become with Professor Lee, but she knew she liked him – a lot. Nevertheless, even talking to her best buddy about it was a little too uncomfortable. Somehow she knew it would bother him. "Don't worry about me, silly. Let's talk about you. You have a project due, right?" He nodded, fatigue written across his face. They gathered their books from the table, slipped past the disapproving librarian and headed to the exit.

"Yeah. I was up until three o'clock this morning trying to get this one aspect of the theory I'm working on. I still don't get it. I have to talk to my professor about it today." He paused and looked at her. "Maybe that's what you should do." She looked at him and frowned.

"What?"

"Your problem. Maybe you should just talk to your professor about it and he can help out," he responded as he pushed open the library door for her. Jewel shrugged her shoulders.

"Huh. That's simple. Maybe I should."

Noah Lee was an excellent communicator. His interest in archeology was just one of the many facets attracting her to him over the past few weeks, and it certainly didn't hurt he had gorgeous ice blue eyes and a captivating smile. A mere twelve years older than she, Jewel wondered if there could be a future with him. Trying desperately to keep her mind on her studies while he spoke, her defenses were melting fast.

It had been nearly a week since she had spoken to Jonathan about her situation, but she finally decided to follow Jonathan's advice and confront the professor with her problem.

"Professor Lee," she said after the rest of the students left the classroom. She stood up from her desk and held her books in front of her defensively.

"Yes, Miss Culpepper?" He looked up from his papers and smiled.

"May I speak with you for just a moment, please?" The tremor in her voice betrayed her. She was nervous and uncertain about how to begin the conversation.

"Of course," he said putting papers into his briefcase. "What can I do for you?" He walked around to the front of his desk and sat on the edge, propping one leg up on top of the desk and folding his hands on his lap. Jewel looked at him. She noticed how the muscle in his leg flexed as he moved. Shaking her head, she took a deep breath.

"Professor Lee, I seem to be having a problem with this class."

He leaned forward. "Oh, really? That surprises me, Miss Culpepper. You seem to me to be very comfortable. Your daily work is very good, and you take part in the discussion quite readily."

"Yes, sir," she hesitated. "That's not the problem." She could feel her face flush as she stood there.

"What is it, then? How can I help?" He moved toward her, and flustered, she took a backward step.

"You, sir. You are the problem," she said quickly. She looked down at her feet, hoping to hide her embarrassment. She couldn't. He pulled her chin up to look at him.

"I, Jewel?" He'd never called her Jewel before. It sounded good – really, really good. She closed her eyes trying to block out the smoldering look in his eyes. "How could there be a problem between us?"

"I'm sorry, Professor. I don't know how –." He was standing too close to her now and the scent of his aftershave filled her senses. He slid his arm around her waist and then leaned down and brushed her lips with his.

"I'm afraid you're a problem for me as well, Jewel." She leaned into him as he wrapped his arms around her. His mouth covered hers, and she was suddenly lost in a fog of desire.

Chapter XIV

A Clandestine Relationship

The fire cracked as Noah added another log. He had invited Jewel over to his elaborate apartment in one of the old store fronts renovated as condominiums near the banks of the Mississippi in Saint Paul. The building itself was over a hundred years old. Limestone brick had been sand blasted and re-tucked to promote its original beauty. Noah liked the look of its 19th century architecture. He'd often mentioned he thought he might have been born at the wrong time, and he actually belonged there.

Artifacts from some of the area diggings were shelved in his den, including a large arrowhead collection. He also had another collection – artifacts from the Civil War. An old Rebel cap and jacket hung on a rack near the fireplace; a musket and sword were displayed on the mantel.

This was the first invitation since they had started dating over a month before. It was on the "QT" of course, since it was against university rules for a professor to date one of his students. He always made sure they would never see each other on campus by meeting in the suburbs or somewhere outside the metro, hoping no one they knew would run into them. And Jewel never mentioned her rendezvous with Noah, neither to her roommate, Jill or even to Jonathan. She was falling in love, though she knew it was an impossible situation. She knew her friends – especially Jon – would never understand. Thus far they had met in little coffee shops or restaurants in a suburb or outlying city where they were unknown to anyone. Their relationship was innocent – hand holding, a kiss good night, a touch, but nothing more. Tonight, however, Noah decided to begin a new phase of his plan, which had so far been working well for him. Poking the fire, he smiled to himself as he remembered the look of surprise on her face when she'd read the note he had attached to her assignment. "Darling," he'd said, "Tonight let's take our relationship to a higher level. Meet me at my apartment." Her eyes were wide when she looked up at him. "Another A," he'd told her to cover her reaction from the rest of the class. "Good job, Miss Culpepper." She had thanked. Her face was crimson red as she spoke, but no one seemed to notice. Jewel was always getting A's. Noah chuckled. She was so easy.

There was a knock on the door, and Noah slowly put the poker back in its stand. Looking around to ensure everything was in place, he walked over to the door and peered through the peep hole. Jewel stood in the doorway dressed in simple black chiffon, held up by spaghetti straps. Tendrils of her golden hair fell daintily down to her shoulders, with the rest loosely knotted at the back of her head. Noah stood a moment to look at her. She was so young and so beautiful, but it wasn't her beauty captivating him. Around her neck was an antique ruby and diamond necklace. The Rosenbrand, he thought.

"May I come in?" she asked smiling up at him, leaning to the right to see if she could peek into his apartment.

"Why, of course, Miss Culpepper. I would be honored if you would come into my humble dwelling," he replied in his most genteel manner. He raised her hand and caressed it with his lips. She pulled her hand from his and skirted around him.

"Oh, Noah, this place is beautiful. I would never have thought you could do so much with such an old building!" She walked over to the wall and touched the limestone.

"It just takes a little imagination and a lot of money," he joked. "Come here." He sat down on his couch and patted the pillow next to him. Jewel hesitated then warily sat next to him. He looked at her and touched her cheek with the back of his hand. "Beautiful," he said simply. Jewel felt butterflies in her stomach.

"Noah, I –."

"Shh. Don't say anything." He leaned over and brushed her lips with his. "Jewel," he said her name with such passion. She could not help but melt into his arms. Noah decided he could take her now if he wanted to, but he held back. Pulling away, he stood to his feet. She looked up at him confused.

"Honey, we need to do this right," he said matter-of-factly as he stooped in front of the fire to stir the coals. Taking the poker from its stand, he pushed the logs an inch or two. "I don't want to take advantage of you when I know you are not ready."

"But, Noah, I am ready," she insisted. She smoothed the wrinkles out of her dress and sat up straight. She was still and innocent, but in every way she felt ready for an intimate relationship, especially with Noah Lee.

"No, Darlin', you are not. Let's wait and see what happens from here, okay?"

Jewel had always had to fight boys off, and she thought it strange this wasn't the case with Noah; but because he stopped when he did, she loved him all the more. In all her inexperience, she was sure this was the man she would marry. He stood up and held out his hand to lead her to the dining room where an antique oak table stood decorated with an antique lace tablecloth. Noah's plate was set at the head and Jewel's was at the end in formal Southern fashion. After asking his permission, she moved the setting to sit next to Noah. He held her chair as she sat and offered her a kiss on the cheek. His very touch sent chills up her spine.

Sitting next to each other, they discussed their future adventures together. Jewel had imagined the possibility of taking a trip to Egypt with Noah to discover the pyramids, or traveling to Mexico to study the Incas. She had adventure in her soul, and it thrilled her to think she might be able to accomplish something so grandiose in her lifetime, just like Henry Jones, the great World War II archeologist. She told him that as far as she knew, no one in her family had done anything as exciting since her great, great grandfather who had been in Africa.

"You had relatives in Africa?" Noah asked nonchalantly.

"Yeah. I don't remember much about it. There's a legend claiming he found a huge diamond and brought it to the states, but it was lost during the Civil War in Georgia. My dad told me I was named after it. The Jewel of Africa," she said dramatically, holding up an imaginary marquis. She giggled and then stuffed another piece of lettuce into her mouth.

"Really? That is interesting!" Noah took a bite of his steak. "Of course, you already know my family is from Georgia."

"Why, sah, I nevah would've guessed," she teased with an overdone southern accent.

"You mock me, young lady?" He pointed his fork at her. She smiled at him while she stole a mushroom off his plate.

"Of course," she joked. More serious, she continued. "My family hails from Georgia, too, but we ended getting all split up in the end. My grandfather moved from Macon to Houston, and then my father came up from Texas after his dad died." Noah nodded.

"Do you know anything about their life in Georgia?"

"No. I guess there's a distant cousin living on some property near Macon. That's all I know. Our property just sits there now. I think the mansion is a museum or something. My Great Aunt Jewel deeded it to me on my twenty-first birthday, but I have yet to see it."

"I see. Well, perhaps we should check it out some time in the future," he said nonchalantly. "So what happened to this 'Jewel of Africa'?" He glanced up at her as he played with his salad, hoping he hadn't sounded over interested.

"Honestly? I don't know. It was lost in the Civil War, they say, but the daughter of the man who found it was named after it, and it has been a family tradition to name the first daughters in the family Jewel ever since. There's no record of it anywhere." She fiddled with the gems around her neck as she spoke, unaware of their real worth. They were given to her father at her birth by his Aunt Jewel, and he had kept them in a bedroom drawer, not knowing their value either. Lee wondered if they were real, or just a very good copy. "I was told this necklace came from my great grandfather's discovery." She pulled at the necklace to look at it. Noah knew immediately she was ignorant of the necklace's value.

"I see. Well, tell me, darlin'. What would you do if you ever found that diamond, the Jewel of Africa?" Noah was fishing. He wanted to know what she knew about the jewel. He was certain she knew more than she was telling.

"You know, Noah, because of the legend surrounding my name, I have done quite a bit of research on diamonds over the years. Did you know the first recorded diamond from South Africa, the Cullinan, is still in the Crown Jewels of England today? They say it was the biggest diamond ever found. Now the government of South Africa claims it belongs to them, and it should never have left the country. They'd like to have it back."

"Really?" Noah sat listening quietly.

"Really, it's true! So you know what I'd do with that diamond? I'd give it back to the South African government. It was stolen from their country, and it belongs to those people. As an archeologist, wouldn't you agree?" To Noah, her naiveté was astounding.

"Absolutely, my dear. I do believe something so valuable should go to the most deserving, should it not?" He gave her a winning smile and sipped his coffee. Jewel's eyes sparkled. She felt very much at ease with Noah Lee. It was comforting to know she would marry someone who was her equal.

They had had a very romantic rendezvous, laying on pillows in front of a blazing fire. They'd talked until midnight when he insisted she get home before he was "tempted beyond his control." He practically shoved her out the door. Leaning against it, he yawned, turned out the lights and watched her dance out to her car. His lips curled at the corners. *About time you left,* he thought as he pulled off his shirt and headed for bed.

Jewel fairly floated through the door of her small apartment late that night. She was in a dream world by the time she left his apartment to return to her own. She was happily greeted by her toy poodle, Barney, but also by a disapproving roommate who had fallen asleep on the couch.

"I thought you were dead," Jill said sarcastically.

"Dead? Not hardly! I am in heaven, though," Jewel laughed. She sat in the high-backed wing chair positioned next to the couch. Picking Barney up and setting him in her lap, she tugged at his ears and rubbed his tummy.

"And what brings on this sudden case of euphoria?" asked her roommate.

"I'm in love," Jewel responded. Then looking surprised, she sat up straight in her chair staring at Jill. "I can't believe I said that! I didn't even think it before, but I guess it's true. I am in love!" She held Barney up above her head. His feet tucked under him and his tail wagged cautiously, unsure about whether he should trust her or not. "I'm in love with Noah Lee, Barney!" She stopped and closed her eyes. When she opened them, she was met with a stare from Jill who now towered over her.

"What did you say?"

"I, uh, I –."

"Have you been dating Noah Lee – *the archeology professor Noah Lee?* Are you crazy? You could get expelled and him fired! Are you crazy?"

"I didn't mean to say Noah Lee," Jewel hedged. But she knew what Jill was saying was true. If it hadn't been, why had she been hiding the fact they were dating for so long? It had been over a month. What was more, she knew that Noah knew it, too, and it was for that reason he had been wooing her in his own apartment and anywhere else away from the city. She was caught, and she knew it. She tried covering her mistake.

"Well, it's not as if I'm under aged. I am nearly 23, after all. I can certainly manage my own affairs," she said hotly.

"There's an interesting statement!" Jill looked at her while she chewed the inside of her cheek, her eyes large with disapproval.

"Listen, Noah and I have decided we are going to see what happens. He wouldn't even take me to bed tonight. He said I wasn't ready. Can you imagine a guy telling you he wants to wait because he's concerned about your welfare instead of his own?"

Jill shook her head, but Jewel couldn't tell if she was agreeing with her or just telling Jewel by her own silence what an idiot she was.

"Well?" she asked hopefully. She actually felt relieved she had mentioned it. She had needed to talk to someone about their relationship and Jill was one of her closest friends. "Listen, he's a great guy, Jill. I think we might get married." She looked up at Jill who stood there with a curl at the corner of her lips in stark disagreement.

"Honey, you have your head in the clouds. The man is too old for you and he is way above you in just about every sphere of your life. I think you'd better think about this again. I'm going to bed." Jill picked up her books and headed to the back bedroom. "You'd better think hard and long on this one, kiddo," she said shutting her door.

Jewel sat there with a frown on her face. She had hoped Jill would understand, but she did not. Then, she realized, no one would. She picked up Barney's leash and led him outside to get some fresh air for them both. It took many long hours for Jewel to fall asleep.

Jonathan was waiting for Jewel outside of her apartment the next morning. She had not slept well, but she was not about to tell Jon why. The more she thought about her conversation with her roommate, the more anxious she had become. What would happen if anyone on the faculty found out that Noah was dating her? What if Professor Cole found out? She would be mortified, and as a faculty member, he would be forced to report it to Administration. Finally, and most tragically, what if Jon found out? She again avoided any thought of telling him. Somehow she knew it would hurt him most.

She was quiet as they walked together. Dry snow crunched under their feet, seeming to echo her tragedy. It was a cold December day, a week before winter break. Jonathan could tell by her silence she was in no mood for chit chat, so they just walked together comfortably. He knew their long relationship allowed that.

Jonathan had planned to spend the three weeks vacation up north of the cities with his grandparents, while Jewel had planned to stay near campus in her apartment. Unlike Jewel, Jonathan was a family-oriented person. His parents were very supportive, and he often would visit his grandparents on the family farm near Aitkin, Minnesota. Jewel was sure he'd have a nice Christmas.

Jewel never enjoyed Christmases like she did when she was little. Her brothers, Joe and Tom, continued to be obnoxious; Peter was still trying to be her father; and her mother was there just trying to live out the rest of her life, caring for an invalid husband. It was depressing. She wished she could go north with Jonathan. Then again, if she did, she wouldn't be able to see Noah Lee.

Jewel decided it was best for her relationship with Noah to be available to him during the break. She rejected any thought of his being uncomfortable with their situation. In May she would graduate, and they would continue together as they had. At least, it seemed like a rational plan to her. Or was it? She would have to talk to Noah after her next class.

Noah looked up at Jewel as she entered the classroom. He had seen her from the window just a few minutes before walking with Jonathan, and was surprised at himself when he noticed a twinge of jealousy. He chuckled because he knew she was really putty in his hands by now and knowing the two were really just good friends, the young man would present no real threat. Jewel looked at him longingly before taking her seat.

"All right, ladies and gentlemen," Lee announced, opening the class session, "We have less than one week left before quarter finals. Those of you who plan to continue with Archeology 102 next quarter will be able to use the three-week vacation to prepare your final projects. Those who will not be continuing, though I cannot imagine why you wouldn't," he paused meaningfully, "your papers will be due by the end of this week. You understand your grades will be affected by the time difference. The others will have more time, but they are expected to supply more information and evidence of their findings.

"Please provide the necessary information given to you on your syllabus. Those who are continuing, I have a special assignment for you." He looked over the rim of his glasses while the students squirmed in their seats. Returning some papers to the students, he leaned over each one and gave them words of encouragement or exhortation, depending on the results of their work. Coming up behind Jewel, he leaned over and whispered, "Meet me at my place tonight." A little louder he said, "Good work, Miss Culpepper."

She kept her head down as if looking at the mark he had given her. A fleeting thought came to mind as she wondered if the A+ on the paper was actually an A+ or just a mark based on their relationship. She bit her lip and placed the paper into a folder. After class, instead of staying behind to speak with Noah, Jewel quickly exited the room.

Jonathan was standing at the lunch counter when Jewel came in. When she saw him, she gave a sigh of relief. She needed to clear the air about the situation she was in, even if it did hurt him. Tired from another sleepless night, and worried about the paper she'd received from Noah, she headed for Jonathan's table.

"May I join you?" she asked cautiously, putting the tray on his table. Jonathan looked at her and said nothing. "Jonathan?"

"Yeah, I suppose I could sacrifice a little space for such a waif as you."

"Gee, thanks. Don't put yourself out." She was in no mood for silly jokes. Picking up her tray, she started to walk away.

"Hey, girl, sit down. What's with you? Can't you take a joke?"

"I'm really not in a joking mood, Jon. I have some problems and I don't know who to talk to about them." Again Jonathan said nothing. He looked down at his lunch tray and played with the food on his plate. Jewel would tell him when the time was right, not that he hadn't already guessed. She was in love with someone. She was always in love with someone – else. He took a deep breath and waited for her to break the news.

"Aren't you going to saying anything, Jon? Don't you want to know what's going on with me?"

"Not really," he said matter-of-factly. Shocked, Jewel slumped in her chair.

"Really, not really?"

Jonathan rolled his eyes and stuffed a piece of ham into his mouth. "Well, you may as well tell me, you're going to anyway," he mumbled almost inaudibly.

"Well, if you really don't want to hear it, I won't tell you." Jewel buttered her bread for the second time. Jonathan chewed up his mouthful and swallowed. Putting his fork into his tray, he pushed it away and folded his hands on the table.

"I'm sorry, Jewel. I'm listening."

Tears welled up in Jewel's eyes and she had to pause to keep from bawling. Finally, as a tear made its way down her cheek, she looked at Jonathan hopelessly. "I think I'm in trouble, Jon." Jonathan's face reddened and his eyes grew large.

"You're pregnant?" he asked in horror.

This time Jewel rolled her eyes and laughed, wiping the tear from her cheek. "No, dummy, I'm not pregnant. I've just gotten involved with someone I don't think I should be involved with." Jonathan's lips curled.

"So what's new about that?"

"Jonathan, if you are going to take that tone, I'm leaving." Jewel started to get out of her chair.

"Oh, sit down," he said impatiently. "I said I was listening. Who is it this time?"

"Jonathan!" He shrugged his shoulders. He had heard this same scenario a dozen times over the years. "Okay, I'll tell you, but you mustn't tell a soul, do you understand?" He raised his eyebrows waiting for the rest of her confession. Finally, looking around to see if anyone was listening, she whispered the name, "Noah Lee." Jonathan's eyes squinted and he stared at her.

"You are kidding me!"

"Hush!" she warned in a sharp whisper. "No, I'm not kidding you. Why would I kid about something like that? I really love him, Jonathan, but I don't know what I should do about it."

"And Lee, have you talked to him about this?"

"Of course. We've been dating since September. I know it's against the rules, but he said we'll work it out. I think he wants to marry me, Jon."

"Great! That's just great!" Jonathan stood to his feet and looked down at his friend. "Jewel, you know I care a lot about you, but I just can't deal with this right now. I'll have to really think about what to say about his. You're right, though, you are in big trouble." He picked up his tray and walked off leaving Jewel to stew in her own soup. She pushed her tray away and leaned over the table for a silent cry.

Noah opened the door to his apartment to see a miserable-looking blonde with red eyes standing before him. He reached out and took Jewel into his arms.

"Darlin', what's the matter?"

"Oh, Noah, I just don't know what to do about us. I think we're in terrible trouble here and I just don't know what to do."

He held her for a moment while the door shut, then led her to the couch in the living room. "Sit here, Darlin' and I'll go and get you some hot tea. That'll soothe you." As he started for the kitchen, Jewel stood up again.

"Noah! I don't want to be soothed. We need to talk this out and right now!" she insisted. "We can't go on like this sneaking around so no one sees us. If I'm to be your wife, we need to make some plans." Noah stopped and turned around.

"My wife? I haven't mentioned us getting married."

Jewel looked at him horrified. She had overstepped her boundaries and she knew it. Closing her eyes, she put her hands over her face.

"Noah, I'm so sorry. I didn't mean to – I mean, I know you haven't thought about it. Oh, Noah, I'm so mixed up I don't know what I'm saying."

Immediately Noah knew he had to perform damage control. His mission was becoming compromised. He returned to the living room and sat her next to him. Holding her, he pulled her chin up to into her eyes.

"Darlin', it's not that I haven't thought about it. I have a great deal," he lied. "I just wanted to talk to you about it at the right time. You know I love you."

He kissed her hand, then her forehead. "You're very young, dear girl, so I can understand your confusion. Why don't we talk about it over dinner? I've ordered a pizza, I'm already chilling some wine and you'll feel better after you get somethin' into your stomach."

His beautiful southern drawl hypnotized her again. Enamored by his soft voice and his gentle touch, she acquiesced and leaned into him. His mouth enveloped hers and she was comforted by his strong arms.

The pizza arrived hot and steamy, and its warmth and delicious aroma melted Jewel's distress. After a small glass of wine, she relaxed in front of the fire Noah had built in the fireplace. She had run cold water over her face to get rid of the puffiness around her eyes and she finally felt normal again. It wasn't like her to be so dramatic, and she chided herself. She was usually so pragmatic, so reasonable. Noah brought her another glass of wine.

"No, I really shouldn't," she said half-heartedly refusing the glass. Actually, she thought she could use a good drunk at this moment, but she never had been a drinker, and now was not the time to start.

"It'll be fine. Sip it slowly, and if you feel you shouldn't drive tonight, I'll either take you home or you can sleep here." Jewel flushed at the thought of staying. "On the couch, if you wish." She smiled. She asked Noah if he could forgive her for her outburst, and he assured her he already had.

"Darlin', let's talk about marriage," he said sitting next to her. "I have thought a great deal about it, as I said before, but I don't know if this is the right time. Perhaps we should think about it nearer summer. We could make better plans at that time."

"Are you asking me to marry you, then?"

"I suppose I am. If I was, would you have me?" Lee had successfully avoided the question for a second time. He took her hand and kissed her fingers then turning her hand palm up, he kissed her palm. Jewel loved his touch.

"Oh, Noah, of course I would. I love you so much." Noah pulled her over and cradled her in his arms like he would an infant. He had waited for this moment. He had planned it from the first day he saw her name on the class roster, and here she was in his arms, a ripe peach ready for the picking. All he needed to do now was move his pawn where she needed to be for his next move. The Culpepper family treasure would be his in the end, if he followed his plan carefully.

"And I love you, my sweet Jewel."

Chapter XIV

Christmas Plans

Peter wiped his mouth with a napkin and quietly put it back in his lap as he looked at his little sister with a raised eyebrow. They had met at his office complex for lunch because she had something important to discuss with him. Now here she was, telling him of her plans for the winter break. She and her "friend" would be traveling to Georgia in less than two days to do some research for the archeology project due at the beginning of the next quarter. Her friend's family was from the same area as theirs, and they were going together to study the area in and around Macon.

"So you won't be home for Christmas?" he asked a second time. He couldn't believe she could be so selfish as to not turn up on the most important holiday of the year; at least, in their mother's eyes, it was the most important. "The whole family will be there. Our cousins are coming in from Texas. Dad's coming home from the hospital for the first time in weeks. How could you not be there?"

"Don't look at me with that hurt puppy dog face, Peter. I can't be there. It's important for both my grade and my future. Can't you understand?"

"What about our family's future?"

"The family will do just fine without me, Peter. I promise I'll call and give you all a report on Christmas day." She looked at her watch. "Oh, look at the time. I have to meet No – er – my, my friend to go through the final plans and pack. Can you excuse me, please? Thank you so much for lunch." She stood up and leaned over to kiss Peter's cheek. He moved to avoid her kiss, putting his fork down and sipping his water. He didn't want to speak unless he was calm. He had certainly put up with Jewel's crazy schemes enough since her adolescence. Ever since she turned fourteen, she had been scatterbrained, thoughtless and childish. Now she was just plain selfish and he wasn't quite sure how to address this newest attribute.

"No, Jewel, I will not excuse you. Please sit down."

Shocked by her brother's serious tone of voice, she sat back in her seat. Throwing her purse on the table, she slumped in her chair. "What's wrong now?"

"Jewel, this family has not asked much of you over the past few years since Dad has been ill, but this time I think we must. Who is this person you're flying away with? Is this truly an assignment or is it something else, something you may regret?"

Jewel chewed on the inside of her cheek. "Peter, you are not my father."

"Yes, you remind me quite frequently. However, I am your oldest brother, and I am concerned about you. You know how important this holiday is for Mother. I cannot believe you would consider abandoning her right now. I expect you to have a better excuse than you are running away with a 'friend' to do a college assignment."

"Peter, I am not a liar. I am doing research on our family. I would think even Mother might be appreciative of that. If you don't believe me, call my professor. He has given us this assignment. I've been saving up for a long time for a trip like this, and I think this is the perfect time for it."

"Okay, who is this friend?"

"Well, if you must know, it's Jonathan. He's going with me," she said. She bit her lip realizing indeed she had become a liar, but in this situation, it couldn't be helped. No one could know it was Noah who would be traveling with her.

"Jonathan? And you couldn't bring yourself to saying his name? I thought his family was from up north. When did he find out they were from Georgia?" Jewel simply stared at her brother. She rather felt sorry for him. He had been sorely disappointed by her younger brothers, and now Jewel was letting him down. She looked down at her half-finished meal. She truly had lost her appetite by now.

"It's his mother's side of the family. Anyway, what does it matter? Jonathan's my best friend. If two ADULT friends can't travel together, then someone has a problem," she said, folding her arms across her chest. She had volleyed, now it was Peter's turn.

"Yes, I suppose you're right. Jon is a good man. I guess I'll just have to explain this to Mother, then."

"No, Peter," Jewel said quietly. "I'll tell her. I'm sure she'll understand." She stood to her feet and picked up her purse. "I really do appreciate your concern, Peter. I'll call you from Macon." Peter nodded unhappily. The sharp line of his jaw tensed as she kissed him good bye.

Peter left a twenty dollar bill on the table and went back to his office. Sitting in his executive chair, he stared blankly at his typewriter before starting back to work. Drumming his fingers on his desk top he considered his options. He knew he should trust, but somehow he also knew she was in trouble. Against his better reasoning, he looked up Jonathan's telephone number and made a call. Jonathan's baritone voice answered, and Peter hesitated before he spoke.

"Jonathan? Peter Culpepper here. I hear you're going to Georgia with Jewel?" Jonathan said nothing. Peter knew by his silence it was not Jonathan who was going with his sister to some kind of mysterious rendezvous.

"So it isn't true," Peter answered his own question. Jonathan cleared his throat.

"I'm sorry, who did you say this was?"

"You know very well who this is, Jon, Peter – your best friend's brother? She told me you were traveling to Georgia with her for the holidays. I have a feeling she was telling me less than the truth. Am I correct?"

"She did, huh? Man. What the heck does she think she's doin'?" Jonathan was speechless. He knew Jewel was getting in deeper every day, but he hadn't expected her to drag him into it.

"Do you know with whom she is traveling?" His formal tone was Jonathan's signal that Peter was more than just a little angry with his sister.

"Yeah. I know. I don't think I can tell you, though. She asked me to keep it confidential, and even though she dragged me into this, I don't feel like I can betray her confidence, you know?"

"I understand, Jon. Would you mind meeting with me tonight around six o'clock so we can talk? I have an idea." Peter and Jon made plans to meet for supper in downtown Minneapolis at the Spaghetti Factory on Washington Avenue.

Six o'clock came and went as Jonathan sat in one of the tall booths in the restaurant. His mouth watered as he looked over the menu. He was trying to decide between the chicken cacciatore and the spinach lasagna. This, one of the Twin Cities' best Italian restaurants, had excellent food and a great atmosphere. Jonathan had been looking forward to his meal all day, and the fact Peter was going to pay made it even more appetizing because the university was in receipt of most of his cash, these days. He looked at his watch. Peter was already 10 minutes late, which wasn't like him. He was always punctual, always proper.

Jonathan had never cared much for Jewel's other two brothers, but he had always appreciated the way Peter took care of his family. He had developed a business in marketing and advertising which was already in the Fortune 500 and had set aside money for his siblings' education over the years. Eight years Jonathan's senior, Peter was a hero in Jonathan's eyes, even though he was a real pain to his sister, Jewel.

"Jonathan, I'm sorry to be late," Peter greeted him with a pat on the shoulder and a handshake. He was somewhat breathless, having run across from the parking lot on Washington Avenue to avoid the heavy traffic. "I had to run a couple errands before meeting you."

"That's okay, Peter. I've just been enjoying the ambiance and drooling over the menu." Jonathan smiled up at his host. "Here's one for you." He handed Peter a menu and sat back in his seat waiting to order his meal. Following Peter to the table, the waitress amiably took their drink orders and left the two men to talk. Knowing Peter was concerned about his sister, Jonathan was the first to speak.

"Okay, Peter, what's up?" Jonathan was never one to beat around the bush. He was as straight forward as he was handsome. His unkempt light brown hair and hazel eyes belied his businesslike manner. The waitress interrupted them momentarily as she brought them their beverages and a basket of bread. Talking stopped while she served them.

"Here you go, gentlemen. Is there anything else you need right now?" she asked pleasantly. Both of them gave her a negative shake of their heads. Peter waited for her to leave, and then looked directly at Jonathan with his hands folded on the table.

"Jonathan, I think Jewel has gotten herself into some trouble. Am I correct?"

"Yeah. She has, but I don't quite know what to do about it." Jonathan wanted to tell Peter the truth. He wanted to tell him Jewel was heading for a fall with a guy twelve years her senior – a guy whose career could be damaged irreparably if they continued down the road on which they were heading. He wanted to tell him Jewel was just infatuated with this guy because he was a smooth talker from the south with a history much like her own, and it wasn't the first time she'd fallen for a guy like that. He wanted to tell him Jewel and Noah Lee didn't belong together, that Jewel belonged with him, not Lee. He wanted to tell him, but he could not.

No one knew about his feelings for Jewel. He had hoped she would have seen for herself by now how he'd felt about her ever since high school. She had indeed bloomed into a beautiful gem and he had fallen in love with her. But how could he tell her? She had been too involved with the captain of the football team, the captain of the basketball team, the leader of the Spanish club, et al. She went through more boyfriends than he could count, and now she was "in love" with the archeology professor. He had been near tears when she'd told him, and they had hardly spoken since. He didn't know what to do, and now he was having to face the truth in front of her brother. He suddenly lost his appetite.

"Am I also correct that you have feelings for my sister?" Peter looked him squarely in the eye. How did he know, Jonathan wondered. "Well, do you?"

"Yeah."

"I thought so. I recognized it years ago. She's treated you rather badly over the years, hasn't she?"

"Yeah." What else could he say? Peter was on target and he knew it. Jonathan's face reddened with embarrassment. He was nearly 25 years old, and he should have been able to handle this on his own.

"Okay. I won't pump you about who it is. I'll be able to find out on my own. I just wondered if you would like to take a trip to Georgia."

The waitress interrupted their conversation again with their food. Again she asked if there was anything else she could do for them, and they both shook their heads impatiently, wanting to get back to their conversation. She put the bill on the table and walked away hoping the rich guy would leave her a good tip. Jonathan cut into his lasagna and took a bite before he responded.

"Georgia? You want me to tail her?"

"No, on the contrary. I am going to give Jewel her ticket as a Christmas present. I will also provide yours. You'll be traveling together, you see. She said you would be going. How was I to know it was not you who would be traveling with her? We'll play this right up to the plane departure. The whole family will be there."

"Oh, man, she's not going to like that." Jonathan smiled through a mouthful of lasagna. He took a drink of his Coke before continuing. "What am I supposed to tell my folks?"

"Well, Jon, I guess if you care enough for Jewel, you'll think of something." Peter looked at him matter-of-factly, and left it at that.

Jewel sat at the kitchen table with her mother. Holding Gwen's hand, Jewel looked into her eyes. "Mama, please understand, I'm not going to be here for Christmas. I'm sorry if I hurt you, truly I am, but I really have to be gone the whole next two weeks."

"No, really, Jewel, it's all right. I understand you have your studies." Gwen pulled her hand away from her daughter's and stood up. She didn't understand. She wanted her daughter home like she always was. She had already lost her sons, and now her youngest was leaving the nest. She had heard about this. They called it the "empty-nest" syndrome. She saw a psychologist and he had labeled it for her. The depression she was experiencing was something many women undergo in these latter years of life when all the children leave and they are left alone with or without their mates. Since Joseph was ill, she was mostly alone now, and she looked forward to the Christmas holidays when everyone would be home again. Her hand shook as she scooped coffee into the coffee maker.

"Do you really understand, Mama? We do have to get this project done if I am to continue in this class with a good grade. I hope to work towards a Masters in Archeology by the time I'm done. Then I can teach like my professor."

"We? Is someone else doing this with you?"

"Well, yes, kind of. We make a terrific team, Mama. I can't wait to tell you more about him." Gwen looked down at her coffee cup. Jewel hadn't mentioned a man before, though the Lord knew, she had certainly had her share of boyfriends.

"I see. So you're traveling with a man." Her statement sounded disapproving, and Jewel knew by the tone in her voice that her mother was not pleased with this sudden revelation.

"Well, yes. I'm going with Jonathan. Didn't Peter tell you?" There it was again. The lie. Jewel rolled her eyes. Why had she started this, and how was she going to get out of it?

"No, Peter didn't mention it. So he knew about this?"

"Yes, Mother. I just told him today, so he probably hasn't had a chance to tell you. Nevertheless, I am very excited about it, and I hope you are excited for me. I'm going to Macon to study the Culpepper side." Her mother's eyebrows lifted in surprise.

"For archeology? I've never heard of such a thing."

"Actually, it's just an assignment to finish out the first quarter. Something new Noah, uh, Professor Lee is doing. He's very progressive, Mama." Jewel stood at the counter and popped a cracker into her mouth.

"Hmmm. It sounds like it. Well, your father will be pleased, I'm sure. He always wanted to go to Georgia. I suppose there is nothing I can do about it, then. We'll just have to wait for your report." Gwen turned her back on her daughter and blinked back her tears. She wouldn't allow her daughter to know how disappointed she was. She wouldn't let anyone know.

Peter called Jewel the next day after meeting with Jonathan. He said he had paid for her ticket to Georgia as a Christmas present. Her flight was scheduled for Friday evening, the day after her last final examination at the university. At first Jewel stuttered her response, and then assured Peter it wasn't at all necessary. She had already made plans for the flight. She was going to get the tickets that very afternoon. He simply told her he'd already purchased a round-trip ticket for her, and it was non-refundable. She thanked him weakly, and then hung up the phone. What would she tell Noah?

On December 19th, Jonathan, Peter and the family met Jewel at the airport. Jonathan stood next to her nervously, first standing on one foot and then the other. He had not yet informed her he would be accompanying her on the flight, and he was not looking forward to her reaction. Peter strode up to her confidently and placed a mushy kiss on her cheek. His two kids jumped up and down as they vied for her attention.

"Bye, Auntie Jewel! Have a good time!" her niece Amy called while little Joey, who could yet barely talk, tried to mimic his big sister.

"Bye, bye, Annie Jewa."

Jewel reached down and kissed them both. She threw her arms around her mother and kissed her. "Thanks for understanding, Mama," she whispered. Her mother just nodded and patted her daughter's back. Turning to look at Jonathan, Jewel gave him a sheepish smile. She couldn't say good bye here or Peter would find out she'd lied. She'd wait until the family left. She knew Jonathan would hang around. Out of the corner of her eye, she noticed Noah Lee come around the corner by the departure gate. When he saw her, he sat down with his back to the crowd trying to be inconspicuous. Jewel felt sweat run down her neck.

"Here's your ticket, Sis," Peter said pulling the tickets out of his pocket. He handed a ticket to her. "And here's yours," he continued handing the other ticket to Jonathan. "Merry Christmas, you two."

"What?" Jewel's face turned crimson as she realized what Peter had done. "Jonathan?"

"Yeah, Jewel. Peter called me after he found out our plans and said he'd gotten our tickets for us. Isn't that great?" He put his arm around her shoulders and gave them a hard squeeze. Turning his back on Peter, Jonathan crossed his eyes and made a face at his friend. He mouthed the words, "Better play along!"

Jewel was mortified. Her betrothed was sitting not 100 feet away, and here was her big jerk of a brother playing Rockefeller with her love life. Since when did he become so generous?

"Gee, thanks, Peter," she managed to say. "I, I guess I don't know what to say."

"Don't worry about it, Sis. Jonathan and I had a good talk the other night, and I'm much happier knowing he's going with you to keep you safe. This is the first time you'll be away from home, after all. I wanted to be sure you'd be okay." Peter's eyes sparkled as he realized how much fun he was having.

"Wow, what a setup! Ha! Gee! Wow!" She was dumbfounded. Their conversation was interrupted by the departure announcement. Noah Lee stood to his feet and looked around to see if he could signal Jewel. Jewel had been watching him frequently looking at his watch. He nodded at her impatiently, and now he was tapping the face of the watch and mouthing the words, "Come on!".

"Well," she said almost too happily, "it's time to go!" She picked up her bag, kissed her mother's cheek again, and hugged Peter and the kids, then headed for the gate. Jonathan could hardly believe he was doing this, but the more he'd thought about it, the better he felt. By now he was literally laughing.

"Man, Peter, thanks a lot," Jonathan said shaking Peter's hand. "This means more than you know." Peter watched her as she approached the gate. He noticed the man standing next to her.

"Is that him?"

Jonathan turned slightly to take a look. "Yeah. Noah Lee."

"Noah Lee? The professor at the U?" Peter let go of Jonathan's hand. Jonathan looked back at him with a smirk on his face.

"Yeah. But don't do anything, okay Peter? I think I want to handle this." Peter looked at his sister's friend and nodded.

"Okay. I'll let you handle it, Jon. Just don't let it get out of hand, all right? If things seem to be getting too difficult, call me." Jonathan nodded. He turned to Mrs. Culpepper and shook her hand. She leaned over and kissed his cheek, and he left to join Jewel. Peter watched for Lee's reaction. The man stepped back, looked at Jewel and back at Jonathan, and then stood there in disbelief as Jonathan escorted Jewel onto the plane.

So far Peter's plan was working nicely.

Chapter XV

The Snare

Jewel walked to her seat backwards as she questioned Jonathan. Her angry accusations could be heard all the way to the back of the plane. Jonathan wondered if she'd end up getting thrown off as a disturbance to the other passengers. He didn't say anything as he threw his overnight bag into the luggage rack above his seat. Trying to help Jewel with hers, she tore it out of his hand.

"I'll do it myself, thank you!" she growled.

"Window or isle?" he asked innocently. She looked at him, anger seething from deep within.

"Oh, shut up!" she exclaimed pushing him backwards. She sat down in the seat next to the window. She could see Peter and the kids still standing at the large glass windows waiting for the plane's departure. "I cannot believe you!" she finally said. "What are you doing here? Noah is going to kill me. It wasn't bad enough I had to have him return my ticket, but now he has to put up with you!"

"Gee, thanks. I thought you'd be pleased I didn't rat you out. I could have, you know. It's your own fault for dragging my name into this. I could've been spending a nice, quiet weekend with my grandparents, but nooo. You had to say, 'Jonathan's going with me.' Liar."

Jewel closed her eyes and breathed a heavy sigh. He was right. How could she be angry at him? He had been protecting her. She hadn't had the guts to admit out loud she was going with a gorgeous, mysterious man from the university – someone her brother wouldn't approve of – and they were probably going to rent a wonderful motel room somewhere and experience the most romantic two weeks of her life! It wasn't Jonathan's fault she was too chicken to let out a secret that could mean both of their expulsion from the university; it was hers, and they would just have to make the best of it. Now the problem was Noah. She would have to wait for the plane to take off before she could go find him and explain what had happened.

Jonathan was asleep in no time. He told her he'd had a rough week of finals, and he'd been up every night cramming for his exams. In truth, he hadn't been able to sleep the night before over worrying about this trip. Now he had more than three hours to sleep, and he was going to take advantage of it. Jewel, however, could not sleep. All she could think about was getting back to Noah. Shortly after Jonathan started to snore, she felt a tap on her shoulder. Looking up, she saw a disgruntled Noah Lee looking down at her. He shook Jonathan's shoulder.

"I beg your pardon, sah," he said pouring on his Georgian accent. "I know y'all are friends, but I was wonderin' if y'all wouldn't mind my sittin' with Miss Culpeppah. I thought you'd appreciate usin' my seat up in First Class." Jonathan squinted up at Lee. Seeing Jewel's pleading look, he rolled his eyes and stood up, hitting his head on the overhang.

"Oh, tough break there, fellah. Jes' go on ahead there. The stewardess is expectin' ya. Seat 8A. You kin have my Tom Collins, too, if ya like." Lee smiled at Jonathan wickedly, and sat down next to Jewel. Rubbing the top of his head, Jonathan retreated to First Class. At least he'd be able to get some decent sleep and maybe watch a movie. He was absolutely certain he would drink Lee's drink for him, and maybe another while he was at it.

"Noah, I cannot tell you how sorry I am about this. I had no idea Jonathan was coming until we stood there at the gate. I thought we'd be able to trade the ticket in when we got it and I could sit with you, but Peter set this whole thing up without my knowing any of it." Jewel was practically in tears. Noah patted her hand, still somewhat disgruntled over having to give up his First Class seat to that "boy."

"Nevah you mind, Honey. Once we're in Georgia, things'll be fine.

The plane landed on schedule, and Jonathan, Jewel and Noah deplaned together. Jonathan had barely slept during his three hours in First Class. He could not stop thinking about Noah Lee, a man over twelve years Jewel's senior. Lee was controlling her life when it should be him controlling her life. No, that wasn't right either, he knew, but he wasn't thinking clearly these days. Jewel was on his mind entirely too much.

"After you, sah," Noah dripped.

"No, you go on ahead, Professor Lee, I always show respect to my elders." Smiling down at Jewel, he crossed his eyes. "I know you two have a lot of study and research to do. I'm just along for the ride. I'll just be like a bug on the wall," Jonathan assured him, "a mouse in the corner, a bird on a branch –."

"I got it, Mr. Tyler," Lee sneered. Jonathan may be no more than what he'd promised he'd be, but Lee doubted that was his real intention.

The airport was very crowded, but having frequented it, Noah knew his way around. He took Jewel's hand and led her and Jonathan down through the terminal gates to the taxi station. He would get her to the hotel and have a car rental pick them up there. The three of them crowded into a cab, Jonathan on one side of Jewel, and Noah on the other. Sandwiched between the two of them, Jewel felt like pushing Jonathan out the side door. She thought better of it deciding she would lose him later without committing murder.

Jonathan pulled out their itinerary just as they pulled away from the terminal. Peter had reserved two adjoining rooms for them at the Holiday Inn West on I80, so Jonathan would be able to reach Jewel easily, if needed. Meanwhile, Noah had reserved a beautiful room at the Ramada just across from the Holiday Inn, and he assured Jonathan Jewel would be quite comfortable with him.

"No, that's okay, Prof. Jewel's brother wanted to be sure she had a great time, so he set up the whole thing already. It's part of the itinerary, see?" He shoved the paper into Noah's face. Noah backed away and put his hand up instinctively to keep Jonathan from smothering him.

"Jonathan!" Jewel growled. She could not believe he was acting like such an oaf. She pulled his arm down from in front of her face and jabbed him with her elbow. "I'm sorry, Professor Lee. I don't know what has gotten into my old friend." Her eyes were full of poison darts as she glared at Jonathan. Noah simply gave her a reassuring smile and patted her hand before entwining his fingers with hers. Jonathan, in turn, protectively placed his arm around her shoulder. Jewel's head jutted forward and she sat between the two men feeling miserable.

Arriving at the Ramada, the taxi dropped Noah at the front door and continued across the highway to the Holiday Inn West. Noah stood there looking rather lost as the cab drove away. Jewel was nearly in tears.

Hot, tired, and just plain angry, Jewel threw her suitcase on the bed in her motel room. She couldn't believe she'd just traveled half way across the country to have a wonderful secret rendezvous with the most glorious man in the universe to be stuck there with Jonathan Tyler! She unzipped her Pullman and shoved the top open. Angrily tugging at the hanger, the latch broke off.

"Oh, crap!" she exploded. Throwing all her outfits and the suitcase on the floor she stomped her foot, tore off her clothes and left everything in a pile to take a hot shower.

While Jewel unpacked, Jonathan, sitting on his bed next door, leaned back and sighed. It had been a long, silent trip worrying about Jewel and spying on the two of them on the plane. He was satisfied to see them boxed in with a crying baby sitting behind them and a man who smelled like both a chimney and a barn in front of them. At one point, she almost appeared a little green. Jon had to stifle his laughter as he passed by for the fifth time on his way to the facilities. He had spent more time in the restroom than was normal for anyone. The stewardess had actually asked him if he was all right, and if he needed some antacid or something. He enjoyed the comfort of Lee's first class seat after all. Closing his eyes at the memory, he heard a thump from Jewel's room and an expletive filtering through thin walls. He simply smiled and nestled into his pillows.

Meanwhile, Noah Lee stood at the desk at the Ramada staring at the attendant. He tapped his fingers on the counter, impatient for the answer from the clerk.

"I'm sorry, Sir, there is nothing here in our reservations denoting a reservation for a Ms. Culpepper, and it appears your reservation has been cancelled. The notes say you called in two days ago to cancel a full week's stay, and you would not be coming to Macon after all." The clerk gave him a hopeless look. "And we are completely full due to the holiday, Sir."

Noah leaned forward on his elbow and rubbed his temple with his forefinger. "Do you mean to tell me you don't have so much as a closet left for me? Do you know who I am, Sah?"

"I'm extremely sorry, Sir. Not a hotel in Macon has a thing open. It is winter break, you know. You might check the Chamber of Commerce. There are a number of nice bed and breakfasts available you might try."

The sharp line of Noah's jaw moved up and down as he gritted his teeth. There would be hell to pay when he found out who cancelled his reservation. He picked up his luggage and headed to the nearest payphone to look for a phone book.

Jewel allowed the full force of the shower to beat down on her aching head while the hot water flowing down her body soothed the tense muscles in her shoulders and back. She leaned forward, resting the palms of her hands on the wall and closed her eyes allowing the water to soothe away the frustrating events of the day. She wondered about Jonathan's sudden presence on this trip. Why had he given up his precious time with his grandparents? He could have said no to Peter. It was so unlike him to leave his family on a holiday. She sighed as she stretched her neck. Besides, what was with her brother? Had he sensed something was going on and set things up like this? No, she thought, Peter wasn't that smart. How could he have known about her plans with Noah? She couldn't believe Jon had betrayed her. Not only did she doubt her brother's intelligence, she highly doubted Jonathan's, at this point. Putting her head under the water again, she was so deep in thought she did not hear the telephone ring in the other room.

Noah slammed the receiver down and checked his pockets for another thirty-five cents. "Thirty-five cents for a phone call. Unbelievable," he mumbled. He had tried two hotels and three bed and breakfasts. None of them had an available room. Then he attempted to telephone Jewel in her room to see if she would let him stay with her. He already knew her answer, though. She couldn't do that with Jonathan in the same motel. Nevertheless, she never answered and now he was more furious than before. He took in a deep breath, held it for a few seconds, and then let out the air slowly as he forced himself into perfect control. Gritting his teeth, Lee picked up the receiver, gave the operator his credit card number and dialed information.

Jonathan had fallen asleep and was resting peacefully when he heard a knock on the adjoining door. His eyelids were heavy as he sat up in his bed. "What?" he called.

"Jon, it's me," Jewel said. He scrambled off the bed and tripped over his shoes.

"Wait a minute," he yelled. Slipping his shoes on, he reached the door. "Hi," he said peering down at the angry face of his friend. Seeing the look on her face, he decided it would be best if he said no more.

"Hi," Jewel responded. She pushed her way into his room.

"Won't you come in," he said sarcastically, closing the door. Jewel stood looking at him with one hip jutting out to the left and her arms akimbo, a look of expectancy in her eyes. She had figured out most of the plan with Peter, but something more was up with Jonathan, and she wanted to know what. Her face had dark clouds drawn across it and Jonathan knew he was in for a long talk.

"What's up?" Jonathan asked. Looking at her with innocent eyes, he sat on the edge of the bed and smiled.

"What's up? What's up? That's all you have to say for yourself, what's up?" Jonathan looked side to side and back, as if he wondered who she was talking to. He shrugged his shoulders.

"I guess I don't know what you're talking about Jules. I've been sleeping." He picked up the radio clock to check the time. "Man! It's almost eight o'clock. No wonder I'm hungry." He stood up and grabbed his jacket. "Wanna go out?"

Jewel blinked a number of times, flustered by his calm demeanor. Finally she walked up close enough to him he could feel her breath on his cheek. She looked him straight in the eye. "I don't know what you're up to Jonathan Tyler, but I'll tell you this. I *will* find out." She walked back into her room and slammed the door. She knocked again and he reopened it.

"I'll meet you down stairs in five minutes," she said slamming the door again. Jonathan sat back down on the edge of the bed.

"Man! I don't know if I can keep this up," he told himself aloud. He hadn't seen her so angry since her brother, Tom, ran over her bike with their father's car. He sat for a bit before he got the nerve to head downstairs. He'd seen angry hornets that were calmer than her. He picked up his key and walked out the door. As the elevator doors closed, his phone began to ring.

"Come on! Come on!" Noah growled. Then he gave up. Jonathan wasn't answering either. He calmly replaced the receiver, picked up his luggage and walked outside through the revolving doors. Looking across the highway, he noticed a couple waiting for a cab. Studying them, he realized it was Jonathan opening the taxi cab door for Jewel. He called out to get her attention, but that was more than useless. Flagging a taxi, he threw his luggage inside and got in.

"Follow that cab." Even he couldn't believe he was repeating that old cliché.

"Sir? What cab?"

"That taxi at the Holiday Inn. See it? Catch up and follow them," Noah ordered.

"Yes sir!" The cabbie pushed the meter arm down and moved into traffic. Noah had lived in Macon most of his life, but had never seen traffic this heavy. Urging the driver to hurry, they crossed the median and were soon driving behind Jonathan and Jewel's taxi, following them to a Pizza Hut.

"It figures," Noah mumbled. He believed he'd eaten more pizza since he'd started dating the younger Jewel than he had eaten in his entire life. He palate was raw from tomato acid, he abhorred the taste of mozzarella cheese, and he could barely stand the smell of the girl's favorite meal. Retrieving his luggage from the back seat, he reached for his wallet. Tearing a $10 bill in half, he handed one part to the driver.

"Wait here if you want the rest."

He picked up the luggage and headed into the restaurant leaving the cabbie wondering why the man tore the bill. He would have stayed if the guy had asked him.

The restaurant was crowded. It took Noah a minute to find Jonathan and Jewel, but when he did, he headed straight to their table past the seating hostess. She called out after him, but he ignored her. Setting his suitcases down, he collapsed dramatically into a chair.

"Noah, what are you doing here?" Jewel looked at him shocked.

"I am so glad I found you!" he gasped. "I was nearly destitute!" Jonathan sneered. This guy hadn't been destitute a day in his life. Taking a handkerchief out of his pocket, Noah mopped his brow.

"What's wrong?" Jewel looked alarmed as she touched his arm. Noah knew he'd baited her.

"Someone cancelled my reservations at the Ramada," he said looking at Jonathan directly. Jonathan looked at him without a glimpse of knowledge reflected in his eyes. "There isn't a room anywhere in town. I will have to travel down to a B & B nearly forty miles east of here." The waitress came over with another glass of water. "Thank you, darlin'." He gulped down half the glass of water before continuing his woeful tale. "I don't know what else to do except go on out and try again tomorrow. It'll cost me almost $100.00 just to get there and back." He shook his head. Pitying him, Jewel wanted to hold him to her, she felt so bad about this whole mess.

"Noah, I am so sorry. What are you going to do?"

"I'll jes' have to make the best of a very bad situation," he replied. Jewel thought for a second.

"You could come over to the Holiday Inn and stay in my room," she offered. Hair stood up on the back of Jonathan's neck.

"I don't think Peter would approve of that, Jewel. You know how he is," Jonathan warned.

"Yeah. You're right." Looking from Noah to Jonathan and then back again, she came up with an idea.

"Well, why don't you stay with Jon?" Jonathan straightened up in his chair. "You don't mind, do you Jon." It wasn't a question. Her eyebrows shot up and her mouth formed a tight line.

"I, uh –."

"I thought not. Noah?"

"I'd hate to put you out, young man."

"I bet," Jonathan said under his breath.   Seeing Jewel's look, he recanted. "No, that's fine. It's a double room," he said. *All the better to keep you in my sights, buddy.* He pulled out his room key. "Here. Let yourself in. Room 522."

"But you'll stay with us for supper, won't you Noah?" The professor looked from Jonathan to Jewel. He had a little more work to finish before they returned to the motel. Standing up, he bowed slightly at the waist and took the key.

"I wouldn't think of disturbing your evenin'. You two enjoy your food. I'll just order something from room service." He held out his hand to Jonathan to offer a friendly handshake. Jonathan hesitated just long enough for Jewel to take Noah's hand instead. Noah turned her hand over and kissed it. "You are my rescuer, my dear. This will be a wonderful trip after all." He looked over her hand at Jonathan who sat glaring at the older man. Picking up his suitcases he went back out to the cab. The driver was talking to his dispatcher.

"Yeah. He just took off and let me sit here. So I can't pick up that other fare. Wait, here he comes now." The cabbie hung up the mike and watched Noah in the side mirror as he stepped around the car. Noah opened the door and sat back in the cab.

"The Holiday Inn."

"Where's the other half?"

"You'll get it when we get there." The cabbie, angrier still, sat there with his arms crossed.

"I ain't movin' 'til ye pay me for the first trip." Noah's right eye twitched as he considered his options. He handed the other half to the driver.

"Now can we please leave, Sah?" Seeing the look in Noah's eyes reflected in the rearview mirror, the cabbie realized he might be wise to tread lightly. He put the car into drive and moved out of the parking lot.

Jewel appeared to be very jittery throughout the rest of the next hour. She ate her pizza in near silence and only stared back at Jonathan when he tried to make light of the situation.

"Okay, Jewel. What do you want from me? Do you want me to admit I'm in cahoots with your brother? Fine. Whatever you want. I can't stand it when you're mad at me and I won't stick around for an entire week for the silent treatment. So what do you want?"

"I want the truth." She looked at him sideways, and then looked away again. She was on the brim of tears, and she was trying hard not to let him know it. Jonathan took a bite of pizza as he thought about what to say. Finally, after another gulp of cola, he stood up and faced her.

"Okay, here it is, Babe. I love you. I've been in love with you since high school. I never told you because you always had some jock hangin' around." Jewel's eyes opened in stark disbelief. No one could have been more surprised at his statement than she. "I came on this trip at Peter's request because he already knew it without anyone telling him. As a matter of fact, he was amazed at your insensitivity. He recognized it years ago.

"As far as the professor is concerned, I don't trust him. He's up to something and I'm gonna find out what it is." He pulled $25.00 out of his wallet and tossed it at her. "This should cover the pizza and a ride back to the hotel. Thanks for a swell vacation." He picked up his jacket from the back of the chair and pushed his way through the crowd. Jewel was shocked into silence. She shoved her plate away and sat there very much alone.

Noah had been working on his notes for nearly an hour when he looked at his watch. He knew Jonathan could be walking in very soon and he wanted to get as much research done as possible before he arrived. He examined the record of events he had already recorded over the past ten years. First, J. Reginald Culpepper's flight from South Africa in 1859. He had not registered the jewel with the Transvaal government back then, nor had it been mentioned among the security records of the HMS Alacrity. Noah's great, great grandmother, Mary Lee, had left quite a detailed scenario for her descendants including the names of the characters involved in this story. He flipped through the pages and found mention of a ruby and diamond necklace she had found in Miss Jewel's cedar chest.

There was little he could find out from those older records, but he did find information about a certain jeweler named Jacob Rosenbrand of New York who had also kept a diary of his work. Noah later acquired the diary after a great deal of trouble from Rosenbrand's great niece, whom he'd found in a rest home in Albany, New York, nearly two years before. She died almost immediately after his visit.

The officials hadn't even bothered to do an autopsy; she was nearly 100 years old. They reasoned she had died from old age. Noah figured with no living relatives, no one would care about a missing diary. He had walked out of the nursing home with the diary in his pocket, while the insulin he had slipped into her tea did its final work. The old woman had been an interesting conversationalist for the short time they did have to talk. Too bad, he thought. She might have been able to give him more information about her uncle's estate.

Noah closed his notebook and rubbed tired eyes. He opened his briefcase and loosened the false bottom where he stored his precious research. He had heard the legend of the lost jewel when he was a child. His grandfather had bitterly related the events of the loss of the family farm to the Culpeppers during the Civil War, how his great grandfather had lost his life in battle, and his grandfather had become Fairland's manager, only to be kicked out later because the farm was inherited by some other Culpepper woman who ended up turning it into a museum. The woman had sold off most of the land to corporate investors and hired a curator to keep the Civil War artifacts with her artwork at the museum. The only thing she did not keep was the Rosenbrand necklace, which was passed to her namesake.

He had planned to learn more about the family and then obtain the missing Rosenbrand necklace when he had the opportunity, and then there it was, walking right into his arms. The necklace alone was likely worth a cool million. The Jewel of Africa, if it was ever found, would be priceless. The story, though slightly biased, had so enthralled him he'd started his doctoral thesis on the subject. The finding of the jewel would be his crowning glory, besides making him very rich.

It was by the pure favor of the gods that Jewel was at the university when he started there, but he had not been surprised when she walked into his classroom this past quarter. He congratulated himself on the perfect plan he had developed. The young fool possibly held the key to the mystery of the lost jewel. Lee frowned when he thought about Jonathan. Now, unfortunately, he would have to deal with this extra inconvenience, as well.

Noah knew Jonathan's feelings for Jewel were greater than he was willing to admit even to himself. As far as he knew, Jonathan was here for Jewel's sake to protect her from the "old professor." He smiled to himself as he thought about his plans. It will certainly be an interesting Christmas vacation.

Chapter XVI

Unraveling the Mystery

Jewel barely slept as she thought about the day's activities; her total horror at the airport when she realized Jonathan would be taking Noah's place on the plane, then his final words at the restaurant. Jonathan loved her. She would have stayed awake based on that knowledge alone. She took another look at the slow-moving clock. It was still only half passed three. She had been watching the clock for 15 minutes, and it seemed as if it should be at least a half hour later. Throwing off her blankets, she sat up to turn on the light, thinking perhaps further research might help her get back to sleep.

When Jewel heard about the assignment regarding family heritage from the professor, she had written to the Mercer University's Jack Tarver Library to see if they could help her discover the history behind her family, and maybe find out something about the Culpepper museum at Fairland Farm. Unfortunately, the information she had received from the library revealed nothing really earth shaking about her family. Macon had become the official arsenal of the Confederate government in 1862. Then, in 1863 City Hall had been converted to a hospital. The same year, the government established a gold depository which was directed by a William Butler Johnson. However, in 1865 Major General James H. Wilson occupied the city and Macon was finally under Union control. Jewel found nothing mentioning J. Reginald Culpepper, or his role with the Unionists. He was evidently not a local hero.

Jewel did have some sketchy genealogical information on her family. She knew she was distantly related to Charlemagne through the William Colepeper line, but why this would have been important was certainly beyond her. She would use those facts as part of the introduction for her research paper, she decided.

Of course, she had inherited her great, great grandfather's diary, and had also received legal information on Fairland Farm, her inheritance as the heiress of the name, Jewel. The information mentioned the dimensions of the property, 40 acres by 60. Very little was left of the original acreage. That was all the information she had. Shuffling through the papers strewn across the bed, Jewel picked up a pile and threw them into the air admitting this was a hopeless task, especially at this time in the morning. She leaned her head up against the headboard attached to the wall and reminisced about the plans she and Noah had made that special night they had spent in front of the fire in his apartment.

This was supposed to be such a romantic trip, she thought. She couldn't believe it had gone so wrong. Noah hadn't even called her after she arrived back at the hotel from the restaurant. She reasoned he must have been asleep long before she got there. Sad and tired, she shook her head as she tried to figure things out. No part of the day seemed to make any sense. Closing her eyes, she finally fell asleep sitting up against the headboard with a pen in one hand, and a paper in the other.

Noah's snoring awakened Jonathan from a heavy sleep. It had taken him at least an hour to get to sleep in the first place, and now at – he looked at the clock – four o'clock in the morning, he lay awake once again. "Unbelievable," he said aloud. Peter would definitely hear about this, he told himself. Slipping his jeans on, he stepped into his shoes, grabbed his key and jacket, and then left the room.

Noah turned over and watched the door a full minute before he threw back the covers and left the bed. Stepping over to the adjoining door, he knocked and listened for any response. Hearing nothing, he knocked a little louder and called out Jewel's name. A moment later, she opened the door.

Noah was shocked by what he saw. Jewel's hair was wound around plastic tubes, and her face was greased with cold cream. His stomach flipped, and he hesitated before saying anything.

"Jonathan, I – Oh, Noah!" Startled, she put her hand over her mouth. He was really the last one she was expecting to see. Her arms automatically went up to cover her hair. In spite of his initial repulsion when she opened the door, he stepped into her room, reached out to her and pulled her into his arms.

"Jewel, darlin'. I missed you." He kissed her soundly on the mouth, then held her greasy face and kissed her forehead. Hugging her, he wiped cold cream off his mouth with the back of his hand. Then he pulled away and held her at arm's length. "How are you doin' here all alone?"

"Noah, how kind of you to be concerned. I'm fine, really; but how are you? You've had such a ghastly beginning to your vacation. I thought Jonathan – Oh, never mind. I don't know what I thought." Jewel wrapped her arms around Noah's waist, smearing cold cream across the chest of his silk pajamas. She had forgotten what she looked like, but Noah could not. Looking at the stain on his clothing, he pulled away and sat on the edge of her bed.

"Honey, we're gonna have to work fast today. I plan on goin' to the university to complete some research before going out to your family's farm. Since we have so little time, I wanted to touch base with you to hear your plans."

Jewel stood speechless and a bit flustered for another minute.

"Plans?" She sat on the bed looking at the alarm clock. "It's not even four-thirty."

"Why, yes, darlin'. There's quite a bit to accomplish if you want to find your roots, wouldn't you agree?"

"But I thought you and I could spend a little time together."

"As did I, my love." His response was as smooth as baby oil as he squeezed her hand a bit too tightly. "But your friend is here, remember. We won't be able to spend any time alone together as long as he's with you." He looked at her with the slightest squint to his right eye. "Besides, with what little time we have for research, why waste it on something as trivial as our being alone together. We'll have the rest of our lives." He pushed a rebellious lock of hair away from Jewel's eye.

"Well, okay." Her reluctant reply was not lost on him, but he gave no indication he noticed it. She followed him as he stood to his feet to go back to his room. "Noah," she said. He stepped closer. "Maybe I could just ditch Jonathan for the day. I'll tell him I have to go to the university to do some studying. If you rent a car, you could pick me up there and take me out to Fairland Farm.

Noah smiled. He was indeed a master of manipulation. She said exactly what he had planned for her to say.

"Why, Jewel, honey, I'm surprised you'd be willing to dump your friend like that."

Jewel didn't like the sound of that, it made her feel dirty. Although she hated hurting Jonathan, this was Noah Lee. How could she let him down? Noah noticed her hesitation.

"Don't worry. I think I can work it out. I tell you what. Why don't I meet you on the north side of the Tarver Library at ten-thirty, all right? That way you can get a little more sleep and you can also talk to Jonathan."

He kissed her cheek and escorted her back to bed. Pushing aside the papers she had strewn across the bed, he helped tuck her in. Blowing her a kiss from the doorway, he turned out her light and quickly walked back into Jonathan's room. Jewel lay there, looking up at the ceiling, feeling strangely awkward. Something just didn't seem right. Whatever the problem was, it escaped her and before long, she drifted off to sleep.

Jonathan had gone down to the lobby and asked the front desk clerk where he could get some good donuts. He headed down the street to the Krispy Kreme. He remembered the name from his childhood – a small Krispy Kreme located in Richfield. It had been closed down in the seventies; a great loss to donut lovers in Minneapolis. He also remembered their chocolate-covered, lemon-filled bismarks, and he reckoned it would be a good start to his very early day. He sat on the bus bench on the corner until six o'clock when the shop opened.

After swallowing three donuts and a couple cups of coffee, Jonathan decided to head downtown to look at the sights and do some early morning souvenir shopping. Jewel and the professor could spend the whole week together as far as he was concerned. He was going to enjoy himself with or without her. Jonathan was angry with Peter for talking him into taking part in this scheme, but he was more hurt by the one he loved so much. He would learn to forget her, he thought, even if it took a lifetime.

The next two hours were critical to Noah. He needed to finish reviewing the notes he'd already recorded. The Jewel of Africa still remained a mystery to him, but he scoured his great, great grandmother's diary notes to see if he could at least get a clue as to its location. The stolen Rosenbrand's diary revealed the gem was real, and now he was determined to find it. The time between Culpepper's hiding the jewel and his ancestor's search of the mansion had been relatively short, but she never found it. His ancestor had checked every place that might contain a hiding place. She knew it had to have been hidden somewhere in the library because the night she listened at the kitchen door, she had seen Culpepper walk into the library with the diamond from the staircase above. She also noted he never mentioned the jewel in or out of her presence again before he died.

"That diamond is there, I know it," Noah mumbled. At eight-thirty, he gathered his notes, put everything into his briefcase, then picked up his suitcases and left the room.

Jewel stood on the other side of the door knocking. It was already nine-forty and she was late in leaving her room to meet Noah. At first she'd hesitated talking to Jonathan after last night's altercation, especially if Noah was present. Then, remembering her earlier conversation with Noah, she thought she would at least try to talk to him. Perhaps she could convince him she needed to spend the day at the university while he did some sightseeing. She was sure sightseeing would be extremely boring if one were doing it alone, but surely Jonathan could find something worth doing while she and Noah spent some time together. As she stood by the door reasoning these things through, she realized no one was answering. She looked at her watch. It was after nine-forty already. She only had an hour to get to the library to meet Noah. Still, no one answered. Giving up, she picked up her sweater, backpack and key, and left the hotel by taxi.

The Jack Tauver Library held a great deal of information about both the Culpepper and the Lee families. Noah shut the final volume of the local newspaper artifacts. His great grandmother Mary Lee's obituary reported she'd died in 1869 at the age of 68. The article said she had raised her own children and after the death of her son and his wife, she took in his children, as well. With the help of Maggie O'Neil, she had tried to raise the children at Fairland Farm. Unfortunately, Mary Lee had become ill and they ended up living with her second son, Matthew, where they were given very little.

There had been little inheritance left from their father. After Matthew Lee buried his mother, he derived the story of the "evil Englishman" who had taken away the family farm. This story passed from the first generation to the next, creating an iron root of bitterness in Noah Lee the Fourth that held him like a vice grip. He'd learned to hate the Culpepper name, but that hatred fueled his drive to become the first in his family to obtain a doctoral degree. He wrote his thesis on the archeological and familial findings and legends of the Civil War. He had kept the family records, including his great, great grandmother's journal, vowing he would one day return to the farm to regain what he felt rightfully belonged to him as the last of the Lee clan, including the Jewel of Africa. He understood from the legend his great, great grandmother had risked her life to keep the diamond a secret. Noah would find it, redeem it and tell the world.

Noah's eyes clouded as he thought of the appropriate revenge. He would not only take and sell the hideous gem; he would buy back the farm from those so-called historians and set the record straight. A Socialist at heart, Lee believed Mary Lee, a true believer of the Confederacy, saved her family the only way she knew how – by serving under the oppressive rule of the Englishman and the Unionist regime.

His thoughts were interrupted by the urgency of Jewel's voice.

"Noah! I'm so glad you're here," she gasped, out of breath. She had run in from the taxi outside, hoping she hadn't missed him. She was nearly 20 minutes late. Noah clenched his teeth then smiled and turned to face Jewel.

"Hello, Darlin'. I'm happy you made it." He stood up and gave her a peck on the cheek and gestured toward the books. "I was just tryin' to find out a little about my family. As you know, I jes' have some sketchy information about my great grandparents. I only know my great grandfather, Noah Lee the First, was killed in the War Between the States."

"Did you find out anything more this morning?" She reached for one of the volumes. Noah slapped the cover shut and startled, she pulled her hand back.

"Barely a hint. I did find some information for you, though. Fairland Farm is about five miles southeast of the city, and as you told me, there is a museum. All we have to do is drive down and look through the place. There should be plenty there for your paper." He turned away from her to gather his things. Jewel agreed and glanced down at the newspaper annals. She was surprised to see her great great grandfather's name in one of the articles.

"I'll come back here tomorrow, then," she said looking back as Noah took her by the arm and led her away from the stacks.

"Fine, Darlin'. I'll help you with it tomorrow."

Noah didn't say much on the way out to Fairland Farm, which was all right with Jewel. She simply enjoyed his company and the scenery. She could certainly understand why J. Reginald Culpepper would bring his bride here.

Macon's boundaries had stretched far enough southeast that much of the farmland had been swallowed up by concrete and housing. Fairland Farm was a gem, though, still standing proudly among the magnolia trees. The peach orchard to the west of the mansion had recovered nicely and was still worked, the gardens were well maintained, and Fairland House Museum stood majestically on a hill seen from the freeway.

Jewel studied the house as they drove up the stone driveway. True to southern colonial charm, bright white paint was offset by contrasting black trim and shutters. The front entry had a massive oak door with a brightly polished brass knocker. The porch overhang was upheld by two large hand-hewn wooden columns. With heavy railings curled at the bottom and led up to the porch, the mansion seemed to invite her in personally as if it held out its own hands to help her up the front steps. A slider swing had been placed on one end while two matching antique oak rockers moved with the breeze on the other. Jewel didn't move for a moment when the car stopped. She felt drawn to the century-old home almost as if she belonged there.

Noah said nothing as he turned off the engine to the little sports car. He, too, was enthralled by the pull of the place, but his was a different feeling – a feeling of both hate and longing. Since he was a boy playing in the fields behind this old mansion, he'd desired to own the place; to once again have Fairland Farm in the hands of his family. The farm rightfully belonged to him and he could hardly wait to tear down the mansion and replace it with a home of his own.

"Oh, Noah, it's just beautiful, isn't it?" Jewel sounded breathless and indeed she was. Noah was startled out of his own reverie.

"Yes. Yes it is," he agreed reluctantly. He quietly opened his car door, shut it and walked around the car to open Jewel's door. He may have been a murderer, but no one would ever be able to say he was not a gentleman. "My dear, shall we go in?"

Jonathan had spent the morning walking through town. He had been angry with Jewel, but he could never stay angry with her for long. He loved her. He had known her nearly all his life and had stuck with her through childhood pranks and teenage crushes. He smiled when he remembered the crush she'd had on her seventh grade art teacher, Mr. Case. She said he reminded her of David McCallum from "The Man from U.N.C.L.E." and she was head over heels in love with him because he was a blue-eyed blonde. Jon shook his head at the memory. He wondered what it was about blue eyes and blonde hair that attracted Jewel. Besides, he was blonde, kind of, and she didn't seem attracted to him. "Whatever," he said aloud.

Hopping onto a downtown bus, he managed to get back to the Holiday Inn to see if he might, by chance, catch her before she and Lee took off. He stopped at the front desk where the manager looked up and greeted him with a smile.

"Hi! Any messages for 522?" Jon asked. The manager checked the box behind him.

"Yes, sir. A long-distance call came in. Here you are, sir." He handed Jonathan the note.

Jonathan took the time to read it before going upstairs.

Jon, call me as soon as possible. I have something important to discuss with you. Peter.

"When did this come in?" Jonathan asked.

The manager took a look at the note and frowned. "I'm sorry, sir, I don't know. It appears the operator neglected to state the time and date."

"That's okay, I'll take care of it. Thanks." Jonathan thoughtfully tapped the note on the edge of the counter before returning to his room. Curious about the seeming urgency of Peter's message, he asked the manager, "Did Miss Culpepper leave?" The manager nodded affirmatively. Disappointed, Jonathan headed for the elevator.

Jonathan noticed the maid had not come to clean the room. "Some fancy hotel," he said to himself. "You can't even get a clean room when you want it." He threw his key on the bed stand and picked up the phone. The phone on the other end only rang once before a receptionist from Peter's office answered. This concerned Jon even more because Peter did not like to receive personal calls at the office. He sat back against the headboard and crossed his long legs to relax.

"This is Peter Culpepper."

"Peter, this is Jonathan. What's going on?"

"Where's Jewel? I've been trying to call her all morning!"

"Calm down, man. I guess she went out with Professor Lee. What's the problem?"

"Jon, I think Jewel might be planning an elopement." Jonathan sat up straight on the side of the bed.

"What? What makes you think that?"

"My mother called me early this morning very upset. She was going through some old mail and found an envelope from the passport agency in Seattle. She's never needed a passport before."

"Peter," Jonathan said sarcastically, "She is an archeology major. Did you think she might someday go to another country to do some work? Besides, Jewel would've told me. She tells me everything."

Peter was not convinced. "Yeah? Then why did Noah Lee quit his job at the U?" he asked urgently.

"When did he quit?"

"Last week. They announced a change in the staff on the news last night. I called a friend of mine who's a faculty member there and he said Lee had some family issues to take care of in Georgia, and he would be unable to finish out the year. I think Jewel was his family issue. Where is she?"

"I don't know. She was s'posed to go to the library to do some research."

Peter sounded exasperated. "I thought you went down there to keep an eye on her." Jonathan didn't answer. He knew Peter was frustrated and he was not going to argue with him now.

"I'll find her, Peter. Don't worry, okay? I don't believe she'd pull something like that now, not without telling me." Peter remained silent on the other end. "I promise I'll call you later." Jonathan listened to the buzz of the dial tone for a second before he realized Peter had hung up on him. He replaced the receiver on its cradle and leaned forward rubbing his tired eyes. He had no real clue as to Jewel's whereabouts, nor did he know where to even start to look. Just then, he heard a knock at the door and, "Maid Service." He let the woman in.

The maid looked around the cluttered room and frowned. Seeing her resentful look, Jonathan said, "Sorry about the mess. I was just going to pick up a little."

"Not to worry, sir. That is why I'm here, isn't it?" she challenged. She brought in clean sheets and pillow cases, placing them on the dresser next to the television. Picking up a bedspread from the floor, she reached down to retrieve a crumpled sheet of paper. Busy looking at a map of the city and a phone book, Jonathan did not take notice of her tossing the paper into a waste basket, but after the bed was made, he did notice her emptying the basket into her cart.

"Say, I didn't throw anything away yesterday. Could I see what it is?"

"Certainly, sir." She pulled the paper back out of the garbage back along with some torn pieces. Giving them to Jonathan, he smoothed out the paper and placed the pieces on the table to rebuild whatever Noah Lee had torn up. Jon gave the maid a tip and excusing her, ushered her out the door.

"Hmm. Looks like a receipt for something. It was missing a piece, but Jonathan could tell it was from a drug store in Minneapolis. The telephone number was clear, so he called it. Then in his best southern drawl, he requested to speak to the pharmacist. Yellow pages in hand, he found the name and number of a near-by pharmacy.

"Hello, sah. This is Noah Lee. I was in your store the othah day to pick up a prescription? And I seem to have misplaced the bottle. Would it be possible for y'all to transfah it to my druggist heah in Macon?"

"Why of course, Mr. Lee. What's the name and number?"

"Yes, could y'all send it to the Walton Drug at 478-555-2000?"

The druggist took the information and promised to transfer the prescription as quickly as possible. Meanwhile, Jonathan reached for the other piece of paper. Lee had scribbled out a picture of what looked like a diamond. He could make out the word "Africa" and then at the bottom of the page, he saw another telephone number. Dialing, he waited for an answer. The woman on the other end of the line had a refined Georgian drawl, not unlike Professor Lee's.

"Fairland Farm Museum. This is Lilly Blackburn. How may I help you?"

"Are you open today?"

"Why, yes sir. We'll be open until four o'clock this afternoon. Excuse me." She covered the receiver with her hand. Jon heard "professor," and "so glad," then she returned to her conversation with Jonathan. "Pardon me, sir. Where were we?"

"Can you give me directions on how to get out there?" The woman asked where he was and then she gave him the instructions. Jon hung up while she was still wishing him a good day.

Rifling through the yellow pages, Jonathan found a number to a rental car service. He'd need to rent a car to get to the drug store and then down to the museum. The urgency in the pit of his stomach gnawed at him. Jewel needed him now more than ever, he was sure of it.

As luck would have it, the car rental was just a few minutes away from the hotel. He reserved a car and called a taxi. Stuffing the prescription receipt into his pocket, he hurried out the door to catch the cab.

Reading glasses slid down Lilly Blackburn's long, thin nose as she continued her dissertation. She tightened the grayed bun pinned at the top of her head, and then pulled at her bra strap to hide it from view. Hoping to express to the professor how much she had enjoyed reading his articles in the local newspaper over the years, she didn't allow either of them to say a word. Noah and Jewel stood at the entrance patiently listening to her as they tried to enter. She remarked about the extensive research he had done on the War Between the States, Fairland Farm itself, and of course, the family's genealogy for which "the museum's Board of Directors will be eternally grateful."

"I'm sure. Thank you. Now may we come in, my dear?"

"But of course, Professor Lee." She opened the gate for them and Jewel stepped through, entranced by what she saw. "I cannot tell you how thrilled I was to learn how you restored your great, great grandmother's memoirs last year after they had been so badly deteriorated; and you plan to donate them to the museum! Doctor Lee, I am just thrilled!"

Noah nervously tried to keep the woman from exposing him to Jewel after he had already told her he knew very little about his family. He pulled the woman aside.

"Yes, yes, my dear. Thank you," he whispered. "But we mustn't let the whole world in on it, must we?" His forced smile captivated the older woman. She ogled him a moment longer before responding.

"Oh, of course not, Doctor Lee," she said in a loud whisper, pushing her heavy glasses back up her nose. "I am just *so* thrilled!"

Noah nodded, tipped his hat and walked away hoping the woman would leave him alone.

"I'm just over here if you need me, Doctor Lee," she called after him.

He needn't have worried about Jewel, though. She had already wandered into the main living room area enthralled by the glory of the home. Oriental rugs decorated hardwood oak floors, tapestries hung on the walls opposite pictures of both Confederate and Union Civil War heroes, and antique settees invited visitors to take a seat. A long, winding staircase leading to the second floor was roped off for repairs. She secretly hoped she might convince the curator to allow her to sneak upstairs for a peek. She noticed Noah enter and smiled at him.

"Noah, isn't it grand?" Those were the only words she could think of to describe it. "I've never seen anything like it. To think my great, great grandfather built this with his own hands."

"His and about a hundred others, my dear. Even back in the 1800's they had carpenters," he replied sarcastically. He looked around the room, disdain filling his heart. "They've found termites in the foundation, you know." Though he really had no idea whether this was true or not, he hoped they really had. He wanted her to understand even great edifices like this one could tumble. His remark went through Jewel like a gunshot, and her look let him know she'd gotten the message. He turned to walk over to the painting across the way.

"This is my great grandfather," he said proudly. "Noah Lee, the First. He was a great supporter of the Confederacy." Jewel joined him placing her hand in his. She was surprised when he pulled away. "Shall we go into the library?"

The car rental dealer seemed to take forever to get Jonathan the car he needed. Noting the drug store on the way over, he realized he would have to backtrack about a half mile to get back on the freeway to get there. When he finally arrived, he nearly ran to the pharmacy window.

"I'm here to pick up a prescription for Noah Lee." Suspicion reflected in the druggist's eyes.

"You're not Noah Lee. I've known Professor Lee since he was knee-high to a grasshopper, and you're not him."

"No, sir. I'm one of his students. He sent me here from the hotel to pick it up. Go ahead. Call if you want. Room 522 at the Holiday Inn West. He should still be there." Jon looked at his watch. "That is, if he hasn't already left for the university. He's scheduled to speak to some faculty there today in, gosh, about 20 minutes." Jonathan looked at his watch feigning concern. "Man! I hope I get back in time."

The druggist looked Jonathan up and down. "You're a student of his? In what class?"

"Archeology, of course. One of the best at the U of M." The druggist considered him for a second.

"All right, young man. I'll give this to you." He handed Jon a small bag containing the medication. "That'll be $13.95." Jonathan's exasperation was evidenced by his frustrated sigh. Putting down the bag, he fished out his billfold and handed the pharmacist a ten and a five dollar bill.

"Keep the change," Jonathan said as he turned to go.

"Young man, remind Dr. Lee to stop and see me before he goes back up north." Jonathan assured the old man he would do so, and left nearly as quickly as he'd come.

Back in the car, Jon pulled out of the parking lot and drove down the block before pulling over again to check the contents of the bag. It was just a small bottle of insulin and a syringe wrapped in cellophane. Jewel never mentioned Lee as being a diabetic. It didn't matter. His sense of urgency was overwhelming, and he knew Jewel was in trouble. He threw the bag into the passenger seat and headed down the freeway entrance ramp towards Fairland Farm.

Noah's cool demeanor concerned Jewel. She followed him into the library while reaching into her backpack to pull out a small book – her great, great grandfather's diary. She looked at him with concern, but thought perhaps he was just tired.

"Noah, is there something wrong? Did I say something to upset you? She asked. He didn't look at her; he simply gazed at the picture of his ancestor.

"No, why would you ask such a silly question?" he responded. He fumbled with something in his pocket. Jewel shrugged, and turned to the book she had retrieved. Leaving through the pages of her grandfather's diary, she stopped near its center. Looking to her left, she stepped over to the middle of the room. Noah watched her carefully.

"My father gave this diary to me," she said looking back at him. "It belonged to my great, great grandfather, and it was passed down to his first daughter, Jewel Victoria Culpepper, and then to every first daughter with the same name in the family line. Somewhere in here is a clue as to the whereabouts of the big diamond he called the Jewel of Africa. He hid it somewhere in this library, I think." She turned to look at the book again. "I've read it a couple times since we got to Georgia, but I haven't really figured anything out."

Noah came up behind her placing his hands on her shoulders. "May I see it?" he asked almost breathlessly. She handed him the book and as he examined it, he turned the delicate pages very carefully. Noah also noted the dog-edged page, now breaking at the slightest touch, observing it was marked especially to bring attention to it. Typical of the penmanship of the day, perfect lettering written with a fountain pen formed the words of an interesting clue.

"What do you think?" Jewel moved to her ancestor's heavy desk and drew her hand over the ornate carving on the top edge. "Any clues?"

"Clues? No, I don't think so," Noah lied. His mind was trying to decipher what he was reading. *Fair land overlooks the picture of God . . ."* He read it again and wondered what it meant. *". . . Where the door is opened by pressing toward the mark."* Noah walked over to the east wall where a picture of Fairland Farm hung facing the opposite side where the bookcases stood. Then walking back to the bookcases, he examined the titles of the old volumes. Shakespeare, Dickens, Twain, and Poe. Two bookcases were full of books collected by Culpepper and his descendants over the past century. Lee practically drooled as he examined the old books until he came upon the family Bible. Pulling it from the corner of the shelf, he thumbed through brittle pages. There was no secret compartment. Disappointment registered on his face as he concentrated on the other books. He jumped at the sound of the curator's voice.

"Doctor Lee! Would you mind not touching the books, Sir?" Miss Blackburn took the Bible from his hands and replaced it on the shelf.

"Oh, pardon me, my deah. I simply could not resist it. I wondered if there was any mention of the family that lived here. An archeologist's curiosity, you understand." His right eye twitched as he spoke to her in smooth tones.

"Of course, Doctor Lee, I do understand. I would suspect your great, great grandmother may have read this very Bible in those early years." Noah bit his lip at the comment hoping Jewel had not heard it."

"Noah? Your great, great grandmother? How could that be?"

Noah turned and gave Jewel a tense smile. He took her arm to lead her outside. "Come, Darlin'. Let's go out to the garden."

"But –."

Noah leaned into her. "Never mind her, Hon. She's a little eccentric." Jewel looked back at the older woman who was left carefully adjusting the books to exactly meet the edge of the shelf.

"If she's eccentric, why is she managing our museum?" Jewel huffed.

The garden met Jewel's every expectation. Gardeners had sculpted the boarder hedges perfectly. Azalea bushes were still full, but the leaves were turning color marking a late fall. Winters were usually short lived in Georgia, but it had been unusually warm at the end of this year. Hedges grew to over six feet tall in some places, hiding some of the flaws in the garden walls surrounding the mansion.

"Be careful of the bees, my dear. They're quite fierce this time of the year in Georgia," Noah lied. He spoke in hushed tones as they walked.

"Really? In December? How strange it is in the South. But don't worry," Jewel touched his cheek with the back of her hand. "I'll be careful. I just want to see every part of this legendary garden." She couldn't say enough about the beauty all around them. "To think my family owns all this! I can hardly believe it. And look at these flowers. Have you ever seen anything so beautiful?" Noah held back a groan as she carried on, and bent over to smell the flowers. He was glad he would not have to share the rest of his life with this babbling idiot.

"As a matter of fact –."

"Oh, of course you have! You grew up in this area, didn't you? How silly of me!" She giggled like an excited little girl. Noah rolled his eyes. Reaching into his pocket he unsheathed the syringe he had already filled with insulin.

"Darlin', watch out for that bee!" he pointed behind her, and she turned without seeing he had a syringe in his hand. He jabbed her arm and shot the entire syringe full of insulin into it before pulling away and hiding it back in his pocket.

"OW! What?" She backed away and looked at him confused.

"Jewel, I didn't just grow up in the area, I grew up here." The tone in his voice changed dramatically. "Right on this very property."

"Excuse me?" she asked rubbing her arm. She wondered what kind of a bee could've stung her so badly.

"I said this is my home. I spent many of my childhood years in and out of this mansion. I was raised in a shack on the perimeter of this property. It should never have left the hands of my ancestors and if I have anything to do with it, it never will again."

Jewel stopped walking and faced him. "Noah, I'm not sure I understand." Her arm throbbed and she had a gnawing feeling in the pit of her stomach something was terribly wrong.

"Jewel is your name, is it not? A name inherited from an ancestor of yours, correct?"

"Yes. You know I was named after a diamond supposedly lost on this very plantation. I told you before." Noah pulled her to him.

"It was lost during that fateful time of the War Between the States." She tried pushing away from him.

"Noah, you're hurting my arm."

"Am I? Please forgive me, my darlin'. I would never want to hurt you." He held her tighter, bent down and kissed her hard on the lips. Fear rose up within her and she again tried to pull away. Suddenly weakened by the insulin surging through her system, her vision blurred and her mind clouded. She grew dizzy and collapsed into his arms. Noah dragged her over to the azalea bushes as she struggled to regain consciousness.

"You really should have been more careful about the bees, my dear. Their sting can be deadly." He kissed the top of her hand and taking the diary from her, let her fall to the ground against the garden wall behind the azaleas. Her body would be unnoticed by anyone unless they walked over her. Stepping away, he reached into his coat pocket for his pipe, filled it with tobacco and lit it. Looking to his left and then to his right, he walked back into the house through the library doors.

Jonathan's drive to the museum seemed to take forever. After nearly an hour of driving through early rush hour traffic, he pulled into Fairland Farm at top speed. Coming to a halt behind a small sports car, he threw the rental into park and ran in through the front door. A guard cordoning off the entryway put up a hand to stop him from going in.

"I'm sorry, Sir. The museum will close in just a few minutes. No one else is allowed in."

"Oh, man, come on! I'm supposed to meet two friends here. Noah Lee and Jewel Culpepper."

The guard laughed. "Culpepper and Lee? That's good. And I'm Jefferson Davis." He stood in front of Jon with arms crossed and feet planted.

"Listen! I gotta get in there!" Jonathan was at the end of his patience. "Okay, pal, I know you won't believe me, but Noah Lee is a friend of mine. It really is a matter of life and death." The guard wouldn't budge, until Jonathan noticed the curator walking over to them. He signaled to her.

"Howard, is there a problem here?"

"Yes, Miss Lilly. This man says he knows Noah Lee." The sneer on his face told his opinion of the story. Miss Blackburn looked at Jonathan and smiled.

"Of course, Sir. I believe Mr. Lee is still in the library. I'll just take you there." Jonathan sniffed at the guard as he went passed.

"Thank you, ma'am," Jonathan said. "I really need to get in there."

Noah stood in front of the bookcase with the Bible in one hand and the diary in the other. He went over the clue about "pressing toward the mark," trying desperately to remember the scripture reference to which it referred. Finally he remembered it was in Philippians. He turned the brittle pages of the old book and found the Apostle Paul's Letter to the Philippians. Checking his watch, he knew he only had a minute before the old battleaxe at the front desk would be kicking him out. He didn't care, for he had already taped the garden door open so he could come back in after the museum had closed. Having walked through this old house enough times to have found the power source to disconnect the alarm, he was confident he could re-enter the museum without a problem. He turned to replace the Bible on the shelf, thinking he would go through the Gideon's Bible in the hotel to check on the reference before returning. His thoughts were interrupted when the library doors opened and Jonathan stood between him and the exit.

"Lee!"

Startled, Noah nearly dropped the Bible on the floor. He turned to face the fierce anger of Jonathan Tyler.

"Why Jonathan, my boy. You startled me." He replaced the Bible and turned to smile amiably at Jonathan.

"Where's Jewel?"

"Why, I am sure I don't know, dear boy." He said "boy" more as a challenge than as a title of respect. "We were supposed to meet at the University, but she never showed up."

Miss Blackburn stood behind Jonathan listening to the conversation. She wondered what had happened to the young woman she had seen earlier. She hadn't noticed the young lady leave, and there had only been one car in the driveway. Jonathan stood motionless for a moment not knowing what to do.

"Excuse me, Professor." Miss Blackburn pushed herself past Jonathan. "I'm sorry to interrupt, but I couldn't help but overhear your conversation.

What happened to the lovely young lady who was with you here earlier? I didn't notice her leaving."

"There was a girl here, with blonde hair, about this tall?" Jonathan held up his hand comparing Jewel's size to his own.

"Why, yes, I do believe that was about what she looked like."

Noah glared at the old woman. "Oh, that woman wasn't really with me. She'd come in with a taxi and left shortly afterward." He smiled stiffly at the two of them and pardoned himself as he tried to pass by. Jonathan grabbed his arm.

"Where's Jewel?" he asked again.

"I don't know what you're talkin' about." Suddenly Lee pulled away and ran to the garden door to escape. With long strides, Jonathan caught up to him and he tackled the older man, pulling him down by the back of his jacket. Noah kicked at Jonathan's chest and forced him off. Crawling out the garden door, Lee again stood up to run. Jonathan caught his leg and pulled him down to the sidewalk. He grabbed Lee's collar.

"Where's Jewel?" Jonathan demanded a third time. Lee pulled up his knee, catching Jonathan in the groin. He fell over in pain, and while he lay doubled over, Lee tried to escape through the garden past the hedges and the azaleas. Jewel's leg, sticking out by the side of the hedge, tripped him as he ran. Jonathan was on top of him in seconds. He pulled Noah to his feet and slammed his fist into Lee's face again and again until Lee toppled backward, unconscious. Seeing Jewel laying behind the azaleas, Jonathan pushed the bushes aside to check her. Kneeling on one knee, he found her pulse still beating, but it was weak and slow. The guard came running from the library with a pistol in hand.

"Call an ambulance!" Jonathan said. The guard did an immediate about face and ran back into the mansion. Jonathan carefully picked up the girl's limp body and brought her into the library where he gently placed her on the sofa under the picture of Fairland Farm. Sweat had broken across her brow and her breathing seemed labored.

"God, Jewel! Please don't die." Jonathan knelt next to her and held her to him. "Please God, don't let her die." His heart was breaking with every faint beat of her heart. Why had he waited so long to tell her his feelings?

They could have spent all this time together. He buried his face in her side and tried to hold back his tears.

Suddenly, the garden doors flew open and Noah Lee stood there, blood streaming from both his nose and a cut next to his right eye. With a large rock in his hands, he held it up over his head and ran toward Jonathan. Jon stood up in time to grab Lee's arms, and with all his strength, forced him back into the bookcases on the opposite wall. Lee tried dropping the rock down on Jonathan's head, but Jon pushed his arms back until it fell from his hands.

The two men pushed against the bookcase and it started to rock. Lee shoved Jonathan back against the desk and the bookcase crashed to the floor. The two men fell atop the desk, where Lee grasped the silver letter opener. Jonathan caught his hand before Lee could shove it into his throat. Searching for something to protect himself with his other hand, he found a paper weight and slammed it into the side of Lee's face. He weakened just enough for Jonathan to push him off.

Lee attacked him again, but Jonathan grasped his wrist and turned his hand to force the letter opener into Lee's stomach. Lee staggered back, looking in shock at the weapon protruding from his abdomen, but as Jonathan leaned against the desk trying to recover, he attacked again. Just then, two shots rang out. The guard hit Lee directly in the shoulder and again in the chest. He staggered back and fell over the bookcase, dead. Jonathan slid down to his knees and watched the man breathe his last breath.

The ambulance had already arrived and two emergency technicians came through the door with a stretcher. Jon crawled over to Lee to check his pockets where he found the empty vile of insulin. As soon as one of the ET's saw what it was, he immediately administered an amp of D50 and started an intravenous tube of glucose to try to restore Jewel's sugar levels. It took only a few minutes before she stirred and opened her eyes. Jonathan stood at the head of the sofa, trying to catch his breath as he looked down at her. His face was the first thing she saw clearly.

"Jonathan? What happened?" Jonathan looked up at the ceiling and threading his fingers through his hair, he finally allowed tears to flow.

* * *

Three days later, Jewel was recovered and fit enough to leave the hospital. When they were finally able to talk alone at the hotel, Jonathan confessed to her the idea Peter and he had concocted to send him down with her just to keep a close eye on her. Although she still smarted from the hurt Noah Lee had caused, she admitted she was relieved they had, but she spent most of the next day in tears. After having thought through the past few months since she met Noah Lee, she realized how foolish she had been, how much she had hurt her family and Jonathan. She needed to call home.

Peter listened to his little sister pour her heart out to him over the phone. After assuring her everything was all right, he let her talk to their mother. It was agreed Peter would take the next flight south to join them in Macon to tie up loose ends.

A detective named O'Connor met Jewel, Peter and Jon at the museum late in the afternoon. The attorney for the estate also joined them as the detective cut through the tape closing off the crime scene. The guard was available to answer any questions while Miss Blackburn was away "resting" in the Macon Home for the mentally challenged. Miss Blackburn had had to be sedated the day of Dr. Lee's death after facing the fact that her secret hero, Noah Lee, a murderer and a fraud, had played a very large part in nearly destroying her dearly-loved museum. She lay in a psych ward totally oblivious to the world.

Jewel stood at the double French doors overlooking the mess in the library. She had been unconscious during most of the events five days before, but she had not realized the museum was left like this. Noah Lee's blood stained the Oriental rug laying near the garden door. The desk had been shoved back from the weight of the battle between Jonathan and Noah, its contents were strewn across the hardwood floor. The bookcase lay on its face with a cracked bulge in its back caused by the rock on which it had fallen. The guard and Jonathan bent over together and picked up the shelf unit, and stood it up against the wall. As Jewel knelt down to pick up the rock, she was amazed at what she saw just to its side. The Jewel of Africa lay glistening in the sunbeam shining through the garden door. Larger than the palm of her hand, the diamond felt heavy as she picked it up.

She gasped. "I can't believe it!"

Still talking to the attorney, her brother overheard her and turned to see what was wrong. Jewel's face, pale from shock, registered her complete surprise. Peter's mouth fell open as he nearly tripped over his own feet trying to get to her.

"Where did this come from?" he asked taking it from her hand.

"Here! Right here on the floor! It must have been in the bookcase." They all gathered around her to look at the long-lost gem, amazed at its size and beauty. "I can't believe it. I've found the Jewel of Africa!"

Jonathan looked back at the bookcase and noticed an opening in the rear of the shelf where the gem had been hiding for over 100 years. He examined the door for some kind of a release and found a small, flat metal hook latched to the corner of the shelf making a perfect hiding place for the jewel. The entire back wall of the bookcase was false so no one could have seen the hiding place unless they knew what they were looking for. Jonathan pushed the little door closed.

"I know how it closed, but how did it open?" Jon asked. He looked back at Peter who joined him to examine the shelf. Jewel remembered the diary and pulled it out of her purse. Noticing the dog-eared page, she turned to it and read the clue. She recognized the picture of Fairland Farm in the description, but "the door is only opened by pressing toward the mark," made no sense to her. Walking over to the bookcase she examined the back and side walls. On the inside left she saw a knot hole engrained in the wood. A scar caused by the rock when the bookcase fell, ran right up to the knot hole. She pushed the mark and the door slid open.

"Look at that! Wow! That guy must have been a genius!" Jon said looking from the front to the back examining the trap door mechanism.

"I guess it runs in the family," Jewel quipped.

Epilogue

The museum property was placed on the market with all its furnishings. Despite the $2.8 million fair-market price attached to the listing, the attorney was assured the estate would sell quickly. It still had a working orchard, and the beauty and history behind the mansion was reason enough for someone to buy it. The stipulations of the estate dictated that the proceeds of Fairland Farm's sale be placed in probate to be divided among the living relatives of J. Reginald Culpepper. The Jewel of Africa, however, had been willed to the only one still living with the name Jewel Victoria, and since Jewel found the diamond, a finder's fee was provided by the estate to her for ten percent of its over $10 million appraised value.

Jonathan's love for Jewel grew, but she had to forget her infatuation for the evil Professor Lee before their relationship could mature. His every free moment was spent wooing her to him, and it was not long before she realized it had been Jonathan who mattered to her all along.

Jonathan did succeed in winning her, and they were married less than a year later. Over eight months passed from the time the Jewel of Africa was found, and it escorted the young couple to South Africa on their honeymoon.

In Jewel's eyes, the diamond was priceless. They would probably never find anyone who could pay for its history. She knew she would never be able to sell it if they did; but neither could she keep it because of the curse that seemed to come with it. Everyone who had been attached to the legend had either been hurt by it or had died, and Jewel could not be held responsible for any more sadness. She had inherited the Jewel of Africa, but she knew it really belonged to the Venda people. She decided she would follow through with the plan she had voiced to Noah Lee nearly a year before – to return the diamond to its native country.

Jewel and Jonathan spent a month visiting South Africa, but before leaving it was determined they would make an annual trip there to visit new friends. Adventure was in their souls, and they could not help but be drawn by the possibility of new discoveries on the "dark continent."

They traveled the Limpopo River to revisit the jungle her great grandfather had discovered over a century before. Visiting the Venda tribe, they were welcomed heartily by the people. Having made arrangements through the American Embassy in Johannesburg, South Africa, Jewel presented the diamond to the chief of the Venda people who still lived in the Limpopo River region. The Vendas accepted her gift and with great joy, they celebrated its return, the young people who returned it, and the prosperity it would bring.

Their trip ended all too quickly, and soon the newlyweds had to leave for home. They headed back down the Limpopo, and flew by bush plane to Johannesburg.

Salty air whipped at Jewel's long hair as they stood together on the deck of their cruise ship, watching the South African coastline fade into the distance.

"Are you sorry?" Jonathan asked.

"Sorry?" she responded. "Why would I be sorry?"

"That was quite a gift you gave to them." Jewel turned to Jonathan and he drew her into his arms.

"No, it wasn't a gift. It was a return of their property. They lost lives over that diamond, and they earned the right to have it. Besides, you're the only gift I want now." They kissed and stood in each other's arms to watch the horizon. She was happy. She had Jonathan, and the Jewel of Africa had come full circle, home at last.

THE END

Now that you have enjoyed "Jewel – Heiress of the Lost Diamond"

here is an excerpt from

The Greatest Love Story

A new novel from

K. J. Culpepper

Coming soon

Gordon Lindstrom, dressed in his best Armani suit and tie, sat uncomfortably on stage before a large-capacity crowd at the Minneapolis Convention Center, a popular meeting hall over the past 40 years in downtown Minneapolis, Minnesota. His long legs stretched out in mutiny against the unwieldy folding chair on which he sat. He smoothed down a rebellious hair on the back of his head, trying to appear the confident businessman.

People mingled on the main floor, preparing for the final meeting of a three-day conference. Folks laughed and cajoled as they stood or leaned over backs of chairs. Others walked up and down crowded isles talking excitedly about the events of the previous two days. Nevertheless, with all their gaiety, he realized they were completely unaware of impending danger around them. Gordon felt it though. Persistent tension hovered over and surrounded him as he quietly watched events unfold.

Gordon remained uneasy as he prepared to speak, and caught himself shuffling note cards from one hand to the other. He again tried to appear calm. Stuffing the cards back into his suit coat pocket, he noticed a slight tremor in his hand. Looking to his left, he smiled at the person sitting next to him and nervously folded his hands on his lap.

Gordon wondered what he was worried about. He had known for over two years that his experiences would culminate soon and mentally chided himself for being concerned. He attempted to shake off the dread he felt, and needing some encouragement, he looked past the podium to find Melanie smiling back at him. She had known longer than he what would happen and what was expected of him. She had learned the lesson well, after years of practice and commitment; now it was Gordon's turn. Her smile was met with a shaky smile of his own, and he responded in kind to her encouraging nod. After 32 years of marriage, marred by severe wounds now healed with nary a scar, they had finally developed a silent communication misunderstood by most. Only a few could only interpret it as love.

The crowd slowly began to return to their seats and Gordon was brought back to the reality of his current situation. "You put your foot in it this time, Lindstrom," he mumbled to himself. The man sitting in the next chair looked at him curiously.

"Excuse me?" he asked. Gordon gave him a sheepish grin.

"Nothing – just talking to myself."

The man grinned back, nodded and looked back down at his program. Gordon adjusted his silk tie and cleared his throat. He had to at least look like he was happy to be here, even though he may not feel it.

Well, King, here I am, he thought. *You told me there would be days like this, but I didn't want to believe you. Sure hope this works out as good as you seem to think it will.* He reached down to flip a piece of lint off his trousers, as if the crowd might notice it. He smirked and rolled his eyes as if to chide himself for his own lack of confidence.

A speaker in the sound system squealed. Gordon's stomach leaped as Wilbur Forrest, president of the World Brotherhood of Business Laymen, began to address the crowd.

"Ladies and gentlemen! Ladies and gentlemen, please take your seats."

The rotund, stout man scratched his stomach then rubbed his hands together appearing anxious to get on with the proceedings. He waited a moment while the crowd settled into their uncomfortable folding chairs on the main floor. "Hush's" and "Be quiet's" sounded from here and there around the room until the crowd finally settled down. He began again.

"Thank you. Ladies and gentlemen, since this is the third and final day of the 2014 National Convention –." He chuckled as the crowd erupted into cheers and applause. Wilbur raised his hands until they quieted. "We of the organizational committee of the World Brotherhood of Business Laymen would like to congratulate you for a job well done." Again the crowd broke into applause. Wilbur waited patiently for the noise to die down before he proceeded with his introductory remarks.

"Our fund drive during the convention on behalf of the devastated people in Kazakhstan and Uzbekistan has had a tremendous response! As you know, these areas have been torn by war and hunger; but we have collected more than $11,000,000.00 over this past year and during this convention!" The crowd responded with another cheer and a great deal of congratulatory applause. He held up his hand until the noise lessened, and then moved closer to the microphone.

"Thank you again. We have one more piece of business before we call upon our keynote speaker for the evening. We are voting on the final draft of the proposal to the Father Church regarding the New World Laymen's Bible, and whether or not to accept the newest revisions recently added to this great work."

The crowd buzzed with excitement, and pride exuded from them as they considered the potential of the project. Scholars and translators from every country in the world had come together in a common bond to revise ancient Biblical transcripts. These revisions would "upgrade" its literary style to avoid offending any society, religion, gender or lifestyle.

Numerous revisions had been made, including additions to the Canonical books and the ancient scrolls found near the Dead Sea, and excerpts from the books of Judas and St. Thomas had been added. Commentaries and literary works from different leaders around the world had also been included. These editorial changes were considered necessary for the political correctness of different countries and religious sects involved, and the revisions were understandable considering how difficult the leaders of some Mid- and Northeastern countries were to control – rebellious, sometimes murderous in their attempts to take over the world. The world was tiring of their antics, and this work, *this* Bible, promised to bring change. *This* Bible was written to speak to every class, every race, and every religion. The savior mentioned in *this* Bible would bring worldwide peace. Political entities throughout Europe had decided who the savior would be, but his identity had still not been introduced to the rest of the world. Nevertheless, leaders of the World Brotherhood of Business Laymen had also identified a possible candidate; a person of great influence and power. Regardless, they were keeping their guesses under wraps.

Wilbur tugged at the waistband of his baggy suit pants and held up a piece of paper.

"People, please take a ballot from the holders in the backs of your chairs and cast your votes." There was a vigorous noise as people grabbed ballots and writing utensils, marked their votes and passed the ballots to the center isle for collection. He thanked them for their quick response and assistance, and then looking back at Gordon, assured them that the ballots would be counted and the result given after the address from their keynote speaker.

"As you may have already heard, folks, our registered keynote speaker, Harold Brewster, was in a horrible car accident a few weeks ago, and is still recovering. Unfortunately, he is not able to be with us tonight." There was a compassionate response as people whispered about the possible loss of another leader of the Association. Too many good men had been lost recently. "Needless to say," Wilbur added in a sympathetic tone, "our thoughts are with him and his family this evening." He paused with feigned concern for Brewster before finishing his introduction. With a lift to his voice, he continued.

"However, a good friend and member of the WBBL, has consented to take his place. You all know him," he said gesturing towards Gordon. His comment was met with a positive buzz from the crowd. "Gordon Lindstrom has been a mighty force in the business world over the past 28 years. As Chairman of the Board to Alpha Communications, he has brought about major takeovers of some of the world's leading communications companies. His innovative business style has been instrumental in the development of over 83,000 jobs. And finally, with Gordon working on the WBBL board, we have plowed ahead in the work of peace in our warring inner cities in the heartland of America and around the world. Please welcome with me, Dr. Gordon Lindstrom!" Wilbur stepped back grinning at Gordon, and exuberantly leading the applause.

Gordon stood up at their resounding welcome, and grasped Wilbur's hand. Then, one after another, people stood to their feet affirming their undying respect for the man. His face reddened, which made him seem older than his 55 years, and he appeared tall to those on the lower floor in front of him, though he was actually inches shorter than two years before. His lean body looked strong as he walked forward stiffly, his well-tailored suit covering scars, a metal brace and a prosthesis. There was yet another noise from the crowd. "He can actually walk," was one of many comments he could hear. Gordon smiled at that. He was indeed lucky to be alive, as they all knew; *but then*, Gordon thought, *luck had nothing to do with it.*

Looking down at the audience again, Gordon searched expectant faces in the crowd before saying a word. Chairs scraped the floor as the audience sat down and quieted to perfect silence. They watched him eagerly. There seemed to be a glow about him, but no one readily identified why. Silver hair, turned recently by traumatic events, shone under hot lights and his ruggedly handsome face captured their attention.

Beginning the speech, his voice cracked from the nerves with which he had been grappling since his arrival, and he had to pause and clear his throat. This was not a great start to his first major public appearance. Little beads of sweat cropped out on his forehead. He mopped his brow with a handkerchief and started again. "Thank you, Wilbur, members, and honored guests. Tonight I want to tell you about my recent journey –." He paused. "– into death." The crowd gasped.

About the Author

KJ Culpepper, a secretary for the State of Minnesota, resides with her husband of 22 years. A wife, mother and grandmother, as well as a licensed minister, when she isn't writing, her spare time is spent ministering in the prisons and jails in and around the Twin Cities area.

KJ served her country during the Vietnam conflict as a yeoman in the Navy. Over the past 30 years, she has pursued a degree in music and Biblical Studies. She has a Bachelor's Degree Theology, and will soon be working on her Master's.

An avid traveler, she has visited 14 of the 50 states and Puerto Rico, as well as the Philippines, Ireland, Belarus, India, Mexico, Canada, Poland and Amsterdam. She loves to write about the people and places she has visited around the world.

KJ's passion is writing Christian fiction, whether it be a historical adventure, or simple romance. Her main purpose is to tell people about the love of God, and her writing always includes that message. Jewel, Heiress of the Lost Diamond is her first published novel. Soon to be released are The Greatest Love Story and Forget Not the Prophets, a two-book series written using characters from the Bible.

Made in the USA
Charleston, SC
20 October 2016